ENTANGLED

Reviewers Love Melissa Brayden

"Melissa Brayden has become one of the most popular novelists of the genre, writing hit after hit of funny, relatable, and very sexy stories for women who love women."—*Afterellen.com*

Back to September

"You can't go wrong with a Melissa Brayden romance. Seriously, you can't. Buy all of her books. Brayden sure has a way of creating an emotional type of compatibility between her leads, making you root for them against all odds. Great settings, cute interactions, and realistic dialogue."—*Bookvark*

Beautiful Dreamer

"I love this book. I want to kiss it on its face. I also want to go to Dreamer's Bay, so I can eat the donuts, hang out on the beaches, and maybe even join in on the Saturday night cornhole game with Devyn and Elizabeth. Instead, I'm going to stick *Beautiful Dreamer* on my to-reread-when-everything-sucks pile, because it's sure to make me happy again and again."—*Smart Bitches Trashy Books*

"[A] perfect summer romance, the kind you want to take to the beach to enjoy as you soak up the sun and sea breeze." —*Rainbow Reflections*

"*Beautiful Dreamer* is a sweet and sexy romance, with the bonus of interesting secondary characters and a cute small-town setting." —*Amanda Chapman, Librarian (Davisville Free Library, RI)*

Love Like This

"I really have to commend Melissa Brayden in her exceptional writing and especially in the way she writes not only the romance but the friendships between the group of women."—*Les Rêveur*

"Brayden upped her game. The characters are remarkably distinct from one another. The secondary characters are rich and wonderfully integrated into the story. The dialogue is crisp and witty." —*Frivolous Reviews*

Sparks Like Ours

"Brayden sets up a flirtatious tit-for-tat that's honest, relatable, and passionate. The women's fears are real, but the loving support from the supporting cast helps them find their way to a happy future. This enjoyable romance is sure to interest readers in the other stories from Seven Shores."—*Publishers Weekly*

"*Sparks Like Ours* is made up of myriad bits of truth that make for a cozy, lovely summer read."—*Queerly Reads*

Hearts Like Hers

"*Hearts Like Hers* has all the ingredients that readers can expect from Ms. Brayden: witty dialogue, heartfelt relationships, hot chemistry and passionate romance."—*Lez Review Books*

"Once again Melissa Brayden stands at the top. She unequivocally is the queen of romance."—*Front Porch Romance*

"*Hearts Like Hers* has a breezy style that makes it a perfect beach read. The romance is paced well, the sex is super hot, and the conflict made perfect sense and honored Autumn and Kate's journeys." —*The Lesbian Review*

Eyes Like Those

"Brayden's story of blossoming love behind the Hollywood scenes provides the right amount of warmth, camaraderie, and drama." —*RT Book Reviews*

"Brayden's writing is just getting better and better. The story is well done, full of well-honed wit and humour, and the characters are complex and interesting."—*Lesbian Reading Room*

"Melissa Brayden knocks it out of the park once again with this fantastic and beautifully written novel."—*Les Reveur*

"Pure Melissa Brayden at her best…Another great read that won't disappoint Brayden's fans. Can't wait for the rest of the series." —*Lez Review Books*

Strawberry Summer

"This small-town second-chance romance is full of tenderness and heart. The 10 Best Romance Books of 2017."—*Vulture*

"*Strawberry Summer* is a tribute to first love and soulmates and growing into the person you're meant to be. I feel like I say this each time I read a new Melissa Brayden offering, but I loved this book so much that I cannot wait to see what she delivers next."—*Smart Bitches, Trashy Books*

"*Strawberry Summer* will suck you in, rip out your heart, and put all the pieces back together by the end, maybe even a little better than they were before."—*The Lesbian Review*

"[A] sweet and charming small-town lesbian romance."—*Pretty Little Book Reviews*

First Position

"Brayden aptly develops the growing relationship between Ana and Natalie, making the emotional payoff that much sweeter. This ably plotted, moving offering will earn its place deep in readers' hearts."—*Publishers Weekly*

Praise for the Soho Loft Series

"The trilogy was enjoyable and definitely worth a read if you're looking for solid romance or interconnected stories about a group of friends."—*The Lesbrary*

Kiss the Girl

"There are romances and there are romances…Melissa Brayden can be relied on to write consistently very sweet, pure romances and delivers again with her newest book *Kiss the Girl*…There are scenes suffused with the sweetest love, some with great sadness or even anger—a whole gamut of emotions that take readers on a gentle roller coaster with a consistent upbeat tone. And at the heart of this book is a hymn to true friendship and human decency."
—*C-Spot Reviews*

"Read it. Embrace it. Do yourself a favor and provide it to yourself as a reward for being awesome. There is nothing about this novel that won't delight any reader, I can guarantee this."—*FarNerdy Book Blog*

Just Three Words

"Another winner from Melissa Brayden. I really connected with Hunter and Sam, and enjoyed watching their relationship develop. The friendship between the four women was heart-warming and real. The dialogue in general was fun and contemporary. I look forward to reading the next book in the series, hope it will be about Mallory!"—*Melina Bickard, Librarian, Waterloo Library (London)*

"A beautiful and downright hilarious tale about two very relatable women looking for love."—*Sharing Is Caring Book Reviews*

Ready or Not

"The chemistry is off the charts. The swoon factor is high. I promise you this book will make you smile. I had such high hopes for this book, and Melissa Brayden leapt right over them."—*The Romantic Reader Blog*

By the Author

Waiting in the Wings

Heart Block

How Sweet It Is

First Position

Strawberry Summer

Beautiful Dreamer

Back to September

To the Moon and Back

Soho Loft Romances:

Kiss the Girl

Just Three Words

Ready or Not

Seven Shores Romances:

Eyes Like Those

Hearts Like Hers

Sparks Like Ours

Love Like This

Tangle Valley Romances:

Entangled

Visit us at www.boldstrokesbooks.com

ENTANGLED

by
Melissa Brayden

2020

ENTANGLED
© 2020 By Melissa Brayden. All Rights Reserved.

ISBN 13: 978-1-63555-709-1

This Trade Paperback Original Is Published By
Bold Strokes Books, Inc.
P.O. Box 249
Valley Falls, NY 12185

First Edition: July 2020

Credits
Editor: Ruth Sternglantz
Production Design: Stacia Seaman
Cover Design by Jeanine Henning

Acknowledgments

On my twenty-first birthday, I was a junior in college. I didn't throw a big party, or attend one. I also didn't drink to excess or do shots with friends at a bar. Instead, I went to a nice restaurant with two people close to me and, to feel extra grown up, ordered "a glass of Cabernet Sauvignon, please." I felt proud of myself, sophisticated, and what was even more exciting? I truly liked the wine. A love affair began that day. I took up wine tasting as a backburner hobby, whenever I had time or the opportunity. I traveled to Napa and Oregon and lingered on some boutique vineyards complete with farm dogs and chickens interspersed with the vines. There's something deeply satisfying about the perfect glass of wine, and I've always somehow tied it in with the feelings we associate with romance. Hence I knew I had a series about wine, a vineyard, and falling in love just waiting to be told.

I hope you enjoy these three books and Joey, Gabriella, and Madison (along with the people most important to them in Whisper Wall).

Behind the scenes, there have been many humans working to make my storytelling life better (and easier). Thank you to Ruth Sternglantz for the pep talks, brainstorming sessions, and careful critiques. To Sandy and Radclyffe for working with me when the world changed and my child was home from school and practically in my lap during the workday. To the proofreaders, we all know I so desperately need. To Jeanine Henning for another stellar series of covers. Stacia Seaman for putting it all together. To all the friends who've shared glasses of reds and whites with me over the years, and to my family for Sunday wine nights on the back patio. Love to you all.

Readers, we've come a long way together. I realized it's been ten years since I wrote my first book and there is nothing else I'd rather be doing. Thank you for all the memories we've shared, and characters and locations we've gotten lost in together. I'm looking forward to so many more romantic adventures between the pages.

Cheers!

For the Risk Takers

PROLOGUE

It was the kind of night that just stuck with you, where everything was relaxed but important at the same time. Autumn had just kicked into gear in Whisper Wall, Oregon, and the leaves blew and tussled, bouncing along on the sidewalk. Inside the Big House on the grounds of Tangle Valley Vineyard, Josephine Wilder poured herself a glass of red and one for her father, Jack, who sat on the edge of his worn-in leather armchair, strumming his guitar like it was a part of him. He'd been playing that thing since Joey was small, but only pulled it out once or twice a month these days, as the vineyard kept him so busy. Joey had pulled her somewhat wavy blond hair into a ponytail earlier that evening before walking down the road, from her private cottage to the Big House where her father lived.

The two of them had dinner together once a week to chat about life and the vineyard operations, and to enjoy a good glass of wine from the vines just yards away. She looked forward to these dinners. The routine centered Joey. With her dad's famous pot roast now wrapped up in the fridge, the dishes neatly rinsed in the sink, they could relax for a bit before Joey headed home and geared up for another day of work in Tangle Valley's tasting room the next morning, when they'd open at ten a.m. sharp for visitors. They were getting closer and closer to this year's harvest, and things were a little hectic with everyone pulling longer hours to pitch in. As the winemaker at Tangle Valley, Jack worked harder than anyone, doing everything in his power to ensure the best wine possible came out of their vineyard that year. It was just as much instinct as it was science, but he had the perfect combination of both, which made him not only successful but decorated. Recently, he'd been diligently testing the sugar levels of the grapes out on the vine to determine the right time to pick. Given, the juice wouldn't see a bottle for a couple of years, but what they did now would heavily influence the final product.

"Hey, Jo, what do you think of this one?" her father asked with a gleam in his eye as he began to strum. She immediately recognized the opening chords of "Rainbow Connection" and smiled. He used to play the song for her when she was a kid and couldn't fall asleep. It never failed to grab her heartstrings and give them a good nostalgic tug.

"Now if we could only get Kermit to sing along," she said, in a nod to her favorite rendition. Her heart squeezed with a familiar pang. She had a few memories of her mother holding her in her lap as her father serenaded them. They were hazy and maybe embellished by how often she pulled them out, but they were there.

That was Jack's cue to toss in a few wildly off-key vocals that were so cringeworthy Joey laughed instead. The best part? As he continued to play, he laughed right along with her. She loved his happy face. Round, with pink cheeks. His eyes always got so small when he smiled that they were almost slits. Jack Wilder certainly knew how to enjoy life, and Joey reminded herself that she needed to steal a page from his book and work on having more fun, which was easier said than accomplished.

"How was business today?" he asked as he played. Joey was Tangle Valley's tasting room manager, a job she absolutely adored. She'd started off pouring wine as soon as she was eighteen and legal to do so and had slowly taken over that part of the business. Sure, she pitched in elsewhere on the vineyard wherever was needed and had some big ideas about where they could take the place next, but her dad didn't often listen. He cared a lot less about the business side of things and preferred instead to make wine, spend time with his friends, and strum his guitar. As the official owner, having inherited the place from his parents, Jack preferred to keep things as they were. Easier that way. He wasn't a risk taker, and that philosophy had served him well. He enjoyed his life as it was, even if that drove Joey a little crazy, imagining all that could be. She, however, came with an ambitious streak. Full of thoughts, plans, and ways to implement them.

"Slow morning," she told him, "but we picked up once the sun finally came out. Both Loretta and I had our hands full when the tour bus stopped in at eleven thirty like clockwork." They expected one to two buses a day minimum. More on the weekends. "But we sold a ton of bottles. One couple ordered a case of the dolcetto to be shipped to Altoona."

He set down his guitar and sipped his wine. "Pinot noir is the star of this place, but man, when folks latch on to the dolcetto, they really latch on."

"It has its own fan club. It's the black cherry. Gets 'em every time." She paused. "Speaking of which, have you given any thought to that restaurant idea I proposed, what was it…oh yes, over a month ago now?" She held up a hand before he could start in, moving toward him with purpose, ready to plead her case and have her voice heard. Joey came up with a lot of ideas for the vineyard, imagining all the great ways they could make the place shine. It didn't have to be all about the wine, and the wine only. She wanted the experience at Tangle Valley to be a memorable one. Their vineyard, in a sea of hundreds in the area, should be the one you couldn't miss. She took a seat on the worn-in leather sofa. "I know a restaurant would do well here and keep people talking about this place. The more foot traffic we have, the bigger the buzz, the larger our reach. People talking about us on the internet is the best form of marketing on the planet. Just think of the Instagram photos of the food alone."

He sighed. "Is this really something you're serious about? An actual restaurant. We make fantastic *wine*."

"True. But farming in the age of climate change is not always predictable. A restaurant can help us take in more money. You said yourself we could use a boost in that department."

"Yeah, but a restaurant? I thought maybe you'd moved past that by now."

"Nope. I have other ideas, too." She fought the urge to drag her notebook out of her bag and outline them in detail. One thing at a time, she reminded herself.

He chuckled. "When is that busy brain of yours *not* churning is the real question."

"Don't mock me for my dreams, Dad," Joey said with a dramatic hand to her side. "What would my mother say?"

Jack looked skyward and blew a kiss up to heaven. "She'd bust me for busting on her precious little girl. The two of you used to gang up on me when you wanted something."

"See? Listen to Mom and give me what I want."

"Another verse? Well, okay!" He grabbed his guitar and burst into another round of "Rainbow Connection," purposely off-key and painful.

Joey covered her eyes and waited him out. "Okay. No more wine for you."

He scoffed. "You can't cut this old man off. I know where we keep it. Take that and I'll grow more." He watched as Joey stood and grabbed her jacket. "You headed home?"

Joey nodded. "Told Loretta I'd open up, and she could join me later. She's been pulling a lot of hours, and she needs a break."

"She's a keeper, that one. How many years has she worked here now?"

Joey did the math. "It's been about twenty-two, I think."

"She'll always have a place here as far as I'm concerned." He whistled low. "That one's family."

"She is." Joey touched her heart. She'd grown up without her own mother past the age of eight, when they'd lost her to cancer that had taken her way too fast. Loretta Daniel had shown up halfway through Joey's childhood, hired to help pour wine in the tasting room. She'd been a nice addition to the vineyard and a calming presence in Joey's life. She had her own daughter, Carly, who was a little bit younger than Joey, but Loretta had gone out of her way to be there for Joey as well.

With a full heart, Joey kissed her father's cheek with a playful smack. "Thanks for the grub. Don't stay up late. And don't have more than two glasses."

"You're a bossy kid. Who raised you?"

"You don't even want to know. And think about the restaurant. I'm serious. This could be a really great thing for all of us."

"I promise." He sighed in surrender. "If we can figure out the logistics, might be a good move in the long run, especially with the damn hotel going in up the road. Keep us relevant."

Joey shrugged and smiled into blue eyes she'd been lucky enough to inherit. She kissed his cheek again because she hadn't expected him to concede so easily, and this felt like a victory. "That's my thought exactly. We need to step up our game if they're going to overshadow our rustic charm with their flash."

"I wish to God they'd just stay outta Whisper Wall. Build a place closer to Portland where they're better suited. Big hotels are for big cities."

"I wish the same." She patted his shoulder. "Gonna check back with you later this week about that restaurant. Be ready. Night. Thanks for dinner and the show."

"Good night, sweet girl."

As she walked home to her cottage, which was situated on the perimeter of the property not far from the Big House, Joey grinned at the progress she'd made. She'd always been ambitious when it came to Tangle Valley. She loved every inch of the vineyard and took great pride in her family's wine, which had developed quite the regional following in Willamette Valley and beyond. Mostly thanks to Jack's award-winning winemaking skills and Uncle Bobby's ability to grow top-notch grapes in this Oregon climate. She hugged herself as she walked, taking in the gentle sway of the vines to her left.

Yes, she was bursting with ideas for Tangle Valley, but she could wait patiently until her dad was ready to hear her out and implement them. He was the kindest man she'd ever met and in many ways was her best friend, but he was measured and wanted to be able to hold something in his hands and turn it over for a while before he was comfortable with it. Joey just had to give him time.

"Hey, you. What's going on?" she asked Uncle Bobby that next morning. As she headed across the property to the tasting room up front, she saw him standing stock-still and white as a sheet on the porch of the Big House. Wasn't like him. He was a mover, a doer.

He shook his head, hand on the back of his neck. His eyes carried the worst kind of terror. "It's Jack. I don't…" He moved his hand from his neck until it covered his mouth. His face went red.

"What about Dad?" Joey asked as she climbed the steps. Her heart began to thud and her palms itched because by the look on Bobby's face it was clear that something was very wrong. He shook his head. Things seemed to be playing out in slow motion, and it took forever for Bobby to speak.

"He's gone, Jo."

"What do you mean? Where did he go?" She looked around the back of the house for a glimpse of his truck, but part of her knew.

"I came by when he didn't show up for work this morning. He's always up and at it by seven, and I hadn't seen him. Found him in his room, and, Jo…I don't know what happened, but we lost him."

"No, we didn't," she said, as if correcting him on a simple miscalculation. "We had our dinner. He played music." She tried to push past her uncle to make her way into the house, but he caught her with one arm, intentionally halting her progress.

"I'm so sorry, JoJo." He looked into her eyes this time, as tears pooled in his. Bobby never cried. Did that mean this was real? Everything felt numb and awful. "I don't know how or why, but we lost him."

"We did?" To her left she heard the awful wail of sirens approaching. Somehow the eerie shrill sound sent a shiver up her spine that snapped her into the unwanted reality. This was really happening. She wasn't in the midst of a dream or an imagined fear or a hallucination. She'd lost her dad. Forever. Her mind stuttered, not fully grasping the meaning of the words or understanding that there was no way to fix this no matter what she did.

She blinked and turned just as the ambulance arrived in front of the Big House. The night before had been their last night together? No. She couldn't accept it.

Her parent, her best friend, and she'd never see him again?

The medical examiner later confirmed what they'd all imagined happened. Jack Wilder had been struck with a fatal heart attack in his sleep at some point during the night, and there was nothing anyone could have done. Joey's entire world crumbled, and for the next few days, she felt like she couldn't see straight. She barely moved from the leather couch in the living room of her parents' house. She floundered, she cried, she grieved full-on. The vineyard had belonged to her grandfather and then her father and uncle, who'd eventually signed over his shares. The farm and the knowledge that it needed her now were the only things keeping her afloat. The whole place reminded her of Jack Wilder, and that made her cling to it all the more. It was all she had of her parents, and she had to take care of it.

Though Joey knew the place like the back of her hand and had lots of opinions, she'd never been tasked with managing anything other than the tasting room. With a large-scale business to run, she now had to figure out how to take the reins at Tangle Valley and do her father proud, all the while limping along with a brave face in place, when she felt like half a human. There were a lot of people looking to her now, and she had to step up to the plate and keep Tangle Valley moving forward, new terrain or not.

The next week, she lay awake night after night, terrified, unable to sleep a wink. Finally, one night, she walked out onto the porch of her cottage, rested her forearms on the railing, and stared out at the thirty-six acres of vines. She'd read books between them, skipped among them as a kid, dreamed dreams, and made plans. That idealistic version of her had to step aside now. She had a vineyard to run and a legacy to protect. This felt like a calling she couldn't turn away from, the task at hand too important. She saw the faces of everyone who'd come before her and vowed silently to make them proud.

She would, too.

CHAPTER ONE

It's so sad. That's what I say. Losing Jack like that."

"The town was floored. That's for sure. Who would have thought?"

"Not me. No, sir. He was a young fella. Here one day. Bam. Gone the next. Not right, I tell you."

"It's all anybody is talking about."

Joey Wilder closed her eyes and turned slightly at the discussion about her father happening somewhere behind her in The Bacon and Biscuit Café that Wednesday morning in September. It was those elderly town gossips again. No surprise there. Still, a pang of grief rose fast and hot in her chest as she waited on her double espresso. It'd been six days since the funeral, and she still felt like she hadn't located her bearings as she drifted through this process. She would, though. She had a lot on her plate to keep her moving forward, and she would focus on that. One task at a time. Stay busy and keep going. It was all she could do.

"I hope that child is doing okay. I should send over some chicken and dumplings. She's had a hard couple of years. First the scandal of that broken engagement, now this."

Joey didn't disagree with the assessment, but she was someone who did her best to remain positive in the midst of even the hardest of times. She wanted badly to turn around and decline the covered dish but understood that wasn't how things worked in Whisper Wall, Oregon. The town was small, driven by the local vineyards, and nestled in the Willamette Valley. Neighborly gestures were what made it go round.

It was Maude Berkland offering the chicken and dumplings in her very recognizable wobbly voice that always reminded Joey of a billy goat. Maude was in her early eighties and had zero concept of discretion when dishing with her equally sassy friends, Thelma, Janet, and Birdie. Those old ladies were thick as thieves and the unofficial town gossips. They'd nicknamed themselves The Old Biddies, and the moniker had caught on. It was how everyone referred to the group of troublemakers. Those four knew everything about everyone and gathered daily to sip coffee, eat pastries, and exchange critical town information. Apparently, Joey's appearance in the café had promoted her family to top headline.

"That poor girl now has all that farmland and all those grapes to figure out what to do with. I don't envy her," Janet McRoberts said. She was the spitfire of the group and the loudest. "Not one bit."

Joey waited patiently at the beige and black counter with the swirly faux-marble design running through it for her to-go order, having tossed in a butter biscuit last minute, because who could resist a warm freshly made biscuit at a place called The Bacon and Biscuit? No one. That's who. They were in the midst of harvest season, and she could afford the extra calories. Hell, she deserved them after the blow from the universe. She tightened the rubber band that held her blond hair in a ponytail and watched the action in the kitchen through glimpses offered by the swinging doors.

"She's a smart cookie, that Josephine. Mark my old lady words. She'll figure it out," Thelma McDougall told the Biddies in what she seemed to think was a whisper. It wasn't even close. Joey forgave her. She was the generous one of the group, always offering hugs and snacks.

"Maybe someday," Maude said with a hearty sigh.

"Here you go, Joey," Clementine said and slid the espresso and warm biscuit bag her way. "I tossed in a couple extra biscuits for the folks back at Tangle Valley."

She lifted the bag. "Feels like you tossed in a lot."

Clem smiled and shrugged. "Harvest time. I know you guys must be hungry. Lots of picking left." They'd gone to high school together, and Clementine had always been a good friend to her. She'd worked at the Biscuit since graduation and had become a fixture of the place. Her sweet smile and cheerful disposition kept the townsfolk coming back. There was talk of her buying the café altogether from Mr. Rothstein, the current owner, who took very little interest in the place. Joey thought it sounded like a great idea. Clem's brand of tenacity and vision was the kind she identified with.

"Thanks, Clem. Big week ahead. You're right."

Clem leaned in. "And Joey? The Biddies mean well—they just have big mouths." She offered a wink.

"That they do."

With her espresso and bag of fresh butter biscuits in hand, Joey headed out of the café, smiling warmly at the Biddies as she passed. "Have a great day, you guys. Don't fill up on biscuits. Lunch is not far off."

The Biddies waved and smiled and blew kisses just like she knew they would before getting back to the business of dishing. Joey headed off into the chilly sunshine of the morning. Close to sixty now at nine a.m. on its way to maybe seventy-three later that day. The conditions were perfect for the continued harvest. If everything went according to plan, they'd have the pinot noir entirely picked by the first week in October.

She pulled Dusty, her truck, down the winding road that led to the vineyard she loved like a member of her family. Along her path, she smiled at the large rustic sign out front announcing Tangle Valley Vineyard, which had been owned and operated by her family for fifty-five years now. Her grandparents had opened the vineyard as a pipe dream once her grandfather had retired from his career as a veterinarian. They'd started with only eight acres back then, which they'd planted by hand themselves, and steadily grew to the nearly forty they had now. They weren't a huge operation, but they certainly weren't a small one. Her father and his brother had grown up on the property and took over, along with Joey's mother, who'd married into the place, once Joey's grandparents had passed.

As she arrived at the top of the hill, the expanse of land came into view in all its beauty. God, Tangle Valley never failed to take her breath away. Joey brought the truck to a halt at the top of the hill and just stared, taking it all in with new eyes. After the reading of the will yesterday, it was official. All of these vines now belonged to Joey. Tangle Valley, the place she loved more than any other, was hers to take care of, nurture, and develop in the name of her family before her, and for those ahead. The sense of responsibility overwhelmed her, but at the same time, she wanted this more than she could articulate.

She tapped the steering wheel and sat back, marveling.

The vineyard, in her opinion, came with a lot of personality. It was all rustic charm and lush farmland. Rows of grapes lined their fields for acres with the Big House off to the right and a series of smaller cottages dotting the outskirts of the property, set aside for members of the staff. Tangle Valley was on the map for its pinot noir, and why wouldn't it be? Their pinot was complex, structured, and fruity. The jury was still out on the tasting notes for last year's batch, as they'd yet to bottle, but the year before had been a good one for the pinot with hints of strawberry, plum, and vanilla. It had won multiple gold medals at not just regional competitions but the San Francisco International Wine Competition as well. Joey had high hopes for last year's haul. Time would tell, as it currently sat in the French barrels that lined the barrel room clear up to the ceiling.

And things were looking up for this year's grape yield, too. The fruit was ripe but still held its acid, which made the grapes come with lots of potential. The one thing they didn't have anymore was their secret weapon, Jack Wilder. He knew every millimeter of his equipment. He took care of the wine like it was his baby, coaxing, nursing, measuring, metering, tasting, and tinkering it to be just right. Hell, he even talked to the barrels, whispering his own encouraging sweet words. Joey had learned a lot from him, but she also knew her own strengths, and chemistry wasn't one of them. She'd barely pulled Cs in science classes. She was better suited to overseeing the operation of the vineyard as a whole, managing the tasting room, talking to the guests, selling their wine, working with distributors and their sales managers, and making sure their marketing was everything it could be. She wasn't a winemaker by nature, and trying to force it to fill her father's shoes would show. She needed to figure something out for them, and fast. Her father's assistant, Deacon, could fill in temporarily, but he was young and lacked the experience they needed.

"You hanging in there, Chipmunk?" Uncle Bobby asked a few hours later as the afternoon sun began to make its descent. The grape pickers were slowly bringing in their final hauls of the day and grabbing a water or cool can of soda from the tubs of ice. She waved to many of the seasonal regulars.

"I'm getting by." Joey slanted a hand over her eyes to keep the sun out. She sat in a rocking chair on the front porch of the Big House, her father's place. "Weird without him griping at us." She laughed affectionately. Bobby did, too.

"Still kinda hard to believe." Bobby shook his head. He used a blue bandana to dab the sweat on the back of his neck after one of the more strenuous days of the season thus far. The weather was cool, but the harvest was hard work. He was her father's younger brother and had always looked up to Jack. Bobby was a good nose-to-the-grindstone kind of guy, and she was grateful to have him by her side. He'd sold his share of the vineyard to Jack years back, preferring to keep his life as simple as possible. All he asked for was a job. For years now, he'd served as vineyard manager and oversaw the farm, the vines, and the growers. A farmer by nature, harvest was his time of year to shine, and in spite of their tragedy, he hadn't let Joey down.

"This place is yours now. What are your plans?"

It was a huge question. Tangle Valley didn't have to be a sleepy winery, and she'd always believed there was more to do. She knew the place could blossom. Her ideas involved a second tasting room, a sit-down cellar reserve tasting experience with food pairing, and that on-site restaurant she'd been pushing for. But she needed to start with their most urgent needs and go from there, because unfortunately, her father had not been the best with money. In fact, after his death, she'd learned things were worse than she'd imagined. While she firmly believed that the changes she had in mind would pay off for the vineyard in the long run, it would certainly be risky to invest what little they did have. "We'll need a winemaker. Deacon can fill in for a while, but he's only been an assistant for a few years." She lowered her voice. "He also doesn't have vision. He's a worker bee."

Bobby nodded. "Couldn't agree more. Want to advertise? Willamette has tons of winemakers who'd kill for a full-time gig at a pretty place like this."

Joey took in the information. Advertising was definitely an option. But she had one idea she wanted to explore first. "What about Madison?"

He whistled low when she brought up her best friend who'd left Willamette for California a few years back and eventually took a cush job off in the Northeast. "She's a big shot in the Finger Lakes these days, isn't she? Can't imagine her coming all the way back home for us."

Honestly, Joey wasn't sure she could either, but Madison was an up-and-comer in the wine world, the kind of innovative winemaker Joey wanted to attract to Tangle Valley. "What's the worst that could happen if I offered her the job? She'd say no, and we move on."

Even though Madison had first moved to Napa and then all the way across the country, she and Joey had still remained in close contact, messaging each other nearly every day and getting together once or twice a year for weekends of wine and long talks, which always served as the best possible reset button. Madison hadn't been able to make it home for the funeral because she was in the midst of her own harvest at the large syndicate winery where she was head winemaker. She'd called Joey almost daily, though, a loyal friend.

"Give her a call, then," Bobby said. "That girl knows what she's doing. She'd be a steal."

Joey shrugged. "It's a long shot."

"Like you said, Chipmunk. Nothing to lose at this point. And you know what? Jack would have liked seeing little Madison take over."

She grinned and walked to the edge of the porch where she'd opened a bottle of pinot and left it to breathe. She poured half a glass and lifted it in the air to her father. She'd tasted this vintage a thousand times, but she never tired of it. Her father's hard work.

That night she called Madison LeGrange.

"I might be dead," Madison said upon answering. She rarely said hello. "You're talking to a dead person who's been through four weeks of cruel manual labor." A pause. "Oh, damn it, JoJo. That's not even funny right now."

"It's okay," Joey said, quick to reassure her. "Someone died recently. Doesn't mean we stop using the English language."

Madison sighed into the phone. "You hangin' in there, buddygirl?" She smiled at the use of the nickname Madison had given her in the fourth grade when buddyboy became popular in their friend group but also didn't seem like Joey.

"I am. Strange around here without Jack bossing everyone around, but we're managing."

Madison was quiet for a moment. "I can only imagine." It'd been thirteen days without her father at this point. One of the most surreal aspects was how she kept finding things—belongings, notes, clothes he'd laid out—exactly as he'd left them. And why wouldn't he? He'd been a healthy, vibrant sixty-two-year-old when he died. The heart attack that took his life within minutes had been the only real health scare he'd ever had. In many ways, Joey kind of thought that might be the best way to live and die: healthy and happy until the moment you're not. No suffering, no decline. She remembered him on his last morning, yammering about how nicely the new vintage of dolcetto was coming along, better than he'd hoped, even, but that the chardonnay lacked balance. Projects he wouldn't ever finish now.

Joey purposefully moved them out of the conversation as the sadness gathered in an uncomfortable ball in her chest. "So, how's the East Coast wine?"

"Well, it's not from Oregon, but we're doing okay. The gewürztraminer is turning out to be the star of the show."

"Bring me a few bottles next time you're here."

"Deal." She sighed. "I miss it, you know. The climate, the scenery, and that pull-yourself-up-by-the-bootstraps fiery spirit of the Willamette folks."

"Well, we happen to think a lot of our wines and want the whole world to know it. Even if we're screaming it obnoxiously."

"Oh, the good old days."

"That's actually why I wanted to speak with you."

"You wanted to debate Oregon and New York varietals? God, let me gear up. Make some notes. Roll my shoulders."

"I want to offer you a job."

The line went silent. Madison was either deciding how to carefully extract herself from the conversation with an excuse like her house was on fire, or she was actually intrigued. As a logical, calm, and thoughtful individual, Madison was likely waiting for more information. "I've already scrubbed the drains at your place as a teenager. Were you guys really that impressed?"

Joey smiled at the memory. Kids who grew up in wine culture knew the value of hard work from a young age. Madison was no different. She'd always elbowed her way to be near the winemaking process, soaking up methods and techniques like the little sponge she was. "I need your brain."

"Are you serious right now? You can't be. Tangle Valley?"

Joey heard shuffling in the background and knew Madison was up and moving, something she did when she had a lot on her mind. "Maddie, I need a winemaker, and you're the best damn winemaker I know. I love your approach to the science. You and I like the same profiles, but most of all, you understand the fruit in a way very few people do. Plus, you're now semi-famous in the wine world, and we could really use that clout."

"Josephine Wilder."

"Yes?"

"Do you really mean it?"

"I do. I'm praying you say yes."

A pause. "I don't know what to say." A longer pause. "Yes, I do. I miss it. Home. A lot, and I've always had a soft spot for Tangle Valley. I grew up on that vineyard."

"And it has a soft spot for you, weirdo." She smiled. "Let's do this together, Maddie. You and me."

A sigh. "We always dreamed about having our own vineyard when we were kids."

Joey thought back warmly to the days they lay between the vines, reading books, talking about cute boys, which was laughable now that they'd both turned out to be gay, and musing about all the things they would do with a vineyard all their own. Hell, Joey still dreamed those dreams, and here she was, with the means to make them all come true. But Madison hadn't said yes yet.

"Tell me your thoughts for Tangle Valley and the future."

Joey quirked her lips. "Is this a reverse job interview?"

"No. Yes. I want to make sure that our visions are still aligned."

"Fine." Joey blew a wayward strand of hair off her forehead. "I want to stick with our current varietals: pinot noir, pinot gris, chardonnay and dolcetto."

"The Fab Four. I can handle that."

"Blends are always optional. Winemaker's choice."

"I like that part," Madison said.

"I want to redecorate our tasting room and add a second one for when the place gets busy on the weekends. I'm thinking dark wood, marble countertops. Classy but rustic."

"You've been trying to get that second tasting room for years."

"So why not go for it?"

"What else?"

"Reserve tastings in the barrel rooms. Tours every two hours on weekends instead of once a day. And…this is the part I think could really make a difference."

"Tell me."

"A restaurant on the grounds. One with not just good food, but amazing." Joey could hear that she was talking fast—she did that when she got excited and her mouth couldn't keep up with her brain. "I'm thinking Italian but don't have any more details worked out. I know that old building we used to use for grape sorting would be perfect, and it's currently just sitting there. We could bring in a contractor and have that place turned around. Hire someone to bring it to life."

"Yeah, that all sounds amazing, but Jo, where are you going to get that kind of cash?"

"Dad had some, and it's mine now. It's not a lot, but if I set out to achieve one thing at a time, I'm hopeful the revenue will catch up." She shook her head, her eyes filling with tears. "Nothing would make Dad happier than seeing it go to make this place sparkle, you know?"

"I do." She heard the strangled quality in Madison's voice and knew she'd been hit with a surge of emotion herself. She'd been family to the Wilders.

"My thoughts are a little scattered right now," Joey explained, "but my vision is a solid one. You can count on me, Maddie, to deliver on my promises. I can't pay you lavishly, but I can pay you a competitive salary."

"Home to Oregon wine country, huh?" After that, Madison didn't say anything for what felt like a whole minute. Joey didn't push. She gave Madison space to work it through in that very scientific brain of hers, a practice she'd learned when dealing with her friend years ago. "Can I think about it? It's a lofty idea and a big decision."

"Yes, of course. The fact that you're even considering the offer is huge."

"It's you, Joey. Of course I'd consider. How could I not?"

Warmth blossomed in Joey's chest. Hearing those words from her best friend helped in the midst of such a gut-wrenching stretch of time. "I wouldn't have been shocked if you'd laughed and promptly declined, so thank you, Mad."

The next morning as Joey dressed, she watched through the window as the seasonal workers assembled for another day of harvest. She had an hour until the tasting room would be open to visitors, and she wanted to put out those fresh chocolates she'd picked up from the new chocolatier in town, The Dark Room. She'd negotiated a killer deal with the owner and could sell by the piece. With the fresh wine crackers out, she high-fived Loretta, who was prepping the wine to have it ready to pour.

"You doing okay, little girl?" Loretta asked as she uncorked fresh bottles from beneath the counter. With gray hair she often wore in a short and neat French braid, Loretta had kind eyes that crinkled at the corners when she smiled, which was a lot. She was a salt of the earth kind of human. Yet despite her motherly disposition, she could drop into conversation a detail about her own sex life that would leave Joey's cheeks flaming. It was part of her charm.

"Everyone asks that," Joey said, knowing she could be perfectly herself with Loretta. No pretense needed. They knew each other that well. "I need to come up with more creative ways to say that my life just took a turn I wasn't emotionally ready for, but I'm trying to stay focused and put one foot in front of the other. Is there a word for that?"

"Nope."

"Then I'm at a loss."

"But your heart hurts," Loretta said, coming up behind Joey and giving her a squeeze. "Hearts gotta hurt sometimes. Let it happen. You just need time."

"Yeah, I know." Joey's eyes filled and she immediately pulled out of the soft touch, knowing it would swallow her if she let herself get mired down. Too much farm to run. Too much work to do. She immediately started making a list to help organize her thoughts and prioritize the tasks at hand. She needed to meet with their distribution rep about rolling out last year's vintage, and then talk with the printer about getting more of those glossy postcards of Tangle Valley to distribute to the bed-and-breakfasts in the area. Her phone rang. She blinked at the readout. Madison.

"Is this bad news?" Joey asked immediately as she slid onto the call. "I've always heard when the jury returns too quickly, that it's bad news for the defendant, and I don't want to go to vineyard jail quite yet."

A pause, then she heard Madison's voice. "Did you commit some sort of crime I'm unaware of? Are you heisting grapes from Fable Brook, one farm over?"

"Why would I steal grapes from Fable Brook?" Joey balked. "The Hollis family is commercializing everything good over there. I don't want those grapes. Their Riesling is dull and undatable."

"Only you date wine."

"I have to date someone, Mad, and wine is dependable. Back on track, though. I didn't expect you to call so soon." She shoved her list aside, wanting to give this call her full focus.

"Me neither, if I'm being honest. But I couldn't sleep last night, so I did that thing where I walk and talk out loud. Sometimes in circles. Remember?"

"Oh, I remember the circle talking. You still do that?"

"It's the only way to make any important decision in life. Out loud, hashing it out, no holds barred. In a circle."

"I prefer lists."

"Right. You date those, too."

"So?" Joey asked, pressing on. Her senses were on high alert, and her stomach tightened uncomfortably. All the sounds around her were extra loud—the machinery in the field, the slight squeaking of the tasting glasses Loretta scrubbed nearby, and the loud thudding of her heart. This was a big moment. "What did you and yourself figure out during your out loud circle conversation?"

"This is the thing, Jo." She heard a slow exhale on the other end of the line. "I can't seem to find a way to say no. I keep trying, too."

"Well, stop that."

"I'd like to accept the job."

"You would?" Joey practically squeaked.

"I need some time to square things away here and make arrangements for myself in Whisper Wall. But yeah. I guess this means I'm coming home."

Joey covered her mouth in shock, elation, and an emotion she couldn't name. Whatever it was, it had the tears that had appeared in her eyes earlier streaming down her cheeks unexpectedly. It was a release, that's what it was. Something good was finally happening.

Madison with her calm brilliance was coming home. She would help keep Tangle Valley afloat. Hell, together they could make it thrive. They were that great of a team. She stared up at the heavens and smiled at her father, who she knew this would please. "Best news ever," she managed.

"And Jo? I think I have an idea for someone to run that restaurant."

❖

The small office that shot off the side of the barrel room had been her father's. It was small and simple, and comprised a desk, his computer, some coffee mugs, and his favorite tasting glass. Jack would toil away in there for hours on his plans for this year's wine as well as years' to come. He'd study climate reports and, along with Bobby, watched the weather like a hawk. Joey had not set foot in there since they'd lost him, but she found her courage. His beat-up denim jacket hung on the back of the chair. She touched the rough fabric on its shoulders. The thing should have been thrown away years ago. Her gaze moved around the room. On top of the smooth wooden desk sat his notebook. She knew it well. Jack Wilder was a note scribbler, and whenever he had a thought about his wine, he wrote it right there in that notebook. She flipped through it, glancing at the dated notations, calculations, and percentages.

The top desk drawer contained way too many paper clips and pencils. In his bottom drawer she found what resembled a tackle box, though her dad hadn't been much of a fisherman. She opened the gray metal container and discovered a jumble of curious papers of all shapes and sizes. What in the world? She glanced behind her as if someone there would be able to explain it. Yet she was alone. Post-its, torn-off pieces of notebook paper, ripped file folders, even the back of what looked to be a takeout menu. Each piece of paper held only a sentence or two. Joey sorted through them, slowly at first, then picking up speed when she understood what they were. Jackisms. All about wine, grapes, and his experience with both as they related to life. She blinked in happy wonder at her new treasure trove and then laughed, her hand covering her heart. These were clever little one-liners, words of wisdom left behind in her father's very distinct handwriting. She picked one up, flipped it over, and read the words.

Rough day? Wine about it. J.W.

Joey grinned at the advice that sounded so much like something her dad would say. She closed the box, not wanting to gobble it all up in one sitting, then opened it again to read just one more.

Chardonnay about you, but I'm ready to unwind with a glass. J.W.

She both laughed and grimaced because that one could use a little work but was also so very perfect because it was him.

She closed the box a final time, vowing to save the Jackisms and read them one at a time when she needed to. Maybe they'd heal her heart or give her a good chuckle. Either way, she was blessed to have found them. Joey raised her gaze and looked over her shoulder at the vineyard through the open double barn doors. In the meantime, she had a workday ahead of her, and the grapes, now being processed, waited for no one.

Joey walked to the big open sliding doors to the barrel room and placed her hands on her hips. "Chardonnay about you, but I better get to work." She laughed. "Nope. That's still awful."

CHAPTER TWO

Well, well. Whisper Wall, Oregon, was turning out to be a great little town full of shops, cafés, and quaint little benches Becca Crawford simply couldn't get enough of. She would need to sit on each of them at some point, pop on her shades, and watch the town go by. She'd arrived two weeks prior and was ready to explore all the area had to offer. The fact that she now lived here was almost too much excitement for her to absorb. This was the kind of place she always hoped she'd land. There were so many cute shops to explore, so many people to meet, and the local culture—which she was well aware centered heavily on wine and its creation—to get to know. Wine was what kept the town afloat. Luckily, she was a casual connoisseur of the stuff herself and liked a good glass of red at the end of her workday. Becca knew firsthand how important it would be for a new business like The Jade to assimilate to the town or city, rather than the other way around. She wanted to be a valuable neighbor, and that meant meeting the locals, making friends, and establishing a role in the community for not just herself but the resort, too.

Becca decided to start with an adorable gift shop in the center of town called The Nifty Nickel. It was a happy-feeling store that smelled of cinnamon, and she secretly liked getting to say the word *nifty*. As she perused the room of seasonal wares, she picked up an autumn wreath that had been hand assembled and marveled at the detail. The price tag, a whopping sixty-five dollars, was a shocker, but worth it for the well-made product. She carried it happily to the front of the store and imagined it greeting her guests at her newly rented home. Well, once she had guests, at least. The idea made her smile, and she was struck with a burst of energy. Step one would be meeting some friends, which could prove to be an uphill battle given her long workdays. As Director of Resort Operations, it was up to her to oversee the running of Elite Resorts' newest crown jewel, The Jade. Even though The Jade wasn't up and running yet, Becca still had a myriad of tasks in front of her that she'd been chipping away at, the most important being staffing the resort in its entirety. Luckily, she was well-suited for the job.

Becca had a reputation as a go-getter with a stellar history of running one financially successful hotel after another. She planned on The Jade being her most successful assignment yet.

"I'll take this autumn wreath," Becca said to the brunette behind the counter. She wore a name tag that said *Brenda Anne* and had a pretty smile.

"Aren't these adorable?" Brenda Anne said. She lit up entirely, which made Becca light up entirely. "We got these in from one of the women in the neighborhood across the way. She does such great work. We've ordered a Christmas batch that should be here by mid-November, she said."

"I'll have to come back for one then. I just moved in and am rebuilding my holiday decoration stockpile."

Brenda Anne's eyes lit up. "You're a new local? I had you pegged for a tourist to our small town."

"No, I'm here permanently."

"Well, that's the best news I've heard since Thursday." Becca didn't ask what had happened Thursday, but she was now intensely curious. "What brings you to Whisper Wall?" She pressed her finger to the side of her cheek. "Let me guess. You're independently wealthy from a recently dispersed trust fund and want to spend your days drinking wine and staring out at the best views in the United States. You're hoping to snag a dashing farmer and settle down with your money."

"No," Becca said in apology. "But that was a very specific guess."

"I like to write short stories, so sometimes my brain gets to motoring on ahead of me." Her eyes went extra wide as if to say: *Can you even believe it?* "Stick to reality, Brenda Anne," she said, chastising herself in a voice that was not her own. "That's what my mama always said."

"Well, I, for one, am impressed with your imagination. But the truth is that I'm here because I've taken the position as general manager of The Jade, going up not too far from here."

She watched as friendly Brenda Anne's smile faltered slightly.

"Oh. You're with the big hotel chain? Oh no." She looked a little crestfallen, but Becca swallowed that and plowed ahead.

"Yes, and so excited to get to know everyone in Whisper Wall. I love it here already."

She accepted Becca's credit card for the wreath and winced as if she had bad news to report. "Lots of folks in the area aren't so happy about the hotel going in. It's all the talk these days. They're… concerned."

Becca resisted the urge to correct *hotel* to *resort*, which is what The Jade was. Yes, she'd heard the murmurings about The Jade and had, of course, read the emails forwarded to her by corporate from the less than excited citizens. Many of the vintners in the area were up in arms about the size and commerciality of The Jade and the damage they felt it would inflict upon their out-of-the-way, rustic vibe. They didn't want anything commercial in their midst. It didn't shock her. But they were overlooking the long list of positives a resort like theirs would bring to them. She decided against having that debate with Brenda Anne, however, in fear of ruining their potential friendship. "I completely understand how they feel. It's my hope that once we're up and running, people will change their minds. We have the potential to attract lots of new visitors who wouldn't come to the area otherwise. Our client base is huge."

Brenda Anne didn't appear convinced but remained polite. She handed Becca her cute little two-handled bag containing the wreath. "I wish you all the best with that. There's a meeting about it next Monday, you know." She frowned as if to sympathize.

Becca paused, mid bag handoff. "A meeting?" People still had those things? What happened to just complaining on the internet?

"Yeah. Where everyone gets together and talks about issues that involve all of us. There's a microphone and the opportunity to sign up to speak."

"And that's happening about the resort?"

Brenda Anne nodded enthusiastically. She grabbed a flyer and handed it off to Becca, who gaped. "Next week at the event center. I'm bringing the cupcakes. Double chocolate with a little dash of espresso. I'm so excited about them. Food and conflict pair well together."

"How wonderful," Becca said, keeping her careful smile in place. They were meeting about the resort? Really? Her spirits dropped, and she let the bag fall to her side. After that, annoyance took over. Why did the locals not understand that this could be a very valuable partnership?

She lifted her purchase, refusing to let any of this bleed over onto perky Brenda Anne. "Thanks for the wreath. I'll definitely be back."

Brenda Anne waved. "Looking forward to it. Happy you're here. Kinda."

Becca hit the sidewalk and demanded her weary smile hold strong. She hit up three more shops in the heart of town, and her reception was the same at each: enthusiastic hospitality until she introduced herself and explained what brought her to Whisper Wall. She watched as each smiling face morphed into one of polite tolerance. It angered her as a businesswoman and hurt her feelings as a human being who was excited to make connections and friends in her new community.

Lost in her thoughts and probably not looking where she was going, she shoulder checked a woman walking in the other direction.

"Oh, God. That was on me," Becca said, turning back and holding a hand out to make sure she'd done no damage.

"Not to worry. I'm still alive and a little more awake, so thank you." The woman was smiling and she was...striking. Pretty. Blond hair, crystal blue eyes. She wore a knit cap on the back of her head. That's when Becca noticed the package she'd knocked clean out of the woman's hands.

"Let me get that."

"I got it." The woman bent down, too, and they laughed about the awkwardness of both kneeling to retrieve the same package. Becca beat her there and handed off the bag. "I'll try to be more alert going forward."

"Citizens everywhere thank you." She dropped to sincerity and added, "Seriously, though. No harm at all." She stood, as did Becca. "Enjoy your day, okay?"

"You, too." She stood and watched the blonde head down the sidewalk. Part of her wondered where she was off to. Another part wanted to go with her. Something in her energy snagged Becca's attention.

She returned to her new home feeling dejected, and wishing she'd finished unpacking the remaining boxes that dotted her open living room and kitchen combo. Becca loved her new place, though, in spite of the boxes. Almost entirely white with exposed dark wooden beams traveling up to a point atop the two-story ceiling in her living area. The house was spacious, full of natural light, and just rustic enough to fit in nicely in wine country.

"Well, I'm home," she announced with a small smile to her empty place. No response, though she knew that would be the case. Sometimes simply speaking her thoughts to inanimate objects like her house made Becca feel a little less lonely, not that she was unhappy. She thought about getting herself a dog, imagining snuggling up with a little guy or girl might be nice. She shrugged, feeling a little solitary. Oh, well.

It was relatively chilly out today and the sun was just beginning to fall behind the trees. She watched the beautiful color stream in through her large picture windows at the back of the house. "Looks like the perfect night for chili to me," she said to exactly no one. With a little Corinne Bailey Rae on Pandora, she tossed together the ingredients, knowing she could feast on that glorious pot of chili for the next few days. Oh! And cornbread would be a nice addition. She would do that next.

As the chili simmered, Becca decided to spend the day poring over résumés both from in town and beyond. She'd need managers, team leaders, trainers, clerks, and much more. Maybe if she got enough accomplished this week, she could visit the neighbors she was most excited about, that adorable little vineyard with the logo of the tangled vines. She could practically walk there and looked forward to exploring not only their wines, but the tasting room itself.

Becca wasn't sure why, but she had a sneaking suspicion she was going to fall in love with that place.

❖

It had been a month since Madison had accepted the position of winemaker for Tangle Valley, and at long last, she was on her way. Joey sat on the wooden steps in front of the Big House and waited. They should be arriving any minute. She ran her palms across her thighs, smoothing her jeans with nervous excitement.

She'd opened a couple of bottles and set them out to breathe, wanting to welcome the new members of the vineyard family appropriately. Around here, that meant with a good glass of wine. Loretta had put out a beautiful cheese board that would complement the wines in their variety, and set up a private table for them off to the side in the tasting room. It hadn't been an especially busy day for foot traffic, but then it was midweek. In fact, their visitor rate was something Joey hoped to improve now that she was at the helm and the chief decision-maker. Her father had always been more interested in the wine, which made sense as it was his passion. But the time had come to think big picture.

When Madison had taken the job, she'd suggested her good friend Gabriella, who also happened to be Madison's ex-girlfriend, as someone who might be a perfect fit to open a restaurant on site. She'd served as head chef in multiple spots in the Finger Lakes, but she'd cooked under many well-known chefs in New York City as well. According to Madison, who she trusted as much as she trusted herself, Gabriella knew food like no one she'd ever known. Better yet? Gabriella was looking to turn a new page and itching for a change of pace. Madison introduced them over the phone, and Joey couldn't believe how well she and Gabriella hit it off. After their chat, Gabriella sent along her very impressive résumé and her ideas for the restaurant, which she envisioned to be Italian, and even had some marketing plans of her own. Joey was impressed but wanted to have a heart to heart with Madison before sealing the deal.

"My only concern is that she was your girlfriend, you know?" Joey said. She'd stood in front of the microwave in the Big House, where she'd been staying in the extra bedroom, which she'd now redecorated and made into her very own master. Every bit as spacious as the original. "Don't you think that might make things a little extra dicey?"

"Oh God, no," Madison said without delay. "We were together for four months and both agreed it was the most ridiculous of arrangements because we make way better friends. We haven't had an awkward moment since."

"Okay." Joey nodded, feeling lighter. "That's good to hear." If Madison felt that confident, who was she to overrule her? She was still friends with Simone, after all, and she'd left Joey at the altar. She closed her eyes at the still potent memory from just three years prior. Luckily, she had come to understand that it had all been for the greater good, as they weren't the best match. She could pass Simone in town and have a more than pleasant conversation these days. That said a lot. "If you're comfortable with the arrangement, I'm ready to move forward and offer Gabriella the job. She and I talked through the logistics. The restaurant will be part of the Tangle Valley Vineyard but she will maintain creative control for as long as she's head chef."

"I think you're making a great decision, and you're going to love Gabriella. I say that because, well, everyone does. It's kind of astounding. As a scientist, I've actually tried to figure it out, but really, she's just very likable, and that's all there is to it. Everyone's sweetheart with a side of sass."

"I can get behind that combination but am definitely hoping for low drama between the exes."

"Trust me. You have nothing to worry about. Unless she brings up Christmas from two years ago—then all bets are off." Joey took a hard swallow. "I'm kidding," Madison said, with a quiet laugh. "I just enjoy imagining that deer in headlights look you sport when someone says something even mildly alarming."

"I'm not doing the deer look," Joey said with a scoff.

"Oh, and now you're scoffing, aren't you? The deer-scoff combo."

The outrage hit. "I am not, Maddie-strange-pants. You don't know everything."

"Oh, the childhood nicknames are out. Is a headlock next? I think I still have the move."

Ah, memories. Joey laughed. "I dare you to try."

"I have a feeling if we're working together, we'll get there eventually. You sure you're up for this? I have a lot of opinions when it comes to wine. Don't get me started on destemming practices."

Joey didn't hesitate. "That's why I want you. You know grapes. You anticipate the way they'll unravel their flavors. I like your instincts. Your precision. I will find a way to deal with the headlocks." She knew Madison was someone who craved autonomy in her work, and she would do her best to give it to her. "We're a team, here, yes. But when it comes to the wine, I will always put your opinion ahead of mine."

A pause hit the line. "Can I confess something to you?" Madison finally asked.

"Always."

"I've loved Tangle Valley since the first day I came over to hang out in fourth grade. I can't wait to get started."

Joey felt the pressure that she'd been carrying on her shoulders slowly melt. She wasn't sure quite how, but it felt almost ordained, the way things were working out. Everything seemed to be happening the way it was meant to. She couldn't help but wonder if Jack Wilder had a little something to do with it. He was taking care of her and Tangle Valley from afar. Maybe her mom was, too. It was a nice thought.

As she sat on the front steps, waiting on Madison and Gabriella to arrive from their cross-country journey, she went over the last touches she'd made to their housing. Madison would take the Sunrise Cottage closest to the Big House, decorated in gray, soft orange, and white. Joey had hired Angela Peters to redecorate the whole place, making it contemporary, yet still rustic enough to fit in nicely on the property. A little farther down the road would be Gabriella's Spring Cottage, which Angela had decorated with touches of sage and yellow. It was warm, welcoming, and came with a fully updated chef's kitchen, which Joey felt was important for Gabriella to have at her disposal. Now all she needed were her new coworkers.

Moments later, a U-Haul followed by a blue pickup truck with a white stripe down the side appeared just on the horizon. Joey stood, placed her hands on her hips, and felt herself beam for the first time in weeks. She waved excitedly as the vehicles pulled to a stop just shy of the Big House.

An absolutely beautiful woman with thick brown hair and soft brown eyes hopped down from behind the wheel of the U-Haul. When she hit the ground, Joey saw that she was petite in stature, a few inches shorter than Joey's average height, but she'd handled that truck like a pro.

"Hi, there! You must be Joey," she said warmly and came around the front of the truck with a great big smile. "Gabriella Russo."

"So great to meet you in person." Joey held out her hand, as Gabriella approached and ignored it entirely, instead opening her arms and pulling Joey into a hug. "Sorry, but this occasion seems big and I'm a hugger." She released Joey. "Do you mind? I guess it's a little late to ask."

Joey laughed. "Not at all." She paused because up close and personal, she realized how beautiful Gabriella was. No. Stunning. With big, wide-set eyes, flawless olive skin, and dark hair that fell in thick layers past her shoulders, she could see why Madison's interest had been piqued years back.

"Stop all the fun until I get there," a voice shouted. Joey laughed and turned to see Madison hop out of the truck. "You two look like old friends already." Joey's heart swelled at the sight of her best friend, here at last.

"Maddie," she said and held open her arms. Madison LeGrange with all her curly brown hair streaked with blond from the sun hadn't changed much over the years. Her blue eyes twinkled when they saw Joey. Their friendship had always been stronger than any she'd ever known, and it was clear that connection persisted.

Madison scampered the rest of the way and pulled Joey into a tight embrace. "I can't believe I'm here. I'm back. Can you believe it?"

"You're not back. You're home," Joey said, banishing the tears that stung her eyes. This was a happy occasion, and she was not about to get over-the-top sappy. She released Madison and shook her head. "We're working together. Can you believe it?" She included Gabriella in the declaration, but she was already lost to the conversation, seemingly mesmerized by the beauty of Tangle Valley. Joey had to admit, if you'd never seen it before, it was something to behold. Rows and rows of beautiful vines that extended for acres until you saw their green and the blue of the sky meet. The air was fresh. The temperatures were mild. Joey couldn't understand why everyone didn't live in Willamette Valley. The wine industry was certainly taking on the big guys from California and Europe, and people were slowly giving the area credit for the quality wines they were turning out year after year. There was no denying that Oregon wine was climbing steadily in popularity, and Tangle Valley was right there in the center of it. It was an exciting time to be in the wine business.

Gabriella shook her head. "The photos don't come close to doing this place justice. Wow. I live here?"

"You do now," Joey said, coming to stand next to her.

"Well, I'm impressed and floored." Gabriella exhaled. "You have no idea how much I need this…serenity. My life's been feeling a little scattered lately." The exuberance had receded from her voice and been replaced by quiet sincerity.

"Well, you've come to the right place for that. I hope you like wine."

Gabriella laughed. "I hear it's all the rage."

"How about a tour?" Madison asked.

"I thought you were going to ask for a tasting first."

"Don't think I didn't want to," Maddie said with a wink. "I'm anxious to taste last year's yield."

"It's not out yet, so you'll be one of the first. I have a sample bottle on hand. We can do a barrel tasting later as well, if you like."

Gabriella seemed to still be taking it all in. "I can't believe this is real. I feel like I've stepped into the pages of a calendar. First that downhill drive onto the property and now this."

Maddie slung an arm around her shoulder. "Get used to it. You live in a Thomas Kinkade painting."

Joey clapped her hands together. "Speaking of living, follow me to your cottages, freshly remodeled, though I promise the paint is dry. I've also left you some fresh baked goods from Loretta—she's so excited you're both here—and of course, I've stocked your places with wine because I'm not a criminal."

"I'm just thrilled to say that I live in a cottage," Gabriella said, as they walked the path along the perimeter that took them to the onsite housing. She added an extra hop in her step and a sway of her hips.

Joey laughed. "I think you're going to like them." Uncle Bobby also had a place on the property, as did Loretta and Deacon. "I thought I'd drop you guys off, let you get situated and refreshed, and maybe we could meet in the tasting room?"

"I think that's the best plan ever," Gabriella said. Joey was beginning to understand that she was a cheerful, positive person. The kind that might be really nice to have around.

"Sounds great to me. I'm ready to get started. Quick question," Madison said.

Joey looked over at her as they walked, her heart just so happy that they were, at long last, here. "What's up?"

"The construction we passed on the turnoff to Tangle Valley. What in the world is that place? It's huge."

Joey bristled. It pained her even to think about the monstrosity down the road. In fact, she'd shoved it from her mind once her father had his heart attack and kept her feelings simmering on the back burner as she worked feverishly to keep the vineyard up and running. But with things moving in the right direction now, it was time to face facts.

"That's the site of a giant hotel going in, brick by brick. It's almost done."

Madison stared at her. "Here? In Whisper Wall?"

"I know. Even worse? It's an Elite Resorts property. The hotel chain?" Joey shook her head in distaste. "The charm of Whisper Wall is rooted in its out of the way, small, quaint look and feel. It's our bread and butter. We're a small town, and people come here on their vacations to get away from the world, drink good wine, look at the lush green landscape, and watch the sunset. The end. We depend on those visitors." She extended her arm in the theoretical direction of the hotel. "The Jade, or whatever it is they're planning to call that thing, is a problem. It's a boil, an eyesore on our"—she gestured to Gabriella—"calendar photo."

Madison grinned. "No problem is too big for the perfect bottle of wine. It's up to us to make sure we produce it and ignore that place."

Gabriella grabbed both Madison's and Joey's arms, grinning down the path at the two cottages, just a short distance apart from each other. "Get out. Seriously?"

"All yours." Joey gestured to the second cottage as Madison approached the first. "I'll see you soon for wine and snacks."

"You're my favorite new friend and boss," Gabriella said, with a celebratory clap. She and Madison thanked Joey and headed into their new homes to say hello and settle in. In the meantime, Joey had a list of tasks still on her daily to-do list, including approving the updates to their labels for last year's vintage, which would be bottled soon. Not far from her mind, however, was what she was going to do about The Jade. She made a point of moving that little obstacle to the top of her list.

❖

If Joey wanted to impress her friends and new colleagues with all the work they'd put into their wines, it seemed to be working. Later that afternoon, the three of them gathered in the corner of the tasting room while Loretta tended to the small number of visitors who lingered shortly before closing.

"Calling it now. I think the dolcetto was my favorite," Gabriella said, admiring the last swallow in her glass. "But I've always been partial to any and all Italian influences. Heritage, you know." She kissed her fingertips in jest.

Joey touched her glass to Gabriella's. "Oh, you know what? We're going to get along. You and me. We're probably going to get into a little trouble, too." She could tell Gabriella liked wine as much as she did.

They'd already done tastings of all four varietals from both last year's yet-to-be-released vintage as well as several of the more popular blends, not to mention the vintage from two years ago, currently in distribution and on the tasting room floor. Madison swirled her glass and took a final sip of near-ready-but-not-quite pinot. "Jack made strides between the two. He deserves a lot of credit." She took another sip and then dumped the rest of the glass in the bucket at the center of the table. If they consumed all the wine Joey had poured that afternoon, they'd be drunk off their asses.

"He wanted to bring the fruit forward. Tweak the acidity levels."

"And he did."

Gabriella set her glass down. "I love it. That's for sure. Mellow, but satisfying." She dumped the rest.

Joey smiled. "My dad would have loved that you used the word satisfying. He believed that's exactly what a good wine should do—not draw huge attention to itself, simply satisfy."

"Well, it's true. Do you know what else I love? That cottage. Joey, I don't know who you paid to get inside my head and mimic my exact style, but they knocked it out of the park."

"Oh, did they?" Madison asked, pointing at her face.

Joey dipped her head. "Madison told me a little more about you, and that helped with the decor, but feel free to make any changes to make it more you." She'd supplied the cottage with basics like curtains and paint but had chosen to leave the intricate details to each inhabitant. Maddie was easy enough. She'd toss a couple paintings of nature on the walls and high-five herself, practical person that she was, but Joey had a feeling Gabriella was different. The details would matter.

"What had me excited is that most of my stuff will match perfectly."

"Flowers," Madison told Joey with a laugh. "Think lots and lots of flowers. Like a bouquet of flowers walked into a room and multiplied like gremlins dipped in water."

Gabriella passed her a look. "We can't all have charts and graphs on our refrigerator."

"Oh, can't we though?" Madison said wistfully.

"People who visit think you're CIA."

Madison grinned and held her now empty glass off to the side, allowing it to dangle from her hand. She seemed so damn sophisticated and put together these days. Wine magazines ran features on her. Young winemakers looked up to her because of all she'd accomplished in her short career. Joey was not only blessed to have her talent on board, but her pride in her friend's accomplishments welled robustly.

Madison watched Joey. Then, finally, "We've had some wine. Can I ask about Simone? I filled Gabriella in on the high points on our drive."

"Of course," Joey said. No, it wasn't her favorite topic in the world, but she did just fine with casual conversations that surrounded her ex and their very public, humiliating ending three years ago. Madison had stood next to Joey on what was to be the happiest day of her life, her wedding day. As maid of honor, she was the one who'd picked Joey up off the floor that afternoon. Literally. She'd collapsed in a heap of shock, despair, and humiliation. Joey had believed Simone to be the love of her life back then. But time helped reveal the reality. In spite of the town gossip chain a mile long, Joey was grateful for the outcome. Her life was okay. She loved her job and her Tangle Valley family, and had great friends. What more did she need?

"So, here's the thing I don't get," Madison said. "Simone leaves you at the altar."

"Yep," Joey said and sipped. Gabriella winced, obviously experiencing empathetic horror.

"Because she wants a bigger life for herself."

"True, again. Simone has always believed that life here is too mundane. She wanted something faster paced than, well, a farm."

"But then she goes and settles down with a veterinarian who's home by five most days. How is that faster paced?"

Joey shrugged. "It used to bother me, too. But you know what? Constance apparently makes Simone happy in a way I wasn't capable."

"Do we hate her?" Gabriella asked, showing that she was, in fact, the best type of friend. "The vet?"

Joey placed a hand over Gabriella's. "No, but you get major points for the offer. Simone is…not my person. That's all. Those two were meant to be. They're honestly very sweet together. I long to hate them, dream about it even. Can't seem to."

"She did one hell of a number on Joey, though." Madison drummed her fingers on the table and shook her head.

"Are you *sure* we don't hate her?" Gabriella asked again in solidarity.

"Still sure. And she did not do a number on me," Joey said, adding another splash of the dolcetto to her glass. "At least nothing long lasting."

"No? I disagree." The expression on Madison's face said that she was attempting to make her point in the gentlest way possible. "When was the last time you dated?"

Joey shrugged. "I couldn't tell you, but I'm busy with this place, Maddie, and I really like it that way." Why was she suddenly so defensive?

"Anyone since Simone?" Gabriella asked, her voice soft. Those big brown friendly eyes helped Joey relax.

"No," she confessed. "I'm not against romance and dating, but… okay, maybe I'm against romance. It hasn't served me well, so I stick to things that have. Friends, wine, Tangle Valley, a good sunset, and the occasional excellent bowl of soup." Madison and Gabriella exchanged a look. "What? You're already exchanging knowing glances. I'm fine."

"You did not just say soup," Madison said.

"I did."

"I'm going to die if my best friend's excitement level peaks at excellent soup. There's more to life." The outrage was clear, but all Joey could do was laugh.

"I believe you're fine." Gabriella smiled. "I don't even know you that well yet, and I can tell as much. Plus, you run one of the most beautiful vineyards I've ever seen, so that means you're more than fine. You're special."

"See?" Joey said and turned like a victor to Madison. "I'm more than fine. Well, outside of losing my dad." Her playful spirits dipped. Sometimes she got caught up in the day and forgot. It was never long, however, until it all came rushing back, like now.

"But you have us here now, and you don't have to shoulder all of this on your own," Madison said and took a moment for a long blink. "I'm a tad tipsy, but can we talk briefly about the harvest anyway?"

Joey didn't hesitate. "We had a good year. The fruit is beautiful. Cooler temps at night served the grapes well, but we never got too cold. The rain cooperated, and the summer was fairly warm and dry."

"Sounds like we're gonna have a lot of good wine coming out of Willamette this year, especially with the weather proving so conducive for pinot."

"I want ours to be at the top of every list. Entered in all the big competitions, too." She could hear the conviction in her own voice. This year without her father would be an important one, and she wanted them to thrive. For him. For herself. For everyone who put in the hard hours at Tangle Valley on the daily.

Maddie met her gaze. "Me, too. We'll take on the world."

"What about food?" Gabriella asked. "What did you think of my preliminary menu for the truck?"

"I loved everything you suggested. Especially the rice ball things. Good God, woman. I've never drooled over an email before."

"Arancini," she said. "Great finger food. Perfect for a truck."

"I'd murder my mother for one of those right now," Madison said.

Joey gasped. "You keep making dead parent jokes."

Madison winced. "Why do I do that?"

"I have no idea. Plus, you love your mother."

"And Gabriella's balls. The rice ones. Hence the internal struggle," Maddie said matter-of-factly.

"My balls bring all the girls to the yard," Gabriella said with sparkle.

Joey laughed and could tell she was in for a ride working with these two.

They'd made the decision to hold off on construction on the restaurant until they had a stronger handle on the direction and flavor, no pun intended. To do so, Gabriella wanted to spend some time at Tangle Valley to get a feel for the vineyard's typical clientele and the local culture. Joey had no problem with going slow, wanting to make sure they did everything they could to achieve the best possible marriage between wine and food. Gabriella did want to get cooking, however, and pitched to Joey the idea of starting off with a food truck on the property and some additional outdoor tables. That way she could test out some dishes, work from a rotating menu, and then migrate to a full-scale sit-down restaurant the following year, maybe using summer to kick it off when the tourists arrived in droves. Joey could already envision the big marketing push now. They'd start with social media and move to heavy local advertising, making an event of the truck's soft opening and then a big smash for the restaurant's grand.

"What's our expected rollout date for the truck?" Madison asked and picked up the pen and small black journal she'd used to record her tasting observations. Leave it to Maddie to stay on top of every detail.

"Well, we're hoping for sometime in the next two weeks, but first we have to buy a truck. I have a lead on a couple not far from here." She nodded toward Gabriella. "Maybe we can take a field trip?"

"I'm in. We'll be women on a mission. Thelma and Louise."

"They don't have the happiest ending, Gabs," Madison supplied.

She frowned. "Bonnie and Clyde."

"Yikes." Madison winced. "Seriously?"

"SpongeBob and Patrick."

Madison raised a shoulder. "Sure."

Joey laughed, getting a feel for what the give-and-take around here was going to feel like now, and she was a fan.

Gabriella turned to Joey. "I'd love to grab lunch somewhere in town and start to get a taste for the local flavors."

"Definitely. I know just the place to start. Now who wants a revisit?" Joey asked and gestured to the array of seven-plus open bottles. Two hands shot in the air. The sun was going down, Loretta was closing up shop in the tasting room, and outside the vines swayed gently in the wind. After all she'd been through lately, Joey needed a night like this one. Being around friends, one old and one new, had her heart feeling lighter. Their chemistry felt right, somehow, and she relaxed with the knowledge that she wasn't on her own. She had a team, and together they would get through this.

CHAPTER THREE

Officing out of a portable building definitely had its drawbacks. Very little space, uncomfortable furniture, and the noise from the resort's construction just outside left Becca feeling more than a little tense. She squeezed the back of her neck, hoping to relieve a little of the pressure, as her final candidate for the position of front desk manager departed.

"What do you think?" Carla Cortez, the assistant resort manager asked. She'd hired Carla first, so she could help staff the place. So far, she'd shown herself to be knowledgeable and eager, a transfer to town herself. They seemed like a great duo, already complementing each other's styles. "He's got the experience, and his leadership philosophies have me excited. I would be pumped for work every day if I worked on his activities team."

With no more interviews scheduled that day, Becca slipped out of her heels. "Right? God, my toes are angry. Do yours ever get angry?"

"Mine bitch at me with a megaphone, the bastards."

"Thank you for getting that." She switched gears. "But I had the same thought, and with a new property, that's exactly the kind of proactive energy we need. I'll call him tomorrow and extend an offer. He's based in Portland, so he'll likely want to relocate, unless he loves commutes."

Carla leaned against the doorframe. "Any plans for the weekend? I'm taking Pete on a hike. You're welcome to join us."

"A hike? Our feet are killing us. How are you rebounding to hiker status. What's in that water bottle?"

"Oh, Becca. I'm hoping the new girl comes tomorrow and hikes for me. She comes every morning, fresh and ready to go."

"I need a new girl. Are they expensive?"

Carla laughed. "I'll tell you one thing—Pete loves her." Pete was Carla's brand-new husband. Though Becca did enjoy a good hike on occasion, she wasn't sure she could stomach the third-wheel status that came with hanging out with the two of them. They'd been married less than a year and resided firmly in the land of Maybe You Two Should Get a Room Now. The dinner she had with them recently had easily been rated PG-13 on their side of the table, and inched its way toward R as the night progressed.

"I appreciate the offer, but I'm not sure I can watch you suck on his face all the way up the mountain. Especially if my new girl didn't come. She often doesn't."

Carla laughed. "But what a fine face it is." They'd spent enough hours together in the past couple of weeks to speak candidly and seemed to have a decent rapport when it came to joking around. "What do you have going in place of us?"

"Nothing concrete. I'm going to spend some time putting my house together. I don't think I can neglect it any longer. After that, I thought I might wander over to that vineyard down the road from here."

"Tangle Valley? Have you taken the winding road that leads to the tasting room that pops you in the head with that scenery? It's breathtaking. Views for days and the people are so nice. Pete and I checked it out when we first drove into town for my interview with you. Fantastic pinot. Best I've had."

"I think you just sold me."

"Oh, and that lady who pours the wine? She's Carly Daniel's mom. Her actual mother." Carla did a little happy dance. "I love me some Carly Daniel, especially when she's in peril and racing around with a gun." Carla demonstrated. "Plus, she's kickass on that game show. Her partners always win the money. I want her to be my friend."

"Well, it's good to have goals. I do like her films." Becca slid back into her heels with a smile and offered Carla a high five on her way out of the office. She had more work to do, but she could do it from home where it was infinitely more comfortable. "Get out of here, Cortez. We're done for the day. But don't get used to it. Once The Jade is up and running, our lives and schedules will no longer be our own. Better say good-bye to Pete. And hire a few extra new girls."

"What?" Carla squeaked.

Becca laughed. "I'm just kidding."

Carla sighed in relief.

"Kind of."

The next morning was chilly but in a really good way. Becca busied herself hanging art around the living room and hallways, doing her best to match themes and colors, and feeling quietly happy with the results. After lunch, she was ready to venture out and knew exactly the place she wanted to hit up first. Not only could she grab a nice glass of wine on a sunny, crisp day, but Tangle Valley, due to its proximity to The Jade, was an ideal neighbor to befriend. Perhaps they could even strike up a partnership that would benefit both businesses. She opened the door to her home and paused. Swinging the door had dislodged a flyer that had been placed in the jamb. She picked up the sheet of light blue paper and frowned at the header in large angry black font. *The Jade Hotel is NOT Your Friend.* She sighed. Okay, first of all, the sentiment hurt her feelings. Second of all, it irked her because it was entirely untrue, and third, The Jade was a *resort*, not a hotel. She shook her head, squeezed the flyer into a ball, and returned inside to throw it away. With her spirits taking a definite hit, she needed that cheerful day out more than ever. Who knew? Maybe she'd even meet a new friend at the vineyard, or at the very least, find a nice spot to have a glass of wine on a weekend.

Minutes later, she pulled her car onto the winding road that eventually led her to the entrance to Tangle Valley Vineyard. She smiled happily at the quaint sign with the swirly font and the tangled vines. As someone in the hospitality industry, she very much appreciated its friendly nature and the way it seemed to greet her with a happy hello. She drove farther onto the property, around a wooded bend and up and over a hill. At the top, she paused. This was what Carla had been referencing. Her breath caught. Laid out in front of her was the money shot, a gorgeous, sweeping view of the property in all its glory. Rows of vines for as far as the eye could see. It was something you'd see in a painting. Becca had always romanticized wine country, and she had to pinch herself now. This was *her life*. She lived just up the road from this gorgeous stretch of land. She felt herself smiling as she drove on, and then brought her car to a stop in the designated parking lot, just as the quaint signpost had instructed. She passed a wave to a friendly looking couple who were retiring to their car probably after a fun afternoon of tasting. They waved back, a little giggly. Yeah, they'd had a glass or two.

She followed the same path to the brick building with the impressive vaulted roof. She passed a couple of outdoor heaters and smiled at several groups on a small patio drinking wine. Not far away, a man played a guitar and sang "Hotel California." She imagined the live music was a weekend feature. Becca made her way inside the tasting room, which was surprisingly modern, yet still came with the heavy feel one would associate with wood, barrels, and industry. The sturdy oak beams across the ceiling contrasted nicely with the marble countertops in a pleasing marriage of new meets old. Becca immediately liked the vibe and feel of the space.

The room wasn't crowded, but it definitely felt alive. Conversation reverberated, and laughter carried across the room. The space blossomed with happiness. There was a group of five twentysomethings doing a tasting together, and their boisterous banter signaled that this was perhaps not their first stop. Becca smiled at them, admiring their fun. Aha, one wore a Bride-to-Be sash, which explained it all, including the limo she saw waiting in the parking lot. Down the counter a bit there were two older couples who looked like they were longtime friends. Behind the counter was a woman in her fifties and a young woman, maybe thirty. Wait. Wasn't that the same woman she'd seen in town? She studied her and yes, definitely. She had her hair pulled back in a ponytail, but several strands were loose and framed her beautiful face. Becca imagined that was on purpose. She listened in as the woman she had trouble taking her eyes off explained to the bachelorette party what they could expect in their next tasting. When she finished, she turned to Becca.

"Hello there," she said with a bright smile. She was pretty, very pretty, and it made Becca pause and gather herself. "Wait. I saw you in town a couple of days ago, right? You dropped your bag near the Nickel?"

"Yes," Becca said, pointing at her. "I thought I was the only one who remembered."

"Not a chance," the woman said and put her hand on her hip. "Well, it's nice to see you again. What can I do for you today? Some wine to take home, a glass to enjoy, or maybe a tasting?"

Becca swallowed and refocused, finding her normal stride again, even though she'd decided that this woman had a fantastic mouth. "I'd love to do a tasting if you have room."

"We always have room." The woman grabbed a glass. She had blue eyes and they sparkled. She seemed in her element, which probably contributed to her zest. This was someone who liked her job, and it showed. "Then you have come to the right place. I have four varietals for you to try and a sneak peek at our upcoming pinot noir if you're diehard."

Becca smiled. She was captivated in the most pleasant way. "I am."

"Time will tell, but that makes you my kind of person. Glad you stopped in today." The woman grinned, and for a moment they just stared. Wow. What was that? Was Becca imagining the powerful pull or was it real? She swallowed and noticed her cheeks warm. Then it seemed as if the woman remembered herself. She blinked, laughed quietly, and pushed forward. "Here's a list of what you can expect. We'll want you prepared." She slid the sheet of paper listing the wines Becca would be trying over to her so she could follow along. She touched the top entry, leaning slightly but noticeably over the counter and into Becca's space. Becca caught the scent of her shampoo. Raspberry, maybe? It complemented her personality wonderfully. "We'll be starting with white today, our pinot gris." She poured a couple of ounces into Becca's glass and straightened, hand on the back of her hip again as she waited for Becca to explore the wine.

"It's beautiful," Becca said, holding it up to the light. She was no wine expert but knew a few things. She noticed the edges of the wine, its color, which was deeper than she was used to on a pinot gris. Not nearly as pale.

The woman gestured to Becca's glass as if reading her mind. "Pinot gris is most typically a lighter wine. Because we're in Oregon, you're going to find this one a little more medium bodied, hence the deeper color. When you taste, you'll catch some crisp green apple, a little bit of lemon, and pear, too. Our particular pinot gris is very fruit forward with bright acidity."

"I'll *catch* those flavors, huh? I like that word."

"When it comes to wine, I have many words," the woman said.

Becca sipped and let the flavors wash over her. She took a second one now that her mouth would be used to the acid. She liked the wine. Crisp and refreshing. In fact, she would probably drink a lot of it on a warm day. As she finished the little bit left in her glass, her hostess moved down the bar to see to a couple of new guests. Becca felt the loss. The two men who had arrived smiled at the woman. Of course they did—she was vibrant and beautiful.

When she returned a few moments later, she held up a bottle of chardonnay, ready to pour. "So, where are you visiting from?"

"Most recently Orlando, but I move around as needed for my job."

"Oh, so you're in town for business?" She was assumed to be a tourist most likely because the town itself was small and their visitor quotient large. Odds were this woman knew the locals on sight, and Becca wasn't one of the familiar faces.

"Yes, but permanently. I'm a new transplant to the area."

The woman paused entirely, as if what Becca had just said had changed everything. She stared at her happily. "Well, in that case, welcome. This is very exciting. Joey Wilder," the woman said and extended her hand.

Becca accepted it and squeezed. "Becca. Crawford." Joey's cheeks flushed pink. That moment they'd shared earlier had been real. Only now that Becca wasn't just a tourist, it seemed to carry more weight.

"Well, Becca, are you living in Whisper Wall?"

She nodded. "I am. Not far from here, actually. We're neighbors, so I thought I'd check the place out. Say hello. I have to tell you, it's absolutely stunning out here, and I've visited quite a few vineyards."

Joey poured the second tasting and set the bottle down. "Isn't it?" She stared out the window as if drinking in the luscious view for the first time. "You'd think having lived here all my life, I'd be used to it. I'm not."

"Really? Your whole life?"

"Yes. This was my grandfather's vineyard originally. Then it was my father's."

"Oh, wow. And now?"

She exhaled. "Mine now, I suppose." Her eyes darkened momentarily and she pointed at Becca's glass. "This one is a little more energetic than you would find in a California chardonnay, and that's because our yearly temperatures are cooler. You'll taste lots of citrus in this one, sage, and fresh-cut hay with a soft floral finish."

"Hay? There's a flavor comparison for hay?"

"Oh, Becca, there definitely is." It was the most casual of sentences, but the way Joey said it made Becca's stomach muscles tighten pleasantly. That, and her vibrant blue eyes.

The funny part? Joey wasn't wrong. Becca tasted actual hay, something she'd never sampled before in her life but knew innately that's what it was. She didn't drink a lot of chardonnay, but this one resonated with her, a winner.

"Be right back." When Joey drifted away again, Becca's gaze traveled with her. She watched the way Joey gestured almost elegantly when she spoke about the wine to the two men. She had slender hands and wrists that complemented her beautiful long blond hair. Maybe it was the wine taking effect or the fact that Becca was out of the house, surrounded by so much beauty. Maybe it was Joey herself. Whatever the secret ingredient, it had Becca warm and happy, on a high. Today was turning out to be a really nice one. She'd made an actual friend.

"Ready for number three?" Joey asked, coming down the bar.

"I am," Becca said and slid her glass forward.

Joey smiled at her as she poured what was now red wine. "You have really pretty eyes, and I'm not embarrassed to tell you that."

"Oh." Becca smiled. "Well, thank you." The compliment lifted her spirits even more. Were they flirting? It felt like it. "Are you trying to get me to buy wine? Level with me."

"Always," Joey said with a wink. "But in this case, it happens to be true. I also like your jacket." Becca glanced down. She'd worn jeans, gray booties, a white V-neck top, and her sleek navy leather jacket. She'd chosen it because it was chilly out but not cold. She was grateful now for the decision. Joey raised an appreciative eyebrow. "Looks expensive."

"I like to splurge once in a while."

"I think it's good to do so. In this case, most definitely." Joey placed the glass in front of Becca. "This is the one people show up for. Our crown jewel, and the triple medal winner, our pinot noir." She held her arms out and shimmied her fingers as if to say *ta-da.*

Becca could tell that Joey took a lot of pride in their wine. She wondered more about the story, glancing down at the tasting notes where she found a list of awards including a gold medal from Oregon Wine Fest. "Wow," Becca said, pointing at the list. "This résumé is impressive."

"So is all our wine."

Becca lifted and swirled her glass. The saturation of purple was modest, which was typical of a pinot noir, a lighter red. She watched as the legs of the wine ran down the side of the glass, indicating its rich alcohol content. She inhaled and then lowered the glass to let her brain filter the aromas.

Joey took it from there. "Very fruit forward, more specifically raspberry and strawberry with hints of vanilla and smoke. It finishes with notes of spice and a little cola."

"I completely get the hint of smoke," Becca said with a small shake of her head. She took another sip, further exploring the flavors and finding Joey's description spot-on. She wasn't sure whether to be proud of herself for finding the flavors so accurately for the first time in her life or pat the winemaker on the back for nailing it.

"My compliments to the chef. Or in this case, the winemaker. Spot-on and fantastic." She admired the glass.

"My father."

"Really? Well, please tell him the wine is delicious."

"He'd love you for it, but he passed last month. I appreciate the compliment on his behalf." Joey smiled through the appearance of loss.

"Oh no. I'm so sorry." Becca was floored. She didn't know what to say. God.

Joey held up a hand. "No, no, no. You don't have to be. You're here. You're drinking our wine, and it's a beautiful Saturday in Willamette Valley. My dad would love all of it, so we have to do that for him. I know I am."

"Okay. Fair enough. Then I am, too."

"Now, I think I'm convinced of your diehard status."

"Thank heavens. I was working hard over here."

Joey grinned. "How about that sneak peek." She produced a bottle without a label of any kind from beneath the counter. "We're not quite to the bottling stage with this vintage yet, but we're getting closer."

"I feel like I just got tickets to a fancy advance screening."

Joey poured. "That's a wonderful way to put it."

The newer vintage was much smokier, which had Joey excited. Not as fruity, but every bit as good. She liked the subtle shift and felt that the wines were still similar enough to be identified as from the same vineyard, but different enough to set them apart. Tangle Valley didn't mess around. "I love it."

"Try it again in a few months, and it'll knock your socks off. "She glanced down. "Are you wearing socks?"

Becca lifted a bootie.

"Even your shoes outclass me."

"Oh, I disagree."

"Well, that's something," Joey said, leaning on the bar. This was fun.

In that moment, the tasting room was hit with the low roar of approaching conversation as a large group appeared. A quick glance behind her told Becca that one of those tour buses she'd passed on occasion had shown up, and Joey and the older woman behind the bar were about to have their hands full. Becca sighed, knowing their moment had likely passed, and she should clear the counter for the new guests. She gestured to the group. "I'll get out of your way."

"Wait. Would you like a glass of something you tried? On the house, of course, to welcome a new neighbor."

"Oh," Becca said, flattered by the offer. "Sure. I would, uh, love a glass of the pinot noir."

"Good choice," Joey said, swapping out the tasting glass for an overly round red wine glass and pouring a healthy amount for Becca. "Will you come back soon? Say yes."

Becca tried not to react to the shiver that brought on. "I definitely will."

"Good. Someone's gotta let you know the ins and outs of this town."

"I was actually hoping a person like that might come along."

"And here I am. You're getting luckier by the minute. For example, watch out for the Biddies, unless you want to wind up the hot gossip item for the week. And make sure to grab one of the wine slushies from Williamson Vineyard three miles from here. They also have fantastic produce and a cute Yorkshire terrier who will boss you around while you shop. His name is Ricardo, and he's harmless but opinionated, so prepare accordingly."

"Well, for tidbits like that, I definitely have to come back." She liked Joey—her spark, and her friendly personality.

Joey grinned in victory but was enveloped by the large group of arriving guests. Becca quietly raised her glass in thanks and drifted to an outdoor table. She blissfully sipped the pinot as she watched the sun set in a wash of beautiful oranges and pinks over the vine filled hillside. She snuggled into her jacket and enjoyed the late afternoon, sneaking glances through the window at Joey, who smiled, laughed, and lit up the whole room.

Yes, she hoped to spend lots more time at Tangle Valley.

❖

After one of the more exciting days of work in a while, Joey, on a high, invited Madison and Gabriella for dinner at the Big House. The two of them were still settling into their new homes, and it was the least Joey could do to help ease the transition. Plus, they had a lot of fun together and had quickly picked up a rhythm. While she'd planned to toss a few steaks in the skillet and baked potatoes in the oven, Gabriella had insisted on cooking for them, and when you had a highly rated chef hell-bent on regaling you with their amazing food, you would be an idiot to say no. With the decadent aromas now permeating her kitchen, Joey knew she'd made the right choice. The wafting garlic was the perfect cap off to an already good day.

"I don't understand how you just toss the pan and everything leaps out and then falls back in perfectly," Joey said in mystification as she watched Gabriella work.

"That is why you pay me millions of dollars."

Joey frowned. "I'm worried you didn't read our agreement."

Gabriella waved her off. "Details to work out once we're up and running."

Madison pointed. "I told you. She's so nice that you don't see her coming. The next thing you know, your house is signed over."

They seemed to have congregated in the kitchen, chatting over the food preparation. It really was a thing to behold, how effortlessly Gabriella threw in spices, flipped the pasta around willy-nilly, and added cheese, cream, or eggs without need to measure. Joey caught Madison watching her with a knowing grin.

"What?" Joey asked. She pointed in a circle. "What's with the face?"

"I'm just wondering why you're twirling your hair like you used to in the sixth grade when you'd had a good day. Something is up with you that you're not saying, and don't argue because I know you, Joey Wilder. Got your number."

"Hair twirling can happen for a lot of reasons, Madison, and some of them are simply hair related. I should know as a chronic hair twirler."

"Except you're also showing off your dimples when you're not expressly meaning to, which means you're preoccupied with something that is making you happy." Madison grinned. "Yep. There's a whole movie playing out in your head, and you can't stop watching it, and you're not sharing the popcorn."

Gabriella pointed at Joey excitedly. "She's right. Your dimples are showing." She adjusted the tie in her hair. "You have really cute dimples, Joey. I'm jealous now. Also, share the popcorn."

Joey raised one shoulder. "I think I just enjoyed my day, and with the way things have gone the past while, I needed a little pick-me-up."

Gabriella squinted. "Okay, who picked you up? I'm starting to side with Maddie."

"No one picked me up." She watched as Gabriella stirred the egg mixture into the hot spaghetti and then topped it with the crisp pancetta she'd set aside. Joey's mouth watered. "Yet."

Two heads swiveled her way. Gabriella paused mid stir, looking like she'd stumbled upon a stash of leprechaun gold. Madison grinned victoriously, surely congratulating herself for knowing Joey so well. With one hand, she made the give-me-more gesture.

Joey took the cue and it all came tumbling out in a fervor. "Okay, fine. A woman came into the tasting room. Our chat was brief and maybe minor in the scheme of life, but you guys"—Joey did a sweet-Jesus head shake—"you should have seen her. Chestnut hair cut to about here." She touched a spot just past her shoulders. "Layered, like if she shook her head, she'd be on one of those commercials for hair products where it all falls perfectly into place."

"Good God," Gabriella said, setting the pan down slowly.

"Seriously. It was like wind machines kicked on as she opened the door to the tasting room, and I could not stop looking at her."

"Did you feel things?" Gabriella asked, placing a hand over her stomach as if she was imagining the moment full-on.

"Yes," Joey said, pointing at her. "A lot of them." She turned to Madison. "She wore this navy leather jacket with a round collar and this zipper that just had me." Joey paused. "This woman knows how to wear a zipper. And I'm gushing like a stupid person, aren't I?"

Gabriella hadn't moved a muscle. "If you don't keep going you will die."

"A horrible death," Madison finished. Another give-me-more gesture.

Joey came around the center counter, the very one she'd grown up playing beneath. "Well, at first I thought she was a tourist. I mean, they all are, right? She was devastatingly beautiful and clearly put together and, yes, there was this obvious, palpable chemistry between us, but I'd likely never see her again, so I didn't invest. Just enjoyed the fun banter." She realized she was gesturing a lot, which she knew was something she only did when she felt something very strongly. "Then she tells me that she's just moved here. As in *here*. Whisper Wall. In town."

"Plot twist," Madison murmured with wide eyes.

Joey nodded. "And so…I'm feeling a little surprised and off-kilter. I mean, what am I supposed to do with this? A mystery woman walks in, makes my day, and proclaims that she's sticking around per-manently."

"Jo, you're not feeling surprised." Maddie ran a hand through her curls. "You're hot for her, and you damn well should be."

"What's her name?" Gabriella asked, plating the carbonara beautifully. "I need to know everything I can about this devastatingly beautiful neighbor. Bring the sexy. Layer it on like her perfect windswept hair."

"Becca." She popped the cork on the chardonnay that would pair wonderfully with the pasta. She liked the sound of the word as she released it from her lips. "It suits her, too. She's sophisticated, yet very personable and friendly. Warm. She also has a tiny freckle right here." She gestured to the side of her right eye.

"What does she do?" Madison asked, allowing Joey to pour her a glass. She swirled the wine and watched it settle. Always working, that one. Madison's mind rarely relaxed, which was likely the reason she'd accomplished so much in so little time.

"We didn't get that far. A tour group showed up, and our conversation was cut short. But I plan to find out. I'm going to guess that, dressed like that, she's a high-powered attorney. We could use a few more around here with all the land sales and disputes." She grinned while setting the table and imagined Becca standing up in a courtroom, decked out in a business suit. She fanned herself because, sweet Lord, please see fit to have mercy. Joey didn't even know she was into that kind of fantasy until now.

"Surely you asked for her number, though, right?" Madison asked. "I mean, that's just basic."

"Didn't we just talk about the fact that I've been out of this game for years? Maybe next time," Joey said. "I'm playing it cool."

"Or chickening out, but we will go with your version."

Gabriella scoffed at Madison. "You leave little Joey alone. She's taking things at her pace, and I love everything about this story. I imagine Becca walking to the bar in slow motion. Mamma mia. That's what my grandmother would say."

"It really was like that," Joey said, nodding very seriously. "You think I'm making that up, but I'm not. She's really pretty, you guys, and put together as hell, and it's the combo of the two that makes me want to make out with her in an orchard somewhere."

"This is so saucy and specific," Gabriella said, placing a plate in front of each setting. She glanced behind her. "Oh, and I have fresh bread with this amazing garlic butter."

"Garlic and butter are the best words," Joey mused, sipping her wine and readying herself for what looked like an out of this world culinary experience that Gabriella had whipped up in no time. Why hadn't she hired a chef to live next door sooner? Biggest misstep of her young life.

It turned out the food was even better than she'd hoped, and Joey felt like she'd floated up somewhere near heaven. She was more than full but somehow needed just a little bit more of that hot bread.

"Gabs, you're getting better and better," Madison said. "Why did we break up again, because that food…No," Madison said, quelling the thought with a slap on the table. "I don't even have words, so I won't belittle you with my failed attempt to appropriately capture the essence." Someone was feeling the wine. Madison left the table and collapsed onto the new couch, which made Joey happy. She loved the Big House and all the memories that came with it of childhood, family, and history, but she also knew how important it was to make it hers now. When the decorator had made over the cottages, Joey had hired her to update the Big House as well. She'd kept all the important components like her grandmother's butcher-block countertop, the core of the kitchen. She'd altered the wall colors, going with an entirely gray and white palette for both the kitchen and living room. The space felt lighter and much more her speed than the heavy browns of the previous decor. She hoped her dad wouldn't mind.

Gabriella, who'd begun to do the dishes unnecessarily, gestured at Madison with a spatula. "Because we were getting ready to kill each other if we didn't change up something and fast." She grinned sweetly. "This is so much nicer, and you're still eating my food. See?"

"Winning," Madison said from the couch, a fist in the air. She blew Gabriella a kiss, which she caught.

Having gotten to know Gabriella better in the days they'd spent together so far, she could see how her and Madison's energies might not have commingled as well romantically. Gabriella was sweet and creative, while Madison was someone who relied heavily on science, facts, schedules, and structure. She didn't get caught up in optimism, preferring pragmatism, always. For Gabriella, that might have been a buzzkill. Their friendship dynamic, however, felt incredibly balanced and supportive.

"How's the wine faring out there in winemaking land?" Joey asked Madison, as she shooed Gabriella out of the kitchen and off dish duty. She'd get to those later, once the others went home.

Madison's eyes lit up at the mention of her new charge. "It's sleeping right now, Joey, but the new grapes are good grapes. We've made friends. They like it here."

"Friendly grapes?" Joey asked.

"The nicest. We're getting to know each other as we make plans to take over the wine world."

Gabriella's eyes went wide with hope. "The little vineyard that could."

Joey laughed. "Sounds about right. Grandpa Wilder started with one seed in the ground, and look out there now. Makes you realize that anything really is possible."

"More than possible," Madison said. Joey admired her for both her confidence and skill set. Winemaking was no easy job. The hours were insane, and the amount of babysitting and trial and error to get all the components balanced was painstakingly difficult.

"Are we shopping tomorrow?" Gabriella asked, picking out a spot for herself on the floor where she began a series of stretches, showing off her lean torso. Joey had no idea how she managed to look so amazing when she was surrounded by food all the time. That just wasn't fair.

"Yeah, I have two of our part-time pourers coming in to back up Loretta in the tasting room. Midmorning okay with you?"

"That gives me time for morning yoga."

"You do yoga?" Joey asked. She always admired those women who could twist themselves into a variety of pretzel-like poses. They seemed so sophisticated and worldly. She wondered if Becca did yoga. "I've never tried it."

"Well, then I'll have to teach you. You'll love it." Gabriella hooked a thumb at Madison. "This one doesn't."

Madison shrugged. "I just feel the time ticking away. I'm supposed to stretch and breathe when my to-do list is just sitting there, dormant and afraid?"

"Yes," Joey and Gabriella said in unison.

"I'd die slowly of impatience. I'd say you'd miss me, but I think you'd be busy breathing in."

"What's it like to be you?" Joey asked.

"It's torture, Jo. You don't want this life." But Madison was laughing when she said it, a sign of healthy self-awareness.

After lounging for an hour, her friends eventually headed out into the night, leaving Joey with the dishes and a feeling of satisfaction. Life seemed so foreign to Joey now, that she took true comfort in establishing new norms. Madison and Gabriella were helping with that, and after her conversation with Becca in the tasting room, she had an extra spring in her step. She'd not detected a spark with anyone since Simone. She'd actually started to think that maybe the romantic part of her life was good and done. She was only in her thirties, and that reality would have been sad, but livable. Today, though? She'd experienced something exciting when she spoke to Becca, looked into her eyes as she tasted the wine. She didn't know what it was exactly, but it had her paying attention. Joey did know one thing for certain. She wanted to feel that way again soon.

CHAPTER FOUR

Joey, I have to confess, this stuff gets me going," Gabriella said and rubbed her hands together as they moved from one end of the used-car dealership to the other in search of the perfect food truck for Tangle Valley. "Virgin Mary, I'm all atingle," she whispered to Joey as they followed Powell Rogers, the sometimes gruff owner of the lot, to truck number two. She did a little dance as if in a boxing ring. Joey smothered a smile. Gabriella was definitely an enthusiastic chef, but she was no pushover. She spoke up for what she wanted, even passionately when called for.

Joey passed Gabriella a look and kept her volume down, not wanting to alert Powell to their plans. "Just let me know how you're feeling about each one as we go."

"Not a problem," Gabriella said, still gearing up for battle.

"Does that help you shop?" Joey asked, pointing at Gabriella's quick moving feet.

"Yes," she said, as if it were universal.

"Got it," Joey said, pressing on. "Do you."

She'd lined up three different trucks for Gabriella to inspect, not knowing exactly what would be most important to her but wanting her chef to have everything she needed for success in the coming months when she'd be relegated to a small workspace. The introduction of the truck and the buzz about its food would hopefully act as introduction to the restaurant the following year.

They'd nixed truck number one already simply because the thing had been used into the ground, was likely on its last leg, and Gabriella felt it was like "a sad little truck that just needed to rest with its mama now."

"Yep. You folks are about to fall in love. The beauty of this next truck is that it's all top of the line equipment, and fully automated," Powell explained with his Budweiser ball cap perched too high on his head like it didn't fit. He'd always worn it like that, and Joey couldn't figure out why he didn't just buy a bigger size, but that was Powell.

"Sounds promising," Gabriella said, ceasing her footwork the second Powell looked their way. They followed him to a maroon colored, medium-sized truck with a single serving window.

Powell clapped his hands. "Beautiful, isn't she? Let's go inside."

Joey followed behind Gabriella who followed behind Powell until they were all three standing in the truck like needy sardines.

"Small," Gabriella pointed out. "It's nice, but I'm Italian and I need room to toss stuff, you know? I'm a toss-arounder. It comes from my mama."

"She's a toss-arounder," Joey said to Powell. "Why don't we give you some space to test it out fully?" Joey signaled for Powell to follow her and left Gabriella in the truck. She popped the service window and looked about. Next, they watched as she mimed some big reaches and cooking-like gestures. She flipped something over in an invisible frying pan and then tossed some ingredients into it in a fury as if time was of the essence. She was totally right about being a toss-arounder. Joey nodded at Powell, who nodded back.

"She's good," he said. "I can tell."

"Right?"

Gabriella called down to them. "No. This one doesn't feel right. I can cook here, but I'm not sure I can *cook* here. There's a difference. Trust me."

"We want the second version of cooking, I think," Joey informed Powell. "Where's the third truck?"

"Back this way," he said. Gabriella scampered down and followed them farther onto the lot. "Last one is kind of in between the two. She has a couple years on her. Not telling you any lies 'bout that. Bigger, though, which you'll like for the, uh, tossing, but not as fancy."

Gabriella wasn't listening. She was already gazing ahead at the blue truck with the oversized service window. "Okay, this is promising." She nodded several times and gestured inward to her chest. "We're bonding."

"Already?" Joey asked.

But Gabriella didn't answer her. She was walking around the truck and nodding some more. She ran a hand across the blue exterior. There was a colorful peace sign on the side that could be painted over. "She's pretty. That's for sure," Gabriella said. "We could put a bottle of wine here with your label," she said, pointing at the peace sign. "I can see it now."

"I like that idea. See what you think about the interior." Joey crossed her arms and waited. She and Powell remained outside and let Gabriella explore the truck on her own. She popped the service window and moved about, making many of the same gestures as before, this time with extra pizzazz, kicking her hip, and making a few fun sound effects—*pop, bang, bam*. Lots of *bam*s.

"Why do you wear your hat like that?" Joey asked, not taking her eyes off the imaginary show.

"Cause I like wearing my hat like this. It's how hats go on my head best."

"Fair enough, I guess. You realize it's perched."

"I like a good perch. Makes me feel tall."

Joey nodded. "Fair enough."

Finally, Gabriella looked up. "It's this one, Joey. I can kill it with this truck."

"I think we have a winner," Joey said to Powell. They didn't have a ton of money budgeted for the truck, given how much the restaurant was going to run the vineyard in the end, but she was hoping to cut a deal. Pennies were too tight not to. The books kept her up at night these days. "What are you asking for it?"

He rubbed his chin. "This one is fifty-nine. Firm."

Joey whistled. "Seems high, given it's not brand new. You said yourself the features aren't top of the line. It's lacking some of the automation." She paused. "I can offer you forty-nine." Gabriella joined them with an even bigger spring in her step. She was practically vibrating with excitement.

Powell shook his head. "No can do, Joey. I can maybe go as low as fifty-five. It'd be a steal for fifty-five and only because I loved your dad and like you a whole lot."

This was getting better. Joey was hoping to stay under fifty, but five thousand more wasn't awful. She prepared to take the deal when Gabriella turned to him with her most winsome smile.

"I have an idea. Hear me out. We give you fifty, a case of wine, and lunch from the truck anytime you want until the restaurant opens. You stop by the truck during business hours and I'll make you up a plate myself. You've never tasted gnocchi like mine."

He blinked.

"The sauce alone will get you going, you know?"

He nodded silently, and Joey covered her smile with her hand.

"Oh, I don't know," Powell said, scratching the back of his neck, which had turned red. The blush began to creep up to his stubbled face until he resembled a smitten tomato. Joey grinned at this new development. Well, well. Powell had a thing for Gabriella, which made total sense.

Gabriella punched his arm. "You're gonna love the meatballs, Powell. Extra parmesan for you." She tossed a glance to Joey, who nodded along.

"Two cases of wine," Joey said.

He swallowed. "Fine. You have yourself a food truck. But I want that wine, and it better be the pinot."

Joey laughed, amazed at what had just transpired. Gabriella just got more and more wonderful the more time she spent with her. "You got it."

As they headed into town for lunch, Joey shook her head and looked over at her new friend. "You smiled at the guy and saved us five thousand dollars. You *smiled.*"

Gabriella, who chair-grooved to the radio in the passenger's seat, nodded. "Sometimes a little kindness goes a long way."

"No. This was different. What's that like? To walk in a room and immediately have everyone fall for you?"

"I have no idea what you're talking about," she said and continued to groove. And what was great about it was that she actually didn't. Gabriella was a looker but didn't seem to know it, at least not fully. "I just think kindness goes a long way and we were nice to him."

"Not five thousand dollars nice. I owe you lunch to celebrate."

Gabriella paused her lip-syncing but continued to dance. "Yes, take me somewhere that uses the local ingredients. I want to familiarize myself with the flavors, bathe in their fresh variety." She gestured as if clutching a handful of vegetables.

"You got it." Joey flipped her turn signal as they approached the town center of Whisper Wall, flanked with gift shops and restaurants and plenty of wine bars. Because she was having such an awesome day, she fell into the groove with Gabriella, shaking her head in unison with the music. Why not? It was a beautiful sunny day in October, they'd just made a killer deal, and Gabriella brought out her playful side.

Minutes later, she pulled Dusty into the parking lot of the Cabernet Club. "You're going to love their broccolini. It's from a farm a mile up the road. In fact, everything here is fresh, and they only carry local wines."

"Including Tangle Valley?" Gabriella asked.

"All four varietals and even our blends."

"Even better."

"I'll be happy to introduce you to their chef, Theodore Quevedo, but I call him Teddy Q. He's amazing. In fact—" But the words died as they stepped inside the restaurant, because there she was, walking toward Joey like a model on a runaway. "Becca," Joey said quietly.

"That's her?" Gabriella whispered.

Joey nodded as subtly as possible. She swallowed and instructed herself to play it cool.

Becca's eyes met Joey's and she broke into a grin. "Hi, Joey. It's good to see you again." She wore a navy dress with a thin beige belt and heels. Very corporate and businessy. Joey loved it on her, even if she did worry she'd be cold. To Becca's right stood a woman dressed in an emerald pantsuit. Colleagues maybe? She secretly hoped that's all they were. Probably at a fancy new law firm. She tried to imagine where those offices might have gone in without her noticing.

Becca gestured to her friend-maybe-colleague. "Carla Cortez, meet Joey, my new friend from Tangle Valley." She turned back to Joey. "I already told her about the amazing wine at your place."

"Hi there," Carla said, shaking Joey's hand. "Trust me. I'll be back again with my husband soon. We're big wine people."

"We'd love that," Joey said. She had a husband. Her stomach tightened and her skin tingled. Her stomach was not the type to do that at all. The excitement of some new stomach action had her off-kilter but still enjoying the ride, and the shade of navy Becca wore really made her hazel eyes especially dreamy. "In fact, you're both invited this weekend. We're debuting our brand-new food truck. Gabriella here is our chef. She has some bites lined up that will knock your socks off."

Gabriella curtsied. "Socks knocking is my specialty. Nice to meet you both."

Becca laughed the most perfect sounding melodious laugh. "The feeling is mutual. I'd love to stop by this weekend and lose my socks." It didn't even seem like she was feigning politeness. She was either a fantastic actress or just as excited as Joey. "Will you be there, too?"

Becca asked, adjusting her focus entirely on Joey. It felt like the world shifted beneath her.

Carla smothered a smile. Gabriella beamed like bright lights on a highway.

"Oh," Joey said. "I will, yes. You'll, uh, find me in the tasting room. I'll be happy to get you set up with a fantastic glass or bottle. Whichever you prefer." Joey was feeling bold. "Maybe even join you for a glass."

Becca didn't hesitate. "I insist."

They stared at each other as the air between them crackled. This was the part where she and Gabriella should head off for a table, and Becca and Carla should take their leave. But no. They stood there, clinging to the moment.

The restaurant door behind Joey opened and she broke contact, turning to see Brenda Anne from the Nifty Nickel step inside. "Getting nippy out there," she said with wide eyes to Joey. "Hey there, Joey. How are you getting on?" She didn't pause. Brenda Anne didn't seem to believe in them. "We got a shipment of those Molly Dolly truffles you love, and I set a box aside for you." Joey grinned, not sure whether she wanted the box for Tangle Valley guests or maybe just for her damn self.

"I'll stop by this afternoon and snatch those ridiculous things from you. My mouth is already watering, just thinking about it."

"I ate six this morning. I just lied. Seven. I ate *seven*." Brenda Anne then looked past Joey to Becca and grinned even brighter. "I see you've met our newest resident. Well, hey there," she said to Becca.

"Hi, Brenda Anne," Becca said back. "I just love my autumn wreath. Makes my door so much more friendly."

"Well, come back. We have more fall decor. Just got a shipment of scarecrows you'll love. It's so nice to see you again. I see more and more progress on that hotel every day."

Joey grimaced as a dark cloud fell over everything at the mention of The Jade. She shook her head adamantly. "A little piece of my heart is stolen with each brick that goes up on that overly fancy money suck." She shook her head again and turned to Becca. "You haven't been here long, but we're known for our charm around here. That means local everything, right down to the ingredients at this restaurant. But there's this huge hotel chain that's about to crush this town's culture and all we have going for it. We don't even have a McDonald's for eight miles, and they're building an Elite hotel just down the road from Tangle Valley."

Becca blinked. Carla stared at the ground.

Gabriella squeezed her wrist, but Joey didn't care. The newcomers needed to be updated on all that was about to be lost to big business in the name of a few extra dollars. Joey sighed with ire. "It's really sickening."

That's when Gabriella inclined her head in the direction of the leather attaché on Becca's shoulder, the one engraved with the words *Elite Resorts*. Joey stared hard, just sure she'd misread the lettering, but no, she hadn't. Good God. Really? She raised her gaze to Becca's as shock strangled the words in her throat.

"Becca Crawford, manager of The Jade, aka the overly fancy, town-crushing resort." She pointed at Carla. "Carla Cortez, assistant manager of town crushing."

Carla waved almost apologetically.

Joey didn't know whether to laugh at the awful joke or cry at the reality that the first woman she'd been excited about in ages was actually an agent of corporate evil. "I don't know what to say." Joey shook her head. "This is embarrassing and awful. I'm not sure which is winning." She held up a finger. "No, awful is. That I'm now sure of."

"I don't think it has to be either," Becca said. "In fact, I think we could find a way to work—"

"I'm so sorry that's your life." Joey shook her head, feeling the indignation rising in her throat. She heard all the reasons The Jade would hurt them, her father's voice chiming in. "There's still time to change course. Save yourself. Brenda Anne, are you hiring?"

"I'm not. No," Brenda Anne said uncomfortably. She'd always been averse to conflict. Bless her heart.

Joey deflated. "Well, that's a shame."

"Joey," Gabriella whispered, trying to rein her in, but Joey was not willing to compromise her convictions just because her sworn enemy turned out to be beautiful, smart, and friendly. There were deal breakers, and anyone advocating for The Jade and its presence in Whisper Wall was an adversary of Joey's and the entire town. That simple. What's more? Her father had been crestfallen when he heard The Jade was going in, and she didn't plan to just roll over and let it happen without having her voice heard. She had to be that voice for him now.

Becca tilted her head in what seemed like sympathy. "I fully understand that you're protective of your town and your business. It makes total sense to me. I just hope you'll keep an open mind about all the good things the resort might bring to the table. I think there are several."

Joey shook her head but remained calm and even keeled. "I think we'll have to agree to disagree."

Becca shrugged. "Well. I hope to change your mind. Enjoy your lunch," she said to Joey and Gabriella. "Brenda Anne, I'll stop by the shop later this week."

"See you then," Brenda Anne said. Joey passed her a look that said *really?* Once Becca and Carla were gone, Brenda Anne stepped forward. "Josephine Wilder, just because we don't like the hotel or resort or whatever it is, that's no cause to be inhospitable."

She wasn't wrong, and Joey could use a good reminding apparently. She was a little surprised at the strength of her own reaction. "You're right. I just get so wound up about it. That place is going to change everything when it opens next month."

"Maybe Becca is right, though," Gabriella offered gently. "Maybe everyone will be surprised in the end. Let's hope for that."

Joey turned to her. "You're an optimistic person, and I love that about you, but no good can come from a giant chain hotel looming over our vines." She shook her head, feeling crestfallen all over again. "Let's eat something sinful like bacon. Maybe it will help me forget what's coming."

Gabriella grinned. "That word is a love button. I just got a hit of dopamine from its mention. We'll get a whole plate of it."

After Gabriella studied every inch of the menu, they ordered two of the best sandwiches ever made. Gabriella selected the toasted BLT with avocado, and Joey went for the Cuban, pickles and all. She only wished she'd been able to enjoy it more. Of course there was also that side of bacon, which helped.

While they ate, Gabriella tossed a look at the kitchen window that faced the interior of the restaurant as if trying to catch a glimpse of the action. "This garlic mayo is made in-house. I can tell. Dying to know what the mystery spice is."

Joey only halfway absorbed the comment and instead moved the brown sugar rimmed potato chips around her plate as if using them to work a puzzle. Only the puzzle had already been solved and it spelled out disappointment.

"You in there?" Gabriella asked. "I get the feeling that mayonnaise and its mysterious makeup aren't exactly on your radar right now. I'm sorry it's played out the way it has with Becca."

"She's the enemy from the evil empire. She's the general manager, which makes her evil empress." Joey sank against the soft backing of the booth, disillusioned.

"Slow down, slugger. I know you're sad. But remember something for me. Becca is not her job."

Joey took comfort in Gabriella's warm, reassuring smile, but that's about as far as it went. She'd already downshifted after learning her new crush could no longer be that. "Doesn't matter. It's water under the chain hotel."

"Think you might be leaping to that conclusion a little early?"

"Nah, but I'll get past it. I just need to act like a disappointed four-year-old for a while."

"Okay. But know I'll be here as cheerleader or pushy woman with a spatula. Whichever works best. I can pivot."

Joey tried to imagine how the spatula thing might play but didn't possess the fortitude.

On the drive home, the car dancing was relegated to a few head bops to the easy listening station. Their party had been busted up by that stupid hotel, too. It damn well ruined everything these days.

CHAPTER FIVE

Friday afternoon finally arrived, and Becca had a hostile meeting to attend and a dog to go meet. Not a ton of afternoons shaped up with such diversity of experience, but hers definitely had.

She had roughly a month until The Jade opened its doors to throngs of guests, and once that happened, her ability to steal a little time for herself wouldn't be so easily won. Today, however, it was important for her to wave a white flag to the citizens of Whisper Wall and attend the town meeting she'd read about on that flyer from The Nifty Nickel. If the town was discussing The Jade and its new presence, well, she wanted to be there to quell their concerns and speak to the other side of things. As nicely as possible. After that, she would shed her work persona and head just outside of town to a small rescue farm for sweet dogs looking for new homes. It just so happened that she was someone in the market for a new friend herself. She liked her new house and her job very much, but she hadn't made the friends she'd hoped she'd make when she moved to Oregon and was feeling…well, lonely. She had an inclination there was a furry little guy or gal out there who might be lonely, too. They could maybe be each other's friend. Wouldn't that be nice? She smiled at the idea as she selected an outfit that would work for both the meeting and the farm: dark dressy jeans, brown boots, a white short-sleeved shirt that she could toss a brown plaid blazer on top of for the meeting and shed as she headed to the farm.

As she drove to the town center, she replayed her last encounter with Joey Wilder over again in her head. She'd done that about eighty-five times now and never felt any better about it. Joey carried such passionate feelings when it came to The Jade that it was going to take time to make her see the benefits. Like it or not, Elite Resorts had gone through all the proper channels to establish a presence in Whisper

Wall because it was growing as a tourist destination by the second. The resort was coming with or without Becca's assistance. If only she could find a way to make the town see the perks that could come from a partnership. She rejected the memory of the abject disappointment in Joey's eyes when she'd last looked at Becca. It had been a true blow, and the sting lingered.

She gave her head a shake and focused on all that was ahead of her. She pulled up to the small building with the simple words *Whisper Wall Events* on the side and smiled at the to-the-point language. This should be fun. Becca took a moment before going in and watched a handful of people head to the meeting. That's when it clicked that the overflowing parking lot indicated there was a great deal of interest in the topic. Becca took a deep breath and headed inside. Alone. To what felt like the lion's den. Once inside the room, which echoed with conversation, she slipped quietly into a cold metal chair toward the back. Shortly after, an older gentleman with a prominent belly stood at a small podium and addressed the room via microphone. Apparently, she'd arrived just in time, having missed out on the chance to grab a few of those snacks along the wall. She now remembered Brenda Anne's double chocolate cupcakes with espresso and vowed to at least try one before fleeing the scene. Plus, that would give her a chance to meet some more of her new neighbors on behalf of The Jade, but also on behalf of herself. This was her home now, and she wanted to get to know everyone. If only they would let her.

"Good afternoon, friends and neighbors. I'm Mitchell McHugh, but most of you know me as Big Mitch." He chuckled at a joke Becca didn't get. Others joined him. She smiled along. "I'm the owner and manager of Twin Grapes, a small vineyard on the eastern perimeter of town. Like you, I'm concerned about the new direction we see our town heading in. Part of our appeal has always been an invitation for folks to get away from their lives and spend some time in Whisper Wall, a gem in Willamette Valley where we have the best damn pinot on earth." That brought on applause. Becca joined in happily. She, too, loved the pinot. "Today is our chance to talk about what the opening of a very commercial property on the hill might mean for us and for the future evolution of our city. If you have something to say, we want to hear it, even if it's just to get it off your chest." Many nodded. Becca did, too. "We're all friends and neighbors here. Just put your name in to speak at the back of the room." Big Mitch consulted his clipboard. "We're going to start with Josephine Wilder from Tangle Valley. Joey?"

Becca blinked in surprise, took a deep inhale, and watched as Joey, dressed in jeans, low-heeled booties, and a navy sweater, approached the microphone. Even from ten rows back Becca could see the shine from her lip gloss and the sparkle in her very blue eyes. They matched her sweater to perfection. She remembered how special she felt when those eyes were happy to see her. The tasting at Tangle Valley, just five days ago, seemed like ancient history.

Joey took a moment to regard the audience. She clenched and unclenched her fists, probably nerves. Finally, she took a deep breath. "The Jade is coming whether we like it or not. Elite Resorts has heard our complaints, they saw our written petition, and don't care. The question is, how are we going to handle it? As a representative of the vineyard closest to the hotel, I'm worried for the flavor of my business. I'm concerned about the effect such a commercial property will have on the rustic, secluded ambiance we've always made our goal. Hell, we even use those terms in our marketing materials." Joey swallowed. She spoke with conviction. And though it seemed public speaking wasn't her favorite, she gained momentum as she went. "I don't want the hotel here and do not plan to support it in any way. I hope you'll stand with me on that front."

Becca swallowed and her stomach turned over. Ouch. It was one thing to be unhappy about something. It was quite another to actively seek and hope for its failure. She glanced around at the faces of the audience members and watched as many took to nodding. This wasn't going well.

Joey shifted her weight and continued. "We have to look out for each other, protect the small inns and bed-and-breakfasts owned by friends and family. As you know, some of them are very nice places to stay, even if they don't come with an Olympic-size pool with a waterfall." Becca suppressed an eye roll. "I don't want to see town square riddled with fast food restaurants, and Walmarts along our country roads. That's not who we are. What I do know is that this town has a lot of heart. We're unique. One of a kind. That's why people love to visit. Let's hold on to that charm no matter who shows up."

Nope. Uh-uh. Becca couldn't let that slide. She stood, found the sign-up sheet, and waited for her turn to speak. She had to change the tone. It was the only way. She listened to another four speakers, each one met with emphatic head nods and applause. The tide was firmly against her, and she needed to change its course.

Finally, Big Mitch returned to the podium. "Next we'll hear from

Ms. Becca Crawford." He looked around the room as her name was likely not recognizable to him, nor to the majority of the attendees. She stood from her seat in the back and walked to the front of the room, feeling the curious gazes firmly on her as she passed. Joey, she noticed, shifted uncomfortably in her seat when she saw Becca and quickly looked away.

She grasped the sides of the podium and relaxed into what she hoped was a warm smile. "Good afternoon, everyone. You may not know me just yet because I'm new to Whisper Wall. My name is Becca, and I'm a Florida transplant who loves wine and procedural TV shows, and is hopefully adopting a dog in about two hours from now." She crossed her fingers. "Wish me luck on that one." Many in the audience smiled back at that. "I'm always pumped for home decorating but somehow never get around to it. There are still boxes along the perimeter of my living room that have started to blend in with the furniture." Several more people smiled. "I love to cook, but I burn things when I get distracted." She shrugged. "Maybe you've been there, too. As for my day job, I'm the general manager of The Jade, the resort going in on the north side of town"—she gestured to Joey—"not far from Tangle Valley, a place I think might be the most beautiful on earth." She tapped the podium. "I tell you all of this because I'm just a person like all of you, and I really happen to love Whisper Wall and everything that makes it unique. I don't want to change anything about it. In fact, I want *more* people to experience its charm and am confident The Jade's arrival will help that happen. More visitors, *different* visitors, who will enjoy your town, your wineries, and will hopefully come back year after year." She looked around the room at the interested faces peering back at her. "Speaking as a person, I just want to be your friend. Speaking as the GM for The Jade, I just want to contribute to everything this town already has working for it, not take anything away. Thank you for letting me speak." She pointed at the back table. "Now I have to steal one of those cupcakes for my ride to the farm to meet some dogs." She was met with a smattering of applause, which, to her surprise, built to a medium-sized reception. She relaxed. It had been worthwhile to introduce herself, which was only reinforced when the meeting concluded and several individuals approached her.

"Irene Strong," a woman said, extending her hand for a shake. Becca accepted it. "We're glad you came out and let us hear your side. It helps to see the person in charge up close and understand that you're just a normal human being like all of us loonies." She laughed. "Anyway, welcome to town."

"It's so nice to meet you," Becca said with a grin, mid cupcake swipe. Others approached, and Becca happily greeted each of them.

"Not saying I love that hotel because I don't, but I liked what you had to say."

"Nice speech. Welcome to Whisper Wall."

"Maybe try unpacking one box every day. That's what I do."

"Well, I'm at least glad to hear you appreciate good wine. That's step one to becoming a local."

Becca exhaled. Not everyone hated her, and that mattered so much, maybe more than it should have. She had to talk a big game at work and was always viewed as a go-getter in the corporate world, taking no prisoners, but underneath it all, she was a people person. She liked having friends. Feeling better, she scanned the space for Joey and saw her speaking with a man across the room. When Joey smiled, her whole face lit up and her cheeks dusted pink with exuberance. Warmth washed over her when she saw Joey laugh. She never did come over to say hello, and that took a bit of the wind out of Becca's sails. She'd hoped they'd find a way to still be friends, even from different sides of this issue. But Joey, who was maybe even more beautiful today than the last two times Becca had seen her, adjusted the leather bag on her arm and walked right out of the room without even a glance in Becca's direction. Becca deflated further but vowed to not give up completely.

She could be patient and would definitely remain friendly. No matter what. Like good wine, sometimes things just took time.

Joey didn't enjoy the ire or the awful feeling in the pit of her stomach. It wasn't like her to carry anger. She was normally a happy, carefree, even cheerful person, but this hotel business had left a definite bad taste in her mouth that she didn't enjoy. As she drove home from the meeting, she thought back on the speech she gave, and how Becca Crawford had taken the floor and done everything in her power to dismantle every shred of Joey's argument, using her charm and charisma to do so.

She'd done a half-decent job of it, too, as much as Joey hated to admit it. She'd spoken with eloquence and poise, looking so put together in that plaid jacket, which was of course accentuated by her chestnut hair, which she'd worn down. Joey gripped the steering wheel with extra force while her conflicting emotions about Becca duked it out like second graders in a playground scuffle. She didn't know Becca well, but she certainly came with a list of impressive traits, if only she was using them for good and not evil. How was Joey supposed to reconcile the fact that she actually liked her opposition?

When she returned to Tangle Valley, she found Gabriella staring dreamily at the new truck, which had been washed, detailed, and delivered to the vineyard with an actual giant bow on the side. He'd even found a guy to paint the Tangle Valley logo in place of the peace sign. Score one for Powell.

"Isn't she gorgeous?" Gabriella held up her hands in a gesture that reminded Joey of early morning game shows from her youth.

Joey laughed. "You two look like you were destined for each other. I can just see all the memories ahead."

"There will be plenty. I think I'm going to call her Jolene because of your name and also because Dolly Parton would love this truck. That's who this sweet but fierce little lady reminds me of."

Joey nodded, struggling to connect the two but loving every second of Gabriella's enthusiasm. "Gabriella and Jolene has a nice ring to it. Do you think we'll be up and serving by lunch?"

"Easily," Gabriella said, patting Jolene gently. "All the paperwork with the city was submitted and approved. We're in the food business now legally." She pointed at Joey. "Just prepare yourself for the amazing aromas that will be wafting past the tasting room come eleven a.m."

Joey's mouth watered automatically. "I'm going to be dreaming tonight about the arancini I sampled and fantasizing about our next one-on-one rendezvous."

"Oh là là." Gabriella winked. "Take note. I'm making you and Madison a sampler platter of all the truck's bites for lunch tomorrow, so leave room at breakfast. No heavy biscuits or anything."

"God, I don't know, Gabriella. You make life so hard."

She smiled as she made her way into the main building and the tasting room. Things were really starting to shape up. It was so gratifying to see one of her dreams for Tangle Valley begin to shift into place. She'd already had some contractors out to discuss that second tasting room and had a meeting set up with a designer who would be instrumental in making sure the space matched the vibe of the rest of the vineyard property. Next, she wanted to see what they could do about turning that old barn on the far side of the property into something romantic for weddings or special events. It honestly wouldn't take too much work to convert it into something truly beautiful.

Since it was just past lunchtime on a Friday, guests were few and far between. Business would pick up again in a couple of hours, but for now Joey could use this time to pull in more bottles and work on scheduling with Loretta, who she could hear washing glasses in the back. Joey paused. Alone at a table, not far from the bar, sat Madison. She stared out the window as she chewed on a pencil, so lost in thought that she'd not even heard Joey enter.

Joey approached, grinned, and placed a hand on her hip. "There she sat, pondering the world's great mysteries, ready to take on any obstacle that comes her way. She was Madison LeGrange."

Madison turned and didn't miss a beat. Her blue eyes sparkled brightly. "If you're talking about tannin concentration, then most definitely. About to make those suckers my bitch."

"Language, missy. You can't fucking talk that way in here."

Madison covered her ears. "And now I'm scandalized. Joey Wilder is floating f-bombs like the tooth fairy dropping change. What is happening? This is not normal behavior."

"I'm fired up today," Joey said as she rounded the counter to behind the bar. She checked the bottles below the counter and did a quick count. They also needed more tasting crackers.

"And why is that?" Madison spun around and pointed her pencil. "Oh, right. The town meeting about the hotel you hate because Jack did. How'd that go?"

"She was there."

"The beautiful, sophisticated sellout?"

"Yes, and that's the perfect word for her, a sellout."

Madison winced. "I was being playfully hyperbolic, but if you want to go there, I'll indulge. What was she wearing? Did you notice? Because that would tell me a lot."

"Maddie," Joey said, scolding her. "This is not the time and that isn't the point." A pause. "A really awesome brown plaid jacket with matching boots. The thing looked like it was tailor cut to her figure. It probably was." Joey slapped her own cheek. "What is wrong with me?"

Madison set her notebook aside and came to sit at the bar across from Joey. "You're a smitten kitten. I know that flushed cheek look well, and it was that way before you slapped it. You had that look when you first started mooning over Simone back in high school. You'd stare at her across geometry class with pink cheeks and longing in your sweet little Joey eyes."

"Exactly." Joey nodded. "And look where that got me. Publicly humiliated and alone. Best to avoid any and all flushing. Wouldn't you say?"

"I wouldn't. You're grown now and can handle it."

"But why would I want to?"

"Pink up, buttercup."

Joey shrugged and uncorked a bottle of dolcetto to let it breathe. "It's a nonissue. She works for The Jade, my least favorite thing."

"Her job can be your least favorite, but she can be your one and only."

Joey gestured with the cork. "She cannot. She can't even borrow sugar." She paused. "Well, maybe once, but there will be no ongoing sugar sharing. That would be over the limit."

"God, can you imagine someone pushing the sugar limits? Brown plaid jackets be damned. There will be no condiment back-and-forth." Madison made her eyes wide and headed back to her table. "Now stop talking to me, I need to do some math if you want this wine to taste any good."

"Nah, mediocre wine is all the rage."

"Shut up."

"You shut up."

❖

The Moon and Stars Ranch was a twenty-two-minute drive from the center of town, and Becca made the whole trip with the windows down on her Nissan Juke, enjoying the chilly air as it rushed past. Her ears were now cold, but she didn't care. Cold ears just got her excited to be smack in the middle of fall and the cooler Oregon temperatures, which she already preferred to Orlando's. She savored the sunshine-filled drive as she hummed along badly to Taylor Swift, her total guilty pleasure, like her car. She could easily afford a Range Rover or a BMW, which would certainly be more fitting for the image of the general manager of a multimillion-dollar resort, but when she'd seen the Juke on the road, it had just looked so fun and festive that she had to abandon her professional persona and give in to the inner Becca. She'd gone with yellow and had never felt so at home in a car. It made people smile and children wave when she passed.

She pulled the Juke onto the long dirt road that led to the ranch and smiled as a handful of happy-looking dogs ran and skipped along the fence as she drove. It made her happy to see how much space they had to exercise and play. Luckily, her house came with a fairly decent sized yard for whoever she might adopt. She imagined herself with a smaller dog, though, so she didn't need acres of exercise space. Just enough for some good running.

"Hey, there. Are you Becca?" a man in an actual cowboy hat and boots asked. He removed the hat as she approached, and she saw that he was incredibly handsome. Calendar worthy.

"Yes. That's me. Are you Stephen? Hi."

He held out his hand. "Yes, ma'am." Just then, a border collie mix approached and sniffed her hand timidly. "That's Livewire. She's always the first to vet a new guest. It's pretty much your background check."

Becca offered her hand for sniffing, and Livewire gave her the once-over before wagging her furry tail and scampering off, clearly trusted off leash.

"You've been approved," Stephen said. He had crystal clear blue eyes that carried kindness. "Follow me out to the corral, and you can meet the pack. They're an eclectic crew but friendly."

Becca raised her shoulders to her ears as they walked. "I'm excited and nervous at the same time. I've wanted a dog for so long but knew I needed to wait until I was settled. But today is that day."

Stephen smiled as she spoke. "I know exactly what you're talking about. I feel the same way every time we foster a new rescue." He touched his chest, acknowledging his feelings. "You just want it to go well."

"Yes." She laughed. "I very much do, and I feel it here," she said, touching her jittery midsection. "But it's a good feeling. Anticipation."

"Totally normal." He gestured with his chin to the large open fenced-in area in the distance. "You'll notice some are a little more shy than others. Don't let that fool you. They're all good pups. Just a matter of figuring out if one fits."

"Got it." Becca followed him past the large ranch-style home where they ran into another man along the corral fence. He wore crisp jeans and boots, an honest-to-goodness cowboy.

"Hi there. Welcome," he said and tipped his hat to her.

"Becca, this is my partner, Monty. He's the dog whisperer around here, but don't give him too much out loud credit. The pups can't get enough of him, and he calms the scared ones when they arrive."

Monty flashed a perfect smile. "What can I say? I'm a cuddler."

"Great to meet you." Becca shook Monty's hand, struck by how handsome he was as well. Truly. What was with this place? She didn't know what they were drinking, but she wanted some of it. Monty could be the model for one of those sultry romance novels with the shirtless cowboys on the cover. She also wasn't sure if *partner* meant sidekick, like on a ranch, or *partner in life*. These two would make an unbelievably striking couple. She secretly hoped for it.

"Nice to meet you, ma'am. You're looking for a new best friend, I hear."

"That's my hope." Right on cue a group of excited dogs approached the gate, sensing they were about to get some attention.

"We're currently fostering ten dogs out here on the ranch. All have been hard to place for various reasons." Monty pointed. "This adorable goofball sheds a ton and barks a bit too much for his own good. That gorgeous girl likes to chew things. That one doesn't like being on his own for too long, just to give you a sampling."

Becca shrugged. "We all have our hang-ups. I forget to call my friends on their birthdays. I'm working on it."

"Aren't we all?" Stephen said, joining them along the fence. Monty placed a hand on his lower back, and Becca grinned to herself. Definitely not just ranching partners, which warmed her heart. "Ready to say hello?"

"God, yes. Just look at all these cuties." She laughed at the silly shepherd with the tongue lolling out the side of his mouth.

Monty tossed her a cautionary glance. "Just be prepared to be overrun and jumped all over. Part of life around here."

Becca didn't balk at the warning. "It's my favorite thing."

"I knew I liked you," Monty said and led the way carefully through the gate. Stephen stayed outside the corral and leaned over the fence. She could see a small building in the distance with the door open for the dogs to go in and out, which made her feel good about the care they were clearly receiving. Her attention shifted when four energetic dogs bounded straight for her, dancing side to side, and jumping for her affection. She knelt down, not withholding, and was immediately greeted with kisses and whines as she did her best to greet each dog. "Hi there. Hey. Oh, look at you, Furry Face McGee."

Not far away, a few others looked on with interest, but held their ground. Monty pointed. "Those are the more shy ones." As if overhearing, a white dog with large brown spots, including one over his right eye, approached and sat down. He didn't make it all the way to Becca, but close enough. He was testing the waters.

"Who's this guy?" she asked.

"That's Skywalker, but we call him Sky for short. He likes his ears scratched and for things not to be too noisy." Monty studied him. "We're guessing he's a beagle-Labrador mix, but it's hard to say for certain."

Two of the more boisterous dogs began to wrestle, and Skywalker let out a distinctive bark that made Becca grin. "I'd say there's definitely some beagle in there."

Stephen straightened from the fence. "About that. Remember how we said each had their own hang-up?"

"Let me guess. He's a barker?"

Monty winced. "We prefer the term *crooner*, but yes, Sky can be quite vocal." He furrowed his brow as a thought occurred. "You don't have chickens, do you?"

She squinted. "No chickens."

The men exchanged a glance. Stephen nodded at her. "That's for the best."

She laughed and walked farther into the corral to meet some of the other dogs. They were all incredibly sweet. The little Jack Russell-dachshund mix that continued to prance around like she owned the world would be a good match for Becca. In fact, she was exactly the kind of dog she'd imagined for herself before arriving. Yet for reasons she couldn't quite pinpoint, she just kept glancing back at Sky. He'd been following behind her everywhere she went as if to say, *Don't forget me*, but always stayed a few feet behind as if he wasn't quite sure he should intrude.

"You like him, don't you?" Monty asked from where he stood next to her, hands on his handsome cowboy hips. He patted Sky's head, and the dog closed his eyes, savoring the affection.

She stared at Sky and gave her head a puzzled shake. "There's something about him that's tugging at me." She touched her heart. "But he's bigger than I was hoping for, and according to you, maybe a little louder."

"That's something to factor in. He's not overly energetic, but he does like to play. He's great with a ball." Monty whistled at Stephen and made the throwing gesture. Stephen nodded, ran off, and moments later returned with a small orange rubber ball, which he threw to Monty, who threw it to Sky. To her amazement, he caught it in his mouth seemingly without moving a muscle. Then he did something remarkable. He didn't return the ball to Monty. He brought it to Becca and set it at her feet and took three steps back.

She stared at him in amazement. The moment felt important. "Did he just choose me?" she asked. Her hands started to tingle, and her cheeks felt warm in the fifty-five-degree temperature.

"It's very possible," Monty said with a surprised look on his face. He glanced back at Stephen in amazement. "I've not seen him do that with a stranger. Did you see that?"

Stephen nodded. "I did. He likes you."

She knelt down and stroked his soft head, admiring the brown patch that covered his eye. "Hey there, fella. Maybe we weren't meant to be strangers. What do you think?"

Sky blinked back at her happily. Everything about him said he was a gentle soul. She tossed a look over her shoulder at that Jack Russell-dachshund mix and knew full well she'd have a home in no time, with that spunk and those good looks. When she turned back to Skywalker, he brushed his tongue across her nose as if to say, *Hello there, lady.*

She stood. "So, he barks, has an aversion to any and all chickens as well as loud noises. What else do I need to know?"

Stephen's face sobered. "He comes from a pretty rough life full of neglect. I'll spare you the details, but know he needs some love in his life."

Becca went still and looked down at Sky and his big brown eyes. Bigger than she planned or not, she could give him that love easily. She already felt it. "Sold. I'll take one Skywalker to go, please."

Sky barked his approval, which sealed the deal. They went inside, and Monty and Stephen went over all the essentials about caring for a dog like Sky, and even provided her with what looked to be a week's worth of his favorite food and that orange ball for throwing. When they finished their talk, the men looked at the clock.

"How about a glass of wine to celebrate," Monty said.

"Oh, I don't want to put you out. You probably have ranch things to do." Secretly, she was pleased to be asked. It felt nice after the adversity from earlier in the day.

"C'mon," Stephen said. "This is a momentous day. Your family just got bigger."

"You know? You make a valid point." She enjoyed hanging out with them and eagerly accepted the offer. "It's hard to turn down wine around here. It's all so good."

"Welcome to Willamette Valley," Monty said. "The wine pours from the trees like nectar."

As he poured three glasses, Becca squinted at the bottle. "Tangle Valley," she said, recognizing the tangled vines on the label.

Monty held up the bottle. "I don't know if you've been, but it's beautiful. Wine's fantastic, too."

She accepted the glass of dolcetto, which she loved, but it was no Tangle Valley pinot. "I have been there and fell in love with the place. It's right next to where I work. Well, where I will work once the construction finishes."

Stephen's eyes went wide. "You're working at The Jade?" He nearly came out of his seat like a giddy teenager at a concert. "I'm so excited to see something magnificent and luxurious show up at long last. I'm already planning a spa weekend."

She grinned, thrilled to finally, hear someone local have a positive reaction to the resort. "You let me know when you want to come, and I'll set you up with a special package. Use my manager perks. What else are they for if not for the people who helped you find your dog?"

Monty and Stephen grinned at each other. "You're the best new friend we've made in a while. Stay for dinner," Stephen said. "I make a mean apple pork chop, and then you and Sky can enjoy life together. Until you come back another time. And hopefully many more."

"I would love to stay. What can I do to help?"

"Nothing. Drink your wine, get to know your dog, and enjoy yourself."

Sky barked four times and Becca laughed.

She did enjoy herself. Dinner was not only fantastically prepared, but the conversation was never dull or slow. The three of them riffed effortlessly and laughed a lot. Monty and Stephen had met when both were attending college in San Francisco. They'd fallen in love and moved to Oregon to buy some land and never looked back. The Moon and Stars Ranch was how they made their full-time living, growing not only acres and acres of oats but fresh vegetables as well. It was a fantastic night. She'd done it. Becca had made a new pair of friends, and she really, really liked them. She tried not to celebrate outwardly, but it felt nice to spend time with other people, not that Carla wasn't great.

"You mentioned during dinner that you're single. How is that possible?" Monty asked as they cleared the table together. He was so good-looking with his sandy blond hair falling onto his forehead that it almost hurt to look at him.

She scrunched up one eye. "Probably because I've been married to my job for far too long. I'm good at it, but sometimes in my line of work, the men ascend the rankings faster than the women, so I fought like hell to make sure I stayed relevant. Plus, my last relationship wasn't the best." Monty winced. "Yeah. Then when I heard The Jade was going up, I leapt at the chance to open the property. I like the idea of a slower pace as my priorities shift. I want to do a few things for me." She handed a plate to Stephen.

He studied her. "You could date."

"I could. Who knows? Maybe I'll meet someone organically." She tried not to think about Joey. "I'm not in a rush."

"Oh, I feel like a challenge has been extended," Stephen said to Monty with a bounce of his eyebrows.

Monty nodded back seriously. "Oh yeah. A gauntlet has been thrown down. We shall prove our skills."

She laughed. "No. No gauntlet. Nothing to prove either." She winced apologetically. "Setups can be awkward. Forced."

"Or magnificent. You're forgetting the potential. We'll keep our eyes open." Monty offered a wink. "You do the same with your mind."

"I'm terrified and trying not to be." *But there's Joey*, her mind supplied.

When it was time to go, Becca felt a ball of excitement gather in her chest. Her palms were hot, and there was a smile on her face she couldn't erase. This was the start of a new adventure, and her life would likely never be the same. Monty leashed up Sky and sat with him for a few moments, whispering to him privately. Becca was touched by the love these men showed each dog and grateful she'd come to them for Sky.

Monty stood and grinned at her. "I think he's all set for his new home."

Becca took the leash he offered her and knelt down. "Want to come with me?" she asked him.

He didn't answer outright, but the way he shifted his two front paws back and forth said he was excited. She gave him a few reassuring pets, kissed his cheek, and they were ready. She thanked the guys with hugs and promised she'd call with any and every question. In fact, they insisted.

With Skywalker riding shotgun, Becca drove them home.

Home, she thought happily with one hand on Sky's warm back. Soft tunes played on the radio. The stars shone brightly overhead as if smiling down on the new little family. Yes, it was definitely starting to feel like home.

CHAPTER SIX

Every time the door to the tasting room opened, the savory aromas wafting in from Jolene, the food truck outside, nearly brought Joey to her knees. Gabriella had been up early prepping everything she would need—homemade pasta, her arancini filling, cured meats. Her prep even included a crisply ironed white chef's coat.

"I can't make good food if I don't look good," she'd said earlier that morning as she'd stood next to the pretty blue truck, admiring the sky.

"You always look good," Joey said, still a little sleepy. "You're literally one of the prettiest people I've ever seen in person. Even first thing in the morning, which is not fair, so I hate you. I'm not apologizing either."

"So we're fighting?"

"We can be done now. I've forgiven you."

"That was close. I adore you, so it cancels out the hate. Bam. What do you think of that?" She placed a hand on her hip. "I do love the morning, though. I use it to plan menus. It's perfect for creating."

"What are we having today?" They'd discussed a rotating menu for the truck, offering different items each week but using it to figure out what the fan favorites were for the eventual restaurant menu. They'd have the better part of a year before all the moving parts lined up and the restaurant was a reality. It would be small but memorable with Gabriella at the helm.

"We're starting today with arancini filled with a white wine risotto and fontina cheese, and the Goodfella, which is a slider topped with salami, pepperoni, prosciutto, mozzarella, roasted red peppers, and a vinaigrette you'd elbow your infant for."

"I have no infant."

"Even better, because you're not gonna wanna share the not-your-mama's cannoli I'm serving today. The shells are, of course, homemade."

"Listen to you. You make trucks fancy."

"Gotta keep up with the delicious wine." She gestured to the tasting room, just yards away. "I actually chose my flavors alongside Tangle Valley sips. I had a bottle of each of your varietals open. I didn't get drunk, though."

Joey nodded. "Great restraint."

Gabriella closed one eye. "Maybe a little drunk."

"Well, that's okay, too," Joey said with a wink. She took note of the fact that Gabriella was very put together as she reported for work. Fluffed and sparkly. She even had her nails done, something Joey never gave much thought to but that looked beautiful on Gabriella's elegant hands.

Back in the tasting room, Joey celebrated Jolene's reception. The food truck had only been open for a couple of hours now, but from the buzz she'd overheard at the bar, it was a smash hit. Their guests were gushing, and the advertising they'd done to promote the truck's opening had paid off. Joey estimated they had triple their typical traffic for a Saturday. She'd even set up their outdoor bar for folks to purchase glasses of wine, and the line was never empty. She grinned to herself as she moved about the grounds, saying hello to guests and helping to clear stray glasses. She'd wisely scheduled several of her part-time pourers as reinforcements in the tasting room, which freed her up to move around and fill in as needed.

"This place is hoppin'," Loretta said as they passed each other in the storage room. She had two bottles of pinot gris in her hands and was headed in the direction of the tasters.

"Right? It's been a while since we've been this busy. I will not complain about my feet, which are already killing me. It's good pain."

Loretta turned back from where she stood at the door. Her eyes carried that fierce sentimentality that she was known for. "Your dad would love this."

Joey felt the wistful pang, but she was also hit with something else. Pride. She hadn't fallen on her face, and the winery was still up and functioning, and doing quite well.

"Ton of people out there," a voice behind them said.

They turned. "Hey, Uncle Bobby."

"Think I'm gonna get a fourth cornhole game set up. People are waiting in line for a turn."

Joey shook her head. "Everyone loves a good game of cornhole with their chardonnay."

"Ain't that the damn truth." He gestured with his chin in Joey's direction. "When the crowd dies down, I challenge you to a match."

Joey laughed, remembering playing against her uncle when she was a kid. It had been a while since they'd battled it out. "I'm game. But it's good that we're waiting until the guests are gone. Wouldn't want to hurt your ego in front of them."

Her uncle's eyes flashed steely and competitive like she knew they would. He was a total sweetheart until it came to competition. He'd toss his ball cap on the ground when he didn't do well, his signature tantrum. "Oh, you're trash-talking now. Reminds me of my brother."

"Always," Joey said, standing taller. Loretta shook her head, enjoying their back-and-forth, before going back to work. Joey followed suit and headed out to the patio where Matt Tremore played on his guitar and sang a slow rendition of "Brown Eyed Girl" into the microphone. A crooner, that guy. She walked across the lawn to the food truck where she could see Gabriella and Lynn, the part-time pourer they'd placed on cashier duty today, laughing through the window with a couple at the front of the line. She continued her stroll and found Deacon, Madison's assistant, gearing up for the next tour of the vineyard's grounds. Madison was likely at work in the barrel room if she had to guess. She'd been pulling long hours since she'd arrived at Tangle Valley. That was Madison—a total workaholic, lost in measurements and sampling.

"Oh, hello there," Joey said to a medium-sized dog who approached her slowly on the edge of the patio, the part still kissed by the sun. In another two hours, the whole thing would be overtaken by shade and markedly chillier. The dog's tail wagged gently and he looked up at Joey with a curious stare. He was mostly white with brown patches all over his body, and a big round one over his eye. It suited him. Joey loved getting to see all the dogs on the patio week to week. She knew most of them. Not this handsome dude, though.

"That's Sky," his owner said from somewhere behind Joey. "He's a friendly fella."

Joey gave the dog a hearty scratch. "I can tell. He has the sweetest eyes ever." She looked back and met the gaze of Sky's person, and froze. Her body went warm and still when she saw Becca staring back at her, and then cold once she remembered the whole story. But Joey caught herself. She was the hostess here and treated every single Tangle Valley guest with respect. Today was no different.

"Hi." She forced a conservative smile.

Becca sat forward and grinned back. "I know I'm not your favorite person, but I hope it's okay that I'm here. I saw a flyer for the opening of the food truck, and well, it was such a pretty day out." She gestured to Sky. "And this guy didn't want to be left behind, so here we are. You don't have chickens, do you?"

"I'm sorry?"

"Never mind."

"Well, we're glad you came, regardless of…the rest." That felt awkward to say. As fired up as Joey was about The Jade, she wasn't the type to run headfirst into confrontation. Plus, her position didn't lend itself to being inhospitable.

"About *the rest*, I know you're skeptical."

"I am," Joey said, straightening. Sky returned to Becca and lay at her feet.

"But we had such a nice chat the last time I was here. Is there no way we could be friends in spite of our differences?"

Joey shifted her weight from one foot to the other, lost in those hazel eyes and the soft tug brought on by Becca's bottom lip. The breeze caught her chestnut hair and tousled it. She wore a different jacket today, an army-green military-looking number that she rocked like no one else could.

Becca held up a hand. "Tell you what. You don't have to decide right now. How about that?"

"Okay." Joey wasn't sure where Becca was going with this.

"But can we have a glass of wine? As foes, I mean."

"You're asking me to have angry wine with you?"

"Yes. Furious wine, if you prefer."

Damn it. That softened her and she didn't want it to. Why did Becca have to be so personable? "Maybe sometime." Joey would have leapt at that opportunity just a week ago, but now she had her walls up.

"How about right now? Provided you have a few minutes to be angry."

Oh, man. Cue the war of feelings. Beautiful woman. Capitalist enemy. Adorable dog. Charm-sucking yuppie trap. What was she supposed to do here? "Maybe I could work that out."

Becca sat back in her chair and nodded her understanding. "I hear the pinot is good."

"Your sources are stellar." Joey looked around and saw that everything seemed to be under control, and well, she was due for a break. Was she really considering this? Just then, Sky-the-dog returned and nuzzled her hand with a quiet whine, as if saying, *Oh, won't you please sit with us so I can be your forever friend?*

Becca saw the effect he had on Joey and grinned. He was clearly on the payroll.

"One glass," Joey said, "and only because sitting down sounds nice about now. But I retain anger rights."

Becca nodded. "One glass it is, and I would expect nothing different." Joey stole a bottle of pinot from behind the outdoor bar and brought it to Becca's table, where she poured herself a glass and topped off Becca's.

They sat there a moment and let things settle.

"You gave a great speech the other day at the meeting." Becca sipped her wine as Sky sat to her left.

"Thank you. Is this the dog you mentioned during yours?"

"So you *were* listening." She slid a strand of chestnut hair behind her ear. "I wasn't sure."

"Of course I was. Taking detailed notes, even."

"Yes. His full name is Skywalker and his favorite thing is apparently sitting on the couch and watching television. We're good at it. Champions, really. But loud noises are a no-go."

"Good thing we're a quiet little vineyard."

"And he seems to like the music." A pause. Becca seemed to make a decision. "We're not at war, you know. Can we maybe start over? Find a way to be friends again, like that first day? Lose the anger clause."

Joey sighed, as the bricks began to fall from her walls. "Okay, but that doesn't change how I feel about The Jade."

"You're not a fan. So stipulated."

"Not enough." She gestured higher.

"You hate The Jade and its existence more than anything in the totality of Planet Earth."

Joey laughed and pointed downward. She really liked staring at Becca Crawford.

"You have a hearty dose of dislike for The Jade and the greedy corporation that brought it here."

"Ding, ding, ding." Behind her, Matt broke into "I'm Yours," and Joey smiled. She loved Jason Mraz.

Becca met her gaze, which caused Joey's stomach muscles to tighten. "Well, just know that I'm aware of your feelings and hell-bent on changing them. If you haven't noticed, I can be persuasive."

"I've noticed a lot."

Becca seemed to enjoy that comment. She'd left a subtle lip print on her glass that made Joey's stomach flutter. Sexy.

"You know, they finished the lobby yesterday, and it's perfect. Lots of light colors and large windows. It's entirely cheerful, which," she said, making a sweeping gesture to the land around them, "will send our guests into the world happy, ready to drink wine and carouse."

"Carouse?" Joey asked with a laugh. "You don't often hear that word."

"A shame. It's a nice word, I think."

Well, now it was. Joey swallowed. "Have you eaten?"

"I have." Becca tossed a glance over at the truck. "Gabriella and I had a nice chat. She's a natural up there, tossing things to and fro and holding a conversation easily at the same time. She says there's a restaurant on the way."

"That's true. In the works as we speak."

"I'm excited for that, and I didn't realize that she was new to town as well." She lifted a shoulder. "Nice not to be the only recent transplant, you know?"

"I can imagine." Gabriella and Becca were bonding, and a trickle of jealousy snuck in. Joey shifted in her seat. She wasn't sure which woman she was jealous of, however. Well, yes she was, too, and didn't like it. She shook it off. "Are you settling in, getting the boxes taken care of?"

Becca laughed. "No."

"Well, you gotta do something about that. You don't want to get a reputation as the town box lady, do you?"

"Mildly tempting, but no."

Joey squinted. "Give me the status."

"I have eleven boxes left. The problem is at the end of the day I'm exhausted and accept their place in my life. The boxes are my friends, and as someone who tends to assign feelings to inanimate objects, that practice has extended their lease."

"Well, stop that right away."

"Easier said than done. I've stopped short of naming them."

"That's something." Joey pursed her lips in thought. "You could be unpacking them right now, you know."

"Yes, but then I wouldn't be here talking to you, and I happen to really like getting to know you better. Are you married?"

Joey nearly spit out her wine. She took a moment. "Definitely not married. Guess you haven't been in town long enough. Give it time."

Becca didn't seem to understand the reference, which was a good thing. It was nice to have at least one person not know about her personal scandal.

"In a serious, committed relationship then. Is he around here somewhere?" Becca made a show of looking behind her, then under her chair.

Joey winced. "You'll be looking for a long time. He doesn't exist." She pointed at Becca. "And you know that, because before I knew you were behind the controls at The Jade, you and I flirted." Joey was a little surprised she'd just blurted that out. Yet here they were.

Becca didn't seem fazed. Joey was beginning to think that very little ruffled her feathers. She was the epitome of cool, calm, collected, and yep, still hot as hell. "We did. It was fun. Now you hate me and it's awful." She leaned forward. "Let's go back to the flirting. Definitely preferable, and we were pretty good at it."

"I won't argue that point." Joey tapped her finger on the side of her glass. It was hard to resist Becca's suggestion with her sitting right there, giving off such a warm and friendly vibe. Why couldn't Becca just have been a self-involved corporate money-grubber, like Joey had imagined Elite's people to be? "Maybe we could be friendly."

Becca smiled and didn't push. "What do people do for fun in Whisper Wall, besides drink small samples of wine and discuss them?"

"Food is also pretty major. We all get out of bed early for any kind of festival devoted to the worship of a specific food. You missed Waffle Fest a few months back. Here a waffle, there a waffle. It was a syrupy good time." She took a sip.

"God, I'll count the days until it cycles back around. What's next?"

"Wassail Fest in late November."

Becca squinted. "Do all the festivals start with *W*?"

She laughed. "Nope. Just the luck of the calendar."

"Well, I'll definitely attend any and all festivals. I love meeting new people. Probably why I gravitated toward the hospitality industry. You?"

"Born into it, remember? But it has given me a chance to come out of my shell. I'm an introvert naturally, though." She pointed at herself. "You probably noticed. My social energy runs out, and I'm a dormouse." Why was she all of a sudden so talkative? This was supposed to be a polite drink. She stared at the truth juice in her glass and knew the answer.

"Well, you'd never know it, and you happen to be much better looking than a dormouse. Your hair alone tops that of a small rodent."

Joey nodded, enjoying their back-and-forth and allowing herself to relax. "I brush it daily."

"It shows." Another sip. Becca held up her glass. "Know what I'm noticing, this time around?"

"Tell me." Joey lived for wine talk, and the way Becca held her hand out as she searched for the words to describe the flavors had her gripped. She could watch her grapple for days, almost like she tasted something amazing and just had to figure out what it was.

"I want to say brown sugar. It reminds me of my childhood, but it's very subtle."

Joey sat taller, energized. "Yes. I've had that same thought. My father never explicitly said brown sugar, but it's there, right?"

Becca made a show of wiping her brow. "I'm always so nervous talking wine to people who know wine. I'm glad I wasn't out of left field."

"Nothing to worry about. There's no wrong impression when you taste wine. You let it settle, you take it in, and you say what comes to you." Becca blinked, almost like the words had been stolen. "Did I lose you with that one?" Joey asked after a few seconds.

"Oh. No. I was just…enjoying listening to you talk about what you love." She glanced at the table. This was Joey's first glimpse of Becca off her very sure footing. She relished getting a peek behind the perfectly put together curtain. She also wanted to say something to help even them out.

"It's one of the few areas in life where I can fully employ confidence. I know wine and I know Tangle Valley. The rest of life? Well, let's just say I always misjudge the hug or handshake question. Lean in for the wrong thing every damn time. I'm the worst and shouldn't be allowed out in public."

Becca laughed. "Don't be ashamed of that. It's earnest."

"It's sad."

"Special delivery for hungry people." Joey turned just as Gabriella set down a plate with a cannoli for each of them.

Joey practically vibrated happiness. "Those look amazing."

Gabriella moved her hand in a circle around the scene. "So does this conversation, which is why it deserves reinforcements." She hooked a thumb at the truck. "Now quit talking to me, dammit. I have amazing food to cultivate."

They watched her go, her pressed chef's coat now showing signs of her hard work. "A cannoli for your thoughts," Becca said, holding up the plate in temptation.

Joey shrugged. "I can admit it. Angry wine has been fun."

Sky lifted his head and looked up at Joey from his spot next to Becca's chair. "I think Skywalker agrees with you. He also wants a bite of cannoli." Becca obliged, feeding him a tear-off. He wolfed it down, which made Becca laugh. She looked up, the gold flecks in her eyes sparkling with amusement. "He sends his compliments to Chef Gabriella."

Joey motioned to the bustling vineyard. "Everyone else does. He's a trendy dog."

"Hear that?" Becca said, giving Sky a good scratching. "This woman thinks you're with it." Becca stood and smiled reluctantly. "I should probably take this big guy and get him some real food."

"Probably better for him than the pinot." Joey stood, too, and gathered their now empty glasses.

"I can't imagine that being the case for anyone. Thanks for hanging out with us, Joey. Angry or not." She reached into her pocket and produced a business card. "In case you need anything. A spare tire, a joke, or maybe just a couple of eggs for a cake you're making."

Joey accepted the card, saw the words *The Jade* scrawled across the top in a modern script, and suppressed a sad shake of her head. Instead she focused on the name *Rebecca Crawford*, which seemed friendlier, exciting even. She held it up. "For eggs."

"Will I see you again?"

"Oh, you never know. This town is pretty small, and you're welcome here anytime."

Becca squinted. "I can't decide if that's code for *I'd like you to come back again* or *If you do, I'll try my best to be nice.*"

"Well," Joey said with a shrug, "it could go a lot of ways."

Becca seemed to accept that and gave Sky's leash a tiny tug to signal their departure. "I enjoyed today. Thanks for not killing me."

Joey nodded. "Anytime."

As Becca headed off down the well-worn path that led to the vineyard's guest parking, words she hadn't planned on fled Joey's lips. "It was code for come back."

Becca stopped, turned, and broke into a supermodel grin as the wind hit. It was one of the most beautiful images Joey had ever seen. "Good to know. I will be."

"What the hell are you doing right now?" Joey mumbled to herself as she watched after Becca. The view of her ass made Joey's stomach flutter and her thighs tighten. Her cheeks flashed hot in betrayal.

"So what the hell *are* you doing?" Gabriella asked from several feet away. "I saw every minute of that, and it was glorious."

"Wait. What did I miss?" Madison asked, arriving in the area between them. She followed Joey's gaze to Becca Crawford driving away in a Nissan Juke and whistled low. "I see. I always arrive too late. Fill me in?"

Joey glanced back at the tasting room, which had been hit by a big boom of new arrivals. She pointed at her friends. "Meet me in the big barn at seven, and I'll tell you all about it. It's problematic because I'm a weak individual."

"Why I like you," Gabriella said. "You have a pulse."

Joey grimaced. "Seven o'clock. I'll bring the wine."

"The big barn it is," Madison said. "Little Joey Wilder," she said with a knowing gleam in her eye as she wandered away back to the barrel room.

❖

Becca clipped off Sky's leash and watched as he bounded into her living room and up onto her comfy leather couch, which he had apparently declared the best place for sitting and snoozing in the sun that cascaded through the large picture windows. He threw back his head and bellowed, beagle style, before collapsing onto his side in surrender. Becca could imagine how the barking and bellowing could be a problem for anyone who lived in an apartment. She'd take out his orange ball later and give him a workout in the backyard, but for now she'd let him rest.

"You were so well behaved in front of my friend," she told him and placed a kiss on the side of his head. And then another one because she'd truly grown to adore him. She loved how warm and smooth he was. "You are a stellar individual," she told him. He reciprocated with a lick across her face. "Nice one." She sat next to him on the couch, and unprompted, he snuggled his big body against her side. Who would have guessed from their tentative introduction that he would be such a lover?

Becca knew she had a lot to organize as opening approached. There were trainings and systems to set up, vendors to schedule, and meetings to sit in on and conduct. God help her. She needed to outline in writing everything about the upcoming week, to keep her head on straight. There would be time for that later that night. For now, she wanted to sit with Sky, decompress from their afternoon out, and ruminate over her conversation with Joey, who she now knew was actually a Josephine. She grinned, thinking the name pretty, but also feeling that Joey fit her better. "Joey Wilder," she murmured, liking the way the name felt on her lips. The woman had definitely snagged Becca's attention in a way no one had before. She was beautiful and stubborn and quick witted. A killer combination, even if she was on the wrong side of things.

Becca's phone, which she had deposited on the coffee table, vibrated in notification. Probably Louise from corporate in Orlando. She reached for the phone, imagining this was about securing rooms for the out-of-town leadership team who would arrive shortly to assist with opening.

She was wrong.

Instead she found a text from her new debonair cowboy friends.

Becks. We call you that now. We found someone you need to meet. Sending our love to Sky. This is Monty, by the way.

She smiled at the text and snuggled in. "It's your foster dads," she told her dog. "We're friends now. It's a whole lovefest."

Who is this mystery person I need to meet? she typed back.

No questions. Do you trust us?

Becca exchanged a look with Sky. "Do you vouch for these two? I'm serious. I don't know about this. But it would be nice to meet a new friend."

Sky showed her his belly.

"Good enough." She returned to her phone and typed out a response. *Fine. When and where, cowboys? My calendar is flexible until opening.*

CHAPTER SEVEN

W e've gathered in the name of star-crossed lovers. Spill," Madison said from on top of a bale of hay inside their biggest barn on the property.

"Can't we ease in first? The weather was nice today."

"I'm not here for weather chatter," Madison said.

Gabriella nodded seriously. "We're here for lurid romance."

"I don't have any of that."

Gabriella narrowed her focus. "You've got close."

Joey grinned. It was dark out and chilly enough that they all wore their warm coats. Joey happened to like her red and black checkered belted number quite a lot and had her hands stuffed in her pockets. They'd used this barn for storage of various farm-related materials and tools, but at Joey's request, the farmhands had begun to clear the space in preparation for the overhaul she had in store for it. She could already see the gorgeous receptions that would one day take place in the exact spot where they sat.

Joey adjusted on her bale of hay and pulled a leg beneath her. Gabriella sat on the ground, leaning her back against a bale, already sipping a glass of dolcetto, looking exhausted and happy from her first day of service.

"I've lost my damn mind, that's what," Joey remarked, half proud of herself and half horrified.

Gabriella shook her head. "In the most delicious way. I totally get what you see in Becca Crawford. She's sexy as hell, all put together, and glamorous." She shook her head. "Double damn on a silver platter of hot."

Joey raised an eyebrow. "I can't argue there. It's the rest of it that gets me all bothered."

Madison covered her eyes in frustration. "Josephine. The hotel is opening. You can bang your head against the wall all you want, but all you'll have then is a hurt head. Is that what you want?"

She squinted. "Well, no one wants a hurt head."

"Exactly," Gabriella said, picking up the baton. "You know what would be much nicer? A happy heart."

Joey stared at her. "You're a Hallmark commercial tonight."

Madison laughed. "Listen to Hallmark, JoJo. What's the deal with the whole hotel thing? Can we back up to that?"

"If you want."

Madison pressed on. "You're like a dog with a bone. Don't get angry at me for asking," she said, her voice softer, "but is this maybe more about your dad than it is you?"

Joey immediately sobered from the earlier banter, as the fun slipped away. "Maybe," she said quite honestly. It was a question she'd been asking herself over the last few days. "I don't like the idea of The Jade in Whisper Wall either, but it was such a sticking point for him, you know? He wanted to see this area preserved the way it was, and part of me is fighting for that on his behalf."

Gabriella nodded in sympathy. "Noble of you, but it's okay if you like Becca, too. You're not betraying your dad."

Madison nodded. "In fact, Jack would want you to live your life to its fullest. He would get it. That's the kind of person he was."

Joey considered her friends' words. She had to admit, they rang true. Yet at the same time, she felt this…call. "I have to be the watchdog for Tangle Valley now."

Madison winced. "That's a lot of pressure."

"You can't control the world," Gabriella said. "Definitely not a large corporation. I say you cut yourself a break and get to know this hotel hottie. She's actually really nice. We chatted."

"Should we call her up right now?" Madison asked with a glint in her eye. "I can drag over another bale."

Joey held up a hand. "No, no, no. We absolutely shouldn't." She sighed. "I have a lot going on right now."

"Can't argue with that," Madison said.

"So I think I'm going to work on a friendship with Becca. Nothing more."

"For now," Madison said into her glass. Joey blew off the comment, but Madison caught it. "It's been years since Simone. And a horse just walked by. Hop on."

"Take a *ride*," Gabriella said, drawing the last word out with a grin.

"You two are tag-teaming me," Joey said, gesturing with her wineglass at the pair. "You're a no-good duo and you know it." She grabbed a folded plaid blanket from the pile of three she'd carried out and noted its scratchy goodness. All farm blankets were a tad scratchy. It was a rule.

"We still do *some* things well together," Gabriella said. "But listen, if you want to take it slow, I applaud you. That's the responsible way to go about it, just a little less exciting for me, but that's not our goal." She shrugged. "Becca's not going anywhere and neither are you."

"Thank you for getting that."

"Now tell me all about your talk today." Gabriella leaned in. "And emphasize any sexy parts. No. Embellish them."

Madison rolled her eyes as Joey launched into the tale. "It started with her dog…"

Later that night, Joey couldn't sleep. She turned onto her side, her back, her stomach until she finally threw the covers off and sat up in the dark room. The problem was she kept flashing on her afternoon and that undeniable push-pull tension she'd experienced in Becca's presence. Her skin tingled in sensitivity and her mind went places racier than she was used to. Was it possible that their opposing sides had made their dynamic…even hotter? There was now something forbidden about Becca that had Joey shifting uncomfortably in the tank top and panties she'd worn to bed. She remembered the flecks of gold in Becca's eyes. She visualized the way she sometimes ran a hand through her hair. She bit her lip when she thought about the sexy way Becca formed her words and the intelligent manner in which she communicated. Her body responded. The temperature in the room rose. She visualized Becca doing the most decadent of things to her body, and it responded readily.

Oh, this was most definitely getting complicated.

❖

Whisper Wall, Oregon, had an entire restaurant dedicated entirely to French fries, and Becca was here for it. The place was called I Only Have Fries for You, which made it only more perfect in Becca's eyes. Inside there were famous paintings in which the subjects had been swapped out for a fry wearing sunglasses. *Girl with a Pearl Earring* was now a fry, as were the *Mona Lisa* and many others. She marveled at the genius and grinned in support.

Once she looked at the menu, which was only a fourth the size of a regular menu, Becca found the restaurant's name fitting because they legitimately offered nothing else. She'd arrived for her setup a few minutes early because first impressions mattered, and she'd never want anyone waiting on her.

"What about a side salad?" she asked the server while she waited on her date. While Becca had made it clear to the cowboys that a romance with this woman was unlikely, she'd shut her mouth and agreed to keep an open mind when they'd argued. The only problem was her mind was otherwise preoccupied with someone else.

"No salads," the server said. He was a glasses-wearing teenager in a red T-shirt with a container of overflowing French fries depicted on the front. He wore a name tag that read *Kevin* and refused to participate in a single vocal shift or facial expression, which had Becca intrigued and up for the challenge.

"A burger?" she asked with a grin.

"God, no," he deadpanned.

"Chicken strips. I do love a good strip."

"Nope."

"How about another potato product? There are so many. Loaded baked? Tater Tots?"

"No."

"You could ask the chef, Kevin." Now she was just messing with him.

He touched her menu. "Just the fries. And toppings and sauces. All we got."

She pointed at the menu. "Let's hope I can mustard up the courage to order."

Kevin blinked. Nothing.

"You know what? I'm going to wait for my date to arrive before ordering the fries. Ketchup with you later?"

He nodded curtly, turned on his heel, and headed to the front of the restaurant. She wondered if the constant fry service had scared away his zest for life. Shame. Just then, in total contrast to Kevin, a perky individual bounded her way into the restaurant. She stood at the front of the room and scanned the nearby tables, which signaled Becca that this might be her date, Emmaline. She had the same dark curly hair as the woman in the photo.

She held up her hand, waved tentatively, and smiled, to which the woman pointed back and skipped her way over. She was certainly very cheerful. Becca easily gave her that. Must have been having a fantastic day.

"Are you Becca? You look just the way Stephen said you would. I love your hair." She hooked her bag around the back of the chair. "And your jacket. Just look at you." She placed a hand on her hip and just stared before sliding into the chair across from Becca's.

"Oh, well, thank you. You must be Emmaline. Great to meet you."

"Right? It's wonderful to meet new people, and going on dates is just an exciting way to meet people in a separate, more intimate manner. Wouldn't you say?" She supposed that was true. Interesting way to phrase it, though. Becca opened her mouth to answer but didn't get very far. "Dates are just stuperific. I made up that word. Don't think I'm dumb for it." She shrugged. "It's just this thing I do a lot. I love to make up words. We need so many more of them. Wouldn't you agree?"

That was a lot to take in, and Becca did her best to turn her reaction around quickly, having learned from past experience. "I think there's always room for more, and I would never think you dumb for adding to the world's vocabulary." She swallowed. "It's a good word, stuperific. And dates can be fun, yes."

"Tell me when you knew you were gay."

"What? Weren't we just talking about words?"

"That's another thing I do. I leap around to keep the conversation fresh and exciting." She demonstrated leaping with the saltshaker, then folded her hands on top of the table and waited.

Becca stared back. "Maybe we should order first."

"We only have fries," Kevin said, appearing out of nowhere. How did he manage that? He studied them, pen poised and ready for the order.

"I'll take...the fries," Becca said gleefully. Why did she enjoy Kevin's lack of surprise so damn much? Kevin simply made her happy.

"I'll have the fries, as well," Emmaline said. "I'll follow your lead."

Becca laughed because there weren't really any other options.

"You get your choice of three of our marvelous dipping sauces," Kevin said as if he was the most bored human in the dullest moment of his very laborious existence. He offered a half-hearted gesture in the direction of the wall listing their choices. "Might I suggest the garlic aioli? Or perhaps our nacho fries? What about some chili on top? The choice is yours."

Oh yeah. He'd been forced to memorize that. "Do you know what an aioli is, Kevin?" Becca asked.

"No," he deadpanned.

"Just checking." They picked their sauces, and Kevin trudged away to French fry purgatory.

"Now, where were we?" Emmaline asked with really wide eyes.

"Why don't we back up?" Becca offered. "Get to know the basics. How do you know Stephen and Monty?"

"That's an easy question right there. I make dog food in my kitchen and took them a sample. I'm hoping to mass produce one day. I just adore dogs, don't you?"

"Yes," Becca said, seizing on the commonality. Relief settled. "I just love my new guy, Sky, who I adopted from the ranch. He's a mixed breed and just the sweetest boy. What's your dog's name? Or do you have more than one?"

"Oh, I don't have any pets. I just like seeing dogs when I'm out and about, on their leashes, being pooches." She made what could only be described as a pouty little dog face. "I'm a hardcore fan of the species. I do have a poster in my bedroom of three dogs, however."

"Perfect," Becca said, nodding, trying not to question any of this. "And you're capitalizing on a passion. That's the way to do it. I admire you."

"I'm over dog food now, though. Onward and upward. I want a job where I can work with people in crisis. You know?" She gestured a lot with her hands, grasping at the air.

"As in the health and wellness field?"

"Or they somehow lost their keys and need help." She placed an earnest hand on her chest. "I could be that person."

"Interesting. I suppose you could."

"You're pretty. Has anyone ever told you that before?" Emmaline asked. "So glad I found you." She licked her bottom lip. "If you ever lose your keys, come to Mama."

Mayday. What was happening right now? Becca bit the inside of her lip hard because a woman she'd known for all of six minutes had just said those words out loud. She wasn't sure whether this was the most hilarious encounter ever or the most horrifying. One thing was for sure, she could not look away and longed for a journal to take notes.

"Well, look who it is! Hi, Becca Crawford. We meet again."

Becca turned at the sound of a friendly voice floating their way from across the restaurant and grinned widely at Gabriella from Tangle Valley, who waved enthusiastically. Behind her walked Joey and another woman she'd not met. She watched as the two women turned and said something quietly to Joey, who, to Becca's surprise, headed toward her.

"Three times in one week. We're out of hand," Becca said.

Joey smiled and shrugged. "A dose of small-town life for you. You can't escape anyone around here. Enjoying yourself?"

"Oh, immensely."

Joey looked to Emmaline. "I don't think we've met. Are you a colleague of Becca's?"

Becca gestured to her date. "No, no. This is Emmaline. She will, however, help you find your keys."

"Nice to meet you. I'm Joey Wild—"

"We're on a date tonight," Emmaline supplied. "A romantic one. We've also both agreed that we like dates a lot. What about you?"

"Oh." A pause. An unreadable expression came over Joey's face. One thing was for sure, the authentic smile had dimmed. "I think dates can be nice. If you're in the mood to go on a date." She looked at Becca with what almost seemed like regret. Becca felt a pang of it herself, because Joey was now witnessing her on a kind of date, and it would likely send the entirely wrong message. Why had she agreed to this again? Because it had seemed like a nice way to meet more people. Sigh. She now saw the possible ramifications turn into her reality.

"This is a cute place," she said, making a show of looking all around at the overabundance of French fry decor, while her real goal was to steer them as far away from the topic of the date as possible. Especially since she had zero interest in Emmaline.

Joey nodded. "I love it. We don't have a fry festival in this town yet, but I'm feeling like it's imminent." Joey's blond hair was parted on the side and swept down her forehead. It was a really sexy look, but what was even more effective was that she didn't seem to be trying for that.

Becca hooked a thumb. "I'm not sure if you've met Kevin, but he should maybe not be ambassador."

"I heard that," Kevin said blandly, as he tromped over and delivered their fries. "Will you be joining the table?" he asked Joey.

"Oh no. I wouldn't want to intrude on their evening."

"And it's a date, so…" Emmaline said, placing her hand on top of Becca's in a cringeworthy show of possession she'd definitely not earned in their twelve minutes' acquaintance.

"I think you mentioned that," Joey said politely. "And I'm intruding, so I'll return to my friends." She held up a hand as she backed away. "Enjoy your night."

Becca smiled but it was entirely forced and she hoped Joey saw her unhappiness at the now awkward situation. Once Joey turned to go, Becca closed her eyes briefly. She'd done nothing wrong, yet she felt like she'd crashed and burned horribly in Joey's eyes. Again. She popped a fry into her mouth and felt the smallest bit better because God apparently worked in their kitchen.

"These things are amazing," she said to Emmaline, dipping a second fry in the sweet chili mayonnaise that came on the tray of sauces. "How's the jalapeño ranch sauce?"

"I'm enjoying it, but it reminds me a lot of my dead ex-husband. I can't wait to tell you all about him. First, there was his run-in with a teacup poodle in 2001 that started the whole thing off."

And here we go. Becca ate her fries while nodding and smiling and doing her best to appear alarmed, sympathetic, and interested in the harrowing tales of Ronnie, who'd died from poor living habits. All the while, she stole glances across the restaurant at the three friends. Joey in particular. Her whole face lit up when she laughed, which she was doing a lot tonight, and Becca couldn't help but smile, too. It was contagious, Joey's happiness.

"It's not that positive a detail, though. He had trouble breathing on that ski slope."

Becca refocused and killed the smile. "No doubt. God, I can't even imagine. Poor Ronnie. Again."

"Well, don't feel too bad. He was arrested a week later for chasing our neighbor with a slingshot."

Becca swallowed a laugh. She was barely successful, and looked around for the destined-to-be-there hidden camera. There didn't seem to be one. She sobered. "Well, that's unfortunate."

"Not for the neighbor. Hey," Emmaline said, leaning forward, "you want to ditch this fry shack and take a visit to my apartment? I have peppermint schnapps and a fantastic collection of Christina Aguilera. I can be your genie in a bottle." In that moment, her dark hair seemed alarmingly curly and her eyeballs nearly swirled.

"Oh. You're the nicest for that offer, but I'm afraid I'm not feeling so energetic tonight, Emmaline. I think I better head home after."

But she didn't make it there anytime soon. Emmaline had another half dozen stories to tell and personal questions to ask, not that Becca answered any of them. At least it gave her plenty of time to kill the amazing fries and sample all six dipping sauces, which came with a lot more depth than her date.

After finally bidding Emmaline good night with a friendly hug in the parking lot, Becca leaned against her Juke and began a group text to Monty and Stephen, demanding answers. "Please tell me you don't truly think I'd be compatible with this woman."

Before she could straighten, her phone rang. Monty. "Becca, we thought she was great until she became a lunatic."

Stephen took the phone. "She duped us. She stopped by for coffee and told one wild story after another this afternoon. I wanted to send a *run fast* text to cancel your date, but Monty thought we should let you decide."

"I owe you my firstborn," Monty shouted in the distance. "I'm so sorry. How were the fries?"

"The one bright spot," she called back. That wasn't true. The second bright spot was currently still inside that restaurant having a fantastic night out with her friends. Becca's heart tugged as she thought of the cringeworthy exchange earlier.

"Want to come over for some wine and chatting?" Stephen asked. "We could turn this night around with my famous cheese plate. I add grapes. That's key."

"Tempting, but I think I want to wear yoga pants and snuggle my doggo."

He sighed. "Sorry about tonight. We should have vetted her more. We heard *lesbian* and pounced."

"Common problem."

"You're a class act, Crawford. Get together soon, then?"

She placed a hand on her hip and grinned. "I might be on your doorstep as early as tomorrow."

"Bring Skywalker. We'll get him some exercise in the corral with his old friends."

"You're on."

❖

"I'm just saying that a BLT is only a partial sandwich. It's missing the middle part," Madison argued. "The important part."

Gabriella shook her head. "It most certainly is not. It's all about the bacon. The protein. How do you not understand this?"

Madison balked. "Bacon is an add-on. It goes on top of the burger. It can't hold its own, and if you keep claiming it can, we're going to arm wrestle."

Joey shook her head. "If you two wrestle, I'm putting it online and letting the Biddies run with it."

"That will just make me famous," Gabriella pointed out. "Because I will use my stirring arm and dazzle the viewers."

Madison nodded. "We probably need to come up with terms."

Joey smiled as her friends continued their argument as they left the restaurant. All things considered, she'd had a great time with her friends and devoured way more fries than a human was allotted in a week. Now all she wanted to do was go home and unwind with a glass of port from Fable Brook next door. Check out the competition, boring and bland as they were. The only problem was that the crux of that report was a lie. Becca had been on a date, and that little announcement had surprised Joey, tugged at her, and messed with her head. She was jealous, pure and simple, which made her the most basic of people.

As they spilled into the parking lot, Joey paused. There she was, leaning up against the cutest car. She didn't expect Becca Crawford to drive something cute. Her ride would be sleek, expensive, and probably black. This thing was a very friendly yellow, and it softened something in the center of Joey's chest—her earlier resolve. As they approached, Becca clicked off her call and turned. When she saw Joey, she shifted her weight, looked at the concrete, and back up again. Was she nervous? Distantly, she heard that Gabriella and Madison's banter had gone quiet.

"About in there…" Becca began.

"What are you doing tomorrow?" Joey asked, stopping in front of her. She was all of a sudden brazen and harnessing the moment, clinging to what might be short-lived fortitude.

Becca seemed surprised by the question and took a moment to take inventory. "I have work, but after that I'm free. Is there another event at the vineyard?"

"No, nothing in particular." She rocked back on her heels, feeling silly and a little vulnerable now as she waited. Gabriella and Madison hadn't so much as breathed.

But Becca made up for whatever confidence Joey lacked, saying,

"Maybe you can show me around town a bit? I mean, I've seen all the high points, but I have a feeling you know the secret spots."

"All of them, and pride myself on it. After work, then?"

"I'll pick you up at six."

"Do you think that's okay with…" Joey gestured behind her to the restaurant.

"Emmaline? Oh, she doesn't have a vote."

"Cool. See you then." Joey headed back to her friends, amazed and terrified by what she'd just done. It wasn't exactly sleeping with the enemy, but it wasn't far off. On the other hand, neither of them had called it a date, so maybe it wasn't.

"Did you ask Becca on a date?" Madison asked, as they embarked on their drive back to Tangle Valley.

"No." She watched the darkened town through her window as Madison drove.

"Did so," Gabriella supplied quietly from the back seat. "That conversation was tension coiled, too."

Joey peeked over the top of the seat. "Now you're exaggerating."

"Am not," Gabriella finished emphatically. "The jealousy factor just took your chemistry and quadrupled it." She shook her head and fanned herself. "I need to tell Loretta."

Madison tossed a glance over her shoulder. "Not if I get to her first."

"You guys are gossiping about me with Loretta now?" Joey looked between them, incredulous.

Gabriella fielded this one. "She's really wise and loves a good love story."

"I hardly think this is a love story," Joey said. "We just have good conversation while I admire how pretty her hair is."

"And how you want to run your fingers through it before getting down to business," Madison filled in, not taking her eyes off the road.

"Well, at least I did before I knew what her job was. Complicated now. My hands are confused about what they want."

Madison ignored her. "Regardless, it has all the ingredients of an impressive love story. I'm not the romantic in this car, but I can spot formulas. Conflict, tension, a will-they-won't-they storyline. I already popped the popcorn."

"I'm eating it," Gabriella said. "Pass the sexy butter."

Madison nodded wistfully. "Big fan of sexy butter."

Joey kinda liked it, too. Butter was warm and smooth like Becca's skin and, okay, enough of that. "Let's not get ahead of ourselves. It's two friends walking through a town."

"On their journey to love," Gabriella whispered.

Joey shook her head. "You're trouble."

"You love me." Silence. Then, "God, this sexy popcorn is good."

CHAPTER EIGHT

H ello, gorgeous," Becca murmured. She stood in what would be her office in just a few short weeks, grinning at how nicely the place was coming along. The Jade, decorated in whites, creams, and of course pale jade, felt spacious, bright, opulent, and modern, all the things it had been forecast to be by corporate. While they weren't quite ready for guests, the resort had been granted its certificate of occupancy, and Becca had moved her work world from the temporary portable to the wing just to the right of the front desk. They'd placed her solid oak desk earlier that day, and she had gotten right to work. She still had food vendor agreements to process, training manuals to sign off on, team leader one-on-ones to conduct, and the spa to check in on. That area was apparently running behind schedule, making her wonder if they'd have spa services available their first week.

"I think it's a true loss," Becca voiced to Maria Rubins, the Vice President of Resorts for the western division. They'd scheduled an afternoon call to go over fallback options. "Vouchers for disgruntled spa hopefuls would be a nice touch, but honestly, Maria, I think we need to push to make sure we finish on schedule. Whatever it takes."

"I completely agree," Maria said. "How are we looking on bookings?"

"We're completely at capacity for the first twelve weeks. The social media marketing pushes have done wonders, and that foldout brochure is breathtaking."

"Excellent. I'll touch base with our development team and see what the word is on the spa's prospects for opening." A pause. "So, how are you doing otherwise? All settled in?"

"Nearly. The town is gorgeous and quaint and just makes me smile at least once an hour." She chuckled. "I wish I could say I did the same for them, but our presence has been deemed an intrusion."

"I've heard." Maria laughed. "They don't know what's coming. Once those extra tourist dollars show up, they'll suddenly be a lot more friendly."

"I'm going to hope for that. I'm just holding my breath, waiting for opening to get here."

"Hang in there. You're my champ, Becca. Master of all resort ops. The Jade is going to be a huge property for Elite, and with you at the helm, it's going to shine."

"That's the goal." She ran her newly manicured hand across those vendor contracts. "But I'm going to call it a day, do a little exploring in town, and get back at it later tonight."

"Have a drink for me, and remember we need to catch a game soon."

Becca loved baseball and hoped to see a Dodgers game at some point now that she was on the West Coast. "Only if we get one of everything from the snack bar." She shook her head. "I care way too much about food."

"You just understand what life is all about. Have fun and I'll circle back tomorrow after I talk to Development."

"I'll wait to hear."

She hung up and quickly found a mirror in her bag to check her hair and the subtle makeup she'd applied. Twenty minutes later, Becca straightened her forest-green moto jacket before entering the tasting room at Tangle Valley. She'd volunteered to drive them into town and from there she'd follow Joey's well-seasoned tour through Whisper Wall.

The tasting room was close to closing for the day, and Loretta, who seemed to be in charge of the room alongside Joey, tended to what seemed to be the last group of the day.

"Hey," Joey said, popping up from behind the counter.

"Whoa." Becca placed a hand over her rapidly beating heart. She took a moment to breathe. "Didn't see you there."

"That was the goal. I like to hide and scare the guests as they arrive." Joey said it as if it was the most natural thing in the world.

"Creative. I can see the Yelp reviews now." That's when she noticed Joey herself. She wore a navy ribbed top that hugged the gentle curve of her torso down to her hips and made her eyes pop deep blue. Becca's stomach did a shimmy-shake, and her face heated. Still not quite clear if they were headed out on a date or not, she wasn't sure a compliment was appropriate. She went for it anyway. "You look really beautiful."

Joey blew her off. "I do not. I'm just me." There was still a guard up around her. She lowered it occasionally, but it never stayed down for long. "Ready to go?"

"Yes. I've been looking forward to this all day."

"That excited to get to know Whisper Wall?"

"Whisper Wall," she said, meeting Joey's gaze in order to communicate that she was referring to so much more, "is intriguing, breathtaking, and fun. I like what I know of it so far, and I'd like to get to learn more about it."

"Whisper Wall," Joey said, blinking at her skeptically.

Becca scoffed. "What else would I be talking about?" She headed to the door and heard Joey gasp behind her. When Becca turned around, she saw her grinning. Yeah, Joey could hold her own.

"Where to first?" Becca asked, once she was behind the wheel of the Juke. She had the heat on low as the last sliver of daylight faded.

"Well, every town tour has to start with a stop at the honky-tonk."

Becca smirked. "I can't tell if you're kidding or not."

"I never kid about neon and beer. Write that down." Joey shook her head innocently and Becca marveled at the way her whole demeanor shifted when she got a gleam in her eye. Joey pointed at the road ahead. "Head toward town center, and I'll give you directions to Patsy's Boot and Scoot once we're there. The Scoot, for short."

"Okay, it seems we're doing this," Becca said.

As they drove, she took in the scent of what had to be Joey's perfume or lotion. Whatever it was reminded her once again of fresh raspberries topping a bowl of vanilla ice cream. They passed through the main drag as the lights from the shops glowed along the now darkened streets. Green streetlamps that curled downward helped light their path in warm greeting. They hit darkness for a bit, and then out of nowhere, over a hill, a stand-alone building appeared with a tall pink neon sign in the shape of curvy woman.

"Oh, my." Becca exhaled.

"That's Patsy," Joey said, dipping her head down far enough to see the sign through the windshield. She dropped her tone and said, "Let me caution you. She does not look like that anymore."

"No?"

"Oh no."

"We should meet her."

Joey's eyes met hers in the darkened car and they stared for a beat. Becca liked the way it made her body hum. She'd not felt that before and wanted to hold on to it a while longer. "Stay tuned."

Joey opened the door, and after watching after her a moment, Becca did the same, following her through the dirt parking lot and into Patsy's, which lived up to the sign in its dedication to neon. The interior of the place glowed with a plethora of bright signs along the walls in pinks, greens, oranges, reds, and blues. Even the liquor bottles behind the bar glowed in the dim lighting.

"Not too busy yet," Joey said over the music, Miranda Lambert singing about damaging someone's property. Becca grinned and bopped her head along, taking note that even in the early evening, there were already people on the dance floor, shuffling back and forth, or maybe that was the scooting. "You should see this place later tonight. Hard to find a place on the dance floor and it'll be three deep at the bar."

"Brewskis?" the extremely tall bartender asked. Yep, that was what they called a full mustache and crisp jeans. Becca had no idea what kind of ironing that must require, but color her impressed.

Joey nodded, and two Michelobs were slid down the bar as if it was a foregone conclusion that's what they wanted. "Are you a regular?" Becca asked, taking a seat next to Joey at the bar. "I'm hoping you say yes."

Joey drank from the longneck bottle sweating in her hand. "I used to frequent Patsy's more when I was younger. Not as backwoods as it might first appear. They're actually a very progressive group of people. This is Oregon, after all."

"Josephine Wilder, just where in hell have you been?" The question was loud and shrill and warm. Becca peered down the bar to see a rather plump woman with a ton of red hair piled on top of her head make her way toward them with a friendly smile on her painted lips and a pointed sway of her hips.

"Patsy," Joey told her, "opened this place when God was a baby."

"A honky-tonk OG."

"In the flesh. She's going to grab your face. Gear up."

Becca only had a moment to prepare.

"Hey there, Patsy," Joey said.

Her face was instantly grabbed. "Baby girl, stop making me miss you so hard. You gotta come on out for a scoot more often."

"I do miss it. Been busy at work."

Patsy placed a hand on her hip. "Don't I know it. Still can't believe about Jack. I have to remind myself I won't be seeing his face coming in for a cold one."

Joey nodded, but Becca noticed a dip in her smile. Yeah, she was in some pain. Becca could only imagine if she lost one of her parents. Joey couldn't have been much over thirty and now had the weight of the world on her shoulders, both through grief and her new responsibilities at the vineyard. As someone who liked to fix things, all she wanted was to make the world a little easier for Joey, who she didn't even know all that well yet.

"And who is this?" Patsy asked, shifting her focus to Becca. She had on the brightest pink lipstick Becca had ever seen, but somehow it worked for her, amplifying her sass.

"This is my friend Becca Crawford. Probably *Rebecca*, but we haven't gotten that far. She's the general manager of The Jade, that awful hotel going in on the edge of town?"

"That's me. Rebecca. The hateful general manager," Becca said, extending her hand.

Patsy bypassed it and grabbed her by the face instead. "We hate that hotel. But you're still cute enough to keep."

Becca inclined her head from side to side in acceptance, still mid face grab. "That's something."

"Have some snacks and get to scootin', you two. Is this a date?" Patsy slid a bowl of mixed nuts their way and crowed at someone else down the bar, not waiting for an answer. The woman knew how to work a room.

"You heard the woman," Becca said, pointing after Patsy and adopting the same sassy tone. "Answer the question."

Joey's eyebrows rose. "You want to know if we're on a date?"

A pause. Becca felt uncharacteristically vulnerable. "Well, are we?"

"I can't date you. You come with The Jade."

"So then it's not."

Joey scoffed. "We're like the Hatfields and McCoys. Harry Potter and Voldemort. Daenerys and Cersei."

"Those last two would be smokin' together, and you still haven't answered the question."

"Well...the beer is really good." Joey stared into it with a smile that clearly acknowledged her blatant dodge and weave.

Becca leaned over. "Joey, I love a good chase. I'm up for it." She watched as Joey swallowed. "As long as I have your blessing."

Joey's eyes found hers. "I would never stop you from your sincere aspiration in life." She gestured behind her. "Now we should probably scoot so we can see some more of Whisper Wall."

"You want us to dance? Really? I thought we were just touring." She checked out the dance floor and saw a dozen or so people dancing in a synchronized line.

"You don't dance?" Joey asked, backing up to the floor with a grin that seemed to halfway entice, halfway challenge.

"It just so happens I love to dance." She'd just never *line* danced before, but surely she could make the adjustment, give it a shot. Becca prided herself on her go-with-the-flow confident outlook, and she would simply harness that now. She joined Joey in the line and watched the others for direction. She shifted her hips with the group but then missed a turn, which made her laugh.

Joey grinned over her shoulder. She had her hair in a loose braid, with a few wayward strands framing her face. "You keeping up?"

"Not yet," Becca said, still two steps behind everyone but recognizing the pattern. As she turned, she swore she saw Joey's gaze drop to her ass. She smiled.

"What?" Joey asked, her cheeks turning adorably red.

"I saw that."

"You didn't see anything. I'm dancing, and you're behind the beat."

She was, but just as she found her groove, the music changed on them to a much slower song, and everyone around them coupled up, shifting to a two-step.

"Do me the honor?" A man in a blue-collared shirt extended his hand to Becca.

Joey took a step between them. "She's with me tonight, Frank." Becca raised an eyebrow as Joey took her hand and led her away. Without a word, Joey rested one arm around the back of Becca's neck and linked their other hands between them in proper two-step position.

"Totally a date," she said in Joey's ear, as a song about a neon moon played on.

"Yeah, well…" was all Joey gave back. It was plenty.

The talking faded into the mist as they danced because Becca became aware of their proximity. It dismantled her normally careful composure. Tonight, she was entirely affected and watched helplessly as the control she always craved was stripped from her with each passing moment. With Joey pressed up against her as they stepped across the dance floor in a slow, impeccably timed shuffle, the rest of the world faded at the edges. She enjoyed the way Joey's hair inadvertently tickled her neck. She memorized the feel of Joey in her arms, and she reveled in the warmth from her body. She savored the raspberry vanilla combo that would forever mean Joey Wilder to her, for now and always.

When the final notes of the song clung and faded, Joey stepped back and met Becca's gaze. Her eyes were wide and her lips parted, almost as if she'd just experienced what Becca had.

"Where should we go now?" Joey asked quietly.

"I don't know, but I think I'd follow you anywhere."

Joey hadn't set out to feel what she was feeling. That hadn't been the goal tonight, but at the same time, she noticed herself stepping toward feelings for once, instead of away. That wasn't her usual MO, especially after the way she and Simone ended.

She navigated and watched Becca as she drove them to Maraschino's, where they could surely cool off via ice cream. She needed it, too, because watching Becca drive had been a bad idea. Her perfect profile and the little freckle to the side of her upper lip sent Joey to dreamy places that quickly moved to steamy places and more. Becca's chestnut hair, its long layers, had her fantasizing again about what it would be like to thread her fingers through that hair as she kissed those lip-glossed lips, taking that lip gloss out entirely. She shifted in her seat, feeling overly sensitive all over.

Maybe it also hadn't been a good idea to dance the way they had, but it wasn't like she was going to let Frankie McCluster from high school dance with Becca pressed against him while she watched from the bar. The memory of that dance had her hands itching and her face heated. She shifted in her seat again, aware of the compounded effect low in her body.

"Is this the place?" Becca asked, leaning forward to get a better view of the brown building with the bright blue roof with a straw sticking out of the top. "Because I like it. It's almost as cute as you."

The compliment sent Joey a hit of energy. "Well, thank you for that. And what was it you asked?" Her mind had blanked out on her.

"Is this the place?"

Joey laughed. "Yes! Sorry. Welcome to Maraschino's, home of the best soda fountain in the West." Joey gestured grandly to the building. "Because it's off the main drag, the tourists, God love 'em, don't hit this place up as hard, and we get to keep it all to ourselves. A hidden gem."

"All part of the master plan to keep the town preserved and stagnant for all time?"

"That was a good one. Got any more?"

Becca slid her hands into the pockets of that expensive leather coat she looked so chic in. "Always. But I'd much rather have an ice cream soda with you."

"Nice save," Joey said with a wink. "This coat is nice on you." She touched the hem.

Becca grinned and looked down. "I took a risk."

"They always seem to pay off when it comes to your clothes."

Becca seemed to stand taller. "Thank you."

"Anytime," Joey said, opening the door for her date. She took the liberty of finding them a two-top near the soda bar once inside. Playing tour guide had Joey seeing this place through a newcomer's eyes, and that made her spirits light, much like the fun vibe of the shop itself. The decor was adorable, with a row of silver stools with blue leather seats lining the checkered bar. Throwback illustrations from soda fountains of yesteryear lined the wall. The sounds of zaps, buzzes, and dings underscored the oldies tunes that were piped in on the stereo system. That was because there was an adjacent room devoted entirely to arcade games, which bucked the sixties vibe, but were a big moneymaker for the owners.

"What are we drinking?" asked their young server, who wore a handkerchief tied around her neck.

Becca held out a hand to Joey. "You do the honors for both of us. I trust you."

Wasn't hard. "We'll take two brown cows with two scoops, and add the chocolate sauce on top." She turned to Becca. "It's an extra seventy-five cents."

"Then we have to have it. I want the best. Always."

The waitress laughed and left them. Joey sat back, excited they'd stopped in and enjoying herself so very much. "Did you grow up rich?"

Becca winced. "*Comfortable* is a more accurate word. My parents were both accountants with well-known firms. I didn't get the numbers gene, though." She laughed as if remembering something.

"I used to spend my free time inviting anyone and everyone into my room for imaginary tea and coffee and made sure the experience was a pleasurable one."

Joey shook her head. "Look at you. In the hospitality business from day one."

"You, too, though, right?"

"It wound up that way when my father realized I wasn't the best at chemistry and wouldn't be taking over his job anytime soon. Winemaking wasn't for me. *Wine* was, however, and I love introducing our work to new people."

"You were a fantastic guide when I first came in. The perfect blend of friendly and knowledgeable." She gave her head a little shake. "And beautiful. Don't think I didn't take that part away with me."

"Thank you." Joey batted her lashes.

"I couldn't take my eyes off you."

Oh, that made everything squeeze pleasantly, uncomfortably, and back again. Joey met Becca in her honesty. "Yeah, I had a similar experience when you sat down." She exhaled slowly. "Plus, I really liked you once we started talking. That is, until your evil empire was revealed. Why do you have to work for the empire again?"

Becca smiled a genuine smile. "I'm going to change your mind about The Jade."

Joey leaned in. "Impossible. I'm here for you, and you alone."

Becca sat back in her chair. Her smile dimmed in a good way, a smoldering one. "I'm not going to pretend that wasn't a really attention-getting sentence."

Joey leaned into the momentum and didn't allow herself to think too actively. This was fun. Becca was beautiful, intelligent, and funny. But Joey had questions. "What about your date the other night? We have to rewind. Is it...serious? Do you call her nightly?"

Becca laughed. "It's serious for the gay cowboys who set me up in the first place. I love them, but they received a talking-to."

Joey leaned in and rested her chin in her palm, meeting Becca's gaze. "Those boys are the sweetest. I can't imagine they'd purposefully screw with you. They just don't know what you like."

"What? You? Because it's true."

Joey shook her head. "Maybe the smoothest thing you've ever said to me, and there have been several."

"I feel a personal challenge at hand, but I've always been type A."

"Who am I to get in the way of your ambition?"

"Two amazing brown cows with two scoops and added chocolate sauce," their server said and placed a curvy glass in front of each of them.

"Oh, hello, sexy," Becca said, examining the magnificent drink.

Joey winked. "You're welcome."

"You're not kidding." Becca dug in, then gestured to her dish with a spoon, dropping to a whisper to say, "Maraschino's is importing crack-laced ice cream into their shop."

Joey whispered back, "They just make it fresh each day. You can't beat homemade."

They ate and chatted until they were ready to burst. She loved the ice cream, but she wasn't quite ready to say good night to Becca.

Becca sat back. "You've led me across a dance floor two steps at a time and introduced me to the illegal homemade vanilla ice cream. I don't know how we can top this."

"Take a walk with me? It will stop me from curling up in a sugar coma if I can burn off some energy."

"All right," Becca said. "But only for coma-dodging purposes, and you'll owe me. I'm like the godfather."

"Free glass of pinot the next time you visit?"

"Sold." Becca smiled and her eyes crinkled slightly at the sides. It was a great look. All of Becca's were. Joey's physical attraction to Becca flew off the graph entirely. She hadn't known herself to have a type, but she did now, and it looked just like Becca Crawford. Even the evil empire would have trouble toppling the things Joey was feeling. Damn it.

"When will that be?" she asked as they exited the restaurant, bypassed the Juke, and headed down the sidewalk. They were in a less crowded part of town, which afforded them space to walk beneath the streetlights all on their own.

"You already can't wait to see me. I must be doing okay."

"You definitely receive an A for the human factor, but the employment skews your average," Joey said, hands in her pockets, keeping her gaze firmly on the path ahead of them. Easier that way.

"I'm going to focus on the A. You also get one, but a skewed average for the judgmental factor."

"Gasp out loud," Joey said. "I'm not judgmental." They passed the olive oil shop she loved so much, and though it was closed for the night, she took a deep inhale and melted at the wonderful payoff. "Side note. You definitely want to give that place a try."

Becca glanced back. "Olive You. Cute name."

"The products are even better. Back to the judgment."

"Ah, your sharp criticism and rush to conviction regarding The Jade."

Joey scoffed. "I'd hardly call it a rush."

"I would."

"Feisty."

"A truth teller," Becca countered. "The fact of the matter is you don't know what effect the resort's opening will have on Whisper Wall or on Tangle Valley Vineyards. You're up in arms, and it's all for nothing. Trust me."

Joey didn't do that a ton, but maybe there was wiggle room. She marinated on the request as she walked. "There's the tiniest sliver of possibility that the resort won't kill everything I love about where I live."

Becca nodded. "Let's cling to that. I can work with a sliver, and when all is said and done, I think you're going to be surprised. I'm actually expecting a fruit basket."

"You're ambitious and maybe delusional."

"Am I delusional in thinking that there's something happening between us that neither one of us expected?"

Joey gave her head the smallest of shakes. "I wasn't expecting you to just go there. Shouldn't we warm up?"

"Then you forgot the ambitious part."

Neither said anything for a moment. They walked the quiet section of the street, listening to the buzz of the streetlights overhead as Joey decided whether to punt the ball or go for it. Her father's analogy. "Of course there's something happening," she said as if it was the most natural thing in the world, when the truth was that her heart was impersonating a jackhammer and there was nothing everyday about the bursts of excitement she experienced when Becca was around that, to be honest, she could really use in her life these days.

With a hand on her arm, Becca turned her so that they were facing each other beneath the shadowy awning of a closed boutique. "Joey," was all she said.

It was all she needed to say. The look in Becca's eyes communicated the rest. Joey felt the word all over, her name on Becca's lips. She took one step forward, eliminating the already small distance between them. It was her way of meeting Becca halfway, and hopefully showing her that—

Becca's lips captured hers before she could complete the thought. Everything else went still, like the universe had a pause button for everything but this kiss, which, sweet moscato, was better than any kiss should have the power to be. Her lips moved over Becca's, and she savored not only their contact but the chain reaction it sent through her body. Everything warmed, her fingertips tingled, her stomach flip-flopped, and her body craved. She cradled Becca's face in her hands as they kissed, slow, measured, and wonderful in the shadows. A shadowy kiss. That's how she would always remember it. Becca tasted sweet like the chocolate sauce. She'd always remember that, too.

And then, so very sadly, it was over.

Joey's eyes were still closed, however. She needed them to be, so she could cling to it all for just a few seconds longer. When she opened them again, the world was still there waiting for her, and so was Becca.

"I just took the liberty," Becca said in half explanation, half apology. She seemed pleased with herself.

Joey touched her lips. "Is that what they call it? Whatever it was…" She shook her head and offered Becca a smile. "We might be mortal enemies, but we sure can—"

"Kiss like we were meant to always kiss."

Joey exhaled and met Becca's gaze in the dim light. "Yeah, what you just said." She stepped forward so that she was smack in the middle of Becca's space. She inclined her face upward, enjoying the edge Becca had on her in the height department. Joey watched as she took a breath and leveled a sexy stare. Chemistry was a real and very definite thing. Very slowly, in the silence of the moment, Joey used her forefinger to carefully lift and move a strand of hair off Becca's forehead. She wanted her so very badly. "What are we going to do with this?" she asked.

"I could write up a proposal," Becca said back sincerely.

That did it. The comment entirely fit everything Joey knew and found sexy in Becca. Joey cracked a smile, and the charge in the air around them relaxed until they were just…them. Two people enjoying a night out and wondering what lay ahead. The question mark intoxicated.

"I look forward to reading it." She stole a lingering kiss and pressed on down the sidewalk. "Follow me. The tour continues." Becca didn't hesitate. Joey showed her the old post office with only one customer window, and the numerous tasting rooms where one could sample tons of local wine in one swoop, and finally one of her favorite places, the used-book shop that her grandmother used to bring her to when she was small and let her pick out any book in the whole store. Joey would hug the book to her chest and head off into the vineyard, finding a comfy spot between the vines, and lose herself in whatever fairy tale was in store. The practice had always made the vines feel extra magical to Joey.

"I absolutely adore the image of a little blond girl, lying on her back, reading a book between grapevines."

"Well, that was most afternoons after school, so adore away. After fifth grade, Madison would often join me with a book of her own." Joey touched her chin as they walked. "Let me guess. Childhood Becca shopped at Bergdorf's and scheduled playdates in her appointment book."

Becca laughed. "Well, I was more of a Carrington's kind of girl, but close enough. My mom said I woke up earlier than I had to every day of preschool because I didn't want to be late."

"Tell me you carried a briefcase."

"I preferred the term attaché."

"Can we kiss some more?" Joey was only half kidding. Everything about Becca's polished persona got her hot and bothered and ready to unbutton a few business suits. "Thank God," she said, as Becca moved toward her. They seemed to be kissing their way down Maple Avenue, which could honestly use the excitement. Becca pressed her lips to Joey's, and she angled for better access. "Yep. Still every bit as good as the last time."

Becca touched her lips. "I'm glad I hold up."

"More than hold up. You make my head swimmy, and that beer I had was hours ago." A pause as conflict bubbled within her. "I can't go home with you tonight," Joey said. "I'm not the type." She held up a hand before Becca could speak. "Don't get me wrong. I'd love to be that girl tonight and let you just…pencil me in, you know?" She widened her eyes. "God, that sounds bad. And a little sexy." She touched her forehead. "But no. That would be a bad idea."

"Do you need me here for this discussion?" Becca asked, amused and moving her hand in a circle. "I could honestly listen all night, but I seem superfluous."

Joey winced. "Sometimes I process out loud. More so when I'm nervous."

"I make you nervous? I wouldn't have guessed that, but I think that's good."

"I think I like it, too. Jury is out."

Becca studied Joey and raised a perfectly sculpted eyebrow. "You sure you don't want to come over?"

"Not at all sure." Joey bit the inside of her lip. "But I'll do the smart thing instead, and stay on the safe side of the road tonight. Plus, I can't have people thinking I endorse you and all the abject commercialism you stand for."

"It's true. I'm awful." Joey winced along with her. "Shall I drive you home?"

She bumped her shoulder into Becca's. "Yes. But first, I want to say…I'm sorry. For not being so nice to you early on. I can resent The Jade, but that doesn't have to transfer to you. You're a good person."

"I appreciate that." The wind picked up and somehow made the moment seem destined. Becca shrugged. "Maybe in the end, you won't hate either of us." An idea seemed to occur to her. "We open in nine days. Want to come by for an early tour next week?"

"You want me to set foot in Satan's Palace?" she asked with a squeak.

"You won't turn to ash upon entry. I'll make special arrangements."

Joey softened, trying to be big about The Jade's impending opening. "I suppose it's the neighborly thing to do."

"Great. Then it's a date."

"Is it, though?" Joey asked playfully as they approached the car. "We seem to struggle to define ours."

"Not anymore. You're going on a date to The Jade. With me. Don't argue."

"We're already having our first fight? Feels fast."

Becca laughed. "Come over tonight, then, and we can make up."

"Still a no."

Becca turned to her in earnest. "For the record, I'm only kidding. You have nothing but my utmost respect, and I would never want you to do anything you weren't one hundred percent sure of."

"I know." Joey offered a soft smile. "I very much appreciate that."

That didn't mean that on the drive home Joey didn't think about what would have happened if she'd come to a different conclusion for their evening. She imagined how the sidewalk kissing might feel if they both knew they didn't have to stop. She ruminated on how her fingertips would feel across Becca's warm, smooth skin. She fantasized about removing Becca's clothing one piece at a time, and swallowed back her desire.

"You okay over there?" Becca asked as they drove. "You got quiet."

"Just a little bit tired." Lies, all lies. Joey likely wouldn't sleep, her body too keyed up.

When they pulled into the vineyard, now quiet and sleepy with no one in sight, Joey was ready to hop out of the car and quickly take her leave. These swirling feelings left her vulnerable—to what, she wasn't sure. But Becca opened her car door before Joey.

"I'll walk you up. It's dark out."

"You don't have to do that," Joey said, hopping out of the car.

"I'd like to."

The gesture was a simple one, but sweet, and it resonated with Joey. They walked in silence up the four stairs to the Big House as an owl hooted somewhere in the distance. Joey turned around to say good night, only to find herself compelled to do so much more. She went up on tiptoes, encircled her arms around Becca's neck, and blinked up at her.

"Good night, Joey," Becca said, standing there looking into Joey's eyes. She brushed her lips softly against Joey's. Sweet. Romantic. Perfect.

"Good night."

The early November moon that bathed them in enough light to see by hung steady and strong in the sky overhead as Joey excused herself into the house. As she closed the door and leaned back against it, her fingertips hovered over her lips, still holding on to the wonderful sensation.

"This could be tricky," she whispered to the quiet living room.

CHAPTER NINE

With Sky frolicking like a puppy in the corral with his old buddies, Becca sipped from the fresh apple cider Stephen had not only poured for her but apparently crafted himself from apples grown on the property. These guys were like two amazing Martha Stewarts dressed as pinup cowboys, and she was keeping them forever.

"Of course we know Joey," Monty said. "The whole town knows her. She's like everyone's second daughter around here. We used to be understandably jealous until we realized she was also likable."

"Joey?" Stephen joined them in the outdoor seating arrangement overlooking the Moon and Stars Ranch. "She's a blue-eyed spark plug, that girl. I once saw her convince Missy Jean Tomlinson to come down twenty whole dollars on the oatmeal cookie and spirit gift basket she was selling at Waffle Fest just by batting her eyes and saying please."

Becca nodded. "I'd knock twenty off for those eyes, too. Have you ever seen her talk about wine?" She slid to the edge of her chair. "It's my absolute favorite thing she does. Her entire face lights up and the knowledge she imparts and the words she uses tell me how intelligent she is." She shook her head. "I'm way beyond a crush and have no time to do anything about it because of the resort's demands, and it's maddening."

"The opening sucking up your time?" Monty asked. He reached for the bottle of rosé they'd left to chill in a metal bucket and set to opening it for all of them. A good chaser to the cider. It was nippy out, but beautiful and sunny, making the rosé a perfect choice. She imagined Joey might think so, too.

"Yes," Becca told him. "The Jade itself is ready and waiting for the big day. The staff is in the final stages of training. Corporate sent some of our best managers to facilitate, but I've been running around making sure all the smaller details are in place for them. The vendor situation has been a nightmare because, let's be honest, we're a bit of a drive from Portland." She shook her head as the details of her week came back to her. "So now we're counting the hours until our first guest checks in, with events happening on the grounds all week to promote the big day. I don't know when I'll have time to sleep much less find a way to lay eyes on Joey until she's scheduled to come by, but it's all I really want to do."

Monty sipped and considered. "Might force you to go slower anyway."

Becca felt the sides of her mouth tug. "I suppose there's nothing wrong with slow in the long run." She watched Sky leap and run in the corral, charging one direction and then changing course and going the opposite way. "Is it crazy that I don't seem to have the capacity to?" She turned back around and faced them. "I don't think I've met anyone that I was this attracted to but at the same time liked so much as a person."

"It's like looking in a mirror," Monty said, and then grinned at Stephen, who blew him a kiss.

Becca kept going. "I really appreciate how fired up she gets in protecting a vineyard that's been in her family for years. I also like that being confrontational seems to take her wildly outside of her comfort zone, which tells me she's kind-hearted. I think a lot about the way she expresses herself and how she uses her hands with such flourish to illustrate a point."

"Do you also think about her naked?" Stephen asked. Monty swatted him and passed him a look. "What?" Stephen looked back at him. "It's not like I do, but it's a strong litmus test for Becca's plight, which is fraught."

Monty stared at him. "You've been using *fraught* in too many sentences lately."

"Because I, too, am fraught with delight about the word," Stephen replied.

Becca laughed. The more she got to know these two, the more they let their guard down around her and showed her their true selves, petty banter and all.

"I'm not answering that," Becca told Stephen diplomatically.

"That means she totally imagines her naked like I used to do about you," Stephen said, satisfied. "She might be doing so right now."

"You behave," Monty said, and then refocused on Becca. "If you're into Joey Wilder, I say pursue Joey Wilder. Just understand the girl has experienced a lot of loss." He exchanged a glance with Stephen.

"Yeah. What do you know about that? I don't have specific details other than she lost her dad."

"Her mom, too, when she was a kid," Stephen said. "But the real scandal hit much later."

Monty picked up from there. "It was weeks before we bought the ranch and moved to Whisper Wall, about three years back?" Stephen nodded his agreement and Monty continued, "But a group of older ladies at The Bacon and Biscuit told me that Joey was left at the altar in a scandal three times as big as the town. The sad thing was that they'd planned this massive wedding and invited hundreds, which also meant everyone was there to see Joey's devastation."

"What?" Becca couldn't believe what she was hearing and stood there for a moment in mystification. "Who would leave Joey at the altar? Are they insane?"

"It was the florist, Simone," Monty said, seeming to recall the details. "She's beautiful, with this great skin, but I've never really gotten the impression that she's very deep, you know? She seems kind, though, and now she's madly in love with this veterinarian, Constance. She's been great to our rescues, so I have nothing bad to say about her at all."

Stephen frowned. "She could work on her shoe choice. Hiking boots galore."

"You're going to hell on a super slide," Monty said. "You know that, right? Good thing you're attractive."

Stephen seemed pleased with the assessment. "I think Joey's better off. Plus, now she has you to whisk her away to happiness and forever."

She laughed, but even she knew that forever was a lofty concept in this day and age. "I just know that I want to gobble up more time with her."

"Jaded. And that's not even a pun."

She balked. "What? I am not. Listen, I'm an adult woman who is well versed on the contemporary dating scene. Some people fall in love and live life together. Others invest in a relationship that does or does not work out. Sometimes a hookup satisfies." She shrugged. "I see the benefits of each of those options."

Monty looked over at Stephen. "Damn, you're right. Jaded."

Becca rolled her eyes and took a healthy swallow of the rosé. "Who knew gay cowboys subscribed to a Hallmark ideology?"

"We knew," the men said in unison. Perfect.

She scoffed. "I'm just saying Joey could be a lot of things in the end. I won't presume. All I know is that she feels…significant."

"Oh, I'm feeling myself getting attached already," Stephen said.

Monty pretended to dab a tear, and then snapped out of it. "Now. Who wants to get these dogs some exercise?"

"You do," Stephen said. "I spent all morning on a tractor and need to sit here and stare at my kingdom."

Monty popped his cowboy hat on his head. "The tractor vision alone shall see me through."

Becca laughed, admiring their life together. Maybe settling down wasn't as out of reach as she had once resigned herself to. Stephen and Monty had it all, and she found herself coveting that affection, even the daily teasing. They loved each other, and wouldn't that be nice? To love someone and know without a doubt that they'd be there every morning. Her rock. Her anchor. She'd like to be that for someone, too. She tucked that wistful wondering away, understanding that everything happened in its proper time. Yet she had an inkling that something noteworthy was happening in her life. This chapter, in small-town Oregon of all places, felt different than all the others.

❖

Joey stood in one of the prettiest hotel lobbies she'd ever seen and gaped. Yes, actually gaped. The Jade made a startlingly beautiful first impression. The opulent floors were slate, and the cream-colored brick walls led up to a ceiling multiple stories high and braced by white beams that seemed to be more for aesthetic appeal than structure. The lobby furniture was a mixture of white and gray, which completed the design perfectly. The vibe was rustic meets contemporary, and it had been executed expertly.

"Wow," Joey murmured, turning in a circle. She'd agreed to meet Becca just after lunch for a personal tour of the resort before its opening the following day. The main doors had been unlocked and she'd let herself in.

"You're here," Becca said, appearing from a hallway behind the empty reception desk. "Hi." She wore dark jeans, heels, and a starched navy dress shirt that was…everything. Becca Crawford could make a potato sack look good if she wore it. Joey rolled her lips in and reminded herself that the resort was supposed to be her focus today. But, damn. Becca was stealing the show.

"Hey there." She smiled and turned in a circle. "It's breathtaking."

Becca placed her hands on her hips and grinned with pride. "I think so, too." There were voices coming from a hallway to Joey's right. Becca gestured. "Housekeeping training is under way. In fact, lots of training sessions are in progress all throughout the property."

"You sure you have time for me? You have your hands full."

"Always. That's the thing about hospitality. It never sleeps, as you well know."

Joey dipped her head. "The grapes never sleep, but the people go away when we put out the Closed sign."

Becca tapped her cheek with one finger. "Gotta get one of those. Want to walk around a bit?"

"Of course." Joey slipped her hands into the pocket of her forest-green peacoat. "I'd be lying if I said I wasn't curious about the infamous Jade."

"You two are going to be friends." She inhaled deeply as if smelling freshly brewed coffee. "I can just feel it."

Oh, Joey was feeling things, too. Just not as appropriate.

They moved through the hotel section by section with Becca acting as tour guide, pointing out little details along the way, like how all the art was selected to be modern but with a nod to local culture. Much of it did come with a wine motif, which was a nice touch. Joey enjoyed the tour quite a bit for a myriad of reasons. One was most certainly the way Becca used her elegant hands and wrists to gesture. Joey's stomach flutters were at an all-time high.

"Let's head to the top," Becca said and used her key card to access the elevator's highest floor.

"This place is enormous," Joey mused, as they stepped out to the view from the large picture window in the hallway.

"You're not wrong," Becca said, coming up behind her. "We have more than four hundred rooms spread out over fourteen floors, a restaurant, two bars, a full-service spa, and a luxury pool with a lazy river along with cabana service in the summer. But I think you're going to like the view from the penthouse suite most of all."

"Oh yeah?" She followed Becca to the end of the hall. "I glimpsed the pool on the way in. It's magnificent."

"You could always come stay for a night," Becca said, letting them into the penthouse. "Take advantage of the pool. Order a cocktail."

"That sounds like a scandalous invitation."

"I don't have a clue what you're talking about," Becca said like the innocent she wasn't.

"Wow." Joey stopped in her tracks, derailed from the flirtatious back-and-forth. She stood inside one of the most beautiful luxury suites she'd ever seen. Everything was decorated in shades of gray, light green, and cream. A modern fireplace stood in the corner of the room, which was made up almost entirely of windows. Joey walked to one and grinned because she found herself looking down on Tangle Valley in all its beauty. Her heart squeezed with pride. "Now, this view? Even better."

"I thought you'd like it. That's why I brought you up here." Becca stood alongside her, and Joey savored their proximity. In fact, now it was all she could concentrate on. "Can I ask a question?"

Joey turned, prepared for the where-is-this-going talk that she was not at all prepared to have. "You can. I'll answer as best I can."

"You always smell so wonderful, like fresh raspberries and vanilla. What is it?"

Joey smothered the laugh that threatened. "Just…soap, I suppose."

"I like your soap company. I may invest."

The compliment left Joey feeling confident, bolstered. She'd missed Becca, but being in her presence now drove home just how much. "I could say the same for the people who make all of your suits and jackets." Yes, her gaze moved across Becca's entire body because she was an obvious rake now, and embracing that.

Becca smiled and raised an eyebrow. "Well, well. I thought we'd be all business today, and now look at us."

Joey let her shoulders sag and the truth come tumbling out. "We're the worst. I've wanted to touch you since the moment you walked into the lobby." Her hands slid inside Becca's jacket to her waist. Becca's gorgeous lips parted, and that was everything.

She held her composure and touched Joey's cheek. "Every time I see you, I think you're even more sexy than the last time. It's insane."

"You're good with words."

Becca leaned in. "But do we really need them right now?"

Joey shook her head and accepted the kiss hungrily. What she wouldn't give to be able to pop the buttons on that dress shirt of Becca's and see the breasts beneath the starched fabric. She could already tell they were perfect just from the way they filled out the shirt. Becca's warm and skilled mouth had her hazy and lost. The lustful thoughts of Becca's breasts and allowing her thumbs to touch their undersides left Joey wet. The longer they kissed, the more Joey craved, the more her fingers itched to touch, and the more she wanted to see. To taste. With her tongue in Becca's mouth, she ordered herself to pull back before they were naked and well beyond the ability to stop.

"Cease-fire," she practically hollered as she wrenched her mouth away. Oh, good. There was the air. She'd thought it had gone.

Becca grinned. "That's the first time anyone's yelled that in the midst of a kiss with me."

Joey placed an open hand on her chest. "I can't be held responsible for what comes out of my mouth when we're doing that," she said, gesturing back and forth between them. "That just isn't fair."

"You could yell, *Peanut butter and jelly is my favorite*, and I'd still want to kiss you again. I'd probably buy you a jar of each to say thank you."

"I guess I should have yelled, *Diamond stud earrings*, in that case."

Becca grinned. "There's always next time."

"When is that going to be exactly?" Joey asked in all seriousness. "I keep a pretty up-to-date calendar."

"I have a feeling it will be soon." Becca took her hand and kissed it, her eyes darkening. "You got a little handsy back there." She shot a glance down at her own shirt and back to Joey.

Joey narrowed her gaze. "Trust me, I know. I'm out of control."

"No, you're not. You're alluring."

She hadn't been called that a lot, but the look on Becca's face said she meant it. It gave Joey unexpected confidence to embrace her desires. Feeling wonderfully brazen, she stepped into Becca's space and ran her fingertips lightly over Becca's breasts through the shirt. She enjoyed the way Becca closed her eyes and exhaled at being touched so intimately. And then something happened Joey hadn't planned on. Becca wordlessly unbuttoned the shirt and parted the sides, revealing a pale yellow satin bra and the tops of gorgeous breasts. Becca had beautiful skin, a shade more olive than Joey's. She swallowed. The invitation was not in question, nor was Joey's acceptance. They were at Becca's workplace, Joey reminded herself, but the resort was closed and they were behind locked doors. But a minute was all she needed.

She traced the outline of the bra with a fingertip, first one side, then the other. She kissed the soft tops of Becca's breasts and lifted with her hands from below, touching Becca's nipples with her thumbs through the satin. Becca moaned quietly, making the exchange feel incredibly intimate and raw. She pulled one cup down, freeing a breast, seeing it for the first time, and then capturing that nipple in her mouth. Becca hissed as Joey's lips sucked and her teeth scraped. Joey freed the second breast and paid it the same attention. She bit down lightly and noticed Becca steadying herself with a hand against the window as Joey enjoyed herself, lost in a haze of wonderful sensations. With one arm wrapped around Becca's waist, she used her free hand and mouth to touch, maneuver, trace, and massage.

"I don't think I can take much more," Becca said, her voice weak and breathless. She sounded so different. It was hot. "God."

Joey straightened and took in the gorgeous view that had nothing to do with the windows. Becca with her shirt around her elbows and her breasts on display was an image she wouldn't forget. Ever. She placed a final kiss and helped Becca back into her shirt, which was a total shame.

"Shall we continue that tour?" Becca asked in a still shaky voice. There was a beat before they both broke into laughter.

"Sure. Why not? I can regroup. Can you?"

"What are you talking about?" Becca asked, regaining her poise in spite of her flushed cheeks. "I'm a professional." She then blinked pointedly and shook her head to communicate comically that it was all bravado.

"Great. Then let's give it a shot."

They tried the tour—they *did*—but the second half definitely took on a different tone than the first. Small touches as they moved through the space evolved into stolen kisses when they were confident they were alone, long looks in the elevator and small head shakes when they both seemed to remember what they'd done in the penthouse. Joey did take away from the tour that the hotel offered something new that was lacking in Whisper Wall, and it would certainly attract a very specific type of visitor—those with funds to afford the stay. If she was keeping an open mind and thinking more like a businessperson than someone fiercely protecting the culture in the area, she could see that there might be something to gain from the ritzy Jade opening its doors.

"Want to talk business for a few minutes?" Becca asked.

That had Joey's interest piqued. "Of course."

"Follow me into my office," Becca said, leading the way back through the impressive lobby. Joey took a seat in one of two leather armchairs across from Becca's neatly organized desk.

"I'm feeling fancy. You get that I'm a girl who grew up on a farm, right?"

"I do. I also get that you're no shrinking violet when it comes to Tangle Valley's interests."

"True."

"So I submitted a proposal to my corporate VP. It describes an effort to go out of our way to highlight the local wines in the area. Give them a platform but at the same time enrich the guests' experience."

Joey sat up a little straighter, pleased with where this seemed to be heading, but also surprised. "Obviously, I really like that idea. I think it brings the local flavor to your guests, both literally and figuratively. They can have the big-box commercial wine at home."

"My thinking exactly." She adjusted her dress shirt, which made Joey hold back a grin, as she'd been the reason it was out of place. "I suggested a reciprocal relationship with the vineyard down the road, however. I told them about the wine, the pinot specifically, and that I'd like to feature it in our restaurant. Maybe in return, you give our guests a discount when they visit or maybe a two-for-one tasting."

Joey took in the information. With a resort the size of The Jade, that could mean quite the bump in sales. Not only that, but the discount would probably up their daily visitor count, which would influence their future mail orders and monthly memberships. This would minimize the risk of any new venture. She could move forward with the restaurant! She remained calm. "I think we'd be agreeable to a reciprocal relationship."

Becca smiled. "I'm so glad to hear that. Beyond that, I'd like to recommend we carry Tangle Valley as our house wine. Not only is it fantastic, but you're our literal next door neighbor. That part I need corporate's approval on."

Joey's eyes went wide without her permission. So much for that poker face. "That's…even better." She leaned forward, still in disbelief, already doing the math in her head. "How many rooms did you say this place had again?"

"Four hundred twenty-two."

"That's a lot of rooms."

Becca laughed at what had to be a dazed expression on Joey's face. "And they house multiple guests and turn over frequently."

"That's a large number of humans and a lot of wine. I need to say thank you in a businessy manner."

"Well, don't yet," Becca said. "Not until the ink is dry, but everything is looking favorable for a fortunate partnership."

Joey pointed at her. "Yes, that's how you do it." She took on her most serious expression. "I look forward to our most fortunate partnership." Inside she was celebrating, dancing, cartwheeling like a maniac.

Becca's eyes sparkled. "You're really cute right now. I don't even have the words."

"No, no. You have to stay businessy."

"Sorry," Becca said, adjusting. She stood and extended her hand. "I look forward to our partnership, as well."

"I'll see myself out," Joey said, like the buttoned-up corporate types surely did. She turned back to Becca, who still stood behind the desk. Joey nodded once, properly. "Ms. Crawford."

Becca nodded back. "Ms. Wilder."

She grinned as she exited the office, thrilled with so many of the things that had happened in the last sixty minutes. Because she couldn't help it, she peeked her head around the corner and grinned at Becca, this time as herself. "The penthouse?" She closed her eyes. "Yeah. To be continued?"

"God, yes," Becca said and blew her a kiss.

As Joey returned to Dusty for her very short drive up the road, she allowed herself to marinate in the happiness that came with today, which was not something she did too often. Happiness was fleeting, and when it inevitably receded, the loss was too great. She'd been young when her mother died, but it had affected her greatly. She'd learned that lesson again the hard way on her wedding day and never quite returned to herself. The loss of her father was also a blow she had not seen coming. So while she reveled in the day's happiness, she also remained realistic. She wasn't naive, nor was she a glutton for further punishment.

"Why are you grinning like a cartoon character who got hit by a two-by-four?" Madison asked through the open barn doors. She had her curly brown hair pulled back in a ponytail, which showed off her blond streaks. She was currently on a ladder doing some sort of tinkering with their destemming hopper. The thing had been giving them trouble on and off throughout the harvest.

"I seem to be in my own world. Is that thing salvageable?"

"Bobby seems to think so. I think it's a parts issue, so we're going to call the guy." She winced. "I'm sorry about this, but it's probably going to be a chunk of change. This model isn't exactly new, so the parts are going to be harder to come by."

It seemed like the financial obligations never ended. But that was vineyard life for you. If the hopper wasn't broken, the cooling systems were. If they weren't on the fritz, the wind machines were dying, or the industrial dishwasher in the tasting room needed replacing. It all amounted to dollar signs that she'd been aware of in the past, but nothing like she was now that the decisions were hers. The burden was almost suffocating. Joey now had other people's incomes to worry about, the wine to market, and the family's reputation to protect.

Needing her father's guidance in some way, she headed straight for the metal box she'd stored away in a locked closet in the barrel room and fished out a scrap of paper.

Merlot and behold, when it rains, it pours. What can you do? Break out the s'mores. J.W.

Joey laughed and shook her head. Really? Just like the others, it was so awful that it was wonderful, and just what she needed to hear. Her dad never let her down. "I'll work on that," she murmured to the universe.

"You're on fire today," Loretta told her an hour later during a lull between guests. "Sales are up nearly twenty percent. Just did a quick tally."

"Well, the hopper needs an expensive part, which means we have to hustle, and I have to sparkle." She showed off her most winsome smile.

Loretta placed her back against the marble countertop. "You doing okay, sweet Jo? You have a lot on your plate now."

Joey paused, mid counter wipe. With anyone else, she could scoff and say she was fine. Loretta was different. Loretta knew her inside and out. She'd helped raise Joey right alongside her own daughter, Carly. She was the mom Joey never had, and when Loretta smiled at her, it all came out. "I am. But I miss Dad so very much," she said, as her lip trembled. She tried to smile through it, but the traitorous tears overwhelmed her.

"Oh, my girl. Come here," Loretta said and pulled her into a tight hug. "We all do. I keep waiting for him to walk through the tasting room in his muddy boots and make me fuss at him."

Joey laughed. "He never knew how dirty he got out there. Loved it too much to care."

"We hold him here, you know," Loretta said, touching her heart.

Joey nodded. "I just want to make sure I don't screw up everything he worked so hard for, you know? And it just feels like I'm falling short."

Loretta touched her chin. "I don't think that's possible. You're Josephine Wilder, and you were born to take this place to great heights. I've always known that. He did, too. Told me so, in fact."

"Really?"

Loretta nodded. "One night, he said that he loved Tangle Valley more than words could describe and that the place was in his blood. But that you had your eye on the bigger picture in a way he never did. He knew the future was right here." She pushed a finger into Joey's shoulder. "With you."

Joey shook her head and pointed at her now wet face. "Well, now you've done it."

Loretta waved her off. "Nah. Those are tears of love. The best kind."

Joey paused and circled back to something Loretta had said. "One night?"

Loretta polished a wineglass. "What's that?"

"You said one night." Surely it wasn't possible. "Did you and Dad have something I didn't know about?"

Loretta smiled and continued polishing that glass. Not a word escaped her lips.

"Damn," Joey said, shocked she'd somehow missed this but happy for her father. "Maybe one day we can talk about that?"

"Maybe so," Loretta said. There was a heaviness in the way she said it that told Joey Loretta was struggling with the loss, just as much as she was. "I'd like that."

Joey left it there, marveling at the revelation for hours to come. Her day was a busy one, but as it progressed, she found her footing, her groove even. She waited until the tasting room closed down for the night, helped Loretta get everything turned around for the next day, met with Gabriella about the initial design plans for the restaurant, and said good night to the darkened vineyard as she hopped inside Dusty.

She pulled to a stop in front of the one-story house she knew to be Becca's and killed the engine. Rain began to pelt her windshield. She squeezed the steering wheel. Now or never. It wasn't like Joey to take such a large leap without a guaranteed net, but someone once told her to make s'mores when times got tough, and she couldn't deny that insightful wisdom.

She exited the truck and made her way up the walk as the rain picked up, catching her as she hurried. Damp and a little nervous, she raised her fist to knock.

CHAPTER TEN

B ecca had been home from the resort for an hour and still wore her work clothes because there were more important things to focus on first. She always devoted that initial chunk of time home to Skywalker, for kisses, pats, and of course ball throwing in the backyard. She was lucky enough to have a medium-sized yard with enough room for Sky to run. She'd brought him inside once the ominous rain clouds rolled in, and after a few dozen more throws indoors, he'd retired to his oversized dog bed in the corner of her dining area.

It was a surprise to hear a knock at her front door, and Becca wondered if her neighbor Lana needed something. She ran her fingers through her hair to be sure she was presentable and opened the door with a friendly smile. Well, look at that. She didn't have to put it on any longer when she saw Joey standing on her doorstep looking amazing. Becca's smile easily slid into the genuine variety. Her stomach tightened pleasantly. She'd had trouble getting Joey off her mind all day.

"This has to be one of my favorite surprises ever."

Joey's eyes met hers, and the electricity between them danced like lightening in the sky. "I felt we left a few things…unfinished." Becca swallowed, enjoying the emboldened side of Joey she'd experienced for the first time that day. "So I thought I'd see what kind of night you were having and—"

Becca silenced her with a searing kiss that came with zero buildup, walking Joey backward on the porch. Just beyond where they stood, the rain fell fast and hard, pelting the roof and raining sideways on them as they kissed. Joey had her by the face. Becca's arms encircled the woman she'd been fantasizing about for far too long now. Thunder struck, low and melodious. Becca pulled back and enjoyed the grin that appeared on Joey's lips, the answer she'd sought. The sideways rain had Becca's shirt wet on one side. They needed more shelter.

She took Joey by the hand and pulled her inside. Once they closed the door, the storm outside seemed quieter. "Your hair got caught," Joey said, reaching up and touching a strand of Becca's wet hair.

"So did yours."

"I don't care." Joey tugged slightly on her shirttail, and Becca wondered if Joey knew she was doing it, what she wanted, but that was as far as she got. Becca struggled to construct a thought, given the way her body reacted to Joey's mouth, now on hers again. Her center ached, and her hands itched to touch Joey, take her places.

"Are we on the same page?" Becca asked, stepping back and placing both hands on her head because she didn't know what else to do with them until she had clearance.

Joey settled a hand against Becca's shoulder and backed her farther into the room. She nodded wordlessly. Yes. God. Joey eased Becca onto the couch, into a seated position. She killed the lamp next to them, the only light in the room with evening setting in outside. Thunder struck as Joey climbed into Becca's lap, kissed her expertly, and then paused to pull her shirt over her head.

"Oh," Becca said quietly. Her eyes moved across Joey's skin, illuminated by the moon and then a flash of lightning. Her breasts were round and much fuller than she would have guessed. Joey didn't accentuate them in the clothes she wore but should maybe rethink that because these were amazing. Her mouth watered, but she remained still, waiting, letting Joey set their pace. And she did. Joey slid one strap of her black bra down her shoulder. Becca throbbed with anticipation, enjoying the slow tease. The next strap came down, too. Finally, Joey reached behind her and unclasped the bra, freeing her breasts in gorgeous greeting. Becca's hands moved to them immediately. She sucked a nipple into her mouth and listened to Joey gasp. The inspiration propelled her. Her hands moved to Joey's warm back as her mouth bathed each breast in attention. She wanted to go slow, but that didn't seem possible. It was only a few moments before Joey's hips began to slowly rock in tantalizing rhythm. Becca smoothed her hands up Joey's thighs, watching Joey's breasts sway as she moved against her, and wishing away the rest of her clothes. Becca could help in that department and did, unbuttoning Joey's jeans, sliding her zipper all the way down. Another flash of lightning hit and lit up Joey's face, revealing the darkness in her blue eyes, full of longing and need.

Becca ran a finger along the waistband of her panties. Black as well. Had Joey known what they would do tonight? Had she prepared? The thought had Becca even more turned on. She shifted uncomfortably. She was wet and her body on fire. She urged Joey up onto her knees, which allowed Becca to pull her jeans down just enough, over her thighs. She wasn't patient enough for more. Holding Joey at the waist, Becca dipped her head and kissed her intimately through very damp fabric. Joey moaned and pressed her hips in, searching for purchase, rocking in earnest. Becca sat taller for better access, slid her hand down the front of Joey's underwear, and closed her eyes at the wetness she encountered.

"That's what you do to me," Joey managed, bracing herself with one arm against the back of the couch, and then the second. Becca sucked a nipple into her mouth and released it. She moved her fingers in a soft circle, teasing Joey intimately. "Sweet heaven," Joey whispered. Her eyes were closed and she shook her head. With her hips, Joey followed the lazy motion of Becca's fingers in the most erotic of dances. Becca drank in the sight. As their rhythm increased, so did Joey's breathing. Becca slid inside, pulling a sharp gasp from Joey, who felt so good, Becca swore softly. Joey rocked against her hand, moving faster, riding it, giving Becca the best view of the most gorgeous breasts she'd ever seen. She kissed one as Joey climbed higher. She pulled a nipple into her mouth and swirled it. Joey rose and fell faster, bucking. Finally, Becca pressed her thumb upward, causing Joey to cry out. She clung to Becca's shoulder's as Becca moved in and out of her, hoping to prolong the pleasure. When Joey's body finally went slack, her forehead pressed into Becca's shoulder, Becca lowered her onto the couch, removed her jeans the rest of the way, and tossed them to the floor. Joey laughed. "Whoa."

Becca slid on top and closed her eyes at the feel of Joey's almost naked body beneath hers.

Joey thumbed the lapel of her shirt. "Not only are you still wearing clothes, you're wearing *work* clothes."

"Welcome to Becca, where we dress for the office way too much of the time."

"I have the best idea."

"I love your ideas."

"Let's take them off," Joey whispered, just as a clap of thunder reverberated through the house. The hungry look in her eyes made her impossible to resist.

Becca stood and, for the second time that day, unbuttoned her shirt for Joey Wilder. She dropped it to the floor as Joey bit her bottom lip, seemingly enjoying the reveal. She left her yellow bra on and stepped out of her pants.

"Good God," she heard Joey murmur as she stood there in her matching lingerie.

Becca unclasped her bra, revealing her breasts. Once she did, Joey was up and moving. With a hand behind Becca's head, Joey pulled her mouth down, crushing it to hers. Becca heard her own voice murmur in satisfaction. With Joey's tongue doing wondrous things in her mouth, Becca felt every part of her body cry out for attention. And then she received it. Joey's lips were on her neck, then her collarbone. Joey's hands cupped her breasts, and then lifted them to her mouth where she reminded Becca all over again how powerful that afternoon had been. This time, however, she let herself go. She allowed herself to get lost in the sensations Joey's mouth urged and conjured. Her hips began to move and the quiet moans she heard were hers. Joey slipped a hand between her legs and touched her lightly through the yellow bikinis she still wore. The touch was too light, torturously so, but God, she loved to be tortured.

"I want to be on top of you," Joey whispered, kissing her neck again, cupping her between her legs where she throbbed endlessly.

Becca wordlessly took her by the hand and led her through the living room to the nearby master. There were more windows in her bedroom, which meant she could see Joey better as the sky outside had not completely darkened. Joey's skin, her curves, her exquisite body were something to behold. Becca sat on the bed and looked up at Joey, her blond hair a beautiful halo. With her thumbs, she slid Joey's underwear down her legs, stood, and did the same with her own. Joey kissed her as she eased her back onto the bed and slowly climbed on top. Skin to skin, they began to move in delicious rhythm at long last, Joey's hips between Becca's legs. It felt like heaven on earth, like Joey belonged there. As they moved, Becca felt the pressure build rapidly, amazed at how fast it was all going. She didn't react this acutely to anyone, never had, yet lacked the control to slow down her own responses. When Joey slid down the bed, parted Becca's legs, and licked her center, Becca nearly exploded. With two well-placed swipes of Joey's tongue, she quickly did, her back arching like a bow as a powerful tidal wave of pleasure crashed into her with abandon.

She was no match for the onslaught of pleasure and surrendered to it, reveling in the payout, holding tight to the comforter beneath her. Joey continued to stroke her intimately, which kept the surges coming until the attention was too much.

"You have to stop," she breathed. "I can't take more."

"But it's so good," Joey said, smiling at her as she climbed back up the bed. She laid her cheek on Becca's chest and touched a pebbled nipple with her finger. "I love your breasts. You need to know that I'm never not thinking about them when we're together." She covered her eyes. "You're getting a lot of detail tonight. Too much."

Becca stroked her hair. "That knowledge is going to make mundane conversation a little harder."

"Try it in my shoes." They shared a smile and a kiss and Joey settled more firmly on top. She looked down at Becca with what seemed to be a mixture of affection and intrigue.

"What?" Becca asked.

"You're a tightrope without a net, but you feel so good."

Becca eased her hands up Joey's back and down again, loving the feeling of her weight pressing down. "Take another step. I have you."

The words seemed to strike a chord, which was good because Becca meant them.

Joey smiled and slid a strand of hair behind Becca's ear. "I think this was a pretty big step onto that wire." She laughed. "You took me on your couch in the middle of a thunderstorm."

"I took you, huh?" She liked the phrase.

Joey closed her eyes. "You so did."

"Monumental," Becca said in wholehearted agreement. "A night I will never forget. Will there be more?" She knew it was a big question. Were they moving toward something real, or was Joey biding her time, merely enjoying herself?

"I mean, I hope so." Joey glanced away as she said it, making it clear she felt vulnerable around the question. "Do you?"

Becca nodded and rolled them over so they lay on their sides facing each other. "You don't have to be afraid of me, Joey. I'm really pretty boring." She gestured around her bedroom. "See? Those paintings are from Bed Bath and Beyond. That one's a painting of a vase over there. A vase. You can't get any more basic than that."

That coaxed a laugh and lightened the mood. Joey's eyes were beautiful in the moonlight. The rain outside seemed to have ebbed, as if intertwined with their trajectory. "Becca Crawford. From the second you walked into Tangle Valley, I knew there was nothing basic about you. You're sophisticated and sexy and controversial and—all right, I'll admit—pretty wonderful."

"That was hard for you," Becca said, enjoying this.

"Yeah, but it's getting easier."

"I can tell. You're letting your guard down a little at a time. I love it." Becca ran her forefinger along Joey's cheek. "You're also putting your outrage to the side. Nary a town speech in weeks."

"Yeah, well, maybe that outrage was a little premature." She held up a finger. "Still doesn't mean I love The Jade."

"You don't have to keep saying so. I'm aware." Becca eased her thigh between Joey's, angled upward, and watched her eyes flutter. "So noted in the record books for posterity. You know what else is going in the books? Your hands." She covered her eyes. "What they did to me earlier."

"You like my hands," Becca said. Joey nodded wholeheartedly. "Then allow me to introduce you to my mouth." She moved down the bed as a brand new clap of thunder struck.

❖

The next afternoon, Joey moved through town like there was air beneath her feet, a spring in her step, and rhythm in her walk. A happy soundtrack underscored her day, and she grinned at herself, giddy from the night before and the tawdry time she'd shared with Becca Crawford, sexy executive.

She hadn't planned on staying the entire night at Becca's, but she hadn't been able to bring herself to leave. Not when Becca alternated between sweetly holding her close and taking her body to such heights. She'd make up the sleep another time.

This afternoon, she had a mission, and that was to buy up everything on her holiday decorating shopping list to get the vineyard ready for the season. The Nifty Nickel was a great place to start because Brenda Anne always had a variety of fantastic seasonal decor.

"Well, hello there, Josephine."

She looked up and smiled at Thelma, one of the Biddies. Only she seemed to be out on her own today. "Hey, Thelma. Good to see you."

"You, too." They continued their joint perusal of the store's goods for several moments before Thelma jumped back in, not taking her eyes off the Frosty the Snowman figurine she held. "Someone saw your light blue truck outside the home of the manager of the giant hotel."

"Did they now?" Joey looked up from the tissue paper. "Well, that's interesting."

"I thought so. Are you two an item?" Thelma feigned new interest in a shiny red Christmas ornament across the room, but Joey wasn't fooled. She was gathering intel to take back to the Biddies, who would drop little nuggets of gossip all over town like the hearsay fairies they were. Didn't little old ladies used to have other things to do? Whatever happened to bridge club and bake sales?

"We are not an item," Joey told her. "We're just people. Would you look at that? Nutcrackers are two for one. Good gracious, that's exciting." And it was true. She and Becca weren't an item. Becca had every right to date other people, though the thought made Joey instantly nauseous. She would have to explore that reaction later.

"But you *are* special friends? I think that's so sweet if you're special friends." Brenda Anne's eyes went wide, and she swiveled her focus to Joey as if watching an exciting tennis match.

"Thank you, Thelma, for that show of genuine support," Joey said politely. "I think that ornament would look beautiful on your tree. You should buy it." Brenda Anne swiveled right back to Thelma.

"Does Ms. Crawford have a tree up?" Thelma asked.

Oh, this woman was a pro. "You should ask *her*. She's very open about all things related to home decorating." Brenda Anne smothered a smile and waited on Thelma's response, probably wishing for a snack with her show.

"I could. But it's you I ran into, and I'm just so glad, too. You're such a nice girl, Joey Wilder. Have always thought so."

Joey wasn't falling for flattery. She'd been the talk of the town once and didn't plan to be again. "But someone told you my truck was at her place and you want confirmation. Nice girl or not, right?"

"Well, no. Just making the talk, as they say." Thelma raised what appeared to be an innocent shoulder in explanation. Lies. That shoulder had motives.

Joey smiled. "Well, aren't you sweet?"

Thelma smiled back. Brenda Anne joined in. It was a smilefest.

"I just love the holidays." Joey rounded the corner of the display to examine the many different colored garland options. The tree for the tasting room was enormous and the garland was in need of replacement. "Brenda Anne, do you have any more of the silver? I'll need about four more packages if I'm going to make this work."

"I should have some in the back. I'll just check."

The bell above the door rang, signaling a new arrival. With the holidays in progress, the streets of Whisper Wall bustled like no other time of year. People had things to buy and gatherings to plan for. "Hi, Brenda Anne. I have thirty minutes for lunch, so I've come for that holiday wreath you mentioned. Time to pull down the one from the fall, as much as I love it."

Joey froze. She knew that voice well, and at an any other time her heart would have squeezed in excitement to see Becca outside of any official plans, but this was definitely not the most opportune of times, given Thelma and her supersleuth skills. To avoid drawing any further attention, Joey kept her head down and continued to peruse the garland like she was born to evaluate decorations for a living. Maybe Thelma wouldn't notice Becca's arrival in the shop.

"Hello there, Ms. Crawford. Remember me? I'm Thelma McDougall. We met at the town meeting that time Joey was all worked up and got the pink cheeks."

"Hi, Thelma. Good to see you," Becca said brightly. She had her hospitality voice on. Joey liked that she could now recognize the difference. "Getting cold out there."

"Isn't it, though? I had to cover my flower garden last night to protect it from the cold rain. I bet it's given the wine folk a hard time. Is that the case, Joey?"

Joey raised her head and smiled as breezily as she could. "Uncle Bobby had the fans on to keep the freeze away."

"Hi," Becca said in surprise, tilting her head curiously at having missed Joey's presence in the shop. "Didn't expect to see you this afternoon."

Joey feigned surprise of her own as if her tinsel shopping had hidden Becca's arrival entirely. She was a wearing a black pantsuit today that was slim-fitting and perfect on her. Joey swallowed a wave of attraction. Not the time for it with a Biddy to deal with. "Wow. Hi, Ms. Crawford." Becca squinted, probably wondering why in hell they were so formal after a night of getting it on. "How are things at The Jade this beautiful afternoon?"

Becca took a minute with the wooden quality of the question, but rebounded with impressive form. "Busy. But we're ready for our grand opening this weekend."

"A reception, I heard," Thelma said. "Sounds fancier than my designer luggage."

"I don't know about that, but you and your luggage are certainly invited. Come and have a glass of champagne and help christen the resort properly." She turned to Joey. "I'm actually glad I ran into you. You left this." And from her pocket she pulled a silver hoop earring and held it out to Joey, who closed her eyes. Thelma beamed like a six-year-old presented with the bicycle they'd always wanted. She let out a quiet squeal and scurried from the store, arms working overtime like a mall walker on a mission.

Joey shook her head and leveled a stare at Becca. "If you weren't so gorgeous, I'd be really frustrated at you for that."

Becca looked from the door back to Joey. "Did I miss something? What was all that about?"

Brenda Anne laughed from her spot behind the cash register. "I think you both just got played by a Biddy. A shrewd one."

"You gotta watch out for the Biddies," Joey said, very seriously. "Never feed them details. They're like gremlins at midnight."

Becca winced, realizing her mistake. "Still learning the town, I suppose. I'm really sorry."

Joey waved her off. "Meh. It's okay. They were bound to get to us sooner or later. The embezzlement at the bingo hall is days old at this point, and no one's been hauled to jail for public intoxication in weeks. They need fodder."

The bell chimed again and Clementine from The Bacon and Biscuit popped into the store. She smiled widely when she saw Becca and Joey. "Congrats on the new romance, guys. I had no idea. Never would have imagined it after that fiery town meeting."

Joey squinted. "I'm sorry, what?"

Clementine hooked a thumb behind her. "Ran into Thelma outside. She told me all about it. Called you lovebirds."

"Lord help me," Joey deadpanned.

"It's better than your old nickname," Brenda Anne offered feebly.

"What's your old nickname?" Becca asked. Joey didn't have the heart to say the word and gestured for Brenda Anne to go ahead.

Brenda Anne leaned forward toward Becca as if including her in a secret. "Jilted. That's what they called her around town after, well, you know. They meant it as a joke. Everyone did."

Joey sighed. "Because of the whole left-at-the-altar thing."

"No, I get it," Becca said with disdain. "Seems like a *mean* joke, though."

"It was. Sometimes I hate this town," Clementine said, shaking her head. She'd always been a kind soul, and Joey was grateful for their friendship. But Clem had never made a secret of her frustrations with injustice and mean people. She was a good-hearted human.

"I'm sorry they did that," Becca said, with true sadness visible in her eyes.

"Oh, it's okay. They thought I was laughing with them, I guess." Joey played it off like it was the smallest of incidents that she'd *so* moved beyond. *Pshhh.* Barely even thought about the full-blown humiliation, much less the life-altering heartbreak.

Becca looked at her. "It's not."

Joey glanced at Brenda Anne, who had the same sympathetic look on her face. Clementine shook her head, and Joey was right back there again, remembering what it felt like to be the pitiful one in town, the abandoned, the unwanted, and the devastated. She swallowed and tried to pull herself out of it before she spiraled. "Find that garland?" she asked Brenda Anne brightly, who nodded and slid the boxes across the counter.

"Certainly did. It'll look beautiful on your tree."

"I think so, too." Joey added her own shopping additions to the pile and handed over her credit card. Her cheeks felt hot and not in a good way. She wondered if the other three were exchanging glances about her now as she signed the slip, wondering if she was okay, and what they should say to make her feel better. She hated it. "The tasting room is going to look amazing by the end of the week. Loretta is a whiz at decorating schemes, and I pitch in. You'll have to stop by," she told Brenda Anne. "You, too," she said over her shoulder to Clem. She smiled at Becca and held up her bagged items. "I better get back to work before Loretta sends out a search party."

Becca followed her to the door. "Will I see you later?" she asked. She lightly touched Joey's hand, which made Joey melt and forget all the discomfort of the past few minutes.

"Well, are you free after work for a little decorating at Tangle Valley? We'll be having hot mulled wine and carols as we work."

"I've never had hot wine before. I think I need to."

"You do." Joey did a little hand touching of her own and did her best to make eyes. Probably something she should practice. "See you after hours."

"That sounds scandalous. Don't tell the Biddies."

Joey locked an imaginary key in front of her lips. "Our secret." She headed for the door.

"For now," Becca said, with confidence. It sent a delicious shiver down Joey's spine, and she took a last look at Becca in her black suit.

Sweet Lord. 'Twas the season, indeed.

CHAPTER ELEVEN

The early evening could best be described as blustery, but in the best way possible when one was decorating for the holidays. November had always been a chilly but beautiful month in Whisper Wall and Joey's favorite time of year. The grapes were in process, which meant new wine was on the way under Madison's strict supervision. People wore jackets and scarves and smiled at one another for a beat longer. Families and coworkers traveled together to the tasting room, which always became more crowded when the cold weather moved in, since the outdoor tables became less popular. Plus, Joey loved the aroma of hot mulled wine, which they sold by the mug daily in the late fall and winter. Experiencing it all without her father was not only awful, but strange. To ease the pain, she did her best to focus on the new aspects of her life: working with her friends, her new responsibilities at the vineyard, and now…maybe Becca, too.

"Who knew you could string up a tree so impressively?" Madison asked Gabriella, hand on her hip as upbeat Christmas music played over the sound system. Joey had put together the playlist herself. No, it wasn't quite December yet, but they geared up early for the holidays at Tangle Valley so their guests could enjoy them to their fullest. Gabriella had been put on twinkly lights duty and had the tree looking fabulous in no time. She spaced the strands perfectly, a true pro. "Did you go to tree school and never say?"

"Of course I attended tree school. Who didn't?" Gabriella reported from on top of the ladder leading up the sixteen-foot tree. "You should have taken advantage of more of my hidden talents."

"Now you tell me."

The two were great at easygoing banter, even about their past relationship, which seemed to be as casual a conversation for them as what was on television that night. It perplexed and impressed Joey, equally.

"You guys never celebrated a Christmas together?" Joey asked. "As a couple, I mean. Sometimes I feel weird talking about your romantic relationship because I never witnessed you as a couple. I have no idea why I'm saying these things out loud. Sometimes I misplace my filter."

Gabriella took a last appraising look at her work and came down the ladder. "Well, it was one of the darkest times in my life," she deadpanned.

Madison swatted her arm as she hopped to the ground. "She's going to believe you. She's Joey and she does that. Fix it."

Gabriella laughed. "Fine. No, it's not weird. I have a handful of exes, but this one was a keeper because she's a knucklehead, but a nice one. No other reason."

"She once had *nice knucklehead* embroidered on a pillow for me," Madison said. "And no, we casually dated through a Christmas once but were broken up as a couple by the time the next one rolled around. I don't think I ever saw her tree."

"It is certainly impressive the way you two get along so well," Loretta offered, as she hung the festive red bows she'd made herself, evenly spaced as always, below the bar. She turned around to them as the music shifted to "Jingle Bells." "Shows true maturity."

"I'm a mature knucklehead," Madison said, adjusting a garland. "I like the progress."

"Thank you, Loretta. Given your wisdom, I take that as a compliment. One of us is definitely more mature than the other, however, but we'll let that go." Gabriella winked.

"I'm not even going to argue that point," Madison said wisely. She poured another mug of the hot mulled wine. "This batch is amazing. Your father's recipe really holds up."

"The secret is in the brown sugar, he always said."

Loretta nodded. "He was right."

Joey grinned, knowing if her dad were around, he would have tromped through at the end and offered to help, knowing full well there'd be little to do other than sip the mulled wine and enjoy the splendor around him. "That's actually my grandfather's recipe. Handed down."

"Well, that makes it even cooler," Madison said and lifted her mug.

The door opened and they all turned. Becca smiled tentatively as she entered, wearing jeans, tall boots, and a maroon sweater. Joey tried not to gawk. Work Becca was sexy as hell, but Casual Becca was swoonworthy in a whole separate manner. It was hard to pick a favorite. Pretty much whichever one was in front of her at the time won out.

"Hey, guys," she said, popping on a Santa hat from her bag, which scored her mega points. "Things certainly seem fun in here."

"And they just got more fun," Madison murmured quietly with a sly grin in place.

All heads swiveled to Joey in happy surprise, because of course she hadn't told them Becca was coming. What if she hadn't been able to make it? She would have felt silly. But with her friends now eyeing her proudly, she leapt into action. "Hey, Becca. Glad you could make it."

"I was worried because there was a wave of fires to put out and three unexpected phone calls from Orlando, but I fought them off bravely. Didn't want to miss this." She looked around. "What can I do?"

"How are you with snow stencils? These windows could use a few holiday designs."

"We're about to find out," Becca said. She approached Joey for the can of snow and stole a quick kiss as she passed. The room didn't break into applause, but it was close. Suddenly, everyone was decorating with a little more gusto and had a festive pep in their stride. They drank the wine, sashayed to the music, and turned the tasting room into a true wonderland.

As Becca filled her mug a second time, Joey let her arm linger on Becca's waist as she passed. Yes, it was blatantly affectionate behavior in front of her friends, but Joey didn't care. Madison caught the intimacy of the touch and passed Joey a questioning gaze to which she merely shrugged. When Becca held her stare with Joey just a little too long after they inspected the window art, Gabriella grinned in approval and awe. When they shared a quick kiss behind the bar, her friends had had enough. With Becca's back to them as she strung a strand of twinkly lights along the wall behind the bar, Joey's friends went for it.

"What the hell?" Madison mouthed, silently. She gestured back and forth between Joey and Becca.

Joey grinned. "It's been good," she mouthed back. Gabriella sang along loudly to the music to cover their exchange. She didn't have the most on-key of singing voices, but she made up for it in volume.

"Have you two..." Gabriella mouthed, moving her finger back

and forth, as Madison picked up the singing in her place. Even Loretta jumped in, lending her soprano as she followed the conversation with rapt interest.

Joey nodded. "Last night," she mouthed and offered two hearty okay signs as endorsements. Her friends exploded in celebration, which looked a lot like Muppets when they danced. Joey held out her hands to calm them, not wanting Becca to pick up on the dishing happening literally behind her back.

"Is this high enough?" Becca asked, turning around mid Muppet dance. She quirked her head as the dancers froze. "What's going on?"

"Gabriella is a dancer," Joey offered quickly. "As well as a chef. She's both. She was just teaching Madison this one move."

"And me, too." Loretta performed an enthusiastic but poorly executed Running Man.

"Oh." Becca nodded as if it wasn't insane. "Well, that's definitely a...unique approach."

"Isn't it, though?" Gabriella said. "I take pride in my work."

Joey had to give it to Gabriella. She committed.

"But yes, the lights look beautiful," Joey said. "In fact, the whole place does. Go team."

Becca climbed down the ladder, and Joey only allowed herself a moment to check out her ass because she did have a modicum of restraint. She remembered gripping it in the throes, and okay, that was probably enough trotting down memory lane in public.

"Your face is red, Jo," Madison said slyly. "Want some water? It might help that beet-red face. Some might even call you Tomato Face. I won't, though." She was enjoying tonight far too much. It reminded Joey of when they were kids and Maddie relished it when embarrassed Joey was called to the front of the cafeteria stage on awards night and honored for perfect attendance.

"Thank you, Madison." Joey passed her friend a chastising stare, took the offered bottle of water, and swallowed some down.

"Will I see you all at the opening Friday?" Becca asked the group as they consolidated the empty decor boxes.

"Wouldn't miss it," Gabriella said, looking between Becca and Joey like a proud mom. "I've missed too much already."

Joey sent her a wide-eyed-blink combo.

"We'll *all* be there," Madison added. "Now we're going to get out of here and let you two...mingle. It is the holiday season after all. Warm and jolly."

"And sexy," Gabriella whispered to the ground.

Loretta kissed Joey's cheek. "Good night, you sweet girls. See you tomorrow, Joey. Don't stay up too late now." Her gaze landed on Becca. "Or do. Your decision. You only live once, right?"

Becca raised an amused eyebrow as the three people Joey enjoyed most scurried from the room, leaving Joey, Becca, and Judy Garland. "They know about last night," Becca said, simply.

"They know," Joey said back with a wince. "I'm bad at keeping secrets from Madison, and now from Gabriella, and Loretta has always been a second mother who can read me like a book with large print." She took a deep breath. "I'm sorry."

Becca laughed quietly and leaned against the bar. "They're your friends, your people. You can tell them anything you want."

"Really? You sure about that?" Joey asked, stepping into Becca's space. "I can tell them that as sophisticated as you are, you make the cutest little noises when you're turned on?"

Becca's mouth fell open. "Well, maybe not that." A pause. "I do?" She slipped her arms around Joey's waist and pulled her in. "Much better."

Joey nodded vehemently. "You really do. It's…inexplicably hot."

"No one has ever told me that before. But to be fair, I was a little out of my depth last night."

"Why is that?" Joey asked, already knowing the answer if Becca's experience had been anything like her own.

"I think the chemistry might be a little more compelling than I'm used to."

Joey nodded. "We combusted last night, but I do take part of the blame for showing up on your doorstep so unexpectedly." Joey reached behind Becca and found her mug. She put a little space between them because it was starting again, that ever-present tingling that made her want to touch Becca and kiss her and…more. This conversation might be too important for distractions.

"Blame is not the word. Let's go with credit, because I wouldn't change a thing."

"Good." Joey was feeling shy again, but she wanted to know more about Becca, and this was the perfect opening. "You mentioned people you've been with in the past. Anyone special recently?"

"Oh, the requisite talk about the past is here." Becca straightened. "Is that bad?"

"Not at all. It's just not pretty."

"Oh, my. Is there a scandal in the mix?"

"No, but there's an ex-husband and an ex-girlfriend. Neither of whom is a big fan of mine, if I'm being honest, and I'm not sure I completely blame them."

"Oh, Becca, what did you do to them? Erect hotels in their hometowns, too?"

Becca raised her eyebrows and sighed. "Well, my ex-husband, Blake, felt like I wasn't meeting him halfway. I wasn't. I was gay as the day is long and just took my time realizing that." She shook her head ruefully. "He hates me for breaking his heart and stealing two years of his life. We divorced when I was twenty-four." A pause. "I'm thirty-six now, by the way."

"An older woman. I'm so worldly."

Becca laughed. "How old are you?"

"I'm thirty as of three months ago, which means I'm a settled adult, right?"

"You seem like an adult to me, especially yesterday."

"Good. And I don't think you should beat yourself up about the demise of Blake and Becca, which is one of the better couple names I've heard. What about the girlfriend? Feel like telling me about her?"

"Eve." Becca's brow creased as this one seemed to be more complicated. "We met at a hospitality conference in New Orleans and hit it off. Dated long distance for a year. She quit her job, moved to Orlando, and spent the next two years hating the city, hating her job, and hating me for not being unhappy along with her." Becca shook her head as if being yanked back there.

"So not the best introduction to life together."

"No. I started working a ton just to avoid her, and she felt it. Called me selfish and asked me to move out. Of my own house. I'd had that place for years."

"Oh no. And did you?"

"Sadly, I did. I loved that house. She also took my car. I'm a country song now. Listen to me." She laughed ruefully. "What about you?"

"Me?" Joey scoffed. "Not much to report. Pretty boring." She went about straightening the decor as the focus shifted uncomfortably to her. That snowman statue should probably look to the left a bit more. Yep, much better.

"You haven't dated recently?" Becca asked.

"Not at all. No."

"But you were going to get married?"

"Yes. Three years ago. You seemed to already know the story in the Nickel earlier. Everyone does, so I'm not surprised you were updated."

"I heard the basics, but not from you."

"That's fair." Joey paused, put her hand on her hip, turned, and told it to Becca straight. Just easier to get it all out there. "I planned to marry my childhood sweetheart, who I was very much in love with. Simone. She decided moments before that I wasn't forever material and is now very much involved with someone who I would have to agree is an upgrade."

Becca blinked at her. "Surely you don't really think that."

"Have you met Constance?"

"No. But she works at the practice I visited with Sky."

"She's athletic, tall, beautiful, kind, and she's a veterinarian." Joey held out an emphatic hand. "She helps adorable creatures when they're sick. I'd leave me for her, too."

"I don't care who she is. She's not you." Becca said it without hesitation as if it was as true as the sun rising each morning.

For a moment, it robbed Joey of her ability to speak. And finally, she melted. "That was a really sweet thing to say."

Becca looked her straight in the eye. "I'm not trying to be sweet. I just tell it like it is. I'm still getting to know you, but I can't look away. You're stunning. You're incredibly intelligent, full of pep and spirit and more than a little spitfire in the best way. You're also thoughtful and overflowing with this energy I find completely addictive."

They stared at each other. Joey could hear her own heartbeat as she turned the words over in her mind.

"Me?" she asked quietly.

Becca nodded. "You."

Joey moved to Becca and kissed her, long and thorough, her heart soaring. "That's what I have to say to that," Joey murmured as she pulled back, her mouth but a centimeter from Becca's as they breathed the same air. She stared into those beautiful hazel eyes. "I don't know where you came from, but I'm trying not to question any of this."

Becca's eyes held understanding. "You can trust me, Joey. I mean what I say."

Joey nodded. She was beginning to. With each moment they spent together, another wall came down. On one hand, she hated how vulnerable that made her, but on another, she felt alive for the first time in years. "Dance with me?"

Becca turned her head and passed Joey a sideways look. "Here?"

Joey held up one finger, walked to the switch on the wall, and killed the overhead lights in the tasting room, leaving the space dark with the exception of the twinkling lights on the Christmas tree and around the room. "The Christmas Song" played as Joey held out her hand to Becca, who took it wordlessly. She wrapped an arm around Becca's neck and held their joined hands near her heart as they danced slow and close.

For Joey, this felt like an important moment, a turning point of sorts. Her feelings for Becca startled her, and she had to decide whether she was capable of facing them fully. She looked up and met Becca's gaze, watching as she smiled down at her. As the song came to its conclusion, Becca caught Joey's mouth in a kiss that quickly turned hungry.

"I don't think you've seen the Big House yet," Joey said, breathless and happy.

Becca shook her head. "Feels like a shame."

The tour was quick and to the point, ending in the recently remodeled new master bedroom. They didn't go over the paint colors or new finishes in favor of taking each other's clothes off. Becca wore matching black lingerie that made Joey want her so badly she forgot to take her time. With her hand between Becca's legs, she walked her backward to the bed and had her delicious way with her, taking in every detail with new reverence. This wasn't a hookup. Becca was beginning to matter. When she said Joey's name moments before she came, Joey memorized the sound. It was everything.

Becca didn't stay over that night because there was work the next day and she had Sky to think about, but Joey stayed at her place the night after. They stayed up late, naked in Becca's bed, just talking.

"You've never been to Europe?" Becca asked, as Joey traced a pattern on her stomach, loving how smooth her skin felt.

"No, but I plan to visit wine country in France sometime within the next five years. Madison says I'd go nuts for some of the lesser known boutique wineries in that region. What's something you've never done but want to?"

Becca kissed her chin. "That's easy. Play on a sports team. I don't want to be the star. I just want to help. Maybe softball or soccer."

Joey fell onto her back. "I couldn't take it if you wore a uniform." She went back up on her elbow. "Do you understand what that would do to me?" She fell flat again with a labored sigh.

A pause.

"Now I think I have to." Becca laughed quietly. The sheet only came to her waist, and Joey loved the view of her topless. In fact, it might be her favorite of images. "Are there rec leagues in town?"

Joey nodded. "New sign-up is in the spring."

"Did I really just turn you on?" Becca asked in her ear. "Be honest."

She had, but the whispered question doubled the effect. Becca slid down the bed and nestled her hips between Joey's legs. Joey's eyes slammed shut when Becca kissed her and proceeded to take her to new heights.

"Home run," Joey hissed, collapsing in satisfaction after.

Becca laughed and pulled her close as they worked their way toward sleep. Once the first glimpse of sunlight slipped in through Becca's oversized windows, Joey watched as Becca, naked and unaware of her beauty, moved about, showering and prepping for work. Skywalker came to the side of the bed and swiped a tongue across Joey's nose. It felt everyday, domestic, as if somehow, Joey just belonged in their midst. She snuggled into the warmth of the covers for a few more minutes before she, too, would need to get ready for work at Tangle Valley. First, she smiled to herself. It amazed her that she was able to feel happiness in the moment, when things at the vineyard were so daunting, when she'd lost a close family member and best friend. Yet, Becca's presence in her life helped her through it.

Becca's hairdryer switched on as Joey pulled the covers to her chin. Somehow, the happiness bled through it all. That had to mean something.

❖

Becca wasn't the type to get nervous. She preferred the term excited, anticipating, even. And that's where she hovered that Friday in late November when Elite Resorts was set to debut their new crown jewel, The Jade. She'd arrived at The Jade two hours earlier than normal and spent some time alone, moving through the space, admiring all the final touches that had turned the building into undeniable modern opulence. They'd decorate for the holidays the day after Thanksgiving, but for now, she absorbed the space as it was intended. She knew there would never be another time when the space would feel as dormant. In less than an hour, the staff would arrive and never again leave. The first guests would check in, and that revolving door would continue to spin for years into the future.

"It feels special, doesn't it?" Carla asked. Becca turned and smiled at her second-in-command, who she happened to respect a great deal. She nodded, taking note of how fantastic Carla looked in her green designer suit. Becca had opted for black with a green dress shirt beneath, all in honor of the color jade, of course. The staff uniforms followed the same color scheme.

"It really does. This is the third resort I've served as GM for, but the first one I've opened personally. I feel so connected to it, somehow. Is that crazy?"

"Not crazy at all. It's your baby."

"Our baby."

Carla seemed to appreciate being included. She held out her hands to the pristine lobby. "Just add guests."

Becca folded her arms in satisfaction. "They're heading here now, you know. On planes, in cars, all pointed in this direction."

Carla came and stood shoulder to shoulder with Becca as they surveyed their hard work about to take off. "Let's give them the time of their lives."

"Deal," Becca said, returning Carla's fist bump.

Six hours later, the grand opening of The Jade was in full effect. Complimentary wine and champagne flowed to anyone over twenty-one, passed hors d'oeuvres floated through the lobby on trays, and a quartet played a set of standards.

Becca busied herself greeting not only the hotel guests but members of the community who'd come out to either support the resort or simply get an up close look at it. If the controversy from Whisper Wall continued, no one mentioned it today. Everyone was full of compliments and smiles, and why wouldn't they be? Elite had spent a ton on this reception to make sure everyone went out and told their friends all about how fantastic it was. All the while, Becca kept an eye on the door for Joey and her close friends.

"Welcome to The Jade. Did you have a chance to sip some wine?" Becca asked an older couple.

"Oh, we're not guests," the woman said, clutching her husband's arm with one hand, and her purse with the other. "We just came to say hello. Lookie-loos is all. We live in town, so you don't have to give us your wine."

"That makes you our neighbors—incredibly important guests today. Please eat and drink all you want, and definitely take a tour. My name is Becca Crawford, and I'm the general manager."

"Oh, well, it's nice to meet you," the man said. "You have a real good-looking hotel here."

"Thank you. I'd love it if you'd stay and celebrate with us. Gregory over there is pouring three different varietals. There's food moving around the room." She leaned in. "I'd personally recommend the shrimp crostini."

"Oh my goodness," the woman said. "I'm a shrimp fan. Don't mind if I do."

They headed off toward the center of the lobby as Becca turned just in time to greet the next guest, smile in place, only to see Joey standing there.

"Look at you."

"What?" Becca asked. She could feel herself beaming.

"You're really great at this," Joey said, shaking her head.

Everything in Becca exhaled in happiness. "You think so?" She'd never lacked for confidence when it came to her job, yet hearing that she'd impressed Joey bolstered her in a way she wouldn't have predicted.

"You're really wonderful with the guests and have a serenity to the way you speak to them. I'm taking notes." She moved her hands through the air as if marking a headline. "Be. More. Serene."

Becca laughed. "I've seen you in action. You don't need to be. Bubbly works better for you."

Joey looked around at the celebration in progress. "I had no idea it would be this fancy. We'd have dressed up more."

Joey wore a beautiful V-neck knit top, deep blue in color, dark jeans, and brown booties with a slight heel. "You look fantastic, and it would have been a shame if you'd changed anything about yourself in this moment."

"Well, if you put your foot down," Joey said with wide eyes. "Flatterer. Clearly trying to get me to stay here."

"First of all, I only tell the truth. Even when it gets me into trouble. And second of all, we're booked solid for weeks. But I can put you up personally if you need somewhere to stay. I don't even charge."

"I might. I hear there's personal attention."

"Oh, full service," Becca said very quietly.

They exchanged a heated look that had Becca flashing back to leaving for work with Joey still naked in her bed just forty-eight hours ago. She definitely wouldn't mind a repeat of that scenario. She hadn't seen her since, making Joey a sight for sore eyes. To bring them out of it, because they were at her opening, she looked around the lobby. "You said *we* earlier. Did you bring your friends?"

Joey gestured behind Becca with her chin. "Madison is checking out the wine you're serving, and Gabriella is chasing the waiters around like a curious puppy to scope the menu. Wine and food. They're in their element."

"Madison will be happy to see that we're pouring the Tangle Valley pinot noir, among other brands."

"Are you really?" Joey's face lit up. "That's fantastic." She dropped her volume and added, "Any word on the house wine deal? Do we have paperwork? A contract?"

"Not yet. But it feels like a formality at this point. I told you they loved the idea of featuring a local vineyard."

"Because it was a great idea. I'm just thrilled we're your closest neighbor."

"Luckily, you have the wine to back it up. A match."

Carla strolled by and delivered a glass of wine to Joey. "Ms. Wilder, I thought you might enjoy this glass from Tangle Valley."

Joey laughed and shook her head. "Oh, you guys are good." Carla winked and drifted away. Joey pointed after her. "Impressive."

"We do our best," Becca told her. "I better…"

"Go. Yes. Be professional and awesome." Joey leaned in on her toes and whispered in Becca's ear, "And don't think at all about me imagining our next time together."

Becca swallowed. Suddenly the room looked different, felt different. Joey, however, appeared pleased. "You did that on purpose," Becca mouthed as she walked away, now flushed and loving it.

Joey shrugged innocently and sipped her wine as Gabriella returned to her side with a plate.

Becca continued to play hostess, grinning as the Biddies bustled past in a foursome, chattering away just like always. They were a tight and formidable group, that was for sure. Thelma waved at Becca proudly as if seeing a best friend on the playground. She waved back. That afternoon she saw lots of familiar faces. The cowboys, Loretta, Brenda Anne, and even Big Mitch McHugh, who'd run the town meeting regarding The Jade. Seemed they were all making friends with the place, which was exactly what she'd hoped for.

The opening was a smash success, with the reception wrapping up late afternoon. Beyond that, they had a few kinks to work out in day-to-day operations. Their reservation system seized up temporarily, several rooms reported no hot water, which was cleared up by maintenance in under an hour, and the valet lot was nearly overrun, making them come up with a plan B for now and the future. All helpful exercises for her staff. By midevening, when Becca leaned back in her leather executive chair and slipped out of her three-inch Manolos, the shoes she'd been wearing for fourteen hours now, she nearly cried with relief. She loved mingling with guests and assisting her staff. Both were huge parts of her job, but at the end of a day that had required her to be so explicitly *on*, she was depleted of every ounce of energy. She missed her dog. She wondered what Joey was up to and longed for any means to decompress.

She typed as much to Joey moments later and was intrigued by the text she received back.

Listen to me carefully. Grab your dog and find your way to the closest vineyard. Relaxation awaits.

Text messages didn't get more tempting, and Becca's lips curled into a smile. With her last ounce of energy, she forced herself out of the chair, checked in with her front desk supervisor to be sure there were no emergencies to mitigate, and said good night to Carla, who she scolded and instructed to get out of there. They'd both put in a long day after weeks of grueling preparation. They'd need the downtime to make it through the rest of the week. Their department supervisors would handle it from here.

After a bath of dog kisses, and a healthy wrestling session, which she of course lost, Becca and Sky pulled up in front of the Big House and looked up at the warm glow of light inside. The house was more than cozy, it was welcoming. The kind of place that made you want to hug yourself.

Skywalker bounded up the stairs, bellowed four times, and Joey opened the door for him automatically. She wore leggings and a blue funnel neck sweatshirt that screamed cuddly. "Hi, guys," she said, hand on her hip.

"Hi, you," Becca said, in what sounded like her tired, scratchy voice. Too much talking, apparently.

Joey stole a quick kiss and opened the door for Becca to enter. "Did you at least get to have a glass of wine at the reception?"

"I did not. Wasn't sure it was the best look, but I did sip some of the hot cider."

"Then you deserve a libation," Joey said and presented Becca with an already poured glass. "I know you like our current vintage, but this is a reserve from four years ago that I guarantee will knock your socks off. My father didn't mess around that year, and it shows. I have a handful of cases left that I ration out only to very special visitors."

Becca took a sip, let the flavors settle, and took a second. Wow. The wine was smooth and deeply satisfying. "Oh, I really like that." She stared at the glass and took a third sip. It warmed her up from the cold nicely, as did the fire she saw in the beautiful fireplace across the room. Sky had already curled up on the couch closest to the fire. The image could have been a painting. Becca felt her body slowly releasing tension just being here. Joey wasn't kidding about the relaxation.

"What about a nice soak?" Joey said and took Becca's hand.

"What do you mean? Are we going swimming?" she asked, as they climbed the stairs.

"Wait for it."

Becca did and it was worth the crazy day she'd had. An oversized claw-foot tub, nearly three quarters full with hot water running, welcomed them. The whole room smelled wonderfully of lavender, probably from the expanse of bubbles basking along the surface of the water.

"For you," Joey said. "Decompress."

"You ran me a bath?"

Joey looked at her proudly. "Mm-hmm. Interested?"

She could have kissed Joey. In fact, she did. "You are the best... person," she said, realizing that she was short a noun. Joey wasn't officially her girlfriend, though the way they'd been carrying on, it would be strange of either one of them to date someone else, but now the lack of definition was all she could think about. Joey dating someone else. She didn't like the concept at all. She opened her mouth to tell her so, but the sight of Joey pulling her shirt over her head stopped Becca short.

She blinked and readjusted. Seeing the look on her face, Joey paused midbutton on her jeans. "I thought you might want company, but if not, I can—"

"Oh, I definitely want company," Becca said in wonder as Joey stepped out of her jeans and then began to unfasten her bra. Becca bit the inside of her lip as Joey's breasts were revealed to her. A normal person would take their own clothes off and slip into the bath, but Becca was transfixed as she watched Joey slide her underwear down her legs, leaving her naked and gorgeous. She'd never tire of that visual. Joey felt the water and stepped into the tub, piling her blond hair on top of her head with a clip from the shelf behind her.

"You coming?" Joey asked with a smile.

Becca grinned and removed her clothes as Joey watched from the tub, her arms stretched out across the back of it like she owned the place, which she actually did. Becca eased herself into the tub across from Joey, closing her eyes at the feel of the extra-hot water caressing her skin. The tub was big enough for the both of them, but just, which made it perfect. Becca dangled her wineglass outside the tub and rested her neck on the curved porcelain behind her. "If you'd told me this is what I'd be leaving work for, I'd have been here much sooner."

"I wasn't about to cut the opening short for you. It was a big day, and I figured you should enjoy it. Count the money. Laugh maniacally."

Becca shook her head at Joey's ribbing of The Jade. The tone of it had progressed over the weeks from hostile to tense to playful, and Becca now welcomed the digs and even gave some back. "We can't all stomp fruit with our feet for cash."

"Touché," Joey said and slid her leg along Becca's. A pause. "You do realize that's not actually how the grapes are crushed here, right?"

Becca laughed. "Yes, but it's disappointing. You have such cute feet."

Joey wiggled her toes along the surface of the water, which seemed to give her an idea. As Becca sipped her near-perfect glass of wine, Joey pulled Becca's right foot into her lap beneath the water and went to work on it. Becca took a deep inhale as muscles all over her body began to kick loose. She had no idea she'd wound up so tightly, but the pressure points Joey expertly accessed on the bottom of her foot proved otherwise. "Did you go to school for this? Never mind. You should *open* a school. Joey's Professional Heaven Sending. That's what you'll call it."

"I could. Naming it that might give the wrong impression of the type of service I'm offering, but you're the business executive," Joey said with a wink.

"Scratch that. You're forbidden to call it that. It's now called Get a Foot Massage Here."

"Oh, much more straightforward. I like it."

"But maybe those heaven sending services can be set aside for special clients."

"Even better." Joey's eyes met Becca's and darkened, signaling her mind had traveled somewhere hot. Becca loved that she could read her so easily now. She took another sip of wine and let the flavors settle on her tongue. Wine made her feel sexy. Drinking it on a vineyard only amplified the effect. Drinking wine on a vineyard while in a bathtub with Josephine Wilder took it out of the realm of modern measurement.

"I want to do things to you," Becca said, simply.

Joey blinked and her lips parted.

Becca nodded. "I'm planning on it."

Joey attempted a smile but never quite made it there. She shifted her position as if uncomfortable, another tell that her body was already responding. Becca knew she could affect Joey with just her words. She'd seen it happen. She drank from her glass and stared hungrily at the tops of Joey's round breasts, bathed in bubbles. Every now and then she caught a glimpse of a nipple.

"I want to make you come," Becca said. "Give you pleasure."

Joey shook her head. "You're supposed to be relaxing, you know."

"I can't actually think of anything better, though. Sitting in a bathtub with you might be the highlight of my year."

"Well, who am I to argue how to end your day?"

The water that had felt amazing was almost too hot now, the bathroom full of steam. Joey must have felt it, too. She downed the last of her wine and left the glass on the shelf behind her. She stood, revealing her body, her curves, wet and pink from the tub. Becca let her exit and open the door to allow the steam to escape. She allowed herself the luxury of watching Joey towel off for only a moment before she joined her at the sink, where she took the clip out of her hair. It fell soft and silky onto her shoulders. As the steam faded from the mirror, Becca slid her hands around Joey's waist, which brought everything else to a halt. They watched each other in the mirror with hungry eyes. Becca took the towel Joey had wrapped around herself and let it fall to the floor. From behind, she cradled Joey's breasts, closing her eyes at the wonderful feel of the weight of them in her hands. She pressed them back against Joey's body and listened to the way her breath caught, watching her eyes slam shut in the mirror. Becca was sweating from the steam and lost in a haze of lavender. She dropped her palms to Joey's ribs, her stomach, and down the front of her thighs and around behind to her perfect ass. Joey's head dropped forward, and she laid her hands flat on the countertop as Becca caressed her slowly. She knew very well that Joey came fast when she was turned on and that it wouldn't take much. She ran her hand along the inside of one thigh first, and then the other, holding Joey with one arm around the waist when she started to tremble. Joey bent farther over the counter as Becca touched her between her legs lightly. Joey jerked and sucked air. Becca had fantastic access to her neck and kissed the back of it, the side, as she stroked long and slow. The quiet noises coming from Joey were new and matched the rhythm Becca had established. With her fingers, she pushed inside, which increased the volume of Joey's sounds. She watched in the mirror, mesmerized, as Joey's breasts swayed. She thrust into Joey with her fingers from behind, using her other hand to tease her from the front until Joey shot up straight, gripping the countertop as she tumbled over the edge with a beautiful cry.

Becca would never think of lavender the same way again.

Joey, looking like a woman on a mission, turned, backed Becca up against the wall, and sank to her knees. The sensations hit immediately as Joey's warm mouth went to work. Becca's eyes fluttered closed, and she gripped the wall for support. Suddenly, she didn't feel tired at all.

Chapter Twelve

It was two days after Thanksgiving, and Joey sat on top of an oak barrel as evening crept in. Across from her on a stack of hay bales, Gabriella sat cross-legged. Madison chose to stretch out on the concrete floor, back against the bales, as they shot the breeze and caught up on all they'd missed during the Thanksgiving break. The sun had just descended on what had been a lazy day on the vineyard, as the majority of staff had recently traveled back from wherever their holiday had taken them. As for Joey, she'd enjoyed a turkey dinner prepared by Loretta, who'd insisted, since her daughter was tied up with a show in New York. Uncle Bobby and Madison had joined them, and the foursome did their best to enjoy each other's company without dwelling too much on the empty chair at the head of the table that no one had felt comfortable filling just yet.

Tonight felt like a good time to regroup with her friends, however, before jumping back into work, which would bring an inevitable uptick in visitors as the holidays approached. To bolster their evening, Madison had brought the three of them a thermos of hot mulled wine she happily poured into cozy mugs. The spices were fresh and aromatic, making Joey's soul squeeze when she inhaled deeply from her cup. The warmth radiated through her gloves, reminding her how much she loved the colder months. Before her first sip, she thought of her parents back in the day, newly married and working on putting Tangle Valley, an up and comer in the Oregon wine scene, firmly on the map. She sent a silent cheers up to them now, remembering what big shoes they were all trying to fill.

She'd turned on one of the metal portable heaters she'd talked her father into purchasing, in spite of the coats and hats and gloves they'd piled on. Yes, it was cold outside, but the old barn was becoming a nice place to unwind and catch up. She'd half-heartedly suggested they relax in the Big House but was relieved when her friends suggested the barn. It was becoming their time, their place, and she liked that.

Gabriella was newly home from spending Thanksgiving in Connecticut with family, first generation Italians. "The food, you guys, was off the charts. My grandma Ursula has the best stuffed olive recipe, but that was just the tip of the iceberg. We *showed up* for Thanksgiving. All of us. Two tables of food, entirely covered in dishes of all kinds. Pastas, eggplants, antipasto platters, and my mother's spinach lasagna, which I would happily die at the feet of. Almost sinful, except it wasn't."

"And how many of those were your dishes?"

"Nine or seventeen. Not that many," Gabriella said with a wink. She dusted off her shoulder with pride. "What? I had to show them up. I'm the chef. My Tuscan rib eye was the talk of the neighborhood, though." She sipped her wine. "Speaking of things cooking, is Becca back from Georgia yet?"

Madison grinned. "Oh, Gabriella, I can safely say that she's not. I know this because Joey says as much every few hours. She's but half a human without her soul mate." She reached across and gave Joey's boot a shake in solidarity.

Joey balked. "You guys, I have never said Becca was my soul mate."

"Out loud," Madison corrected. "You forgot that part."

"It's just that I haven't seen her in four days now, and yes, I can admit that I miss her. A lot." She shook her head as she searched for the words. "It feels strange to say, given it's only been a couple of months for us, but four days feel like four years. It's disarming."

"Don't cast this as anything but normal when you care about someone. I, personally, like seeing you so invested," Madison said. "It looks good on you after the last few years of tumbleweeds."

"Hey!" Joey bit out.

"The utter truth. But you deserve a break from strife and heartache."

Gabriella held up her glass. "Have the good sex. That's what I say."

"Feels really nice," Joey marveled. "I'm not going to downplay it. I miss her smile. The way her hair tickles my shoulder when we kiss." Joey lifted her shoulders as if doing so would take her back there, to those magical moments she'd shared with Becca.

"You're going to make it until she's back. I promise you," Gabriella said as if this was the most vital of causes. "Then you and Sexy Execsy will kiss and bound through the vines, laughing and holding hands."

Madison blinked a few times. "God, I want to be you, Gabriella. If that's how you see the world, let me wear your unicorn glasses. How can we make that happen?"

Joey grinned. Madison, who had been practical and levelheaded since the day Joey met her, sometimes struggled to see the world beyond science and logic. "Please make that happen for her. She needs to do a little skipping of her own."

Gabriella sat taller and moved her hands in a circle around each other. "You just gotta relax, Maddie, and the butterflies and unicorns of life will find you, too, one day."

Joey laughed. "Don't dissect them when they do."

Gabriella pointed at Joey in reinforcement. "Yes, listen to her. Embrace your inner unicorn, Madison."

Madison raised her mug in acquiescence and then mumbled into it, "I might need that on a T-shirt."

"Don't tempt me." Gabriella looked behind her, remembering something. "Oh, damn. I brought cake."

Madison's mouth fell open. "You brought cake and you're just now saying so? We've been sitting here for ten minutes. Cakeless."

"Gabs," Joey said, leaning in, "if you bring cake, you should be screaming that all the way to the barn with the pan raised above your head in victory."

Gabriella nodded. "Got it. Next time? Screaming from a distance." She pulled the foil off the dish and presented the wonder that was her work. "It's pumpkin and apple with a cream cheese frosting I perfected when I was sous chef for Aiden McHenry at Albondiga in Manhattan."

"Oh my God. Really?" Joey felt her face light up. "I love his show. I still can't believe you worked with him. When I saw that on your résumé, I knew we had to have you. I'm just lucky you're willing to slum it."

Gabriella looked skyward. "He was actually the last man I considered before scrapping the whole concept of them."

"Why have you never informed me that you dated Aiden McHenry? I feel like that's key information." Madison accepted the slice of cake, complete with a stainless-steel fork. Gabriella came prepared.

"Dated is the wrong word."

"Oh. Well, then. So you had a hot hookup with Aiden McHenry?" Joey asked, mouth agape.

"Sadly, I did. And I would not use the words hot or anything close." She took a moment to enjoy her cake because, as Joey had found, angels had kissed it into existence. Good God. Gabriella dabbed the frosting from her face. "Fantastic body. Lots of ambition in bed. Talked a big game about it beforehand. Did nothing for me. That's when I knew I had to be out." She shook her head as if it was just so clear now. "Hooked up with a random girl from the restaurant two weeks later and thought my world sparked into magnificent color."

"Unicorn color," Madison said. "How am I doing?"

Gabriella grinned. "Better."

"I'm ambitious, too."

Gabriella pointed at Joey with her fork. "So I get how one person can change everything you think you know about yourself. Who knew I was gay?"

Madison raised her hand and they laughed.

Gabriella turned back to Joey. "When is she back?"

"Tomorrow. Apparently, Carla's been great while she was away, but she'll have a lot of things at The Jade that will need her attention when she's back. Hoping we can steal some time, though."

Gabriella eyed her knowingly. "Please. I've seen you two together. If you're in the same town, there'll be no keeping you apart, little magnets that you are."

Joey beamed, liking the sound of that. She could get used to it even, which felt reckless and terrifying. She moved past it. Maybe they'd drive to Portland this weekend, hit up a food and wine tour. She'd also like to see that new indie film Loretta's daughter, Carly, had out. Of course all of those activities involved a little sex-laden extracurricular afterward. Joey thrummed with excitement.

There'll be no keeping you apart. Joey heard the words again and refused to examine the natural question too closely. What if something did?

❖

Thanksgiving in Georgia had been lovely, relaxing, and a nice break from the day-to-day grind. Not only that, but it had given Becca a chance to reconnect with her parents, her little brother, Paul, and his wife, Lara. They'd laughed together, eaten fantastic food, and she and her sister-in-law had cleaned up at charades, per usual. Yet throughout all the good, a large piece of Becca felt like it was back in Whisper Wall on a vineyard there, and she ached to return.

After a quick trip to see the cowboys and pick up Skywalker, who knocked her over, stood on her chest, and peppered her with sloppy kisses, she headed home. If she played her cards right, she'd have time to swing by Tangle Valley for a short visit before heading into the resort for the remaining portion of the workday. After leaving so much on Carla's shoulders, it only seemed right that she take over her share as soon as possible. Carla would take the same number of days off at Christmas, leaving Becca to handle things at The Jade, a tradeoff they'd agreed upon before the grand opening.

As she let Sky off his leash and watched him bound through his living room, greeting each piece of furniture by jumping on top of it to make sure nothing had changed, her phone vibrated. Hoping for Joey but getting Carla, Becca clicked over.

"I'm on the ground and getting my doggo situated," she said upon answering. "How are things?"

Carla chucked ruefully. "I hoped you'd ask. Jean-Luc, the chef? His girlfriend broke up with him, so he's crying in the kitchen and calling her a cheating whore in a voice probably too loud for a four-star restaurant, all the while wielding a knife. The staff is literally in hiding. As you can imagine, the food is not making it out in a timely manner."

"Fabulous." Becca squinted and began pacing the length of her kitchen.

"But wait, there's more."

"Oh. Okay." She braced herself.

"Our less-than-reliable front desk manager called in sick, so I'm covering things there with our attendants. Rudy, the valet, has filed a sexual harassment complaint against Frank from housekeeping and is refusing to be at work when Frank is. Both are angry and demanding to speak with you, though HR wants to be briefed first. Also, we're having that hot water issue on the sixth floor again. A woman reported it to the front desk in a towel. I'm not even making that up. Plus—"

"You know what? I think that's plenty." Becca closed her eyes and pinched the bridge of her nose. That Tangle Valley visit was going to have to wait. Damn it. But when it rained, it poured. "I'll be there in ten and we can make a punch list. Don't let anything else happen. You put that resort on notice and hold it up with your shoulders if you have to."

Carla sighed. "I'll threaten the building within an inch of its life. See you soon. Happy you're back. As in, really happy."

"Me, too." She clicked off the call, knelt, and gave her dog a kiss on the brown spot encircling his eye. God, she loved that patch of fur. "What a welcome, huh? I have a feeling you're going to be asleep within five minutes. I'll see you soon, okay? We'll catch up and see what that pesky squeaky bone has to say about things." Another kiss for Sky before grabbing her bag with an overdramatic sigh.

The sun was down when Becca came up for air next.

She headed out to the parking lot, feeling an ache on the back of her neck and tension binding her muscles up in bunches. It had been a long day of travel and then a killer one to follow at the resort. The hot water was up and running on the sixth floor, and they'd managed to call in the assistant front desk manager to cover things up front. She'd began an investigation of the Rudy/Frank complaint and had looped in their HR manager, Sebastian, who would handle it from there. Becca was on fumes.

"There she is."

Becca turned, searching for the voice in the parking lot, knowing who it belonged to. Everything in her celebrated. And then there she was. Joey sat on Dusty's folded down tailgate, one leg beneath her, one dangling down.

"What in the world?" Becca said, grinning and changing course. Joey hopped down and waited, her own smile growing. She pulled Joey into her arms and just held her there, absorbing the feel of her, inhaling her scent, and savoring Joey's soft hair beneath her cheek.

Joey released her and stepped back, her eyes sparkling. "I've missed you." She went up on her toes and kissed Becca's lips. "And these," she said, kissing them again. "These shouldn't leave again anytime soon."

Becca laughed. "God, I've missed you, too." She shook her head. "This was harder than I thought it would be. The phone calls were nice, but not the same."

Joey rocked back on her heels. "Turns out you're getting attached to me."

"It's true." Becca knew it was easier for Joey to phrase it that way rather than stating that she was getting attached to Becca. They were sinking in further with each other, but she'd noticed that Joey still clung to safety, and that made sense the more Becca learned about her. This Simone had really done a number, and losing both her parents along the way hadn't helped. She didn't trust the universe. But Becca could be patient. She longed to be Joey's safe place to fall. Trust took time, and luckily, Becca had that to give. "Next time, maybe you can come with me. Meet the family."

"Really?"

Becca nodded. "You'd love my kid brother, Paul. Pauly, as I like to call him. You both have that same earnest sense of humor."

"I think you might have just called me naive."

"Never. You just come with a big heart. One of your best features."

"Oh, that's much smoother. Let's go with that characterization for Paul and me. What did you read on the plane?"

Becca laughed. "What did I read? Where did that come from?"

"Yeah"—Joey slid onto her truck bed and Becca joined her, heels and all—"I was imagining you in your seat and realized I had no idea what you'd do on a plane to occupy yourself. How could that be? Plane behavior is huge. It says so much about a person. How can I continue to date someone if I don't know anything about their plane behavior?" She shrugged. "That was my early morning train of thought, anyway. Your daily glimpse of Joey."

She'd missed that daily glimpse. Becca stared at her as she spoke, just so happy to be in her presence today. She never got tired of the way Joey's blue eyes lit up when excitement struck, and now that the topic was Becca, herself, that felt next-level. "Well, allow me to put that curiosity to sleep. On the plane, I did a little listening to music to keep me calm." She winced. "I don't love the takeoffs and landings. They make me nervous."

Joey shook her head. "I never would have guessed that."

"Next, I read some of the customer service reports to see how we're doing in our first weeks open and then perused a few résumés for seasonal workers because Carla and I are going to need to pull in a few more folks for the three weeks leading to Christmas. After that, I closed my eyes and thought about coming home. About you. A lot about you."

Joey took a moment and slid a strand of hair behind her ear. "That's unexpected plane behavior. The me part."

"Your little glimpse of Becca."

"No novels, huh?" Joey asked, backtracking. "I was trying to decide if you were a Grisham type or maybe a romance novel reader."

"I do like Bristow. She has a new one out featuring two women, you know?"

"It's next on my to-read pile. Gabriella is finishing it now."

Becca bumped Joey's shoulder. "Maybe we can read it together."

Joey bumped her back. "You have a date. We can read a little every night before bed." Becca smirked and Joey caught it. "Except we likely wouldn't get to the book, knowing us."

Becca shook her head. "Nope."

"Then whenever we have time."

"Deal." They shared a moment just looking at each other, happy to be in each other's presence again. The feelings Becca was experiencing for Joey were powerful and ever evolving. She lusted after her, yes, but she also just liked spending time with her, getting her opinions on things happening at work, or hearing her joke about the friendly rivalry with the other vineyards. It was a friendship and romance blossoming at once. Becca had never had that before.

"Where did you go just now?" Joey asked quietly.

"Somewhere really, really nice. Come home with me?"

Joey nodded. The banter from earlier had receded and something heavier, more important had settled in its place. They made love to each other that night. It wasn't just sex. Their touches carried reverence; their kisses communicated a promise of things to come. She slept with her arms wrapped around Joey from behind, holding her close and beginning to understand that she didn't want to ever let her go.

CHAPTER THIRTEEN

I'm about to throw this book across the room," Joey declared in fury. "That's about to happen, so you better prepare yourself." From her spot on the couch in the Big House, she sat with a book in her lap and her feet stretched out. It was Saturday morning, and though Joey needed to head over to the tasting room in just a few minutes, she couldn't seem to stop reading this anger-inducing novel.

"Oh, I know exactly where you are in the book," Becca said with a grin and sipped her coffee from one of Joey's oversized mugs. She had the day off and wore jeans and a long-sleeved white shirt, looking relaxed and beautiful and like she should always be in Joey's kitchen without shoes.

"This is not okay," Joey said, holding up the book in outrage. "And Parker Bristow wants me to forgive this character? Not going to happen. Uh-uh."

"Keep reading. It just might." Becca came around the kitchen counter to stand in front of the island. "You're really cute when you're outraged, though, which means I have to come over there and kiss you."

Well, that melted some of her ire, and Joey lifted her face to receive a kiss she'd actually been craving all morning. "That helps." Joey softened all over. "I can get mad about a lot of things, you know. Downright furious," she said sweetly.

"Oh, I've seen it. You once got a whole town worked up about a new, very well-intended business."

"That place had it coming," she said in jest, pushing herself off the couch and forcing herself to close the damn book. It was just after nine, and they'd open at ten for what she expected to be a busy Saturday. She wanted to chat with Gabriella about the day's menu so she could market it to the guests. She also needed to make sure their guitarist had everything he needed. Heaters would need to be arranged and set up for those who opted to drink wine with a view. She loved the fancy new ones they'd recently put out with actual fire blazing inside.

"Leaving me?" Becca asked.

"I must." She held out her arms. "People need wine. I must make sure they have it. You good?"

Becca held up her own copy of *Back to September*, the Parker Bristow romance they were reading together. "Gonna find out how it ends if it takes me all morning."

"I'm more than a little jealous, except I'm not speaking to the author anymore, so never mind."

Becca laughed and stole Joey's spot on the couch, looking more than a little cozy with the sun shining in on her through the large picture window that looked out on the vines. She seemed so at home in the Big House these days. They spent nights together lately more than they didn't, and normalcy began to creep in. Joey now expected to see Becca in the bathroom as she got ready for the day each morning or sitting on the back deck admiring the vineyard with a glass of red after her workday. Often barefoot, which Joey never knew she found sexy until Becca Crawford walked into her life. Similarly, she'd spent a great deal of time at Becca's place and was used to Skywalker's constant presence at her side, Becca's overly complicated coffeemaker, and the way Becca's sheets smelled wonderfully like her.

She grinned, walked to Becca, and kissed her good-bye, lingering an extra few seconds or so. "Will you be by later?"

"Count on it. Gabriella is doing a breaded zucchini dish with this marinara dipping sauce with fresh parsley and extra garlic that I've been dreaming about since she mentioned it yesterday."

"Oh, that's right." Joey's mouth watered. She loved waking up to the wonderful aromas coming from Gabriella's mobile kitchen. She'd miss them once the restaurant went up, but maybe there was a compromise in there somewhere. The truck, Jolene, had the vineyard guests clamoring for small bites to go with their wine, and Gabriella seemed to have bonded with her. Maybe she didn't have to go away entirely.

"We're putting the mulled wine on sale today, too," Joey informed Becca as she grabbed her bag.

Becca covered her eyes. "That stuff is highly addictive. Does it have to go away when the holidays end?"

"Well, yes. Because half of the appeal is its scarcity any other time of year."

"It's like you were born for business."

"Maybe I should open up a hotel," Joey said, placing her forefinger against her cheek. "I'll call it The Amethyst, and Marla—my assistant—and I will manage it."

"Don't you dare. I don't care how cute you are."

Joey blew Becca a kiss and headed off to work, content in the knowledge that there was so much to look forward to when they closed shop later that day. Her life was so very different than just six months ago, but she was learning to embrace the positive, casting out her fear of change.

As she made the short walk in the frosty air to the tasting room, she shoved her hands into her pockets and looked up at the blue sky. "What do you think, Dad? Do you like her?" She shook her head and grinned. "I really, really do."

Later that afternoon, she ran into two more people who shared the sentiment.

"Well, if it isn't the Moon and Stars cowboys," Joey said, as she walked down the bar and smiled at the boys. Damn, they were good-looking, but even more so when you realized how much good they did for animals. Getting to know Skywalker and how amazing he was really drove home the importance of their work. "I'm happy you stopped in."

"We heard the mulled wine was back, from Clementine at the Biscuit. We had some at the Wassail Fest last year and couldn't resist a detour."

She smiled at their subterfuge. "It had nothing to do with Becca?"

"We might be checking in on her a little bit," Stephen said. Monty tried to nudge him subtly but Joey didn't miss much.

She grinned. "You're scoping me out."

Monty held his thumb and forefinger a short distance apart.

She laughed. "Fair enough. I'd probably do the same for my friend. But you guys know me."

Monty tilted his head from side to side. "We know Joey, local friend and neighbor, but now you're Becca's Joey."

"That's different," Stephen said. "We're here to see *that* Joey Wilder."

Joey nodded. "Why do I feel like I'm on a job interview?"

"You're not in the slightest," Monty said.

"Just a little," Stephen deadpanned.

"I should have dressed nicer." That earned her a laugh. "Want to do a tasting since you're here anyway?" Any chance to pimp her wine.

"How about two mugs of the mulled wine while we pepper you with questions?" Stephen asked, clearly the one leading the mission today. From outside, she could hear their guitarist strike up a rendition of "God Rest Ye Merry Gentlemen."

"Deal." Joey poured their wine, then held out her hands and gestured toward herself, not quite sure what was about to come her way.

"Are you in the market for love?" Monty asked.

The couple next to them at the counter swiveled in interest. With all eyes in near proximity on her, Joey swallowed. "I wasn't. I was actually just barely holding it together. I still feel that way when I look at all I have on my plate. But"—she shrugged—"Becca makes it all feel better, and I guess I want to see where that leads."

The men exchanged a glance and turned back, both dripping with sympathy.

Joey regarded them. "Look, I didn't mean for you to feel bad for me. I've had plenty of that in life already, and it's my least favorite place to be."

"But we do feel awful for you. You've been through a lot," Monty said.

"But not enough to get out of questioning," Stephen added, holding strong. It really was sexy the way his hair curled a little in front like Superman. She wondered how they could use these guys in ads for the vineyard someday.

"I would never presume." Joey held up a finger because another group of hers was mid-tasting and ready to move on to their next varietal. She quickly took care of the cheerful group from Seattle, who were staying at The Jade coincidentally enough, and returned to Stephen and Monty.

They jumped right back in. "What are your long-term goals?" Monty asked.

Joey considered the question. "Well, I plan to run Tangle Valley Vineyard for the rest of my life. It's my legacy, and the place on earth I love more than all others. Outside that, some people would call me a mess. I can admit to that. I lost my mother to illness when I was eight." She felt the emotion begin to rise uncomfortably in her throat. She resisted it with all she had. "My fiancée ditched me for another woman, and the whole town watched with popcorn and whispers. And now my father is gone, too. Something I never saw coming."

"Who could have?" Stephen said, shaking his head.

"Now, I have a lot on my shoulders. Becca Crawford didn't show up at the most opportune of times, but I also think that might have been by design, you know?" Monty nodded as she pressed on, trying to explain something she wasn't sure she understood herself. "I needed Becca, and in a way, I think she needed me, too." She sighed. "But if you're asking for guarantees about anything, I have to be honest and say I don't have any, guys. I'm operating at a one-day-at-a-time kind of place in my life, and it's all I can do. But I know this. She matters to me." She made sure to look each of them in the eye. "I'm not playing around with her heart, or leading her on, or just out for a good time. I'm earnest, and I'm trying. I just don't have all the answers." She lifted one shoulder and let it fall. "I'm doing the best that I can."

When she finished, Stephen set down his mug, his eyes wide. "Well, that's all any of us can do, right? I'm satisfied with that."

"Sweetheart, I don't know you," the woman from Seattle said, leaning over, "but I'd let my son date you in a heartbeat." The woman pointed at Joey and went back to her glass.

"Thank you," Joey said, surprisingly touched by the show of support.

Monty smiled at her warmly. "I think you're good people, Joey. You two want to come over to our place for dinner next week?"

She nodded and felt a smile blossom. Relief settled in her chest. She seemed to have passed the test. "I'll bring the wine."

"What is happening over here?" Becca asked loudly, standing behind the cowboys. "A couple of ruffians show up, and you're serving them?"

"They mean business," Joey said, pointing at them. "I got a good grilling on the side."

Becca exchanged a wide-eyed, apologetic look with Joey. The cowboys looked like they wanted to shrink into their hats that now resided in their laps.

"Well, well. So this is what it's like having surrogate brothers."

"That's exactly it," Monty said, seizing on the characterization. "We care, is all. About both of you now." A pause. "We're also nosy. I can admit that."

Becca put her arms around them. "I appreciate it, boys, but I think all is well. I'm a big girl."

"So am I," Joey said. "Well, most of the time. If you'll excuse me, I'm needed down the bar." Seeing guests in need of assistance, she set out to pour. As she discussed the wine, she stole glances of Becca, Monty, and Stephen as they laughed and cheered with their mugs. She grinned. There was a fantastic food truck out front, new wine being processed several buildings down, and sun shining overhead. So why was Joey absolutely terrified?

❖

"You're quiet tonight," Becca said, coming to stand behind Joey, who sat with a notepad at the kitchen table. She picked up a handful of Joey's hair and let it gently fall back onto her neck.

Joey dropped her head back and looked up at Becca with a soft smile. "Just trying to get some of my thoughts down on paper. We have a busy season ahead of us, and I don't want the plans I have to fall by the wayside. We should start the building renovation in the spring if everything goes according to schedule. I'd also love to look at adding that second tasting room, but honestly? I don't know that it's a smart move given our balance sheet." She shook her head. "Money's tighter than I would have imagined."

"Does that have you concerned?"

"Yes and no. I feel like the deal with The Jade is going to help a lot. At least, I hope it will."

"Oh, I think so. I'm just waiting on the go-ahead from corporate, and then we're set to place an order officially. They'll be hoping for special pricing and an agreement that spells out all the terms."

"I anticipated as much and can certainly accommodate."

Becca grinned. "Great. I'll have Carla get with you about some marketing materials to promote the partnership, and then we'll be off and running."

"You don't know how happy that will make me. Once that first order is in hand, I'll sleep easier." Becca had given her a sample order sheet so Joey could understand what they'd be looking at from a numbers perspective, and honestly? It was a hefty number of bottles each month. Without this standing order, she'd be a little more concerned about the state of things. So much of the equipment at Tangle Valley was older, and it was only a matter of time before she'd have to make those replacements, and fast, too. She needed a financial cushion for those occurrences. Still…things were too tight for her comfort level.

"Tell you what. I'll see if I can move things along."

"You think they might think it's a conflict of interest?"

Becca nodded her understanding. "I disclosed our circumstances. I think they're more interested in what makes sense for the resort."

Joey placed a hand over her heart. "Well, that's a relief."

"I don't think you have anything to worry about. Tangle Valley is going to flourish."

She smiled at Becca, loving the sound of that. "From your lips."

Becca spent the evening working, and Joey did the same. She hadn't been wrong, though. Joey was especially quiet, even when they'd set aside their work. "You sure you're okay?" Becca asked. "Want some coffee or tea? A bath?"

Joey shrugged. "No. Just missing my dad, I guess. Feeling it a lot today."

"Come here," Becca said and raised an arm from her spot on the couch. Joey snuggled beneath it.

"This is better," Joey said. "I like that you're able to do that for me. Calm my rocky seas."

"Oh, I'll rock your seas," Becca said, attempting to make Joey smile. Her payoff was small at best. She didn't know what had Joey on edge, but it felt like more than she was admitting to. All Becca wanted was to take it all on herself. She held Joey tight, smoothed her hair, and kissed her temple. "I've got you," she whispered.

She did, too.

The next morning, she placed a call to Maria Rubins, her VP, to see about the status of her vendor proposition for Tangle Valley. Maria had loved the concept when she'd first presented the idea of a partnership and had asked Becca to submit it in writing, which she had.

"Yes," Maria said, followed by the sound of paper shuffling. "I do have an update on that front. There were quite a few backs-and-forths about it in Orlando, but I think we've settled on a green light, only they did make the call to go with another vendor, Fable Brook. They're almost as close as the vineyard you recommended, but they have broader national distribution, which means the guests will be able to find the wines when they go home."

Becca blinked, unsure what to say. "Oh. I'm not sure I would agree with that choice."

"Honestly, it was Craig in Dining's call. He did some research on the various wineries in the area and felt Fable Brook was the best match."

"I'm unsure of that." She'd heard Madison and Joey speak about the steps that Martin Hollis skipped in winemaking, all in favor of commercialization. Fable Brook seemed to lack personality. Hell, even their label was dull. Solid tan with a boring font. The tangled vines on Tangle Valley's label were as eye-catching and memorable as the wine. She'd feel the same way even if she'd never met Joey.

Maria continued, "And I appreciate you being forthcoming about your relationship with the vineyard owner out there, and though I didn't bring it up in our discussions, I think for appearances' sake this might be a good pivot, Becca. You know? Between you and me, and I do consider myself your friend, you now can breathe easier about it looking like favoritism."

Becca nodded, hating every word. She had divulged her relationship with Joey to Maria because transparency was important to her. But Joey or no Joey, Tangle Valley was by far the better partnership. Their proximity alone was a no-brainer, the winery itself was the most picturesque of places to send their guests, but most importantly, their product put Fable Brook to shame.

"I hear you, Maria. I do. I just wish I'd been consulted."

"I trust Craig on this. Give it time. If it doesn't work out, the deal is up in two years, and we can take another look at things."

Becca placed her palm on her forehead. "So I suppose that's it, then."

"I'm afraid so. While I have you, can we go over some of the plans for Christmas Eve?"

"Of course." But Becca had downshifted and had trouble concentrating on anything other than the blow that had just been dealt. She saw her mistake now, and it had been to tell Joey about the possibility before it was a done deal. She'd been so confident that corporate would agree with her that she'd taken that leap. How was she supposed to go back to Joey and explain that there would be no deal? Not only that, but that the deal was happening with one of her competitors instead. When the call ended, she placed the receiver on the cradle and leaned back in her chair, realizing that she had an entire day to get through now and somehow had to regain her focus. It haunted her, the knowledge that she'd have to carry this information home to Joey, so much so that she made up an excuse about a late-night-early-morning combo and stayed the night on her own. She felt sick to her stomach when she clicked the light off. Sky, sensing her unease, nuzzled her hand sweetly. "I'm an idiot," she stated to him plainly. "A big one."

❖

The Scoot was fairly quiet when Joey found a spot at the bar, close to five that evening. Becca had canceled their plans due to an unexpected work commitment, but Joey had been primed to get out. Now that she was on her own, she decided to pay Patsy a visit and see what new beers she'd picked up. It was a hobby of Patsy's to discover the new up-and-coming craft beers and bring back a case or two to sell at the bar before placing a larger order.

"You don't come in enough," Patsy said, then dropped a coaster with the Scoot's logo in front of Joey and topped it with a can of vanilla porter from a Portland microbrewery. She said it like an accusation, and Joey winced because ever since she'd begun spending time with Becca, her old routines had taken a hit. She missed Patsy right back.

"I know, and I plan to remedy that."

Patsy softened and grinned warmly. If Loretta was a second mother to Joey, Patsy was a third. "Then all will be forgiven." She grabbed Joey's face across the bar and kissed her cheek.

"How's your pretty girlfriend?" an older women's voice asked from behind her. Joey turned to see Maude and the rest of the Biddies decked out in boots and cowgirl hats. Oh, that was right. The foursome liked to line dance on Fridays.

"I think you're talking about Becca Crawford, and she's doing really well. The Jade is booked up for the holidays, keeping her on her toes."

"I'm so happy you found someone new," Birdie said, with a pat on Becca's shoulder. Of the four, Birdie was the softest spoken and reminded Joey of everybody's favorite grandma. Without the other three to influence her, Birdie would likely cause a lot less trouble.

"Me, too," Maude said.

Janet nodded wholeheartedly. "Especially now with Simone and Constance tying the knot."

Joey paused her beer midway to her mouth. She'd not heard that news. She watched as the other three Biddies passed Janet a chastising stare.

"What?" Janet asked. "The whole town is talking about it. I figured Josephine knew."

Joey set the beer back on the bar and caught the look on Patsy's face. Her eyebrows drew down and the sides of her mouth pinched in sadness. No—in sympathy, and Joey hated it.

"I didn't know." She forced herself to smile even though the world felt strange. "Good for them. It's about time, right?" Three years to be exact, her brain supplied.

The Biddies exchanged another curious series of looks because Joey wasn't appropriately devastated. Only she was. Just inside. She wasn't in love with Simone anymore, but that battle scar hadn't faded entirely. Joey was once the one planning a wedding with Simone and remembered acutely how excited Simone got each step of the way, as they chose their colors, cake flavors, and attendants. Joey had been more excited for the life they would get to lead together. She'd expanded the cottage on the edge of the Tangle Valley property, the one farthest away from anyone. It sat empty now. Joey couldn't bring herself to repurpose it, even though it would be a nice upgrade for Loretta or Bobby. No one even asked about it, understanding the touchy nature of the topic.

"When?" Joey asked the Biddies with what she was sure was a stupid grin still frozen falsely on her face.

"Oh, I believe I heard the spring," Janet said. "The flowers will be so pretty that time of year. I imagine the wedding would be outdoors, but I don't know."

Of course it would be outdoors. Simone had always imagined an outdoor wedding, and so had Joey. "They will be," Joey declared, feeling everything in her downshift.

"And who knows?" Maude said. "Maybe one day Joey here will be tying the knot herself."

"It will be a big day," Birdie said, trying to turn this thing around. "I look forward to that."

Joey nodded, her words absent. The thing was, she didn't want Simone back. She was no longer in love with her and realized that theirs was a childhood romance that wasn't meant to carry into adulthood. But the anguish hit anyway, hearing about the wedding. Call it unresolved issues, PTSD—whatever it was, Joey felt the acute impact like a runaway train smashing into her unexpectedly. She took another gulp of her beer and stared at the label, feigning interest in the illustration on the packaging of what looked to be a purple phantom. The metaphor resonated as her past trauma reared its ugly head, haunting her all over again.

"Another brewski for you?" Patsy crowed, trying to lighten the mood. The Biddies heard a Tricia Yearwood song they apparently loved and headed off in a furious flurry to scoot.

"Nah." Joey waved her hand. "I think I'll finish this one and head home."

"Are you sure, Joey? Don't let this get you down. Damn it," Patsy muttered, eyeing something over Joey's shoulder. She followed Patsy's gaze to the door where she saw, speak of the damn devil, Simone and Constance smiling and holding hands. They both wore shiny new rings. There wasn't a ton to do in town at night, so the odds hadn't been awful that they'd run into each other. Still. Joey's gaze landed on Simone's, and though she tried to glance away quickly, it was too late.

"Hey, you," Simone said moments later, sliding onto the stool next to Joey's.

And here we go...

"Oh, hi. Good to see you," Joey said, doing her best to play it like she'd not noticed them walk in. "Hey, Constance," Joey tossed over her shoulder to Constance, who stood a few feet away. She waved back with a warm smile. Joey had never been able to hate her, and she'd tried. "How are the animals of Whisper Wall?"

"Passing around a stomach flu, but we press on." She raised a fist to communicate they were fighting the good fight, and Joey raised one back. Nothing had ever felt more awkward.

"How have you been?" Simone asked with extra peppy energy. "I feel like I haven't seen you in ages. Since the funeral, probably."

"Right? Time flies." She took a pull from her beer. "Just doing everything I can to put Tangle Valley on the map."

"This year's pinot." Simone made a *mind blown* gesture and let her hand rest on her chest in reverence. "Your dad was a whiz. And Maddie's taken over, yeah? That's fantastic."

Joey nodded, seizing on the opportunity to brag a little. "And we have an Italian restaurant going in next year."

Simone's brown eyes went wide. "I had no idea. You guys are killing it. But I'm sure no one is surprised."

Joey set her beer down. "Trying to."

"Well," Simone said, as if not sure what else to say. "Great running into you. I'm so glad to hear about all the great things happening."

"Your girlfriend coming by soon?" Patsy asked Joey, looking relatively proud of herself.

Joey blinked, not wanting to play this game, but now roped in. "I don't think we'll see Becca tonight, no."

Simone quirked her head. "Becca Crawford? From the resort?" Simone's smile went still.

Apparently, Constance heard the exchange and moved closer.

"She brought her new dog by. He's adorable and so incredibly smart. I had no idea you two were a thing. That's awesome."

Joey opened her mouth to answer, but the Biddies were back, and Thelma, out of breath from dancing, did it for her. "They're so cute together, too. Saw them shopping at the Nickel and the little smolders back and forth told the whole story. The next hot new couple."

"She seems really nice," Simone said, conservatively. "At least, that's what I've heard." Joey hadn't seriously dated anyone since the breakup, so this surely felt weird to Simone.

Joey, on the other hand, brightened. Thinking about Becca always seemed to have that effect. "It's early, but it's been…really good. I like Becca a lot." Joey extended a hand. "And congratulations to the two of you. I heard the news." She could be mature about this. In fact, she wanted to be.

Simone had the decency to downplay. "Oh, it's not a big deal. But you're sweet. Just thought we'd make it official." The weight of the moment settled, and she and Simone held eye contact for a beat as memories of yesteryear hovered in the air between them. That could have been them in another lifetime.

"Thanks, Joey," Constance said, breaking them out of it.

"Shall we grab a dance?" Simone said to Constance. The warm familiarity between them, while not new at all, still stung. With a happy nod, Constance reached for her hand, and Simone provided it, hanging on to Constance like they were made for each other. Maybe they were.

"Have a nice night, you crazy kids," Joey called after them. They didn't seem to hear, lost in love and celebration. Joey raised her eyebrows, sighed, and slid her credit card to Patsy, deciding to head home for the night, after all. The exchange and the news left her gutted, but even more so because she missed Becca tonight. She hoped her day had been a good one and imagined her elbows-deep in work, locked away in her office. She'd call her in the morning, and maybe they'd make plans for a lunch out together.

As she drove home, despite her desire to avoid the memories, her mind decided to double back to a day on the calendar just three years back. She saw the dress, white lace and long. She remembered the engaging scent of the peonies in her bouquet that smelled subtly of jasmine and rose. There'd been a flute and harp duo who'd played Canon in D as their attendants made their way down the aisle one at a time as everything in Joey soared. Madison had winked at Joey as she processed in advance of her. When the music shifted and it had been

Joey's turn to walk down the aisle, leaving Simone for last, she knew that this was the best day of her life. She clutched her father's arm overflowing with emotion. He smiled at her and they made their way. She took her place and waited, her heart thudding and her eyes full of happy tears. That's when it turned into one of those awful, clichéd television shows, because when it was Simone's turn, and Joey turned, waiting, no one came. The guests were on their feet, Joey was grinning, standing up at the front like an idiot in her dress and fancy hair and the professionally applied makeup Simone had insisted on for them both, but there was no Simone. She'd dug her fingernails into her hands as it became more and more apparent that this wasn't a delay. Simone wasn't coming at all. Heads swiveled in Joey's direction as her guests watched in horror. Her focus fell to the ground when the whispers started.

Days like today made her feel like they'd never truly stopped.

If Joey had had the tiniest inkling that something had been wrong, maybe the whole thing wouldn't have blindsided her so acutely. But Simone had behaved as if everything had been fine.

"I'm so sorry," Simone told her when she'd stopped by the vineyard the next day. "You didn't deserve this, Joey. This is all on me. I never should have let it come to our wedding day. I thought I could do it." She touched her heart. "But this right here? My heart? It's with someone else, and it would be wrong to pretend otherwise for another moment longer."

Constance had only been in Whisper Wall for a few months at that point. She'd joined the local practice and quietly made friends, Simone being one of them. In the months after the wedding, Joey had glimpsed them here or there, holding hands as they always did and looking lovingly into each other's eyes over dinner or drinks. To their credit, they'd always toned it down when they saw Joey, but at that point, it didn't really matter. All eyes were on her as the world watched to see how she would handle any given run-in, which had her leaving group events early or turning down invitations altogether.

"That's not you anymore," she whispered to herself as she drove, squeezing the steering wheel, searching for air. She had her friends, her job, and now Becca, who was more wonderful than she could even imagine. Life had so many new and exciting possibilities. She wiped the tears from her cheek and tried not to think about the fact that she had so very much to lose.

CHAPTER FOURTEEN

Something didn't feel right. Joey was half asleep, but even through the haze she could sense it. It crept up her neck and poked at her until she finally released any attempt at slumber. When her full faculties returned to her, she smelled the smoke first, overpowering right from the start. Her brain didn't quite know what to do with the discovery. Why did her house smell so smoky? And not the good campfire kind, either. This wasn't a dream. Something was most definitely wrong. Her smoke detector hadn't gone off, but what in the world was happening? She pushed herself out of bed just as a loud banging could be heard at her front door. Someone was trying to get in, but she had the door deadbolted. She groggily checked the spot next to her, but found it empty because, that's right, Becca had slept at her place after working late. Joey was on her own.

She followed the sound of the *bang, bang, bang* down the stairs, unlatched and opened the door to find Gabriella standing on the porch in a pair of sweatpants and a long-sleeved T-shirt, phone in hand. "There's a fire," she said immediately, her eyes wide with fear. "You weren't answering your phone, but I can see it from my place. It's the back acres. Bobby took the truck to find out. I'm on the phone with 9-1-1. Yes, Tangle Valley Vineyard," Gabriella said into the phone.

The information hit Joey fast and knocked her off her game. Her brain stuttered and attempted to understand. "There's a fire on the property? Ours?"

"Yes, and we have to hurry. We need to get Madison and Loretta and put some distance between us and the blaze."

That's when Joey's instincts kicked in. She slipped into the shoes she kept by the door and ran out of the house. She pointed to Gabriella.

"Will you wake the others and take them to the entrance? The base of the hill at minimum."

"Yes. Where are you going?"

"To help Bobby." She didn't wait for a response and took off toward her truck. They had water supplies and sprinkler systems all over the property. She heard them leap into action as she drove, windows down, which meant Bobby was on it, but would it be enough? As she neared the back acreage, the orange glow grew wider and taller. This was no small fire. What she saw in front of her was catastrophic. Her heart seized painfully as she watched the vines burn, each second lasting a lifetime. The smell of smoke overpowered her as she leapt from the cab of her truck and held a hand to shield her eyes, trying to see Bobby. She could hear multiple voices but saw no one through the thick smoke the wind blew into her eyes, burning them. She'd heard of entire acreages being taken out by wildfires, but the conditions just weren't right for that. What in the world was happening, and how did she stop it? Joey ducked low, choking on the smoke, and then finally backed away, attempting to right herself, get her bearings back before going back in.

Then she saw him.

Bobby stood on the extended ladder on his truck near the edge of the field, spraying water with their industrial hose. At first she exhaled in relief. Temporary. It was like trying to shoot down a fighter jet with a pellet gun. Her heart fell. Joey followed the perimeter of the field, finally making it close enough to communicate with her uncle. "What happened?" Joey yelled over the hiss of the blaze. She fisted her hands in her hair as she looked over the expanse of all they were losing. Each moment that passed took more and more of Tangle Valley. She saw it all slipping through her fingers like sand. As the fire raged, she flashed on the vineyard of her youth, green, vibrant, and thriving. There was nothing she could do to protect it.

The fire department arrived not long after and went to work. Neighbors gathered. They brought blankets and flashlights and hot chocolate in thermoses while they waited together as friends, as members of a hardworking community, for word. For Joey, who was forced to join them, it felt as if everything was happening in one of those horrific slow-motion sequences from a film. Madison paced, probably understanding more than anyone the larger implications for next year's yield. While Joey knew there would be immeasurable consequences to the vineyard, it was her childhood, her family's legacy that she saw up in flames. Madison saw the here and now.

"Hey, Joey. Just a quick update." She blinked in anticipation at one of the firemen she knew from school. "I think we have the fire under control. Shouldn't be long now." Jason Brewster had been two years ahead of her in high school. All the girls had had a massive crush on him, and here he was, fighting the fire that just flipped the script on Tangle Valley. She never would have imagined this moment in the psychology class they'd once taken together.

"How much did we lose?" she asked, terrified of his answer.

He hesitated, his turnout gear sooty and smudged. "It's not for me to say officially."

"What's your unofficial opinion?" she asked.

"Hard to say. Maybe seven?"

She closed her eyes and accepted the full brunt of his statement. Seven acres. This was bad. She couldn't afford to lose seven.

"You'll replant," George Mackenzie, her neighbor, said from where he stood nearby. "This is a setback, but you'll rebound. We got your back."

His wife squeezed Joey's shoulders from behind. "You're going to get through this and be just fine. You have all of us."

The other neighbors nodded and chimed in.

"Not to worry."

"Anything you need, you let us know."

Gabriella wrapped her arms around Joey. "This sucks, but I got you. We all do."

Madison stared out at the fields, which were now touched by the early morning light, a haunted look on her face. When she saw she was being watched, she sent Joey a reassuring smile. "It's okay," she mouthed. Joey nodded back but her eyes were filled with tears as grief gripped her like a vise.

But it hadn't been seven acres. Jason had been wrong. That's what she learned that afternoon as they assessed the charred remains of the back fields. It was closer to ten. On a thirty-six acre vineyard, she'd lost damn near a third of everything. She wanted so badly to wake up from this awful nightmare but couldn't seem to make it happen.

Bobby sat at her kitchen table with his hat in his hands. "Fire chief said they found a charred makeshift ashtray out there. They're thinking teenagers."

Joey shook her head and sipped what tasted like defeatist coffee.

Nothing could cheer her up. "I bet you anything it was that teenage Hollis kid from Fable Brook and his idiot friends. How many times have you chased them off the property?"

"Too many. He just laughs and ambles away. Parents don't care, either."

"Can we sue?" It was a legitimate question.

Bobby shrugged. "Can't prove anything. Not like we have security cameras in the back ten." He shook his head. "Now we gotta look ahead. It'll take years to get those acres back to what they used to be. Can we make it on twenty-six, still pay our workers, and make the restaurant happen?" he asked.

She sighed. "You're asking about money."

"Yeah. That was always my brother's department. I grow the grapes. He makes the juice and runs the business. Less grapes now. That's a real problem."

"There'll be the insurance payment, but overall, this is really going to hurt. Dad was an optimist and his policy covered the bare minimum. He didn't keep a lot in the bank, either. You can't instantly replace ten acres of mature vines." She shook her head.

"Damn well can't. Damn it." Bobby squeezed the ball cap he held in his hands, dropped his head back, seemingly in as much disbelief as she was. They'd been hit so hard lately. This latest blow didn't seem fair.

"The restaurant will have to be put on hold. I don't have any room to breathe now." Joey had never been more preoccupied with money in her entire life, and in just twenty-four hours, things had gotten exponentially worse. She knew her options. Buy grapes from another farm to replace what they would have yielded next year, or scale back their operation. A death sentence. She would need to consult with Madison first, but she had a feeling they'd be purchasing those grapes. She sighed and so did their bank account. At least she had the deal with The Jade in the works. She had guarantees on a portion of this year's bottles, and that went a long way.

"You know what? We're gonna be okay," she said, placing an arm on her uncle's shoulder. "We just have to get creative for a while."

"I trust you, Chipmunk. You know that, right?"

She nodded. "I do. You take care of those fields and let me worry about the rest."

He met her eyes tearfully, which hurt. Bobby wasn't the emotional type. He opened his mouth to speak, but no words came out. He tried again. "I see my brother in you." He pointed at her heart. "He's right there."

Her throat ached with emotion, and she placed a hand on her chest, gripping the fabric of her shirt, and nodded. Finally, out of necessity, Joey turned away, refusing to break down. She had to stay strong for the vineyard and the people who worked hard every day for it to thrive. She squeezed Bobby's hand as she passed him and made her way to the window where the smoke still hovered and clung.

❖

Becca woke feeling emotionally hungover and a little nauseous. When her conversation with Maria came rushing back to her, she remembered exactly why. The Tangle Valley deal was a no-go, and she was going to have to find a way to explain it to Joey, who needed it now more than ever. She pushed herself out of bed with a dry mouth and a headache, not looking forward to the day ahead. She made her way to her bathroom, where she turned on the local radio station to that lively couple that liked to argue way too much for the morning hours. Today, they were arguing about who brewed the best cup of coffee in town. She knew the answer. The Jade did, but the resort was unfortunately not included in the debate. She vowed to make sure that changed with time. In the end, The Bacon and Biscuit won out, which was fine.

She finished getting ready for work, gave her now blow-dried hair a final fluff with her fingertips, and reached to turn off the raucous morning show, when Darby, who was also known as Tater Tot, strangely, segued with a more serious tone. "If you're wondering about the fire last night, we are happy to report that no one was injured." Becca paused, her interest piqued. What fire? "The air is still a little smoky if you're anywhere near Tangle Valley, but that should ease in the next twenty-four hours. Keep those folks in your thoughts, will you? They'll have some rebuilding to do."

Becca went still and then sprang into action.

What in the world? She looked for her phone, fumbling now, her brain ahead of her body. She reminded herself that the report said no one was injured. She focused on that and found space enough to breathe. It didn't kill off any of the dread as she searched her phone, finding a message from Joey that was short but essentially told her not to worry, that they were all okay. Like not worrying could ever happen.

Finally, abandoning the idea of sending a message or calling, Becca kissed Skywalker, who blinked sleepily at her, and hurried to her car. The radio was right—smoke permeated the air, never fading as she drove the short distance to the vineyard. She followed the winding road through the entrance. When she emerged at the top of the hill and looked down on the land below, the view she loved was noticeably marred. The back portion of the vineyard in the distance was black, charred, and ultimately missing. She closed her eyes and let her forehead rest on the steering wheel.

This wasn't fair.

Joey and her family had been through enough.

Disbelief took its turn, followed by resolve. Joey would need her support, her shoulder for comfort, and she was prepared to give it.

A loud knock at the door tore Joey from her thoughts. She and Bobby had fallen into silence, each sitting quietly in the kitchen of the Big House, exhausted, in shock, and sad. When Joey warily answered the door, expecting a neighbor with yet another offering, she found Becca, dressed in a navy and white business suit, standing on her porch, her facial expression dialed to sorrow.

"You heard, huh?"

"I got your text. I can't believe I didn't see it until this morning. God, come here."

She didn't hesitate. Becca pulled Joey into a tight hug, and for the first time since the knock on her door last night, Joey felt like she could exhale. Air seemed accessible for the first time in hours. Becca was here, and she was smart and in charge of so much that her presence allowed Joey to relax. She hadn't fully expected that, but she leaned in to it now. She had her soft place to fall.

"It's awful," she said, when Becca released her. She gestured to the field behind Becca. "We lost ten acres. The vines are gone."

Becca nodded and cradled Joey's face. "Look at me." Joey did. "You'll grow them back. Are you sure *you're* okay?" She smoothed Joey's hair as she nodded. "What can I do? I'm taking the day off. The resort will call if there's an emergency."

Joey studied her, touched. "You can do that? You don't have to— but you can?"

Becca nodded. "Of course I can, and you need me, so I will. This is more important. Even if it's just to make you food. Are you hungry?"

"I forget what food even is." Becca didn't hesitate and headed past Joey, into the house, and straight to the stove with Joey following behind her. "Are you really going to cook right now?"

"Yes, of course I am. You can't face big things on an empty stomach. My mother taught me that, and she's the smartest person I know." She glanced around. "I'm thinking maybe an omelet? Do you have avocado? Hey, Bobby," Becca said, spotting him at the table, hat still in hand. "Would you like an omelet, too? You've had a rough day already."

He sat up straighter like the puppy he was. "Oh. Me? Sure. If you're offering."

"I definitely am."

Joey settled into one of the stools along the counter and watched in awe as Becca raided the fridge and went to work in her had-to-be-expensive business suit. It was a sight to behold. She scrambled the eggs like a boss. She diced the onions, prosciutto, avocado, and tomatoes, tossed them into a pan with tons of cheese, and just when Joey thought she couldn't be any more impressed, Becca flipped the damn omelet in the air and made two more.

"I know my business is in ruin, but I've never wanted you more." Joey blinked in exhaustion but stood by every word.

Bobby coughed at the declaration, and Becca laughed as she carried the plates to the table. The omelets had been perfectly folded. Joey's always seemed to break. But then, she wasn't as polished at anything as Becca Crawford was.

Bobby took a bite and shook his head. "Damn," he said finally, more to his plate than to either one of them. He was never a guy of too many words, so the ones he said mattered. He looked from Becca to Joey and back again, suddenly aware of himself. "Gonna take this out on the porch and get some air if that's okay. See how smoky it still is." They nodded, setting him free. "Thanks for the killer breakfast," he said, raising his plate to Becca. He scurried out of there at lightning speed.

"It's hard for him to see me date," Joey informed Becca. "I'm still seven years old in his eyes."

Becca sat back in her chair. "What would your dad think of me? Sometimes I wonder about that."

Joey paused, a bite of omelet halfway to her mouth. "He'd have to get past the evil empire thing, but after that, he would think you're a pretty cool chick. That I'd leveled up."

Becca pressed her lips around her fork and elegantly slid a bite of her omelet into her mouth. Joey watched, enjoying the view. Becca's mouth was a favorite, even when her brain could barely function. "Is that what you think?" Becca asked, sitting back in her chair. "That I'm a cool chick? I had no idea."

Joey didn't hold back. "Becca, you are the coolest chick I've ever met. That's why I take my clothes off whenever you blink in my direction, and don't think that's not unnerving for me. God, this is good." She shook her head at her plate. "Who knew that omelets help curb devastation?"

"I did. What else can I get you? A nap? Fuzzy slippers? A distraction? I can be that, too, sweetie. Just tell me what you need."

Joey sighed and met Becca's gaze. "Nothing. Just you. That's the craziest part. Having you here makes a real difference."

"I'm glad. And I'm not going anywhere." She pushed her plate to the side, leaving half of her omelet uneaten, which was a crime in this house. Joey let it go. "What do we have to accomplish?"

Joey thought on it, still amazed that the day went on in spite of what had happened. "Well, Loretta doesn't want to close the tasting room. She thinks it's important that we let everyone know we're okay and still open for business. I imagine lots will be stopping in to check things out. Small towns tend to be more curious. Might as well sell them a glass of wine."

"I like the plan."

"Speaking of enterprising, I want to thank you again for putting together that deal with the resort. I'm forcing myself to concentrate on it. It was the one thing that made me feel we could survive all of this. Can you imagine? The Jade, the entity I hated more than anything, is now my savior?" She shook her head. "Life is so unpredictable."

"Oh," Becca said, brushing past the sentiment, "not a big deal."

"It is." Joey grinned. "So thank you." She leaned across the table and kissed Becca, who gave her hand a yank, pulling Joey into her lap where they kissed some more. "I like this jacket," Joey said, running her thumbs over the lapels and using them to pull Becca back in again.

"Put it to work," Becca murmured around the kiss. "I'm yours today, boss lady."

"Seriously?" Another kiss. "You want to pour Tangle Valley wine? We're a scandal now. Well, I should say, *again*."

"It's my dream to pour scandalous wine." Becca kissed the soft spot just under her jaw.

"Hired." She pressed her center against Becca's thigh. "Maybe there is something to this distraction line of thinking. I could lose myself in you for hours. Forget the realities of the world, of today."

Becca passed her an amused look. "I'm available for that kind of hiring as well."

Joey felt that offer low in her body and checked the clock. She smiled ruefully. "We open in an hour, and I need to shower. Later?"

"Of course. I'll be around."

Joey dove in for another long, lingering, and breathtaking kiss that would have to hold her over until later. She climbed off Becca's lap and carried her plate to the sink, scarfing the rest of her omelet as she walked. "Back in fifteen," she told Becca, who had already started gathering the dishes for washing.

"Take your time," Becca said, holding up a plate. "I got this."

Once Joey was alone and standing beneath the hot water stream, the details of the day came rushing back, and the weight upon her shoulders rose to an unbearable level. She gripped the walls for support. Her thoughts felt scattered and disjointed as if pelting her like missiles in a video game. She thought of her father, the fire, stupid Caleb Hollis from Fable Brook, who likely caused this whole thing with his buddies, how wonderful Madison and Gabriella had been last night, and about Becca and The Jade. Her heart swelled with gratitude for Becca, who today had proved to truly have her back. As she stepped out of the shower, she gave herself a stern pep talk. She would reel in those thoughts and focus on only what she had immediately ahead of her. And today, that meant her customers in the tasting room.

An hour later, Loretta smiled at Joey from behind the marble tasting counter. "I told you they'd come."

"You weren't wrong. You can always count on the folks in Whisper Wall."

Whether the town wanted to sneak a peek at the damage or simply support the vineyard during a difficult stretch, they'd certainly shown up in droves. Add them to the usual handful of tourists, and the tasting room was hopping. Joey had called in one of their part-timers, Evan, and had even taken Becca up on her offer to pour, given they were slammed. Between the four of them, they conducted a multitude of tastings, and sales by the glass. Outside, Gabriella had fired up a batch of amazing pumpkin ravioli and spicy calamari that had the smell of smoke taking second place to her fantastic aromas. The line at her truck now stretched past the seating area and showed little sign of easing up. It helped patch up Joey's soul, seeing the outpouring of support.

"This one is my favorite. Give it a whirl," she heard Becca tell the Biddies, her current customers. They'd gathered around, clutching their glasses, ready to listen intently to the tasting notes Becca had to offer. "The pinot noir is what we're known for."

"But you're the manager of that new resort," Maude pointed out. "You moonlighting?"

"She's helping her girlfriend," Thelma supplied knowledgeably. "They're hot and heavy, remember?"

"You looked so pretty at that grand opening with all the cookies and bubbly," Birdie chimed in.

"You're correct. I am the manager of The Jade," Becca told them. "But I love to come out to Tangle Valley whenever I can. Gives me a chance to get out in the community and help out our neighbors. And I get to see Joey, too."

Joey, from off to the side, suppressed a grin.

Thelma leaned in. Her hair carried a definite blue tinge that had not been there the last time Joey had seen her at the Scoot. "Terrible about the fire. So glad no one was hurt." Thelma meant what she said, but Joey knew the fire was also good gossip that would keep the Biddies chatting for the next week. She longed for a time when the Wilder family, or at least what was left of it, wasn't the sympathetic talk of the town.

"I feel the same way," Becca said and pointed to their glasses as she referenced the cheat sheet Joey had supplied her with. "This particular wine is the Tangle Valley crown jewel, and a multiple gold medal winner." She did the same ta-da gesture with her fingers that Joey had executed the first day they met, which made Joey laugh with pride. She loved that it had resonated with Becca. But then again, Joey also remembered everything about that first day herself. It was just nice to hear that Becca did, too.

Joey made her way down the bar to get another group of new arrivals started. They were from California and so sorry to hear about the fire. As she walked them through the tasting, she couldn't help but steal glances at Becca. Ever the professional. Still wearing her pin-striped business suit. Working in Joey's tasting room.

The woman was kind, sexy, and hardworking, it turned out. She also showed up on your doorstep and made a killer omelet when you didn't even realize you needed one. In the midst of a day that had Joey questioning the universe, Becca, she realized, was a blessing to count.

Chapter Fifteen

Becca sat on the steps leading to the Big House. The pinks of the setting sun were almost too beautiful for her heart to handle as she stared at the sky above the expanse of quiet farmland. She had no right to enjoy that sunset. Not while she sat there holding on to a piece of important information she should have divulged nearly two weeks ago now. She hadn't had the courage or the right words to do so with Joey still in recovery mode from the fire. She knew that it had been the wrong move to wait. The guilt practically consumed her, and she realized she had to give the news to Joey. She never should have let this much time pass, but now that she had, her crime was exponentially worse.

She threw the ratty tennis ball for Sky and watched as he tore off through the field, galloping between the rows of sleeping vines, easily retrieved the ball, and bounded back with extra height in his step. "Nice one, buddy." She gave him a good scrubbing behind his ears, knowing how he liked a little extra pressure.

"Sky, you're getting too good," a voice said. "The Olympics are going to call us up, looking for you."

Becca turned and grinned at Gabriella, who approached from the pathway that led to the cottages. "He says he was born to race through wine country. He's a wine dog now."

"Then he hit the jackpot at this place. I have some Italian sausage in my pocket."

Becca quirked her head. "Is that a come-on?"

Gabriella laughed. "It should be. For the dog. Is that okay?"

"Of course. He's going to be even more in love with you now."

Gabriella held out her hand, and Skywalker raced over like he'd won the sausage lottery. He took the chunk Gabriella offered and did his side-to-side dance with his front paws. Gabriella pointed at him. "He's got nightclub skills."

"One of his many talents."

Gabriella joined Becca on the stairs. "You'll be happy to know that I booked a massage at The Jade for later this week."

Becca grinned. "That's fantastic. Marjorie is in charge over there, and I'll make sure she knows you're a friend and valued neighbor."

Gabriella sat a little bit taller. She always brought such a contagious sparkle that it made being in her orbit lots of fun. "That makes me feel incredibly fancy." She gestured to her shoulders. "It's my traps that are aching. I love the truck, but the fast turnaround on the food really takes its toll after a while."

"Does she have a name?"

"You haven't heard? I can safely report that she's Jolene." Gabriella then went on to belt a couple lines of the song, surprising Becca with her beautiful singing voice.

Good God. She pointed at Gabriella. "I love the name and applaud it, but I'm really more pulled in by those pipes. You never mentioned you could sing."

"You never asked."

Becca shook her head. "A singing chef. Tangle Valley just gets more and more interesting, in a good way."

"You're kind to say so. Now, what's going on with you?"

"Me?" Becca squinted. "What do you mean?"

Gabriella moved her pointer finger in a circle. "Your aura, your vibe. Everything feels heavier. Is it work? Homesickness? Please tell me you're not unhappy with how things are going with you and Joey." She tented her hands under her chin. "You guys are the cutest."

"Definitely not. I like her a lot."

"Thank God."

Becca sighed, knowing exactly what it was. She was keeping a secret from Joey and she couldn't stand it.

"Then what is it?" Gabriella asked. "You have a friend in me, you know? Both new transplants to town and all. We gotta stick together."

She met Gabriella's sincere gaze and knew it was true. In that moment, something in her gave way, and after carrying the information around for two weeks now, she had to release it. "Okay. Here goes."

"Listening."

"Do you know the agreement we were working toward, designating Tangle Valley as the official house wine of The Jade?"

"Yes, which is thrilling." Gabriella sat taller. "I can imagine that would mean lots of extra attention for the vineyard. Plus"—she held out her hand to announce a given—"the wine orders themselves."

"It fell through." The words came tumbling out, and Becca jammed her fingers in her hair.

Gabriella blinked. "Oh no," she said quietly.

Becca felt nauseous all over again. She leaned over and wrapped her arms around her knees. "It's awful. Especially since I was stupid enough to let Joey think it was virtually a done deal. I thought it would be."

"Oh, Becca. No. This is bad." She looked behind them, up at the Big House. "Joey is holding on to that deal like it's the one good thing this place has going for it."

She covered her eyes. "I know. And I don't know how to fix it."

Madison came around the side of the house, likely from the barrel room where she'd been checking the tanks. "Hey, guys. Is this day over yet?" Sky dropped a tennis ball at her feet and she gave it an impressive throw. He then turned into the gazelle he was apparently born to be, and Madison took a seat on one of the lower stairs. "What have I missed?" Her dark blue eyes looked to them curiously.

"The Jade isn't going through with the exclusive deal with us, and Becca can't seem to break it to Joey."

The smile faded from Madison's face. For a minute she didn't say anything at all, and it killed Becca. Each of these reactions was only a preview of what she could expect when she told Joey. Not only that, but she felt exponentially more awful because she'd told Joey's best friends first, which had been the total wrong order.

"Why?" Madison asked, bewildered. "This is going to be a blow."

Becca shook her head. "Our VP, the one who oversees the restaurants, did some research and liked what he saw from Fable Brook. Felt they had a larger reach nationally."

"Well, that's because they're four times our size, but who cares about distribution anyway? I though the whole point was to feature good local wine? Emphasis on good."

"They think Fable Brook does both."

"They don't," Madison said. "And I'm not being biased in the least. I know wine, and I know what crap Fable Brook has been turning out the past few years. Notice they don't even bother entering competitions anymore."

"I'm sure corporate doesn't know any of that. But I'm not sure they care."

Gabriella looked crestfallen, her hazel eyes sorrowful. Madison shook her head in anger. Becca wanted to crawl into a hole.

"You have to tell Joey," Gabriella said, lightly touching Becca's knee.

"I just wanted to give her a little time that was free from any more bad news."

"You can't protect her from this," Madison stated matter-of-factly, setting emotion aside. "It's her business. Her life. She needs to know what cards we're dealt, so we can make plans. Without the money from The Jade, she'll have to rethink everything. No restaurant. No expansion. Hell, we'll barely be able to pay our employees." She stood and walked a few feet away in the direction of the vines, speaking quietly. "Fucking Fable Brook. Seriously?"

Becca swallowed and nodded numbly. "Yeah. Okay. I'll tell Joey. I have to."

❖

The sweet smell of Christmas spices, the sounds of holiday carols, and tidings of good cheer were not only present, but the stars of the show that Saturday in Whisper Wall, Oregon. Wassail Fest was bigger and better this year than ever before, and Joey was thrilled to be right in the middle of it, selling hot mulled wine hand over fist. When she'd set up the Tangle Valley booth earlier in the day, she'd done a quick count of vendors on the map she'd been supplied and noticed ten to twelve new ones. Their little town was certainly growing, and she looked forward to the chance to peruse them all later that night when her shift ended.

The streets in the center of town were full of locals and tourists alike, all flooding the area for one very important reason: the celebration of wassail, a beloved warm beverage of the holidays, and pretty much any and all other warm beverages known to man.

Joey'd been working the Tangle Valley booth since the late morning, smiling and selling and reminding everyone she could to stop by the vineyard. The weather had certainly helped the holiday spirit, turning up a chilly afternoon and now evening. With the sun down and the millions of twinkly lights decorating anything in the streets that would stand still, the celebration felt crisp and vibrant. Dickensian carolers in top hats and bonnets strolled the streets, pausing here and there to offer a perfectly harmonized performance. She saw Clementine among them, which made her grin to herself. As someone who was relatively quiet, it didn't seem like Clem's normal fare to wear a bonnet and sing from a songbook, but she was actually quite good and, in an adorable turn of events, seemed to really enjoy it, too.

"For you," Joey said to her friend, who seemed to be on a break between carols. "On the house."

"Are you sure?" Clementine asked. Joey knew she couldn't make much money at The Bacon and Biscuit, and that's what friends were for.

"Of course," Joey said, waving her off. "You guys have kept me entertained and in the holiday spirit all night. Least I can do for the smile you put on my face."

Clem lifted her cup. "Very kind of you. Come by the Biscuit and I'll set you up."

Joey grinned at her. "Deal. But I want my biscuit extra warm."

"You get any time off to enjoy the festival?" Clem asked, sipping the warm wine. "Whoa. This hits the spot."

"Yep. In about twenty minutes, Scott and I"—she gestured to one of her part-timers—"are off the clock, and Loretta and Serena will take over until we close up. Scott will come back and handle that."

"Perfect. And thanks for this. I better fall in line for 'We Wish You a Merry Christmas.'" Clementine lifted her cup as she headed off with her perfectly coifed group for more caroling.

When Loretta arrived to take custody of the booth, Joey rejoiced. She'd always enjoyed Wassail Fest, but this year she'd meet up with Becca, and that meant exploring it through her eyes. There was a carnival set up a couple blocks over in the grassy area adjacent to Pizzamino's, the greasiest pizza joint known to man. She was scheduled to meet Becca, Madison, and Gabriella on the carnival grounds to hopefully play a little Skee-Ball and get their photo taken in the snow globe. What Joey had her heart set on? A giant s'more! She wondered how Becca felt about them. Maybe they'd share. The concept of Becca with marshmallow and chocolate all over her made Joey grin.

As she walked the streets of the festival, she purposefully took in the pink-cheeked, smiling faces of everyone she passed. Everyone seemed so much friendlier during the holidays, and that helped, well, everything. Joey smiled back, snuggling into her puffy purple jacket. It had been a decent three weeks since the fire, and she was just starting to breathe again. Christmas was now upon them, just four days away, and if she focused on that, she could hold on to the newfound air. Plus, she found herself clinging to every last happy thing in her life, and trying desperately not to miss her father too much. She'd never experienced a Christmas without his loud *Ho, ho, ho* whenever she walked into the Big House, or the sound of his guitar strumming carols when he hadn't heard her enter and was simply singing for himself. Instead of embracing the tears all the time, Joey looked harder at her blessings. This festival was one of them.

She passed booths selling popcorn, funnel cake, banana bread, and even freshly smoked brisket plates that made her mouth water. The carolers sang "White Christmas" next from atop the makeshift stage in the center of the festivities. She stood a moment and listened by herself, letting the music envelop her. Powell Rogers from the car dealership sang bass beneath a top hat and muttonchops, like he was born to perform.

Finally, she moved on and turned the corner and headed into the carnival section of the festival. She spotted Becca and her friends right off, standing a few feet away from The Scrambler. The riders on board screamed with horrified delight as they were whisked forward and then back and around again at a high rate of speed. Gabriella waved a giant turkey leg at her and leapt in the air to say hello. Madison grinned from beneath an adorable wool cap that had her curls on display as they tumbled down her back, and there was Becca, waiting patiently with two cups of hot chocolate, each under a pile of whipped cream she knew for a fact was homemade by Edith McHugh, who had perfected the art. Everyone talked about her prowess with a whisk.

"Funny meeting you three here," Joey said, strolling up, hands in her pockets. She'd found her people and relaxed automatically.

"For you," Becca said, handing one of the hot chocolates off to Joey with a happy smile.

"It's like you read my mind. Chocolate all the way."

Becca grinned and looked skyward. "It's possible I've spent a little time with you lately."

Joey narrowed her gaze. "I think I've been accused of chocolate overindulgence."

"Well, you did eat about eleven of Loretta's homemade chocolate chunk Santa cookies before the rest of them even made it to the platter," Gabriella said, as if piecing together a puzzle.

"That's true," Joey said nonchalantly. "I stand by and heartily subscribe to the you snooze, you lose philosophy."

Madison gaped. "Except it was nine a.m., and none of us had even been by yet."

"I don't see the problem."

Becca laughed and pointed at Joey. "First of all, you definitely have one. Secondly, you have whipped cream on your nose, which makes just about anything forgivable."

Joey knew very well that if they weren't in public, Becca would have kissed that whipped cream away for her, so she let herself imagine it even if only for a moment, because where would *that* lead them? She was pretty sure the answer was naked in front of the fireplace, where they'd spent a lot of time lately. The heat from the daydream did more to warm her than her coat and gloves had done all day. She removed the whipped cream from her nose with a laugh and turned to her friends. "Where to next?"

"Gabriella wants to visit the reindeer stable at the North Pole," Madison said and exchanged a wistful look with Joey.

Joey grinned because it had been her and Madison's favorite attraction when they were kids. They would stand in awe at how realistic the stables seemed, with each reindeer able to actually move. As an adult, she could see the repetition in those movements and the slight stutters in the mechanics that she'd been oblivious to as a child. Back then, the stable was pure magic, and she and Maddie would sit and watch for long stretches. She was excited to share the stable with the others now. She turned to Gabriella. "Okay, but understand that Comet is the superior reindeer. You can tell just by watching the display and his adorable eyes."

Madison scoffed. "You say that every year, buddygirl, but you've clearly never paid attention to Dasher, who is watching over all the others like a sweet big brother. Do not let Comet distract you from the main idea."

Gabriella jumped in with a hand out. "Had no idea there was a reindeer war afoot."

"How could there not be if she thinks Comet is the star?" Madison asked in seriousness.

"I can't even with you," Joey said, shaking her head.

Becca laughed and opened her mouth to speak just as Martin Hollis placed a hand on her arm. Joey squinted. Martin, who she'd never liked, grinned widely at Becca. "Ms. Crawford, just wanted to tell you how over the moon we are about partnering with you." He nodded at the others. "Joey," he said respectfully. But she was too busy decoding what he'd just said.

"Thank you," Becca said, pursing her lips. Except she wasn't a lip purser. "I hope you have a nice night."

Martin nodded happily and set off with his wife, Beverly, arm in arm with a skip in their step. She watched after them. They looked like cats who'd been licking the cream. "What was that all about?" Joey asked with a laugh. But the look on Becca's face told Joey there was nothing funny about it.

"Oh, um, stuff for The Jade." Becca's face was red.

"What kind of stuff?" Joey asked. She could feel her friends' eyes on them.

"Maybe that's something we could talk about later," Becca said gently.

Something felt wildly off, and Joey couldn't quite put her finger on what it was, but she was close. She stared off after Martin and Bev, who—if she hadn't been mistaken—had just gloated about something. They were on a high for two people who never smiled a lot and put up with a delinquent son. "Can we talk about it now, though?" Gabriella and Madison seemed to fade away. Whether that was simply Joey's perception or if they actually did give them space wasn't clear. She was too focused on the foreboding sense of dread that seemed to hover over her, a breath away.

Becca rolled her lips in. Joey had never seen her do that before either, which said she was wildly uncomfortable. "Joey," Becca said carefully. Another bad sign.

"Just tell me what's wrong, okay? I'm a big girl." She smiled and shrugged like this was not a big deal. Deep down, she feared she was wrong but couldn't quite look at it head-on. The sense of dread took a step closer, towering over her now.

Becca blinked, looked away and then back at Joey, meeting her gaze. "I wasn't able to make the deal between Tangle Valley and The Jade come to fruition the way I thought I could."

"Oh," Joey said. The implications were upon her immediately. Fuck. This was bad. No, awful. She felt like the air had been kicked right out of her. Those big orders wouldn't be coming their way. The vineyard's name wouldn't be dropped to every guest who sat down for a glass of wine. With the fire, and the lackluster insurance payout, which turned out to be even smaller than she'd expected, what was she supposed to do?

"Joey, I'm really sorry. We'll, of course, still carry the wine."

"I don't understand," Joey said, finally. "You told me it was as good as done."

Becca shifted her weight. "It was. I thought. They loved the concept of featuring a local winery."

"Until they didn't."

Becca hesitated. "No, that's still true." That's when Joey remembered Martin Hollis and his grin. "They just decided to go with Fable Brook instead."

"Fable Brook." Joey blinked and swiveled her head in the direction she'd seen the Hollises walk. "Tell me why?" It didn't add up. "Why in the world would they choose Fable Brook over our wine? It pales in comparison. No character at all."

Becca's voice sounded flat when she replied, "Corporate did their own research and liked that Fable Brook had broader distribution."

This couldn't be the end of it. Joey went into recovery mode, the wheels in her head turning, searching for anything she could do to fix this. "Can I put together a proposal myself? Highlight for them all the ways we're the better choice? I can have it ready in three days. Sooner even, if they need it."

Becca shook her head, stricken. "It's too late for that. They'll reevaluate once the contract is up in a couple of years. For now, it's a dead end, and I feel responsible." Joey had never seen Becca looking so disappointed, but it was as if her brain couldn't focus on that right now. She'd been punched in the eye, and she had to figure out how to see through it first.

Joey let one arm drop, having trouble stomaching the hot chocolate. Her troubles at the vineyard just tripled. A new thought hit. She looked up at Becca, the dread now at full intensity. Her hands went numb, and her stomach turned over. "When did you find out? Yesterday? And you didn't say a word."

"No. Um, I don't think I remember the exact day."

Joey shrugged. "Approximately, then."

There was a long pause. Becca seemed to make a difficult decision.

"Just before the fire," she said quietly. Joey had to replay the sentence to be sure she'd heard it correctly over the sounds of the rides, music, and chatter. But there'd been no mistake.

"That was weeks ago. Becca..." She shook her head in disbelief.

"I wanted to get through the holidays. Let you enjoy them. I figured we'd talk about it after that."

"*You. Figured.*"

Gabriella stepped forward. "She wanted to tell you. I can vouch for that. She was devastated."

Joey stared hard at her friends. "You knew?" She looked to Madison. "Did you?"

Madison slid her hands into the back pockets of her jeans and nodded, regretfully.

And there it was. Her ears buzzed unpleasantly. "You all knew. Of course you did. Why is it always me who ends up looking the sucker? The putz?" she asked the three of them. She nodded a few times as understanding began to rain down.

"I'm really sorry, and no, you're absolutely not a sucker," Becca said.

"Then why do I feel so foolish? Why do I *always* end up feeling foolish? You told my friends. You knew for weeks. Everyone's been waiting for poor Joey to learn the bad news. I'm a joke all over again."

"No, it's not like that at all." Becca took a step forward but Joey dodged her outstretched hand.

"Please don't," she said, feeling the need to protect herself even from an innocent touch. She set her hot chocolate down on the bench beside them, folded her arms, and faced them. "I'll tell you one thing. I don't want to be that girl. I refuse to be. Yet here I am. Poor little Joey." She turned to her friends and back to Becca. "I don't really think I'm up for the festival after all. You all should enjoy it, though."

She walked away without waiting for a response. She heard Gabriella call after her, and then Madison's voice intervening, probably telling her what she knew well about Joey, that she'd need this time on her own.

Joey went home, straight to her bedroom, and stood at the window with the lights off. She felt disappointed, betrayed, and pathetic. All things she'd experienced in her life before, only proving her point that when you put yourself out there, it always came back to bite you. *Always.* Sure, this wasn't a betrayal of the magnitude that she'd experienced with Simone, but it was a sharp reminder of why she'd remained on her own for so long. Tonight was a perfect tap on the shoulder that she'd slipped into old habits that would never serve her well.

After ignoring another apology and check-in message from Becca followed by about eight more, Joey slid into bed. It was strangely empty tonight, but she didn't lament the space. She forced herself to embrace it, instead, and remember why maybe, just maybe, it was better that way.

❖

"You're still here."

Becca looked up at Madison from her spot on the bench. She wasn't sure how long she'd been sitting there alone, two cups of cold hot chocolate next to her, but the crowds had died down and some of the vendors were in cleanup mode. They must have been close to the end of the fest.

"When I downshift, I never quite know what to do with myself."

Madison took a seat and held up the two cups. Becca nodded and Madison tossed them into the nearby trash can. "What's downshifting?" Madison asked.

"Oh. It's, uh, when something jarring happens and you lose your normal ability to handle it." She looked over at Madison. "Have you ever been in an argument and all of sudden you can't seem to make your brain work because your emotions took over? The words to express yourself just aren't there?"

"Oh yeah. Once I had this awful boss, an incredibly sexist vineyard manager with the worst patchy facial hair I've ever seen. I'd lie in bed at night and imagine all the amazing things I'd say to him if I had the chance. I finally got it. We had a blowup that had been a long time coming, and I couldn't remember a single one of them."

"Yes." Becca nodded. "That's because you'd downshifted."

A pause. "When will you upshift?" she asked. Becca realized Madison possessed a no-nonsense way about her that she found refreshing. She wasn't dramatic or falling all over herself to comfort Becca or stand up for Joey. She was just there as a solid friend.

"Still waiting to find out."

They sat in silence a while longer, watching the waning foot traffic. Lots of giggly folks passed by on their way home after too much of the hard wassail, clutching each other with smiles on their faces. Becca had once imagined that might be how their night would end, too, after a little too much fun. Her heart ached that it hadn't.

"You know this has very little to do with the actual deal falling through," Madison said, once a loud group had passed.

Becca nodded. "I do now. After seeing the look on her face. God."

"She'd never say it out loud, but Joey is terrified of letting someone in, giving them enough power to hurt her. She's a wounded bird, and we just gave her a taste of those old wounds."

"Correction. *I* did."

Madison didn't argue, probably because this was all at Becca's hands. She could have been up-front about the deal falling through from the very moment she found out. It certainly would have been more in line with her character. "Is she going to forgive me?" she asked, unable to look at Madison, afraid of her response.

The hesitation said a lot. "She might just need time. This is Joey we're talking about, and she seems strong, but she's a frightened kitten underneath."

The Christmas music had stopped, as had the carousing. The nearby rides were shut down, their whirring sound eerily absent. The festival was quiet, headed to bed for another year. With nothing left to do, Becca stood, lost and gutted.

"I guess I'll go home, love on my dog, and hope tomorrow is better."

"Throw his ball for me, okay?"

Becca nodded and headed off down the street, as city workers chased down wayward trash. The end of a party, which felt like the perfect metaphor for what was happening in her life at this very moment. She shoved her hands into her pockets and walked to her car feeling sad, lonely, and guilt ridden.

CHAPTER SIXTEEN

Becca sat on the porch on a gorgeous Christmas Eve morning. Inside, frustration reigned. She'd accepted the blown-off text messages, respected Joey's request for time on her own, but this had now gone on for too long. With another shake of her head, she knocked on the door to the Big House. This would be her third attempt to get Joey to answer the damn door. She knew she was inside. Loretta had told her as much when she'd stopped first into the tasting room, and Bobby had confirmed when she'd passed him on the path there. Nothing felt right when she and Joey were at odds. Becca needed to fix this and find a way for Joey to understand that she was safe.

"Joey. Please answer the door. I've given you space. I've done what you've asked. Now it's time to have a conversation." A pause. She felt herself begin to crumble. "I miss you, damn it." She knocked again harder, to no avail, and let her palm rest on the oak door. Somehow that made her feel closer to Joey, who she longed for so much it physically hurt. "I know you're angry at me, and you have a right to be. But I want a chance to look you in the eye and apologize." Nothing. "And I don't want to complain, but it happens to be really, really cold out here. I'm starting to not be able to feel my fingers."

"Where are your gloves?" a quiet voice asked on the other side of the door. Joey. Becca grinned and stroked the wood beneath her fingertips.

"I left them in my car because I'm an idiot."

A moment later, the lock clicked, and she heard footsteps retreat. Apparently, Joey had a soft spot for the frozen. Becca didn't hesitate and let herself inside. The house was warm and smoky, which meant a fire burned in the fireplace. She sequestered her memories of the wonderful conversations they'd had in front of it, not to mention more intimate endeavors. She found Joey leaning against the kitchen counter, arms folded, waiting for Becca. She honestly had no idea what she'd find when she did come face-to-face with Joey, but the woman eyeing her now seemed put together, calm, and confident. Her hair was pulled back in a clip, and lazy waves fell around her shoulders. Her thin maroon sweater had been paired with a plaid scarf. In fact, Joey looked beautiful and polished. No broken human in sight. That had to bode well for them, right? Joey had rebounded.

"Thank you for letting me in. I feel like we haven't talked in years." She met Joey's gaze sincerely. "I've hated every second of it."

Joey nodded. "I've been pushing the limit. Sometimes I do that. I shouldn't have ignored your messages for so long."

"You pushing it? You don't say?" Becca grinned, trying for levity and failing. She held up a hand. "It's okay. I know I deserve it. In fact—"

"Before you say anything more, you don't have to apologize. You've said you were sorry about a million times on my voice mail. We can stipulate it as fact."

Becca came around the island and leaned against the counter next to Joey, who felt so far away still. Becca hated it. "All the same, I'm sorry. I want to say so looking straight into your eyes." Joey glanced away uncomfortably. "I hate that the deal didn't happen, and I hate even more that I held that information back. I think I was worried about you and was, in a misguided sense, trying to protect you from it for as long as possible, and now I feel like such an idiot for it."

"Yeah, that's the part that gets me," Joey said, turning back to her. "I'm not a child. You don't have to fear how I'm going to react. Why does everyone do that? I'm stronger than I'd ever imagined."

"I know you are. I didn't mean to insinuate otherwise."

Joey kept going, "And I like you, Becca. A lot. But I don't want to get caught up." She said the words as if she was deciding that maybe she wasn't in the mood for ice cream after all. That casual. That nonchalant. How was it that easy?

Becca was stunned and stuttered, her thoughts suspended, "Get caught up," she repeated, not fully absorbing the meaning behind the words.

"I know myself, and I know that this isn't going to work for me." Joey gestured between them. "So why put off the inevitable? I want us both to be happy, and that means I have to remove myself from this equation."

"No, you don't." Becca stared at Joey hard. "I don't understand what's happening right now. This has all been blown out of proportion. You're ending it? Us? Because of a business deal that fell through? No. Joey, sweetheart, let's just—"

"I don't think we're in a place for nicknames." Her voice was unrecognizable.

"Why are you saying it like you're an instructor and I'm a student that you're educating? We know each other. We're us. Talk to me like I'm Becca. What we have is different. Rare. Haven't you felt it, too?"

Joey sighed. "The problem is that it always ends the same, and I let myself forget that because I was having a good time with you, falling for the fairy tale all over again."

"I'm not Simone."

"No. But you would be."

"God." Becca couldn't believe what she was hearing. "Give me some credit. Hell, give the larger world some. Not everyone is going to burn you."

"Isn't that what I did the past few months? Give you credit." Joey smiled ruefully as if the whole thing had been a learning experience, when what they had was so much more. "Becca."

"Yeah?" There was that delicate, proper voice again. This didn't feel like Joey, but Becca didn't know how to break through this carefully crafted exterior.

"I don't bear you any ill will. I just have to focus on taking care of things around here. Figuring out how to pull us out of trouble again. I have a restaurant to build, a budget to reinvent, and wine to process. Sitting around wondering when the second shoe is going to drop is exhausting, so…" Her eyes shifted behind Becca to the door.

"Who *are* you right now? Joey, please. Talk to me." It was like the old Joey had been swallowed up, and in her place was someone Becca didn't for a second recognize or like. Her stomach churned, and the walls seemed to be moving in on her. She hadn't expected any of this, not even close.

"I already did. And I have things to do."

Unbelievable. "Are you asking me to leave?"

"I think it would be best, given the difficult nature of all of this."

"The difficult nature of a *breakup*, you mean." They stared at each other until Becca's gaze finally fell to the floor. "I'm going to say something first."

Joey nodded. "I think that's fair."

"This is not what I want. Hell, it's not even in the same stratosphere, but if you don't want me in your life anymore, in your bed, your heart, then I guess I have no choice but to leave." She gestured between them. "But I've never had this with someone before. I've never in my life felt this way, and I know deep down that means something." She heard her voice weaken as she said the words. The floor felt like it was giving way beneath her. Her voice began to crack. "And if you're telling me that we're over, then I don't know what I'm supposed to do now. What do I do?"

She saw something shift in Joey's demeanor, a crack in the veneer that lasted only a moment before she straightened, back on track. "You're going to be fine. You're Becca Crawford."

Becca blinked at her, mystified and confused as to where her Joey had gone. She'd give anything to locate her again. She nodded, held Joey's stare, and with her broken heart in tow, headed for the door. She closed it behind her and stood stock-still on the porch. She stared out at the world in front of her and found it hard to put one foot in front of the other. Her vision blurred as she made her way to the Juke. Only once she was inside did she let herself feel it all fully. She placed her head on the steering wheel and cried silently as the sun shone above like it was any other day. As she drove from the dusty parking lot to the hilltop exit of the vineyard, she paused and looked back on its beauty one last time.

She took a picture in her mind, nodded, and drove home in shaky silence.

❖

Inside Josephine Wilder a battle waged like none she'd ever experienced. She wanted nothing more than to run after Becca, bury her face on Becca's shoulder, into the soft strands of her hair, and let Becca take care of the rest. The other half of Joey, the one in careful control now, wouldn't allow that to happen. She gripped the countertop instead and stared down the hallway to the front door that now stood empty. Becca was the one person she simply couldn't turn to anymore. She wouldn't. When those familiar trappings had popped up again, Joey was out. She had to be. She'd lived through the devastation that was Simone and vowed to be smarter because of it. She'd been incredibly successful. Even when Becca walked into her life, she'd proceeded cautiously…until she hadn't. She'd gotten caught up. That was her mistake, letting herself get lost in the everyday happiness until the awful moment hit and reminded her of all that was at stake.

Get out now were the three words that played like an annoying song in her head since the night of the festival. She hated that it hurt Becca so much. The decision hurt her as well, but she wouldn't allow herself to feel it. It was on its way, though—the tidal wave of emotion she wouldn't be able to hold at bay any longer approached like an inevitable day on the calendar.

To Joey's surprise, the front door opened and her heart leapt at the thought of Becca returning. Madison stalked down the hallway instead.

"So? What happened?" she asked. "I saw Becca get in her car and leave. Is she coming back with doughnuts? Say yes. I could use a cruller."

Joey shook her head, biting the inside of her lip hard, a coping mechanism. The pain distracted her from what would inevitably be worse.

Madison placed her hands on her hips. "Jo. What did you do?"

She held up a hand. "Please don't start on me." She moved to the one dirty dish in the sink and made a show of directing her focus there. Yep. That bowl definitely needed scrubbing. So much important scrubbing to do.

Madison eyed her in disbelief. "I thought after a few days, you'd relax out of this defensive position you've got going."

"I think that's just called my life." She paused mid-scrub. "Some people like roller coasters. Thrilling slasher films. Things that get their heart pumping. They do well with the twists and turns. I don't." She scrubbed away, harder. "I'm a happier person when out of the fast lane."

"A relationship is hardly the fast lane. It's part of being human. Stop murdering the bowl. The bowl is an innocent."

Joey scrubbed ferociously, taking out all of the frustration she felt at herself, Becca, and the universe on that poor defenseless dish. Finally, she pushed away from the sink, physically exhausted.

"You okay?" Madison asked quietly, as they stood listening to Joey gasp for air.

"I'm fine," she said, stalking toward the master bedroom.

"You're also a liar," Maddie said, following after her and not giving an inch.

"Why are you stalking me?" Joey said in annoyance and took a sharp left for another lap around the living room instead, Madison hot on her heels. "Stop that."

"I will not." Madison picked up speed which prompted Joey to do the same until they engaged in a full-on game of chase.

"What are you doing? Leave me alone and go make wine." Joey shot a look over her shoulder, brisk-walking through her own house.

Madison passed her an incredulous look. "If you'd stop running from me, maybe. Knock it off, Joey."

"You." Suddenly, they were ten years old again. Joey maneuvered her way into the kitchen like one of those walkers at the mall, arms moving in overtime. Madison mirrored her and came around the opposite side of the island. Just as Joey made an about-face, Madison was upon her. She wrapped her arms around Joey from behind and held her in place with a giant, tight, aggressive bear hug.

"Maddie, this is crazy. Let me go." She wiggled, losing.

"I will not."

"Except you're smothering me."

"You can breathe." The hug continued. Madison's voice was quiet when she said, "I don't know why you think you're unlovable, unworthy. But you're not."

"I know that," Joey said, twisting, but she heard the lack of conviction in her voice. With Madison's arms around her like this, it was somehow harder to look away from the truth, from what she felt down deep in the well of her emotions.

"You're incredibly lovable."

Joey blinked at the surprise tears that sprang into her eyes. "Yeah, okay. You can let me go now."

"Say it."

"No."

Madison rested her chin on the back of Joey's shoulder. "You're smart and wonderful and very much worthy of love."

The tears fell onto Joey's cheeks, hot and traitorous. She stayed very quiet, trying to stay strong and not give herself away. Maddie couldn't see her face, and that was how she wanted to keep it.

"I need you to know that."

Joey nodded silently, and without permission her shoulders began to shake. All of the emotion she'd been holding in for the past week, hell, the past few years began to rain down on her in a torrential storm for the ages. Maddie released her, and as Joey turned around to face her, she felt her face contort, a sob tore from her throat, and she allowed herself to fall into Madison, who was waiting there to catch her. She buried her face in the crook of her best friend's neck and let the tears come, not that she could have stopped them anyway. Madison held her tight, and eventually, with her arms still wrapped around Joey, ushered her to the couch. Unable to regain her composure, Joey curled onto her side and laid her head in Maddie's lap where she shook and sobbed while Maddie stroked her hair.

"Let it out," her friend said, soothingly. "I'm right here. Nowhere to be. I've got you." They must have sat there like that for an hour. Maddie reassuring her, Joey attempting to get it together and failing miserably. She felt vulnerable, exposed, and spent. Good thing it was only Madison there to see.

"I'm sorry," Joey croaked sometime later, once she found her voice. Even to her own ears it sounded raspy and weak.

"Nothing to apologize for." Maddie picked up a strand of Joey's hair and let it fall gently. "Just two chicks on a couch, one of them a little sad."

"I think you meant to say one chick and a train wreck, but I like your version better." Joey attempted a smile that fully manifested. She pushed herself into a sitting position. "Are my eyes bloodshot?"

"Yep. And your nose is red. You're like Santa Claus, sans the beard, after an all-night bender."

Joey nodded. "Totally what I was going for." She sat back against the couch with a sigh. "I'm afraid I'm more of a mess than I realized." She turned her cheek so that it rested against the soft leather couch cushion and peered over at her friend. The stupid tears welled again, and her eyes burned. "What am I gonna do with myself?"

"Let's talk it through."

One of the things she loved about Madison was that she was not simply kind, but a practical problem solver. "Please." The idea of focusing her energy and reining herself in helped her stop the tears. This was good.

"You're going to do *nothing*. That's what I think. When you're not sure which direction you should turn, that's exactly the moment you need to suspend any and all decision-making."

"Okay. That actually helps. It's a relief."

"Give me one word to describe how you're feeling."

"Overwhelmed."

Madison lifted a shoulder, like that solved it. "Then we have to streamline. What do you feel sure of right now?"

"That I need to get the vineyard on its feet and moving in the right direction."

"Then do that. Put all of your energy into that one thing. The rest will be there waiting for you when you're ready."

Joey took a deep breath. Focus on Tangle Valley. She could handle that much. "What about Becca?"

Madison looked thoughtful. "I have a feeling you're going to figure that one out over time."

Joey wasn't as confident. Becca and everything associated with her terrified the hell out of Joey now that she'd experienced the power Becca possessed. "Maybe. Maybe not, though. You know? What then?" She felt the panic rise in her chest.

Madison snapped her fingers. "Focus on the vineyard, weirdo."

Joey smiled at their childhood language. "You're the weirdo."

"I'm not the one soaking a couch."

"Well, when you get all specific..." She felt a small smile blossom.

Her breakdown, the counseling session, and the admission—even to herself—that she wasn't doing as well as she'd claimed had Joey seeing the world realistically. She'd had a rough year, and she needed to take care of herself first. God, she was lucky to have Madison in her life.

When she crawled into bed that night, she was sad, yes, but she could also breathe again. That had to count for something, and when things felt bleak, it was vital to pay attention to the small victories. She wondered about Becca and softly touched the pillow next to her as her heart squeezed uncomfortably. "Have Yourself a Merry Little Christmas" played quietly on her bedside console as midnight hit and Christmas Day arrived. *Focus on what's in front of you. One thing at a time.*

She closed her eyes and drifted off with a hand over her heart. As she felt it beat beneath her fingertips, she thought of her parents and what it would be like to celebrate with them tomorrow. If only. She imagined a Christmas morning where her mother greeted her with open arms and a cup of cider. Her father would get tangled up in ribbon as a joke and lead them in carols with his guitar, as the three of them—her mother, Joey, and Becca—sang along in a post-gift-giving haze.

When Joey opened her eyes the next morning, none of them were there.

Instead, she was alone and scared.

CHAPTER SEVENTEEN

Carla leaned against the doorframe to Becca's office. "Wow."
Becca looked up and around, following Carla's gaze across the perimeter of her office. "What is it?"

"Your office. You've either hired a team of die-hard decorators, or you've been hard at work and have excellent taste."

"The latter," Becca said with a wave of her pen before going back to her paperwork. She'd taken notes during a coaching session with her front desk manager and wanted to organize her thoughts. She'd forgotten about the office's new design. It had just been busywork to quiet her heart and mind.

Carla pointed at the new sitting area in the corner of the room, complete with a white couch with a scalloped back. "That was literally not here forty-eight hours ago."

Becca followed her gaze blandly. "I know. I went shopping." In fact, she'd done more than that. She'd organized her whole house, unpacked every last remaining box, worked with Sky on some new commands, two of which he had mastered, created a five-year career plan, worked on a talent management system for her employees, started a leadership development curriculum to submit to corporate, downed a half dozen bottles of wine in the past week and half, and embarked upon about eighteen other major projects, most of which she had finished. Who knew heartbreak begot ambition? It was apparently what Becca did when she was hurting.

Carla came into the office, closed the door behind her, and sat down. "You're not okay."

"I'm sorry?" Becca asked warily.

"You don't look like yourself. You're not acting like yourself, and it's clear you're not sleeping."

"You're not wrong. It's been a strange time."

"You've been working ungodly hours that are also unnecessary because the resort is in really good shape. The opening kinks have all been worked out. But you have a friend sitting in front of you, not your assistant GM. I'm here for you."

Becca didn't know what to say to that. Normally, she tried to keep her colleagues at a respectable arm's length, but she felt very much adrift. The cowboys were on a Christmas cruise and not due back until the following week, and though Becca had been perfectly fine missing Christmas back home with her family when work called, she now missed them desperately.

"I'm nursing a broken heart," she told Carla.

"Oh," Carla said as her face fell. "Not you and Joey?"

Becca nodded. "We had a hiccup and it scared her off. I didn't see it coming."

"Does this hearken back to the jilted-on-her-wedding-day thing? I heard it was awful. Did you know there were mentions of it in the newspaper? Who puts that kind of stuff out there publicly?"

"A gossipy small town, apparently."

Carla nodded sadly. "So she's gun-shy and backing away. I dated someone like that once."

"What was his deal?"

"Back then it was a her."

"Get out of my office."

"I can't. I'm telling you my commiseration story. Anyway, yes, I dated a woman once, and she was wonderful but wounded, and that made things really hard." Carla studied her manicure as if pulled back into something. "Impossible, really. She didn't trust anyone."

Becca deflated at the report. "I think Joey does battle that kind of thing." While she felt awful speaking about Joey's personal life, she needed to talk it out. "She's had a hard year. She lost her dad, then the fire…and now us."

"Still. I'm worried about *you*. You're a good person, Becca. I'm sorry this has happened. Do you need some time off? I can step in and—"

"No, no, no." She held her hands up over her desk full of file folders. "This is exactly what I need. Keeps my mind busy, you know?"

As if on cue, Becca's cell thrummed in vibration on her desk. She checked the readout, saw Donovan from corporate's name, and slid onto the call. She hadn't seen him in person since the last leader retreat in San Juan. "Donovan, how are things in New Orleans?" As VP of Southeastern resort ops, he homebased from their resort in the Big Easy.

"Hi, Becks. Not so great. Hence my call."

"Uh-oh. What gives?"

He sighed deeply and she imagined him propping his feet up on the desk. "Scooter walked off the job."

Her jaw dropped. She'd never liked the guy, but to have a general manager walk off the job was pretty unheard of. "Didn't see that coming."

"None of us did. I can't give you any more details than that because it's a sensitive HR situation now, but long story short, I need cover."

"Okay, what can I do?"

"I need your insight. Do you think Carla could handle stepping in temporarily until we hire someone? Is she ready?"

"I think she's fully capable." She eyed Carla. "I've been nothing but impressed."

Carla squinted, probably wondering what the hell was going on. "I think she's more than ready to cover a resort. But let's give her this one. I'll come to New Orleans for a while."

There was a pause on the other end of the line. "You would do that?"

"In a heartbeat."

"I'd be thrilled. Let me run it by Maria. If she's good, I'm good."

"Say the word and I'll book travel."

"Give me an hour to make it happen."

She said her good-bye and clicked off the call.

"What in the world is happening?" Carla asked, looking both excited and nervous.

"I think you're about to take this resort for a joyride, and I'm getting out of Dodge for a while." Becca had been drowning, and now someone had thrown her a lifeline, a chance to get away, regroup, and return to Whisper Wall with her wits about her, provided she returned at all. Maybe she'd fall in love with New Orleans in the winter.

❖

The new year, which was supposed to feel like a blank slate, felt anything but awesome. That late morning, Joey walked quietly from the Big House to the tasting room and beat Loretta to work. She moved around the space, gearing up for what would likely be a slow day now that the holidays were over. Everyone had gone back to work and school, and they wouldn't see a big influx of tourists until March. She looked over the tweaks to the new label, which gave more of a pop to the maroon font and a few more tangles in the vines. More swoops.

The business phone rang midperusal, and Joey snatched it up.

"Tangle Valley Vineyard. This is Joey."

"Well, hello there, Head Honcho of the Tangles." Joey laughed, knowing exactly who she was speaking to. "It's Bruno at The Jewel."

"Oh, I know. No one else speaks to me with such personality. It's depressing when it's not you on the line." Bruno, the sommelier at The Crown Jewel, The Jade's in-house restaurant, was always such a gregarious and fun presence. "What can I do for you?"

"Was doing the inventory on our marketing materials and our concierge could use more brochures and discount coupons for tastings. I hand them out with each glass ordered."

"We love that you do. I'll drive some over this afternoon."

"You're a doll."

"So are you."

"Smooches."

She hung up the phone and let the smile drop. The Jade meant one thing to Joey: Becca. She saw those hazel eyes in her mind and felt every part of her react. She shrugged out of the shiver and resumed her study of the graphic proofs. No dice. She was thoroughly off balance and distracted now.

Joey had not seen Becca since the day she had cut things off between them, yet every part of her wanted to. She stood by her decision but also wondered whether she was selling Becca short. Her cry fest with Madison had knocked a few things loose, and she could admit that so much of this was likely her own hang-ups. But she stuck with the plan and concentrated on what she could control, her job.

"Hi, I'm looking for Bruno," Joey told the attendant at The Crown Jewel.

"My love!" Bruno said, coming from the back of the restaurant, which was closed for service between lunch and dinner. They'd only met twice, but he liked to pretend they were long lost wine soul mates, and maybe they were. "I went through six bottles of your pinot at lunch today."

She beamed. "How does that compare with your Fable Brook sales?"

He winced and leaned close to her ear. "Don't tell them, but the feedback on your wine blows theirs away. People have a glass of theirs and switch to something new. The reorder rate?" He shook his head. "Not what it should be."

"That's what I like to hear." All the while they were chatting, Joey kept an eye on the lobby to her left, wondering if Becca would walk through at any moment. She listened for the click of her heels, hoped for them, secretly. "Oh, these are for you," Joey said, producing a stack of vouchers and brochures.

"My angel, thank you."

"You guys seem busy for January." She glanced behind her at the always bustling lobby.

"The spa and the heated pools keep people showing up. Plus, there's a luxurious fireplace in nearly every room."

Joey pointed at him and winked. "Well, it keeps you all on your toes. Send some of them to visit me."

"You have my word."

She waved over her shoulder. "Tell Becca I said hello. Carla, too." The sentence alone made her uneasy, but she had to find a way to exist around Becca Crawford. They were neighbors, after all, and Becca was a good person. There was no reason they couldn't find a way to be friends. The word made her sad and sick to her stomach. *Just focus on what you can control.*

"Carla's in charge these days. Didn't you hear?" Bruno asked.

She turned back. "No. Hear what?"

Bruno winced. "Becca left to head up a resort in New Orleans."

"No. She did?" Joey quirked her head. Her heart thudded. "Since when?"

"She's been gone nearly a week now." He frowned. "We're not sure when she'll be back, if at all, but Carla, the little engine that could, has truly stepped up. She's a force."

Joey was mystified. What was she supposed to do with that information? "Well, I hope it works out, and all is well. For her and this place." Nothing felt right. The room, the sound of her voice, or the way her fingertips had gone numb.

"Me, too."

She said good-bye to Bruno and started for home, only making it as far as the sitting area near the exit of The Jade before dropping hard into one of the fancy expensive armchairs. She blinked at the lobby around her feeling helpless, sad, and worried for Becca.

"Joey?"

She turned and saw Carla studying her from one of the VIP check-in counters. Joey lifted a hand in half-hearted greeting, embarrassed now. Carla made her way over.

"I thought that was you. How are things at my favorite vineyard?" She looked sharp in her suit and fully capable. She just wasn't Becca.

"We're good. Brought some coupons by for Bruno. He said something happened and Becca headed to New Orleans?"

Carla nodded. "They needed some help in a pinch, and I think she…needed some time away."

"Yeah." She paused. "Do you know how long she'll be gone?"

"A month, maybe more. If she likes it there, there's always the chance they'll offer the transfer permanently. She's a hot commodity at Elite."

"Oh no." Joey squeezed her hands together as the information settled. Her heart ached unjustly, because who was she to get a say? She sat there helpless in a lobby hundreds of miles away from Becca. Her own doing. Her instinct was to reach out, call, text, hop a plane, but she had a feeling she was the last person Becca would want to hear from. She turned to Carla. "We broke up," she said blankly.

"I know. I was sad to hear that."

"I don't know what to do. I didn't know about any of this."

"Why don't you send her a message?" Carla said, gently. "That's innocuous enough, right? Just say hi."

Carla had kind eyes, and they somehow made the world slow down. That helped. "What if she doesn't want to hear from me? I wouldn't want to hear from me."

"Then she won't answer. Becca doesn't do anything that she doesn't want to. You know that as well as I do."

"Okay." She nodded. "Maybe I will."

She deliberated fiercely on her short drive home, deciding to just push through. They weren't together anymore. Becca could do as she pleased and Joey would live her own life now. But when she got home and tried to busy herself, the urge to reach out and say something, anything, returned. She shook her head, placed a dish in the sink, and decided to send the damn message and stop living like such a coward. Why did she overthink everything? Which of course, was an ironic topic to subsequently overthink, leaving her in a neurotic cycle. Shaking her head and muttering to herself, Joey composed a short but hopefully sincere text.

I heard about the new gig. Is it nice there? I wish I was with you to hold you and not let go. I miss you so much and just want you to be okay. Both of us.

She paused and studied her work. Nope. She held the backspace button and tried again.

Congrats on the new job. Strange not to have you up the road.

Better. She hit send, nervous and unsure if she should have reached out. Five hours later, she heard back.

Thanks, Joey. It's a whirlwind here. Lots of fires to put out, but managing. You okay?

Joey didn't answer right away. Instead, she opted to take a walk through the vineyard as the sun set, walking one row at a time. She imagined Sky would be staying on the ranch with the cowboys. If she hadn't overturned things with Becca, he'd likely be here with her, walking the vineyard at her side, or maybe she'd be in New Orleans with Becca for a weekend here or there. Both options felt better than this one, yet something held her firmly back from either of those realities. She fired off another text.

I'm okay. Tangle Valley is gearing up for the new year. It misses you.

She watched as the last sliver of sunlight slipped below the horizon. She stood in the dark, alone. With her hands on her hips, she stared up at the universe and asked silently for guidance. Her mind was open, her heart raw. She stood in surrender, asking for a sign, anything to give her soul direction. Where was she supposed to be? What path was hers?

She remained there for what felt like hours, thinking, feeling, hoping. She never got that sign.

What she did receive was a text message, simple and direct. In fact, it was everything.

I miss it right back.

CHAPTER EIGHTEEN

January came and went while Becca spent most of it in a flurry of activity at the resort, undoing so much of what her predecessor had erroneously implemented. Policies not in accordance with corporate, a horrendous lack of checks and balances, and a staff lacking in true hospitality training. It was six a.m. and she'd already been at work for an hour. She'd likely stay into the evening, grabbing meals when she could from their in-house café. The work kept her occupied, and that was best. Her mind wasn't always an easy place to spend time these days. She waved at an older couple heading to breakfast.

Her phone buzzed and she smiled at the readout. Carla.

"You're up early," Carla said.

She squinted through her smile. "And how did you know that?"

"I saw an email come through from you ten minutes ago. Gave you away. You gotta cut yourself a break. Relax. Sleep a little."

"Technology is a betrayer. How's The Jade?" She pivoted past Carla's advice but was grateful that her coworker was now definitely a friend as well.

"Running smoothly. What about La Bella?"

Becca tried not to wince in case anyone was watching. "We're making strides to get back on track."

"Code for chaos."

"Yes, a good description. We don't have the fantastic wine, though."

Carla chucked. "I'm sipping enough after work for both of us. Hanging in there? We miss you here. You miss your life?" Carla asked.

"You've been living mine for weeks now."

"Dodging the question."

She closed her eyes. "I'm managing."

"She was here, you know. Joey. You should have seen the look on her face when I told her you'd left."

Becca opened her eyes again. God, she wanted to know every detail of that interaction but knew it would serve no good purpose. Water under the bridge. "Oh yeah?" She busied herself on the reservations console in front of her, perusing their occupancy level.

"Fix it when you get home. If that's what you want."

She laughed. She'd heard that before. Her younger brother used to make fun movies when they were teenagers, and that was always his favorite go-to solution for most any problem. *Don't worry about it. We'll fix it in post.*

She sighed, abandoning the keyboard. "Not sure it's that simple."

"Becca. What in life is?"

"Good point."

Becca tried to throw herself into work that morning, sifting through the rubble of the GM's office, trying to formulate some sort of order. Yet she couldn't help but drift back to memories of a time when her heart leapt in excitement every time Joey walked into a room. She wondered what she was doing right that very minute. Likely sipping a cup of pecan coffee and looking out over the vines before heading over to work. She wanted to be there, to share their daily schedules, to kiss each other good-bye. She wanted to come home from work to Joey and drink a glass of pinot as they traded stories from their afternoons. Her heart hurt when she gently reminded herself that she would likely never have those things again.

No. Best not to think on it at all.

Where the hell was a person supposed to find cremini mushrooms, and how were those different than regular mushrooms, and why weren't these signs any clearer? Joey studied Gabriella's list of ingredients for that Saturday's menu. Their weekly delivery had apparently shorted them a few items, and Joey, who was heading to the grocery store anyway, agreed to pick up the strays. Only who knew this mushroom quest would be difficulty level ten?

"Oh, I know that look. You're stumped about something."

She glanced up into familiar brown eyes. Simone's. "Do you know which of these is a cremini mushroom?" she asked, automatically, as if they were on one of their shopping trips circa several years ago. Trippy the way it was easy to fall back into an old pattern.

"Hmm." Simone surveyed the options and produced a carton.

"Just like that, huh?"

She gestured to the display. "Just have to take your time and find the right one."

"Right," Joey said. "You would know." What the hell? The snarky comment had flown from her lips before she'd had a moment to censor it. It wasn't like Joey to jab like that. The look on Simone's face and the way she drew back said she was appropriately surprised, as well. Joey shrugged. "No idea where that just came from. Ignore me." She pushed her cart farther down the aisle and fled the scene.

Simone's cart pulled alongside hers and kept up. "I don't want to ignore you," Simone said. "I feel like we've been ignoring each other for years."

"Well, yeah. So?" Joey pushed ahead, making a break for the banana section. Simone, who was the least aggressive person on the planet, was apparently not messing around. She kept pace with Joey as they nearly jogged down the aisle.

"Stop that," Joey told her.

"No." Simone nudged Joey's cart with hers.

"Hey, that's gotta be against store rules." She butted Simone's cart right back, which pulled a glare and seemed to fire her up more. "I will call a manager over here."

"You will not."

Joey made a break for it.

Simone pulled ahead and turned her cart sideways in front of Joey's, blocking her path like a police car maneuver on a high-speed chase. "Well, that seems unnecessary and dangerous."

"It's absolutely necessary," Simone said, exasperated. "We haven't had a real conversation in years and now…"

Joey banged Simone's cart with hers. "And now you're getting married. So what?"

"So…everything!" Simone gave Joey's cart a little kick. "I want to make sure that you're okay. Because I care."

She kicked Simone's cart right back. "No. You want to make sure that you're guilt free, and you are. Live your life. Have babies. I have my own stuff going."

Simone sighed. "Can we sit down together? Put an end to grocery cart wars. I have things to say." She inclined her head toward the front of the store and the small deli with a coffee bar attached, sadly named The Grocery Store Café. It was almost as if they hadn't cared to try.

Joey sighed in indecision. "Really?"

Simone blinked at her, unwavering. "Really."

"I'll meet you there in half an hour. Let me finish my shopping without your Andretti-style maneuverings. You're a menace."

"You have a deal," Simone said, extracting her cart from Joey's path.

"Take it easy," Joey said over her shoulder as she headed off down the aisle. "And don't kill anyone in the meantime. There are children around here."

"No promises," Simone said with a smile as she wheeled away.

Joey did her shopping, taking an extra few minutes just because she was avoiding what had to be a strange and uncomfortable conversation ahead. When it was impossible to delay any longer, she deposited her groceries in the car, grateful for the colder temperatures that would keep them cool, and made her way to the café. When she found Simone, she also found a caramel latte in a mug, completed with a foam swirl. Simone, to her chagrin, knew her too well.

"I took the liberty. I hope you don't mind."

"Not at all," Joey said and slid into her chair with a smile. "What do I owe you?"

"Stop that."

"What?"

Simone's eyes flashed rare exasperation, and she sat forward in her chair. "That impersonal thing you do when you act like we didn't spend half our lives inseparable. I'm allowed to buy you a cup of coffee without us having to settle up." The passion with which Simone said the words was new.

"Okay," Joey said, holding up a conciliatory hand. "Coffee's on you today."

"Thank you," Simone said, sitting back in her chair again. "Now I want to talk about you."

"Oh. Because of the engagement? I'm fine with it. You and Constance were destined. Written in the stars. All that. Are we done?"

"No. This has nothing to do with my life, and everything to do with you and yours. I'm about to get a little nosy here. Fair warning."

Joey hadn't seen this coming. She'd assumed this meeting was about Simone assuaging her getting-married guilt, checking a box to make sure Joey was okay. She squinted. "Why are we talking about me, exactly?"

"Because you're ruining your life, and I can't stand it anymore."

Joey looked around the café in confusion as if searching for something. "I'm ruining my life? Last time I checked, I was attempting to buy mushrooms."

"Don't be a smart-ass. The bigger picture."

"Okay, then I'm trying to pick up where my father left off with the vineyard, and not doing an awful job of it given the circumstances of late. I have a lot of new responsibility on my plate now, Simone. You have no idea. So for you to assume that—"

"I'm talking about Becca."

Joey scoffed, but she was less convincing this time, likely because the topic hit closer to home. She fought the urge to squirm in her chair as Simone watched her knowingly. "Becca's busy, too. The resort is just newly open, and on top of that, she's off filling in at another location right now. I haven't seen her in weeks. Literally since last year."

"You're infuriating, you know that?" Simone's eyes flashed again. "You might be able to get away with this with some people. Madison always was too easy on you, but I'm different." She touched her chest aggressively. "I know that ending our relationship was the right thing to do, but I also know that I did a number on you."

"Would have on anyone," Joey supplied.

"I know." A pause. "I hate the way I allowed it to play out back then, and I'd give anything to go back and do it differently."

"Me, too."

Simone's face showed anguish, and her eyebrows drew in. "I was a selfish coward for not saying something before our wedding day, and I will never forgive myself."

"Well, thank you for admitting that." Joey took a tentative sip of her latte.

"But I can't stand by and watch the damage I've done get in the way of what should be your wonderful, vibrant future." She shook her head. "You have so much in you to give someone, Joey. Don't hold back."

"I'm not. I don't know who you're getting your information from, but I'm fine." She conjured a smile and pretended to use her napkin.

"You're not fine. You're running from your own life."

Simone's words were chipping away at Joey's everything-isdandy exterior. It had taken a lot of work to get it there, and she fought and clawed to keep it. She never would have agreed to sit down with Simone if she'd known the direction the conversation would take. She set down her cup. "What's going on here exactly?"

"I know you ended things with Becca."

"Ah. Of course." Joey shook her head in annoyance. "The Biddies get around. This town. I swear."

"Madison told me."

Joey pulled up short again. "Well, that seems…out of bounds."

"Not when we're all worried about you and care so much."

Joey sighed. "You have a wedding to plan, Simone, so why don't you do that and let me take care of things on my side of the good neighbor fence."

"It's not fair that you lost your mom."

"What?" Joey grappled with the shock of that sentence. Suddenly she was flashing on the important moments of her life that her mother hadn't been present for because the universe had had other ideas. She saw the funeral, her own grief playing out as a child, and her father's heartbreak. A lump rose in her throat.

She pushed back. "Ancient history, but thank you."

Simone didn't falter. "It's not ancient history. I was there. I remember what Mother's Day was like for you year after year."

"Okay, so I struggled. I missed my mom. I still do. So?"

"It's also not fair that you were embarrassed on your wedding day and lost someone you thought was going to be at your side forever."

Joey swallowed, feeling the emotion tumbling toward her, defenseless to stop it. She opened her mouth to argue, but the words weren't there. Instead, the lump grew to the size of this room. She saw the empty aisle and the faces of everyone in town staring up at her in horror. She closed her eyes, wishing the memory away.

"And your dad. He was your best friend."

Joey was aware of the tears that spilled from her eyes. They ran down her cheeks, then her chin. She sat there silently, overcome, but still listening. Simone had her full attention in a strange and unexpected turn of events.

"It absolutely wasn't fair that you lost him, and so very unexpectedly."

Joey nodded at that one and brushed the tears from her face, feeling the full brunt of the grief she'd learned to live with.

"But I want you to listen to me. If Becca Crawford is possibly the one, and I get a sense that others think she might be, then you have to fight like hell to keep her." Simone said the words with such ferocity, that Joey felt them all over. "You look squarely at your hang-ups, recognize that none of them were your fault, and punch them right in the face."

Joey managed a quiet laugh. "You're aggressive today."

"Damn right I am." Simone laughed, too. "This is too important to me. *You* are."

"Yeah, well, that punching directive is easier said than done. I know you mean well, but I just need to focus on what I can manage."

"That's a stupid approach. It's passive and it's past time for that."

Joey blinked. "Madison doesn't think so."

"Then Madison is wussing out, and that's not what you need. Shake it off, Joey, and go after your own happiness for once. Don't lie awake at night and pore over the details of a vineyard that's not going to hold your hand when you've had a hard day, or kiss you good night, or wish you a happy birthday with love in their heart." Simone softened. "Look at me." She did. "Will Becca do those things? Is she that kind of person? You would know more than me."

Joey nodded as thoughts of Becca and how wonderful she was enveloped her. "Yes, she's the best kind of person. She takes care of me and lets me take care of her. We laugh a lot and have the easiest time talking or not talking."

Simone dipped her head and met Joey's gaze. "And it may be weird to hear me say this, but she's really, really hot. Everyone thinks so. Even Constance. Lord help me."

Joey nodded emphatically, aware of the blessing that now felt like a curse. "God, she so is." She covered her eyes briefly in frustration. She missed Becca. She craved her, despite every well-intended effort not to. Why wasn't there a simple off switch?

Simone held out a hand. "Then why are you still sitting here? Go get her."

For the first time in a long while, Joey considered the real possibility of doing just that, which was huge. Her fingertips tingled at what could be hers for the taking, a real shot at happiness. But could she actually take action and make it stick this time? Embark on those terrifying steps out onto the ice that could crack beneath her feet at any moment?

Her lips quivered. "Yeah, I don't know."

Simone's features softened and her voice was sincere when she said, "Listen to me when I tell you that you are very easy to love."

That did it. "You have to stop saying things that make me cry in public."

"I do not. I'll make you cry all day if I get through that stubborn suit you wear."

"I don't own a stubborn suit."

"Fantastic. Then we don't have a problem. Do we?"

Joey sighed. Simone, though she hated it, had a way of getting through to her. Maybe that's what history did to two people, bonded them together. She decided to level with Simone. "Now that I'm out of it, I don't think I can just jump back in."

"Okay, okay. I hear you." Simone nodded, looking thoughtful as if working a puzzle. Finally, she met Joey's eyes. "Remember freshman year of college when you hated calculus with all your heart and vowed to quit school forever and get drunk between the vines?"

"Calculus is my sworn enemy. Of course I do."

"And what did we do to get you through it?"

"I feel like we had that wine."

"After. But first? We went one problem at a time, never looking beyond the numbers in front of us. That's what you have to do."

"Math? No. I refuse."

Simone passed her a look she deserved because it was clear Joey was purposefully deflecting. "Don't look that far ahead. One step only. That's all you have to concentrate on."

She sighed and turned over the idea, examining it. Finally, Joey nodded, feeling guarded, tentative, but not so closed off anymore. Madison's focus-on-what-you-can-control advice had worked in the temporary, but maybe Simone's plan could take it from here.

"So what are you going to do?" Simone asked.

"Well, tomorrow morning, I'm meeting with a contractor. You know her. Ryan from high school."

"Excuse me?"

Joey grinned, feeling lighter. "About the new restaurant. I have a meeting in an hour, not that I can afford it. But I'm going to think about what you said."

"That's all I'm asking."

Joey stood there a moment as a well of something unnamed passed between her and Simone, anchored in their happy and also not so happy history. Simone was getting married. Joey was at the helm of Tangle

Valley. Just look at them. Life was marching forward, and there was nothing any of them could do but hold on. "Thank you for knocking me around, I guess."

Simone grinned back. "Least I could do."

"Say hello to Constance for me." A pause. Joey found her courage. "If I haven't said so, I'm really happy for you two, Simone. She's a nice person."

Now it was Simone's turn to mist up. She stared at the table to gather herself, and then glanced back at Joey. "Thank you. That matters to me more than you know."

They exchanged a weighted smile, and Joey took her leave, feeling beat-up, vulnerable, and more open than was maybe good for her. "Just go with it," she whispered to herself as she started Dusty. "One math problem at a time."

Chapter Nineteen

The Bacon and Biscuit was one of those places you never forgot once you'd visited. When Becca returned to Whisper Wall after her six-week absence, she obviously stopped there first. When she stepped inside, she took a moment to simply inhale the fabulous smell of both baking bread and savory bacon. The restaurant did not mess around when it came to making the most mouthwatering food on the planet.

Clementine was on register today, and Becca stepped right up to the counter, ready with the order she'd kept in her virtual back pocket for weeks now.

"Well, look who's back in town," Clem said with a smile and a twinkle in her eye. She was a quieter presence but knew hospitality and how to make the customers at the Biscuit feel welcome.

"Hi, Clementine. How are things?"

"Full of butter and sass and all the good things in life. What can I get you?"

"Oh, I'll take a hot buttered bacon biscuit with the strawberry jam. Make that extra jam. I'm feeling indulgent."

Clementine rang her up. "That's how you do it. How about a fresh cup of coffee to perk up your morning? I made it myself." She showed off her dimples when she said it.

"I would love that and will pay triple."

"No need. We like our customers happy and coming back. Wait here."

Becca checked her watch, assured that she had plenty of time before she needed to be in her desk chair for her ten a.m. conference call with the corporate resort ops team. There would be a lot to catch up on at The Jade, and she had Carla all ready to sit in on the call. That's when her train of thought derailed because sitting in a booth by the window was Joey with a beautiful brunette Becca had never seen before.

Joey, who must have noticed Becca first, blinked up at her with those big blue soulful eyes. The woman she was meeting with watched in curiosity.

Becca raised a hand in hello. Her heart hammered, picking up speed.

Joey spoke quietly to the woman and then excused herself to the counter. She seemed friendly enough, which was a relief. The last thing Becca would ever want was animosity between them. She'd missed Joey more than she'd ever missed anyone, and seeing her approach now had her stomach fluttering with nerves.

"Hey," Joey said and smoothed her hands down the sides of her jeans. She was nervous, too, which meant they were a pair.

"Hi."

Joey hooked a thumb toward her table. "Just chatting with a contractor. I didn't realize you were back. Hi."

"Just got in last night. Hi again. We're saying that a lot." They stared at each other tentatively. This was uncharted territory, but Becca was very aware of honoring Joey's wishes and staying on the sidelines of her life. She'd had a few weeks to marinate on what that would entail, but she could do it for Joey. It just meant setting her heart and all it was feeling aside.

"And the Big Easy, how was it?" Joey asked.

Becca moved her head from side to side. "I didn't see too much of it. No one threw a single bead at me."

"A travesty." Joey shifted her weight. "The town missed you, you know." Another pause. "I did."

Becca could see that the sentiment was genuine. It touched her and let her know that, God, she hadn't been crazy. She really had mattered to Joey. "You don't know how glad I am to hear that."

"Becca, your order's up. Piping hot," Clementine said from the counter.

"Great. Thanks," she said to Clementine and took the warm white bag she was offered. She held it up to announce her departure. "Well. I'm happy I ran into you." Becca gestured to the table. "And I hope your meeting is a good one." God, that all sounded so formal. She hated that this was who they were now. Weeks back they were snuggling naked in bed and looking to what might be a future. Now they were tiptoeing around each other in a polite competition.

"Thanks! I hope to run into you…soon." Joey's cheeks colored at the declaration, and she seemed aware of it. She quickly scurried away. "And this is a good suit," she said, almost as an afterthought she could not leave off. What it did leave was Becca confused and standing a little taller in her pinstriped navy. She nodded, headed for the door, and stole one last look over her shoulder at Joey, who claimed once last glimpse herself.

What in the world had happened there? She stared at her reflection in her car window as she replayed the encounter. Interesting, indeed.

❖

It was after closing time at Tangle Valley after a successful day that had nearly depleted the dolcetto they had stocked on the floor. Joey would need to check in with Uncle Bobby and have him restock the storage room with fresh cases. Gabriella, still wearing her chef's coat with a dish towel on her shoulder, made her way inside and to the bar.

"That was one of my favorite days working with Jolene. We were one with each other."

Joey offered a smile. "I'm happy to hear you're bonding. I was told by multiple guests that the spinach dumplings were the best they've ever tasted."

Gabriella beamed. "Oh yeah? I was trying something different this time." She kissed her fingers. "I upped the truffle quotient in the parmesan truffle cream."

"Well, it worked."

"Makes it all worthwhile when I hear people like my food. It's why I get up in the morning, ready to go." It was true. Gabriella seemed to attack every day with enthusiastic gusto. She was a perpetual force, driven by the passion she had for her job. "How was your day?"

"It was interesting. Becca's back."

Gabriella perked right up. "You saw her?"

"I did. It was…nice, actually. Is that crazy?"

"Why would it be crazy. You guys have always gotten along. How did you feel, you know, laying eyes on her for the first time in so long."

"I don't know that there's a descriptor. But it was potent. It stuck with me." Joey studied her friend with a thought. "You know how when you're a kid, sometimes you have the best of intentions, but when you leap off that diving board, it's a belly flop? It's not graceful or exciting, and its hurts like hell?"

Gabriella rubbed her stomach absently. "I remember those."

"My first attempt at having something with Becca, I was terrified. I went for it anyway, raced to the edge of that diving board, and I belly flopped."

Gabriella rubbed her stomach again. "I think you have to stop saying that word."

Joey waved her off. "You get the point, though. And now, I have an opportunity to take my time and use the belly—uh, the prior knowledge to formulate a more graceful maneuver."

"A swan dive," Gabriella supplied with flourish. "A beautiful one."

"Yes. That would be the goal. But I would have to do things differently. I showed up on her doorstep and threw myself at her in the middle of a thunderstorm, Gabs."

"Oh, I like that very much."

"No, it was a bad move. It was us leaping in feet first. I need to see if I can go slow this time."

"What are we talking about?" Madison asked, coming into the tasting room rubbing the back of her neck. She'd been working in the tank room all day, tinkering and tasting and tinkering some more, and it showed.

"We are not talking about anything," Joey said, gesturing between her and Madison. "Because *one of us* told Simone way too much."

Gabriella's eyebrows shot up, and Madison had the decency to look guilty.

"Buddy, hear me out." Madison held up a hand. "My heart was in the right place, and I had this tugging that told me that Simone was a key player in all of this, whether we want her to be or not. You needed to hear from her, JoJo."

Joey leveled a look at Madison. "Hearts can be in the right place and still be wildly out of bounds."

"Agreed, but I love you and had to take the risk. How did it go?"

"Horribly. I cried like a child in the grocery store café."

Gabriella held up a finger. "She's leaving off the part where she's gonna swan dive her way back to Becca, so it must have been a helpful conversation."

"I refuse to give her the satisfaction," Joey said, smug.

"I'm in favor of swan diving," Madison said, now energized and taking a seat at the bar. "I'll applaud all day long."

"She's back in town," Joey said and went about wiping the

counter. She felt the corners of her mouth turn up with hope despite her best attempt to appear blandly informative.

"Joey Wilder, you minx and a half. See her yet?" Gabriella asked.

She nodded. "She was at the Biscuit picking up breakfast wearing a business suit and looking like a sophisticated million bucks."

"How'd that go?" Madison asked. "Was she friendly? Was there a hostile vibe? Sometimes pain can shift to anger and back again."

Joey moved a strand of hair behind her ear. "She wasn't hostile at all. She's Becca. She's always friendly even if she's secretly throwing darts at my photo for dropping her over a business deal."

"Belly flop," Gabriella said, and rubbed her stomach.

"Listen, you guys, I'm not saying Becca and I should ride off into the sunset, but I'm going to take a breath and see if I can punch a few of my neuroses in the face, to paraphrase Simone."

"Who in a million years thought we'd be listening to Simone."

"Right?" Joey marveled. She took out the open bottle of pinot and poured three small glasses.

Madison swirled hers automatically and studied the color as if she hadn't seen it a million and nine times. "Now what?"

"Well, that's a valid question. Today I told her she looked good in her suit. So that's something small."

Gabriella's mouth fell open. "You did not."

"Did. And I'm still standing. Now I need to sit with that. Next time, maybe I lean into that same brand of honesty and dip another toe in. Nothing too major."

Gabriella nodded. "I like the water motif we have going here."

"Me, too," Joey said. "I'm really embracing it."

"Rightfully so." They touched glasses in satisfaction and sipped.

"Any word on the restaurant?" Madison asked. Right away, she saw Gabriella perk up.

Joey set down her glass. "I met with the contractor I told you about, the one everyone recommends."

"That Ryan woman, right? She was a few grades ahead of us in school."

"That would be her, yes." Joey turned to Gabriella. "She has her own company now and listened to everything I had in mind"—she gestured between them—"all the details we've brainstormed, and she sent me a budget this morning." Deep breath. "If I can pull a few rabbits out of a hat, we should be able to still make it happen."

Gabriella's eyes went wide. "I'm staying? I'm a Tangle Valley regular?" She screamed, leapt off the stool, and lifted her feet in a fast-paced tap dance celebration, as Joey came around the bar.

"Yes, it's true. We're keeping you," Joey said, embracing Gabriella from the front as Madison hugged her from the side. "We are a cheesy sitcom right now, and I love it."

"Oh, we need a theme song," Gabriella said, her face red from excitement. "I'll work on that, probably after the Sunday rush."

"See? Multitalented," Madison said, ruffling Gabriella's hair. "Movie tonight? Rom-com?"

"Definitely," Joey said with a happy sigh. They'd dragged a projector into the empty building that would one day soon be their restaurant, and the picture took up an entire wall. Gabriella made them all buttery popcorn with parmesan, and Joey supplied the wine. They'd only watched one so far, but Joey had a feeling the tradition might continue. Lighthearted love stories with your friends and snacks? Not a bad night.

Two hours later they laughed and snacked under blankets watching *Imagine Me & You*, a flick Gabriella had shockingly never seen. By the end of the film and romantic journey, Joey was filled with the hope that though love didn't always come easy, without cost, in the end, what could be better?

"Getting any ideas, JoJo?" Madison asked once the lights were on and they folded the blankets.

"One step at a time," she said conservatively with butterflies flitting around in her midsection. She remembered Simone smashing her cart into Joey's and proclaiming her easy to love a short time later. She and Simone had ended badly. She and Becca might, too. But honestly? She wouldn't trade away the memories she had with Simone given the chance. They were part of her. That had to mean something, right? So why was she sidestepping a potential connection that could prove to be just as important? "Maybe I'll swing by The Jade tomorrow. See how our wine is doing."

Gabriella and Madison nodded.

"I'm sure it desperately needs checking on," Madison said.

Gabriella feigned urgency. "Damn it. You better get over there, then. Wine woes are no joke."

"I'll see what I can do. Is there more popcorn?"

Madison held up the empty oversized tin bowl. "Want to lick the bottom?"

"Um, yes."

A pause. "That's what she said," Gabriella whispered.

Joey gasped. "Aren't you supposed to be the sweet one?"

Gabriella covered her grin with her hand. "Sorry."

CHAPTER TWENTY

Joey stared at the orange drink in the fancy coupe glass with a dark purple cherry on a stick lying across the top of it. She was not a fancy cherry on a stick kind of girl. She worked on a farm and drank wine from a tank. She glanced down at her outfit, which she could now see she'd worked too hard on. The black sweater was too low-cut for a Thursday night. She gave it a tug upward. Didn't change much.

"Va-va-voom," Bruno said, rounding the corner into the bar area of The Crown Jewel.

"No va-va-ing," Joey said and sipped her drink and winced internally. Oh, that was sweet. People liked this stuff? Didn't matter. It was a sexy-looking drink, which was why she'd ordered it, having seen a girl group at one of the high tops toasting with them. "I'm just here for a simple beverage, Bruno. Then I must take my leave."

"Oh, you must, must you?"

"Indeed."

He stared at her. "Something's different about you."

"No, I'm just a girl drinking out of a coupe glass at the end of a long day."

He squinted as he walked away. "You're up to something. That's what I think. Must run."

She waved with just her fingers. That was new.

Joey had chosen a seat at the bar very close to the lobby entrance in case Becca walked by. In case? Who was she fooling, she'd planned entirely for Becca to walk by and maybe they could engage in a brief conversation. Couldn't hurt. It wasn't like she was dying to see her but refusing to give in to her craving. She did, however, have her sights set on a very casual exchange. She was not at all a weirdo, either. Why were her palms sweaty? She knew why. Because she was committing to the idea of Becca this time. Something she never allowed herself to do fully before. If she had, a little dustup over the wine deal would have been survivable for them. Couples suffered worse setbacks all the time. If both were committed to making it work, they rode it out. Joey's new goal was that level of commitment, doing it right this time, provided they got that far. For all she knew, she'd scared Becca away for good.

Susie, the bartender, paused in front of Joey. "How's that Winchester 85 working out?"

"It's amazing," Joey said. "My first time trying one."

"Susie, have you seen Bruno?"

Joey froze at the recognizable voice and the click-clack of sophisticated heels. She knew that click-clack. The sound still made her midsection flutter.

Susie paused her martini preparation and pointed around the corner into the restaurant. "Headed that way. High-end guest is apparently ordering some high-dollar wines."

"Yes, that's one of our VIPs and I wanted to make sure—Joey?"

Joey glanced over her left shoulder and grinned, as if *What a surprise, running into Becca Crawford at her very own workplace.* God, she was nervous. "Hi."

"What brings you by? Wait. You're drinking an 85?"

She lifted her glass like she owned it. "I drink cocktails."

"Oh. I've never seen it."

Joey shrugged. "Okay, well, maybe I'm trying new things. Turning over a new leaf."

Becca studied her. "You look…beautiful. Did you curl your hair?"

"A little bit."

Becca's gaze dipped briefly to Joey's cleavage and then away again.

"There's Bruno," Susie said as she poured from the shaker.

"Oh," Becca said, seeming disappointed. "I guess I better—"

"Yeah. Duty calls."

"Will you be here later?" That felt like interest. Maybe Becca didn't hate her.

"No. Just the one drink tonight. I need to head home. But maybe we can grab one together next week?"

"Sure. I'd like that." Becca seemed not only surprised but mystified. Joey didn't blame her. She couldn't imagine trying to decode those mixed signals. That was all her fault, and she still wasn't being all that clear. But she needed to do things in the proper time and correctly.

"That would be grand."

"Grand?" Becca said with a raised eyebrow.

"Sometimes I say *grand*, Becca."

"No you don't. Another new leaf?"

"Maybe," she said, trying to play coy and mysterious and wondering how effective she was. She had an inkling, not very. "I'll let you find Bruno. Have a nice night."

Becca took one last lingering look at Joey, her outfit, and the whole setup before wandering away seeming perplexed.

Five days later when Becca made her way through the lobby of The Jade to find Joey sitting on one of the couches, she blinked in surprise. "Joey?"

"Hey, Becca."

"Well, this is twice in one week. To what do we owe the honor?" Becca wore a belted black dress and heels today. She never disappointed in the fashion department. Yes, these were the things Joey allowed herself to notice again, react to. And God, did she ever have a physical reaction.

"I'm meeting a friend for lunch in the restaurant." It was a lie. She was not a liar, but she was lying now because a black dress had her flummoxed, and she should have prepared a cover story in advance.

"Oh, in that case, I'll let the staff know we're having special guests."

"Please don't," Joey said, standing so that she looked Becca in the eye. "I might get stood up and then it's a whole thing."

"Oh. So a date." Becca's face fell whether she realized it or not. Joey couldn't help but celebrate.

"Not at all. No. Definitely not a date. Very much a friend thing only."

"Okay, okay," Becca said with a grin. Perhaps Joey had put up too much of a protest.

"How was your week?" Joey asked. She was genuinely curious. She hated not knowing the basics of Becca's life that she used to be so intimately connected to. "Did you remember to turn off your straightener?" It had been a running joke when they tried to leave the house together.

"I only went back to check twice this week."

Joey placed a hand on her chest. "I'm feeling very proud of you right now. This is a moment."

They laughed, and when it died, they just stared at each other for a moment. Joey had never felt connected to another person the way she did Becca, and even when she tried to step away, she just…couldn't. Being near her now, laughing with her, just confirmed all of it.

"What about you? How's business?"

"You're not going to believe this, but our visitor rate is up quite a bit."

"Can't imagine why," Becca said and looked up at the ceiling in an *I told you so.*

"It turns out, maybe you know a thing or two about the hospitality industry. I'm not saying everything, but a thing. Or two things."

"Josephine Wilder, I think you just admitted to being wrong."

"Let's not get carried away."

"Too late." This would usually be the point in the conversation when they would sink into a toe-curling kiss, but the barrier she'd put between them remained.

"About that drink," Joey said, feeling the twinge of energy that meant she was taking a tentative step forward. "I was thinking Thursday." She lifted a shoulder. "We can…catch up."

"I would need to move some meetings around that could go late, but I think I can make that work. What about that new place on Center Street. Truth or Dare, I think it's called."

Joey swallowed. "Well, doesn't that just sound ominous."

"Well"—Becca flashed a smile—"I'm feeling brave. Meet you there at seven?"

"Yeah," Joey said, sliding her hand into her back pocket. "I'll see you then." She nodded, turned, and headed for the door.

"Joey?"

"Yep?" She turned back.

"Your lunch with your friend?"

She waved Becca off. "All an act to get to see you." She shrugged. "I can't stand lying."

Becca seemed to suppress a smile. "Understood. See you soon, Joey."

❖

"Do you think she's courting you?" Stephen asked with a squint.

"I think she is," Monty said and put his hands behind his head. "This is a full-on courting scheme. She wants you back. Bad."

After work on Wednesday, Becca needed a sounding board, so

she'd driven out to the ranch unannounced and crashed the cowboys' dinner. Luckily, they always made a ton of food and didn't hesitate to set her a place at their table. With the after-dinner dishes pushed to the side, the three of them sat around the table with Sky and two of the boys' rescues lounging nearby.

"Oh, I wouldn't go that far." She shook her head. "Joey knows what she wants, and it doesn't seem to be a relationship with me. She's made that clear." She sat back and reflected with a shake of her head. "Is my heart broken? Yes. More than I can describe. But, guys? It's like she's peeking through the door again."

"Showing up places where you might be? All classic I-Miss-You signs. She's definitely peeking."

"She'll be stealing looks at you from behind a potted plant next."

Stephen nodded. "Through a newspaper with eye holes cut out."

"Binoculars across a crowded restaurant. I think her heart longs for yours."

"Well, she's not the only one with a few longings." She scrubbed her face. "I miss her so much it physically hurts." She gestured to her body. "All over. I'm tense and unhappy and there's only one reason."

"Well," Monty said, getting serious, "how do you feel about this new turn of events?"

"I have questions, for sure. I mean"—she lifted her hand and let it drop—"what's changed? The biggest part of me is ecstatic, because I hate life without her. My house doesn't feel the same, I still reach for Joey in the middle of the night, and returning to an existence where I don't have plans to see her, to kiss her, to hold her has been awful."

"I sense a *but*."

She nodded. "But is she ready? Or is she just going to slam another door in my face, because I don't want to be right back here again in a few months." She shook her head. "It's not even that I fault her. She's been through so much. I don't want to be just another thing on her list of problems."

Stephen pointed at Monty. "You sound a lot like this guy once did when he wasn't sure if he could ever get me to settle down."

Monty grinned. "Now look at you, a ranch, a husband, and too many dogs. See, Becca? It can happen. Keep an open mind and be patient. That's my advice. Life is a long game. Enjoy the drink with her. No big deal."

"No big deal," she repeated and ran her finger around the rim of her glass, knowing that everything about Joey Wilder was.

❖

Sitting across from Becca at Truth or Dare, Joey had to remind herself that things were different now, and not to fall into old patterns. Slow was the name of the game. She would keep her hands to herself and not so much as touch Becca's foot with her own under the table, something she would have done several times throughout a meal just a couple months back.

She took a deep breath once Becca settled on the bench across from her in the cozy private leather booth. She ignored the fact that Becca's hair seemed a little windblown and that she still wore her white dress shirt from work, one of Joey's favorite looks on her.

"What are we drinking? Winchester 85s?" Becca asked with a wink.

"I ordered a red blend from Stormfoot Cellars. I hope that's okay. If not, I'll drink them both," Joey said with a laugh.

"No, that's perfect. You know what I like, and I prefer you always order the wine, being the expert that you are." They both seemed to catch the use of the word *always*. Becca seemed to regret it and the conversation fell silent as they studied the decor. Joey, hating the silence because it gave her too much time to overthink, jumped in.

"You're probably wondering why I've been weird lately. I practically kicked you out of my house and then started drinking strange cocktails and loitering in your place of business."

Becca smiled the killer smile that made Joey's knees weak. "I did wonder." The glasses arrived and that gave Joey a moment to sip and gather her thoughts.

Finally, she pointed at her face. "I'm someone who seems put together on the outside, but sometimes I'm a mess"—she held up a hand—"and I know you know that because you've seen it, but what I mean is that I hesitate to trust. That's what I did with you. I allowed myself to enjoy us," she said, gesturing between them, "but I held back enough so that when something went wrong, I had one foot easily out the door."

"Yeah, I'd say you were out like that." Becca snapped her fingers and Joey winced. "Not that I didn't play a part. I have a lot of regrets about how I handled the business deal, but I didn't expect to be kicked to the curb over it."

"God, it sounds so awful when you put it that way."

"It was," Becca said. Joey could see it all over her face, and the hurt looking back at Joey slashed at her. She hated that she'd put that hurt there. She downed half her glass of wine. Becca raised her eyebrows.

Joey shook her head vehemently. "It's not who I want to be. Simone crashed her grocery cart into mine and kinda yelled at me about all I'm giving up, and even though I crashed mine back because who does that? I agree with her. I'm blowing it for myself because I'm a coward." She took another big gulp, the glass almost finished. "So if I'm going to do this, I'm going to do this right. The correct way, without guards up, or feet out the door, or holding on to the idea that you're going to desert me at any moment."

Becca seemed to be trying to decode the rambling confession, which even Joey could hear made little sense. "Simone crashed her cart into yours?"

Joey nodded. "Right? And there was nary a Biddy to report on it."

A pause. Becca lifted her glass and sat back against the leather booth. "Are you saying that you regret ending things with me?"

She finished her glass, set it down, and nodded. "Listen, Becca, I don't even know if you'd give me a second chance or even the time of day next week. What I do know is that I'd do so much differently this time. I'd commit to the idea and work through the issues and problems that would arise."

"Because they definitely would," Becca noted. "That's part of life. Of relationships, marriage. People have problems and disagreements all the time."

She nodded. "Right, I know that innately, I just…"

"Self-protect."

Joey nodded. "Marriage?" She met Becca's gaze. "You could see yourself getting married one day?"

"It's what I've always wanted, imagined for myself." She stared at the table for a moment and seemed to make a decision to say more. "You're the only person who I've actually imagined it happening with."

Joey blinked and could have been knocked over by a feather. "Me?"

"You."

She heard Simone's words loud and clear in her mind. *You're very easy to love.*

She swallowed and gathered her courage. "Do you think one day you could fall in love with me?"

"Oh, Joey." She shook her head slowly. "I already am."

"Really?" She couldn't quite believe it, but then, that had been her exact problem all along.

Becca nodded. "I've been trying not to be for months now. It's not really a choice." She raised a hand. "It's just the state of the world, you know?"

"What do you want to do about that?"

"I don't know," Becca said and rolled her lips in.

Joey hadn't said the words back, and Becca had to have noticed. She felt it, though. With everything in her, Joey knew she'd fallen in love with Becca somewhere between that shoulder bump in town and reading romance novels on the couch. It had snuck up on her, but it was there all the same. She opened her mouth, but the important words wouldn't come. They were stuck. She pivoted. "I do. I know what we do about it, I mean."

"And what's that?"

"We take a walk. You tell me about everything I've missed since that day in my kitchen. We put one foot in front of the other."

Becca held on to her skepticism, that much Joey could tell, but she agreed to take that walk. Becca told her about New Orleans and about Skywalker's new habit of stealing her socks and stuffing them, still in a ball, under the couch. She heard about The Jade's fantastic word of mouth and killer reviews on Tripadvisor. She felt like she'd missed so much. Too much.

They strolled in silence a bit, and Joey turned to Becca, feeling nostalgic for simpler times. "This reminds me a little bit of that night we got the ice cream floats."

"The night you had me scootin' across the dance floor in the name of getting to know the town better? Yes, I remember it well."

Joey laughed. "That was a really good night for me. I feel like we started to get to know each other."

Becca took Joey's hand in hers. "We did." It felt so natural that Joey didn't even register the feeling at first. When she did, warmth spread from the center of her chest outward, and she smiled.

"Do you know what I'm looking forward to?" Joey asked.

"Tell me."

"The first signs of spring. The new growth you see happening all over this place. It's like the turning of a page, a fresh start, just like the growing season. It makes me wonder if that's possible for us."

"Maybe," Becca said with a noncommittal gaze, but she was here with Joey, and she loved her, and that had to count for something.

They'd made the loop through the center of town and back to their cars. Joey approached Dusty slowly, clenching and unclenching her fists, knowing that this was the moment she needed to take a step forward, declare herself in some way, but that emotional execution proved too complicated.

Instead, she turned to Becca and met her gaze and held it. Through their silent connection, she did her best to communicate everything that was in her heart, and when she wasn't sure that had worked, she took a step into Becca's space, and once she was there? She felt home. Joey slid her hand beneath Becca's cheek and leaned in slowly, brushing her lips over Becca's. She closed her eyes in unmatched surrender as everything in her world seemed to right itself. Becca kissed her back, deepening the kiss. Joey's heart leapt, and the noisiest parts of her quieted in perfect acquiescence.

"Good night, Joey," Becca said and took one step back.

She blinked, gathering herself. Her instinct was to reach out for Becca and never let go. But she let her walk away, back to her car. That had been her chance to right everything between them. Yet she'd let the moment slip tragically through her fingers.

CHAPTER TWENTY-ONE

With Becca's kiss still on her lips, haunting her, Joey tossed the blanket off her very alert body and stepped into a pair of plaid sleep pants that matched the solid blue T-shirt she'd worn to bed. Next, she found her boots and coat, and headed down the stairs for the door. She needed strength, and she felt a tugging she could no longer ignore.

She didn't take a flashlight. She knew this property as well as she knew herself and trudged through the cold of February until she made it to the cellar where she'd stashed her dad's old tackle box in a cabinet after handing over his office to Madison. She opened the small door, flipped open the lid to the box, and blindly grabbed for the first strip of paper she saw.

She nearly heard his voice when she read the words: *Pour your heart out. It's not good keeping it bottled up. J.W.*

It was his message to her. She knew it without question. She held the paper to her heart and closed her eyes for several seconds as the understanding washed over her. It was as if her father was right there with her, giving her that pesky nudge she needed when she was being a stubborn kid, dragging her feet about doing her homework. She read the words again and again, each time letting go a little bit more, loosening her grip and relinquishing control.

"I saw the light on here. What's going on?"

Joey jumped, then calmed herself when she saw it was only Loretta standing in the doorway to the cellar. "Oh, wow. Did not see you there. God." She exhaled and quirked her head. "It's three a.m. Loretta, what are you doing up?"

She scoffed like that was a silly question. "I'm a night owl. Always have been. I saw the light and just…Well, it was usually Jack out here this late, tinkering with the acid levels or dreaming up some new profile while everyone else slept."

"And you'd join him."

She nodded, subdued. "I'd keep him company. Sure." Loretta absently wrapped her arms around her body, from the cold or old memories. It was hard to interpret which. "Those were some good nights, full of interesting conversation."

"And more." Joey gestured with her head in the direction of the tasting room, one building over. "You as much as said so before."

Loretta sighed and came into the large room. "We were in the early stages of something. I tell you what, when I think of all that time we wasted, dragging our feet, playing coy." She shook her head. "We were foolish, and now it's too late."

The words hit home every bit as powerfully as the ones she held in her hand on that strip of paper. "I don't want to make the same mistake."

"Don't you dare," Loretta said vehemently. "Let me be the one to learn that lesson for the both of us. Life is here, and then it's not, so we have to seize every single moment that is offered to us." She stepped forward on a motherly mission. "If you're not doing that with Becca, then you fix it. You hear me?"

Joey nodded wordlessly as an all-encompassing wave of peace came over her. She accepted what she should have understood all along, that life was messy but so worth living. Hell, messy was even beautiful, wasn't it? When you considered the alternative. Loretta was right. Her father was, too. She was wasting precious time. Keeping her feelings bottled up achieved exactly nothing. Self-preservation was a sham because she wasn't in control of the universe anyway. Her thoughts sped out of control but all in one very defined direction: Becca.

"You think on that," Loretta said, likely perplexed by the look on Joey's joyful face. "I'm going next door to put on some hot cocoa. Helps me sleep. Join me if you want a cup." Joey nodded again and watched as Loretta headed out. She turned back to Joey one last time. "You okay, sweet girl?"

"I feel more than okay."

"Good. Come get that cocoa. There's some of the homemade whipped cream left from earlier today when I sold a few cups. Cold tonight, isn't it?" She rubbed her hands together.

Joey nodded. "Freezing, actually."

Once alone, she stood there a moment and let her feelings settle and her thoughts slow down. Yet when they did, nothing had changed.

She pulled her phone from her coat pocket and walked straight out of the cellar onto the property and kept walking until she stood still between two rows of vines beneath the stars and sky. It was the middle of the night, but Joey couldn't seem to talk herself out of making the call. It was like Loretta said. Don't waste a moment.

She put the phone to her ear and waited, and it wasn't long before a sleepy voice on the other end of the line answered her. "Joey. Are you okay?"

She imagined Becca sitting up in bed, turning the lamp on, Skywalker probably stirring next to her in his dog bed. "I'm so sorry to wake you up. I'm okay."

"Good. What's going on?"

"Have you ever had this urge to do something right then, when it's all consuming, and it's like you can't go another minute until you do the thing?"

"Yeah, I guess I have."

"I love you so much."

A pause. Becca didn't say anything, and that was okay because Joey had more.

"I'm in love with you, and I need you to know it. I get that I've made things difficult and was harder on you than I ever should have been." She took a deep breath. "But I just want to spend the rest of time making it up to you and be the kind of person who works through a problem, and maybe gets a little angry, but definitely doesn't leave." She exhaled. "I don't want to leave you ever again, Becca."

"Where are you right now?"

"I'm standing in the middle of the vineyard like a lunatic, but the thing is, I've never felt more sane."

"I'm coming over."

"What? You don't have to do that. Now?"

"Is there a better time?"

Joey laughed and placed her palm on her forehead and turned around in disbelief. "No. This would be the best one for me. I happen to be very, very available at the moment."

"Don't go anywhere," Becca said and clicked off the call.

Joey returned to the end of the row and stood in the open area between the grapes and the building, hands on her hips in amazement. What a night this had been. It was only a few moments before headlights appeared on top of the hill, and a few moments later, there was Becca. She wore jeans and a red winter jacket she must have tossed on. Her hair was glamorously tousled from the pillow, one of Joey's favorite looks on her. When Becca spotted Joey, she ambled over with a grin on her face.

"Hi," Joey said.

"Say it again."

"Hi."

Becca laughed and shook her head. "Not that."

Joey stepped forward and grabbed Becca by the lapels of her coat. "I'm standing here in the middle of the night and I'm in love with you."

Becca closed her eyes as if to let the words wash over her. When she opened them, their eyes met. "I love you, too."

"I want us to be together, Becca. It feels like we're destined. The minute you walked through those doors, I knew you were someone who was special. In the months that followed, I realized that you were meant to be special *to me*. We're meant to be."

"I know," Becca said, the vibrant moonlight illuminating her eyes. "I was just waiting for you to catch up."

"Kiss me in the freezing cold."

Becca didn't need prompting. She caught Joey's mouth with hers, and she sank into the most wonderful, memorable, heartfelt kiss of her life. The warmth of Becca's mouth and the proximity of her body heated Joey nicely.

"God, I've missed this," Becca said against her mouth before diving in for more.

"What is going on out here?" Joey heard Loretta say. She turned and saw her moving toward them with a thermos of hot chocolate and some stacked cups.

"Hey, Loretta," Becca said. "I just popped in."

Loretta grinned and handed her a cup. "Yeah, you did." She began to divvy up the cocoa. "You two are out here causing a scandal beneath the heavens." She grinned. "The best kind, too."

That's when the moon seemed to get extra bright. Too bright. Joey turned and squinted at the flashlight shining in her eyes. She held up a hand. "Madison?"

"How did you beat me here?" Madison asked and let the beam brush the ground.

"What are you talking about?"

"Time to pick."

Another voice called out, "Oh, Joey's already here. Were they just kissing? I think they were just kissing. Hi, Becca!"

Joey craned her neck to see Gabriella just a few yards behind Madison and Uncle Bobby behind Gabriella. Becca waved. Over her right shoulder, more headlights appeared, as two cars—no, three—approached. Make that four. "Is this what I think this is?" Joey asked, her delight bubbling over because what were the odds?

"It's ice wine time!" Madison called out on a euphoric high. She held up her special thermometer. "Just over sixteen degrees. Let's do this."

"What is happening?" Becca asked. "These people are all showing up to pick grapes? Right now?" She checked her phone. "It's three twenty-six a.m. Did you know about this? Is this why you were awake?"

"I had no idea. The only thing keeping me awake was you." Joey laughed. "I'm just as surprised. When Madison makes the decision, it's a go—a text blast goes out to all those signed up to help pick. It's an event. We'll make gallons of cocoa and open sparkling wine for mimosas, and we stay up all night picking the grapes, and Madison and her crew will take it from there. It has to be close to seventeen degrees."

"And that's tonight?" Becca asked, incredulous and excited. The crowd was growing.

"Yes," Joey said in amazement. "Can you believe it?"

Becca laughed. "I can, actually. It's perfect."

The voices around them grew louder as the number of people rose. Madison organized the grape pickers and offered some brief instruction, but Joey kept her eyes on Becca and her hand firmly in hers. There weren't a million grapes to pick because the batch of ice wine would be limited, but it was still important.

"You sure you want to help?" Joey asked when Madison concluded her speech and the pickers headed out with extra energy bouncing between them. Nearby, Bobby popped a bottle of sparkling wine and let it overflow while Loretta laughed and dodged the spray. There must have been thirty volunteers there and more still arriving. She forgot how much she loved this time of year.

Becca's eyes sparkled in the moonlight. "Nothing could keep me away." Joey went warm in the freezing temperatures and leaned in for a kiss.

"They're in love again," Gabriella said in adoration.

Madison looked up from her clipboard and took a moment to grin. "I saw the kissing and was trying to be breezy, but inside there are cartwheels in progress, and the fact that it happened on ice wine night practically means it's ordained."

"Maddie's cartwheels always remain in her head," Gabriella told Becca.

"Fewer injuries that way," Becca said with a nod of approval.

"Ready to pick some grapes?" Joey asked, unable to erase the grin. She had a feeling it was now a fixture.

"I'll follow you." The way Becca said the words made it clear that she didn't just mean in the picking of grapes. The sentiment comforted Joey like the most snuggly of blankets. Becca was hers and she was Becca's, and there was nothing that she'd let undo that.

They picked and laughed at how ridiculously cold it was and stole glances at each other under the big dark sky, enjoying the renewed feeling of being with each other again. When they glimpsed the sun, the job was done, and with her hand in Becca's she led them up to her bedroom, where they promptly wrapped themselves around each other and fell asleep as the sunlight further illuminated Joey's bedroom.

When Joey opened her eyes a few hours later, she saw Becca gazing at her across the pillow. Her heart swelled. "You're still here. Thank God."

Becca touched her cheek. "Did you think I'd leave?" She shook her head. "Never."

"What about work?"

"I texted Carla and let her know I had a hard night. She's covering for me."

"I love Carla," Joey said. "I need to send her a gift basket to express it properly."

Becca laughed. God, she was beautiful. Joey reached up and touched her hair, elated at her presence, her smile, her body in Joey's bed. They'd thrown their clothes on the floor in exhaustion. Joey still wore bra and panties, which seemed silly now. She eased closer to Becca and savored the feeling of their bodies pressed together. It seemed so clichéd a thought, but everything felt in balance, like she'd come home to her own life again. Becca slipped a hand between Joey's legs and stroked the fabric lightly. The surprise was how turned on Joey already was and how that minimal contact sent shots of pleasure and longing surging through her. "Oh, I've missed you," she said through shallow breaths. It wasn't long before the rest of their clothes joined the pile, and they spent the morning in decadent reunion. Becca's predictive skills and the way she handled Joey's body had not changed, and the way they fit together so perfectly astounded.

"Well, this has been an entirely fantastic morning," Becca said when they were happy and spent.

"I can agree that we've set the bar really high. Do you think tomorrow will live up?"

Becca met her gaze and held it. "If you're here, there's no way it can't."

Everything in Joey melted. When she kissed Becca good-bye before heading down the path, she didn't take it for granted. She understood the importance of their connection and couldn't wait to come home that night.

"What do you think about me picking Sky up a little later while you work? He likes to lounge around the vineyard."

"Are you kidding? He would love that." Becca stole a second kiss. She was showered and fresh and wore a sweater of Joey's that looked amazing on her. "I'll leave the key behind the loose brick. You can keep it."

"Good. I'll need access to him. And other people who live there. A successful businesswoman, for one. Brunette. Amazing lips. Killer smile. Devastatingly sexy hair."

"I'll keep an eye out for her." Another kiss.

"Hey, Becca?"

"Yeah?"

"I love you."

Becca grinned. "I love you, too."

As Joey walked the short distance to the tasting room, she reflected on her year and its many ups and downs. She'd grown up more than she realized was possible over the course of only a few months. She'd learned many of her own weaknesses and how to overcome them. She grappled with grief and the effect it can have on the heart. More importantly, she'd discovered lasting love and how to return it. She passed Gabriella's truck and grinned at the wonderful aromas that now felt like a staple at Tangle Valley. She'd told her to take the day off, but Gabriella's commitment to her food was no joke. She spotted Joey and hopped down.

"Even though I can tell you've had sex, I'm going to bypass the juicy gossip and ask you to try this."

Joey took a bite of the slice of pizza Gabriella handed her and closed her eyes. "Amazing."

"Garlic white pizza with onion and meatball. I've already sold three-quarters of my inventory. Might have to go on the menu. Gotta cook." She dashed back to the truck.

Joey smiled in the tank room at the crusher she saw pressing the grapes for the ice wine, Madison standing off to the side supervising. When she saw Joey, she offered a wave and a couple of celebratory leaps in the air before returning to business mode.

Good God, Joey was beyond blessed to work with her friends.

She stared up at what had turned out to be a gorgeous blue sky, complete with fluffy white clouds. She missed her dad, but she felt like she was turning a page in a book, and the portion of the story that remained was a good one, full of friendship and love and adventures yet to come. With a happy sigh, she joined Loretta behind the bar and picked up a bottle of her family's wine for pouring. She grinned at the guest in front of her. "Welcome to Tangle Valley."

Josephine Wilder had come into her own.

EPILOGUE

Three Months Later

The big day had finally arrived, and wine had never tasted so good. Joey almost hadn't slept the night before. The new pinot was ready to meet the world, and that meant the big release party at Tangle Valley for all their loyal customers. The food was laid out, and Gabriella and her new assistant, Matt, a culinary student, were hard at work turning out more. The vineyard was in tip-top condition under Bobby and his team's care, and the new bottles were ready to meet the world. Joey wished she had a little bow tie for each one. It was a special day, after all. She'd kissed Becca's cheek as she slept and snuck out of bed early to get to work on the festivities.

By noon, the vineyard was hopping. She'd hired a band and a face-painter for the kids. The lunch Gabriella had laid out for their guests was beyond what she'd dreamed possible when she'd brought her on all those months earlier. Eggplant caponata, goat cheese torta, roasted squash, her famous spinach dumplings, toasted pork ravioli, and fresh margherita pizzas.

"I wanted to talk to you about something," Becca said, as she landed next to Joey. She had on jeans, white tennis shoes, and an off-the-shoulder white blouse that would have to be fawned over later. Becca looked too good in it.

"Now, you beautiful weirdo?" she whispered quietly as the Millers approached the outdoor check-in station she'd set up for wine pickup. "Oh, hold on just a sec."

"Holding," Becca said.

"We're here for the guest of honor," Mr. Miller proclaimed loudly.

Joey laughed. "You've come to the right spot." She checked off the Millers' name on her list and handed over their preordered three bottles. "Thank you so much for coming out. I think you're going to love this year's wine. My father outdid himself."

Mrs. Miller grinned. "Tangle Valley has always been our favorite wine. We drive an hour every year for the release. Can we also place an order for an additional case?"

"I'll put you down for one right now and have one of my guys load it into your car when you're ready. In the meantime, enjoy the music, and we have a whole spread for your lunch."

Mr. Miller leaned in. "I have to tell you, the food is a welcome addition. Amazingly good."

Joey leaned in, too. "The least we can do for our VIP wine club members."

The release party was an annual event in the spring, and Joey loved the excitement that surrounded the debut of a new batch. In this case, it would be the very last vintage crafted by her father, which made the day bittersweet. Yet she chose to focus on the celebratory component and kept the smile on her face. He would have loved today, so she would love it for him.

Once they had a moment to themselves, Joey turned to Becca and smiled. "You were saying?"

"Orlando called. They want The Jade to partner with Tangle Valley."

Joey quirked an eyebrow. "How is that possible? Last I heard, Fable Brook, those smug hacks, had a two-year deal."

"I don't think this is common knowledge yet"—Becca dropped her voice and turned her back to the outdoor celebration—"but they filed bankruptcy and quietly ceased operation last week."

"No." Joey could hear her own heart beating. She turned in the direction of the neighboring vineyard. "What happened? Were they really mobsters, and this was all a front? It would explain their lack of knowledge when it comes to good wine."

Becca laughed. "You'd think mobsters right off, I get that. But no, I think they tried to get too big too fast. And I had nothing to do with the offer. Corporate coordinated with Bruno on what local wines were selling in the restaurant and which were favorably reviewed by guests. The dollar amounts told the story."

"They want us to be the wine of The Jade. We're the house wine if I say yes?"

"You would be. You'll have a call coming your way on Monday."

Joey smacked her own forehead and then launched herself into Becca's arms with a laugh. "That's amazing. It's like the end of a movie when the good guys win."

Becca gave her a squeeze and set her back down. "It seems only fitting. I'm so happy for you. This place has earned it. You all have."

"What are we happy about?" Madison asked with a slice of pizza on her plate.

Joey leapt in. "That deal with The Jade—it's happening."

"We're promoted?" Madison set her plate down in happy mystification.

The implications were huge. They'd paid a lot to buy the grapes they needed for the fall, and this would soften the blow. The restaurant would be much easier to finance, and for once, everything looked like it might be okay. Joey could breathe. It felt good.

Gabriella hurried over in her white chef's coat with a curious look on her face. "I'm missing out on something fun." She made the hurry-up gesture. "Include me."

"We're partnering with the evil empire." Becca elbowed her and Joey made a show of correcting herself. "Sorry, The Jade, my favorite resort ever. We're their house wine now." She smiled sweetly at Becca, who rewarded her with a kiss.

"What? Ah!" Gabriella erupted in a grin and hop combo that made the others laugh. "I better finish up with lunch, but when I'm through, we're all having wine. We might get tipsy. Prepare yourselves."

"We would never start without you," Becca said. "You're the most fun tipsy person I know."

"Plus, who would feed us if we wronged you?" Madison asked.

Gabriella pointed at her. "And don't you forget it."

"Well, look at that." Joey stood taller as a guest approached. "Speaking of the restaurant, here comes Ryan. I invited her so she could get a feel for the place."

"Excuse me, what?" Gabriella stared, lips parted. Ryan's dark hair was down and a little wavy today. She wore aviators, jeans, and a navy V-neck T-shirt, which truly showed off her physique. "That's Ryan? The contractor?" she squeaked.

Becca laughed. Madison rolled her eyes. Joey nodded. "That's her. She's something, huh?"

"You think?" Gabriella swallowed and shook her head as if her life had just been changed. "Holy hell."

Joey tapped her lips and exchanged a look with Becca. "You know, I think this project is going to be a little more interesting than I anticipated."

Becca nodded. "Could make for a memorable year ahead."

About the Author

Melissa Brayden (www.melissabrayden.com) is a multi-award-winning romance author, embracing the full-time writer's life in San Antonio, Texas, and enjoying every minute of it.

Melissa enjoys spending time with her family and working really hard at remembering to do the dishes. For personal enjoyment, she throws realistically shaped toys for her Jack Russell terriers and checks out the NYC theater scene as often as possible. She considers herself a reluctant patron of spin class but would much rather be sipping merlot and staring off into space. Coffee, wine, and donuts make her world go round.

Books Available From Bold Strokes Books

Entangled by Melissa Brayden. Becca Crawford is the perfect person to head up the Jade Hotel, if only the captivating owner of the local vineyard would get on board with her plan and stop badmouthing the hotel to everyone in town. (978-1-63555-709-1)

First Do No Harm by Emily Smith. Pierce and Cassidy are about to discover that when it comes to love, sometimes you have to risk it all to have it all. (978-1-63555-699-5)

Kiss Me Every Day by Dena Blake. For Carly Jamison, wishing for a do-over with Wynn Evans was a long shot, actually getting one was a game changer. (978-1-63555-551-6)

Olivia by Genevieve McCluer. In this lesbian Shakespeare adaption with vampires, Olivia is a centuries-old vampire who must fight a strange figure from her past if she wants a chance at happiness. (978-1-63555-701-5)

One Woman's Treasure by Jean Copeland. Daphne's search for discarded antiques and treasures leads to an embarrassing misunderstanding and, ultimately, the opportunity for the romance of a lifetime with Nina. (978-1-63555-652-0)

Silver Ravens by Jane Fletcher. Lori has lost her girlfriend, her home, and her job. Things don't improve when she's kidnapped and taken to fairyland. (978-1-63555-631-5)

Still Not Over You by Jenny Frame, Carsen Taite, and Ali Vali. Old flames die hard in these tales of a second chance at love with the ex you're still not over. (978-1-63555-516-5)

Storm Lines by Jessica L. Webb. Devon is a psychologist who likes rules. Marley is a cop who doesn't. They don't always agree, but both fight to protect a girl immersed in a street drug ring. (978-1-63555-626-1)

The Politics of Love by Jen Jensen. Is it possible to love across the political divide in a hostile world? Conservative Shelley Whitmore and liberal Rand Thomas are about to find out. (978-1-63555-693-3)

All the Paths to You by Morgan Lee Miller. High school sweethearts Quinn Hughes and Kennedy Reed reconnect five years after they break up and realize that their chemistry is all but over. (978-1-63555-662-9)

Arrested Pleasures by Nanisi Barrett D'Arnuck. When charged with a crime she didn't commit, Katherine Lowe faces the question: Which is harder, going to prison or falling in love? (978-1-63555-684-1)

Bonded Love by Renee Roman. Carpenter Blaze Carter suffers an injury that shatters her dreams, and ER nurse Trinity Greene hopes to show her that sometimes love is worth fighting for. (978-1-63555-530-1)

Convergence by Jane C. Esther. With life as they know it on the line, can Aerin McLeary and Olivia Ando's love survive an otherworldly threat to humankind? (978-1-63555-488-5)

Coyote Blues by Karen F. Williams. Riley Dawson, psychotherapist and shape-shifter, has her world turned upside down when Fiona Bell, her one true love, returns. (978-1-63555-558-5)

Drawn by Carsen Taite. Will the clues lead Detective Claire Hanlon to the killer terrorizing Dallas, or will she merely lose her heart to person of interest urban artist Riley Flynn? (978-1-63555-644-5)

Lucky by Kris Bryant. Was Serena Evans's luck really about winning the lottery, or is she about to get even luckier in love? (978-1-63555-510-3)

The Last Days of Autumn by Donna K. Ford. Autumn and Caroline question the fairness of life, the cruelty of loss, and what it means to love as they navigate the complicated minefield of relationships, grief, and life-altering illness. (978-1-63555-672-8)

Three Alarm Response by Erin Dutton. In the midst of tragedy, can these first responders find love and healing? Three stories of courage, bravery, and passion. (978-1-63555-592-9)

Veterinary Partner by Nancy Wheelton. Callie and Lauren are determined to keep their hearts safe but find that taking a chance on love is the safest option of all. (978-1-63555-666-7)